I0703532

COUNTERFEIT

By

Scott L. Miller

Published by NY Book Publishers
www.nybookpublishers.com

PRINTED IN THE UNITED STATES OF AMERICA

Edition: 1, ver 1.00

ISBN- 978-1-964289-01-4

ISBN- 978-1-964289-00-7

DEDICATION

To Robert B. Parker, Jeremiah Healy, John Gardner, and Herman
Melville
Two mentors and all great writers who inspired me

BOOK ONE: THE CALL

The American Dream is, in part, responsible for a great deal of crime and violence because people feel that the country owes them not only a living but a good living.
David Abrahamsen, criminal psychiatrist

SELF-IMPOSED HIBERNATION

I fumbled in the dark for the phone, fighting the knee-jerk fear that something terrible had happened to someone I care about. Again.

I picked up on the first ring. "What? Do you know what time it is?"

A pause, then: "Almos' midnight, Cool Breeze."

I recognized that baritone immediately, and my body went rigid. "You better be suicidal."

"Not in this lifetime. Sorry for the late call. Easy to lose track of time when you're on a stakeout. I have a favor to ask, but I'll call back in the morning—when your head's clear."

"I'm busy in the—," I said as the line went dead in my hand.

How times change.

And how tragedy rearranges us.

The baritone belonged to JoJo Baker, a towering, bald black man with bulging biceps and a nasty scar that serpentined around his left eye and ended well past his cauliflower ear. For months he'd been a major player in some of my worst nightmares, but since I rarely slept these days, he didn't haunt me anymore. Now, his voice brought back memories best left buried.

I imagined Baker parked strategically on some dark street, hunkered down in the front seat of his battered, souped-up black '95 Fleetwood, eating Power bars and drinking stale coffee, enjoying an old Marvin Gaye song with the volume turned low, leafing through the latest *Ring* magazine, a pee jar at his side and the back seat littered with Power

Bar wrappers and old coffee cups while he stalked his latest homicide suspect. At least he's not trying to imprison me for murder this year.

Baker belongs to the night. Me, I wonder if I belong anywhere anymore.

My instinct was to forget about the call, forget about Baker, pull the covers over my head, and go back pretending to sleep, pretending to not think about Kris.

But Baker has a way of getting under your skin, so I got up, checked the front door locks and glass for signs of illegal entry before I returned to bed. No glass on the landing, this time the break-in was internal.

$ $ $

My morning began with an on-line therapy session with a depressed Trans-Alaska pipeline oil rigger living above the Arctic Circle. The feeling of aloneness in the Land of the Midnight Sun can wreak its own brand of havoc on someone prone to depression and stuck in an isolated town named Deadhorse. With the nearest social worker or psychologist or psychiatrist or counselor by any name besides bartender hundreds of miles from his remote outpost and travel difficult under good conditions, a webcam and a good internet connection can do a man down on life a world of good.

I'd logged off from the session and was sipping a glass of juice, staring, like I do every day, out the same windows the man who murdered my girlfriend considered to throw me out of last year when my private line rang.

"Mitchell Adams."

Counterfeit

"How they hangin', Cool Breeze?" I could hear the smooth, bluesy sound of the Robert Cray band in the background as the goose flesh crawled up my arms right on cue and I flashed back to Kris lying on a slab in the city morgue on Clark Avenue.

So much for the dawn of a new day.

"How are you, Detective Baker?" I answered, fighting to keep my voice calm. "It's been a long time."

But not long enough.

Like a bad dream Mutt and Jeff tag team, Baker was the larger-than-life detective with the city of St. Louis who, along with his diminutive partner Detective Francis LeMaster, had dutifully followed the planted evidence last year to make me the fall guy for Kris' murder.

"Look, there's a little brother in city lock-up who could use someone to talk to before he goes ape shit and offs himself. Baker's hushed tone was edged with an odd trace of anguish, like it physically pained him to say the words. "He needs good psych care. I know you the man for the job."

My pause lapsed into an awkward silence.

"If you got the time," Baker said, even softer now.

"What'd he do?"

Baker exhaled deeply and turned off the music. He must have been driving with the windows down, for now I heard car engines and other traffic sounds in the background. I imagined the wheels turning in his big bald head while he decided on a tactic, his trademark toothpick rolling briskly in his mouth under the Fu Manchu mustache. I could see him in his favorite parrot-green sports coat, those massive biceps stretching the sleeves. On the surface Baker appeared to be a throwback to the seventies, but he was the most street-savvy person I've ever met.

"He accused of counterfeitin', armed robbery and shootin' a pregnant security guard in the stomach."

I closed my eyes. "Did he do it?"

"Oh, he a big-time forger, all right. May be the best that ever was. As for the rest, I'll let you decide. Looks bad for the little brother though, with the Chief Prosecuting Attorney hisself descending Mount Olympus to take on this case."

The silence stretched and I sensed uneasiness on the other end of the line. This case seemed personal.

"I knew him when we was in school," Baker admitted, as if reading my thoughts. "But that was a long time ago. The brother ain't never had a break in life, and now this happens. He won't adjust well to prison life, he's already talkin' suicide. If anyone can help him now, it'd be you."

"The Chief Prosecutor will make this case a political football. A full media circus. Racial overtones. The works."

"Uh-huh," Baker said. "A royal cluster fuck." He paused a beat. "Right up your alley, man."

I didn't respond, and Baker sensed my reluctance. "He'll be chained to the interview table, legs and hands shackled, man. This boy, he the runt of the litter. Disabled to boot. A guy like you, you—"

"What's his disability?" I cut in.

Another pause. "You'll know it when you see him."

Ever since Kris' rape and murder, fear and dread tended to lodge in my throat at the merest provocation. Situations I once would have handled with aplomb now made me freeze like a rabbit in the headlights. As a result I'd gone into self-imposed hibernation, seeing only safe clients—garden variety depressives and those with anxiety disorders—and helping good, decent people face the everyday stresses of modern life. My practice was full of social phobia clients: a successful businessman with OCD, the disease of doubt, who compulsively checks under his car every time it hits a bump, fearful he's caused harm to others by accident; West County housewives with agoraphobia, bathroom, germ or other social phobias; and professionals whose careers were cratering because they were afraid of flying or traveling over bridges.

There was nothing wrong with limiting my schedule to those patients, of course. But I did it because I had my *own* social phobia—clients with hot-button issues like marital discord, physical or sexual abuse, and psychoses. These challenging cases used to be my forte, now I refer them to other providers in the group.

Since the early years spent nurturing and building the fledgling practice, I'd done quite well for myself. As clinical director, I receive income every time one of the eight other providers sees a client in the office. This success afforded me the financial freedom to lick my wounds and return to work at my own pace after Kris' murder. It also gave me an easy out to obsess over and nurture my own fears. Including the fear that Detective Baker was buttering me up to take a no-win case that any other provider would decline in a heartbeat.

As a rule, I try to take on a gratis client for roughly every nine paying ones. Along with giving blood, I consider it my "pay it forward" to society. Baker knew that. More important, he knew me. Yes, he'd known what he was doing from the beginning, the bastard.

The familiar tightness in my chest returned.

"Is there anything else about him you're not telling me?" I asked.

"No."

"Listen, there was a time when I'd have been the man for the job … but not anymore. I'm sorry, Detective Baker, but I'm turning you down."

This time he let the silence drag, and I felt uncomfortable waiting for the call to end. Finally, he spoke. "Why you think I called you, Doc?" He didn't wait for me to respond. "That poor little brother needs you or he gonna die. But you need him, too. Look in the mirror, you dumbass. Get your shit together 'fore it's too late."

And with that, for the second time in less than twelve hours, Detective Baker hung up on me.

FLY ON THE WALL

Baker's call behind me, I slogged through invoices, billed third party payers, dictated a few progress notes, and then grabbed a quick lunch at a new Mexican dive down the street. Then, with no afternoon clients, I decided to head downtown to take care of a speeding ticket I'd forgotten to pay. Paying in person meant a stop at the DMV in City Hall, so I headed down Market Street until a traffic backup forced me to stop in the intersection.

A cop stood in the center of the road, directing traffic with his whistle and orange baton like there was something big going on. I had the top down, so I leaned out and called to him.

"What's going on downtown today?"

He blew his whistle and a line of cars stopped. He looked at me, considering whether to answer. "Press conference. News trucks have backed up traffic."

"Is it about the counterfeiter?"

The surprised look that crossed his stubbly face was my answer. He blew the shrill whistle at me, then pointed his baton and ordered my line of cars to proceed through the intersection.

In the rearview mirror, I saw a sleek black motorcade approaching, and before I had a chance to change my mind, I pulled over at the nearest open meter. I was here to pay the ticket anyway, I told myself. It wouldn't hurt to cross the street to watch the press conference and at least find out about the case against Baker's counterfeiter. Kill two birds with one stone, I told myself.

It took no time to get the ticket taken care of and the news crews were still setting up, so I headed for the men's room. The tacos I'd had for lunch were already coming back, and I was afraid it wasn't going to be a friendly visit.

I was minding my own business in a stall when the door to the bathroom opened, and I heard the quick shuffle of footsteps followed by a metallic click. Who locks the door to a public men's room?

"What if it's true?" I heard a man whisper under his breath. That grabbed my attention.

Then a second man: "Not another word."

Somebody was taking a piss, and I heard hard soles scrape against the marble floor as someone strode down the row of stalls. All I could think of was the cute little Amish boy in the movie *Witness*. But with my pants around my ankles, and my tacos ready to return with a vengeance, I couldn't stand and crouch on the toilet seat. Instead, I lifted my feet off the floor as high as I could and said a prayer of thanks for the tight fit between the stall door and side walls. For him to see me, he'd have to go to his knees and peek under my door, but if he tried to push open every stall door, well—he'd know they weren't alone. But that didn't happen.

I never realized how good the acoustics were in old, high-ceilinged marble and tile bathrooms. Makes you think twice about taking care of business, but in this case the acoustics helped me hear most of the exchange, minus certain snippets.

The second man said, "Okay, __________. Tell me what's going on in that big brain of yours."

"Imagine the possibilities if they're good."

"He's lying, ___________. Besides, we'll know soon enough. ________ is on our side."

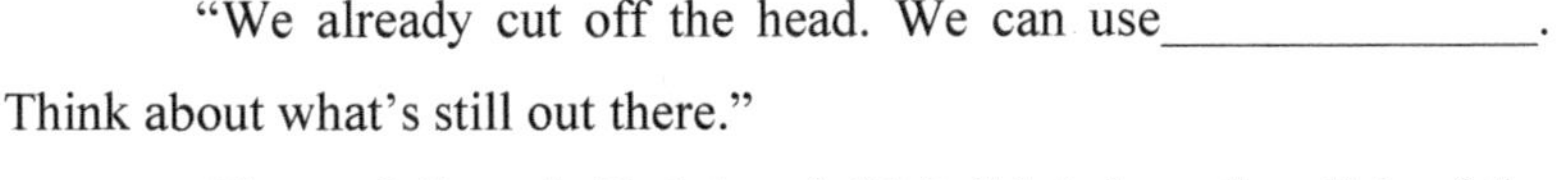

Counterfeit

"We already cut off the head. We can use_______________. Think about what's still out there."

Silence followed. Had they left? I didn't hear the click of the lock. I started to shift on the toilet seat and then my stomach protested, loudly. *Shit—am I about to be dragged from the stall? Is there still Mafia in St. Louis?*

Then the second man: "Okay, I'm with you. What about__________ containment?" Voice rising, he was excited, damn near giddy.

"I can handle my part. The big top is the key."

A silence, then the second man: "I know the right man and you know the right _______."

"Everyone has their price. Let's make it happen."

"You look perfect. Let's go to work."

The latch clicked again, the door swung open, and I was mercifully alone, but covert talk of cutting off heads and containment and paying people off didn't help my digestion. I waited for minutes in silence until someone entered, used a urinal and left.

When I finally left the bathroom, a few people glanced my way but no one appeared to pay me special attention or follow.

Most of the media were now in place and a small crowd had gathered outside for the conference. They stood or paced in front of the massive marble steps, casting sideways glances at the sleek motorcade double parked next to a fire hydrant.

I watched heads turn as two men approached the podium flanked by two strapping young men in dark suits and darker sunglasses. Security. At the podium, a small man in his forties with short receding hair, intense eyes, and precise economical movements whispered non-stop to the other man. The smaller man peeled off, leaving the star of the show at the podium. He had a practiced, movie-star smile, a handsome face, short dirty blonde hair, and penetrating blue eyes that remained fixed on the cameras as if he were about to speak directly to me and everyone else in the world right then and there, like we were best friends. His broad shoulders filled his tailored suit to perfection and he had the square lantern jaw of a prizefighter. A light breeze blew, but his hair remained perfect, unmoved, as if earthly elements such as the weather didn't affect him. He was so confident and polished, I almost expected to see a diamond sparkle of light flash from his pearly whites when he spoke.

"Ladies and gentlemen, it is my pleasure to announce that a sophisticated and dangerous counterfeiting operation was shut down yesterday by our city police force. One arrest was made and a manhunt has begun for at least three other known associates. The man in custody is believed to be the gang's primary counterfeiter and possibly their ringleader.

"It was only through diligent and coordinated police work that this dangerous criminal was apprehended before his gang could contaminate our local economy with their counterfeit currency. During today's initial appearance before Judge Springfield, I requested that the prisoner be held without bond as I believe he presents a major flight risk and public danger. Today the judge ruled in my favor and bond was denied. The prisoner has been remanded to the custody of the US Marshals, pending his judicial hearings and trial. The Marshals have accepted my proposal to house the prisoner in our Gateway St. Louis city jail until the trial. Our city police force is working in conjunction with local Secret Service agents, questioning this man in order to apprehend the others and insure that all the counterfeit monies will be recovered and destroyed. The damage their activities could have caused—both locally and nationally—is significant, and there must be zero tolerance for such crimes against society. I will prosecute these men myself and seek the maximum sentence. Questions?"

A flurry of action followed on the steps of City Hall as reporters jostled for position, hands and mikes waving in the air. They all spoke at once like unruly grade schoolers, eager for face time and a sound bite they could play on the evening news. He chose a waving hand.

Debbie Macklin, a toothpick-thin blonde, elbowed her way to the front of the podium with a self-satisfied smirk. I'd worked with her a number of times when the program manager at Channel Four wanted to air a free professional opinion on a breaking news story that involved mental illness or a case that contained psycho-dynamics considered to be of public interest. She'd interviewed me on topics ranging from Munchausen's By Proxy to prostitution to the psychological dynamics of what drives a woman to cut the fetus from her best friend's belly with a pair of scissors and claim it as her own, ala a metro east murder case that created headlines a few years back. The ham in me used to enjoy the free publicity, the challenge to compress complex issues in easy-to-understand sound bites for the general population.

That person is gone now.

"Congratulations, Mr. Maynard. Good guys one, bad guys nothing. You said these criminals are sophisticated and dangerous. Can you describe the scope of this counterfeiting ring?"

Maynard grinned down at the anorexic reporter, showing at least a hundred perfectly capped white teeth. "Excellent question, Debbie. These men shot and nearly killed a pregnant security guard and her unborn baby when they stole a large quantity of paper and ink the federal government uses to print money. The man we have in custody engraved duplicate plates of the latest United States hundred-dollar bill while working in a printing company on the city's north side. They had the ability and resources to print a great number of bills, but the good news is that the copies are not able to pass for real currency by someone accustomed to handling money. The three men who remain at large should be considered armed and dangerous." He scanned the steps looking to field another question.

Eager reporters pushed forward a second time. Maynard scanned the group until his winning smile landed on another woman. "Yes, Virginia."

Another blonde reporter spoke up, even more energetic and perky than Debbie. "Chief Prosecutor, how long were these criminals operating and how much counterfeit money entered circulation before our police shut them down?"

He smirked, as if he'd anticipated the question. "I'm glad you asked. The stolen paper bundle had the capacity to print a little over twenty-five million dollars of illegal hundred-dollar bills. We have already recovered over twenty-four point five million—"

Maynard paused long enough for the cameras to record the oohs and aahs and whistles from the fourth estate.

"We also seized their master plates, printing press, various related counterfeiting equipment, and an impressive arsenal of unregistered and illegal weapons that included AK-47s and hand grenades. We also confiscated significant quantities of crack cocaine, China White heroin, and methamphetamine."

"What can you tell us about the man who's been charged? Is he the ringleader?" another reporter called out.

"The man in custody is Lonnie Washington, a loner from a broken home on the near north side, a man that behavioral experts from the Secret Service have profiled as a loose cannon, perfect human fodder for a life of crime. We believe he was the brains behind the production of the counterfeit plates and bills."

"And what about his associates?" Debbie asked.

"Three others fled the scene during the raid on the printing company and are wanted for questioning. Their physical descriptions match the other three company employees. They failed to return to their known residences and are assumed to be in hiding. They have not been charged at this time, but it is essential that they step forward now and talk, given the gravity of the crime. We want to verify that the entire counterfeit product has been contained. Chief among them is Earl Mooney. Mr. Mooney owns the building where the bills were produced, and, if involved, may be the money and front man behind the operation."

"Why is the Secret Service involved?" a male reporter called out.

"The prevention of counterfeit currency is the reason the Secret Service was created during the Civil War."

"Can you give us the name of the printing company?" another reporter asked.

"My office is preparing a statement about the arrest and a profile of all the suspects. That will be available within the hour."

"Who are the other two employees?" Debbie shouted.

"We want to question Benny Blades and Tyrone Sparks, two apprentice printers at the company. Given the unique nature of this crime, APBs have been issued on these men and, I remind everyone, they are considered armed and dangerous. We believe these are the principal players, but there may be others. There will be more to this story, and we'll update you as the situation develops. Thank you for your time."

The collection of reporters shouted questions as some followed Maynard, who orchestrated a controlled exit stage right. The two beefcake security men shadowed him while the little man greeted Maynard with a smile and handshake, resuming their private dialogue. The four men disappeared inside the shiny black limousine that immediately pulled away from its illegal parking spot and sped west on Market.

Maynard was smooth. He was smart.

He was the son of a former US president.

He also sounded like the first man I'd heard whisper in the bathroom.

THE REFERRAL KISS OF DEATH

That night I settled deep into my safe, comfortable living room couch to watch the news. I'd made pot stickers and egg drop soup for one while I drank a Tsingtao, the last remaining beer in the house. I was feeling sorry for myself and acted like I didn't know why.

Kris had been a die-hard foodie, and we'd spent a lot of time in the kitchen as she patiently taught me how to cook more than canned soup and frozen pizza. I'd remodeled the whole thing and upgraded the appliances with an eye to the future with her. Now my Sub-Zero contains a bachelor's supply of the four basic food groups along with my standard OJ, soy milk, beer, Tanqueray and Bitter lemon. Before Kris, my old stove served as a towel rack. Now, most days the new one's a much more expensive towel rack.

Her ghost still lingers here—she makes cameo appearances sitting at the kitchen bar stool, on the sofa, in front of the fireplace, on a chaise lounge deckchair that fronts the common ground, and of course, in the bedroom.

I watched the replay of Maynard's speech with no particular interest until he mentioned Lonnie's name. The station had spliced front and side mug shots of a small, thin, clean-shaven black man in his late thirties with a closely cropped Afro, slightly receding hairline, and trimmed sideburns that ended short of his earlobes. His dark, almond-shaped eyes seemed to stare beyond the camera to some distant place filled with immense sorrow. He had a wide sloped nose, prominent cheekbones, and flared nostrils. His jaw rigid, he held his chin up as he displayed his prison number board in front of himself with thin, oddly tattooed hands. The distant look on his face reminded me of a POW or a soldier deep in-country, someone who's seen too much of another world, too much of what men can do to each other, and has little hope of returning home in one piece.

Déjà vu, brother.

At the mention of Earl Mooney's name, a family Polaroid (I thought the self-developing film had gone the way of cassettes and eight-tracks) filled the screen. In it, a gaunt, grinning black man who looked to be in his eighties stood unsteadily in a tiny back yard bathed in bright sunshine. A fat cigar protruded from his thin lips and one scrawny hand gripped a portable oxygen tank while a blue nasal cannula snaked its way up to his sunken face; his other arm draped contentedly around a tiny black woman dressed in a multicolored dashiki and purple turban, her face intentionally blurred for confidentiality purposes. She appeared to be helping him stand. The cachectic man's face and head tilted toward the diminutive woman as if in deference or tribute.

I've done that, too.

The name Benny Blades produced a Glamour Shots close-up on the screen of a handsome young black man, smiling, mid-twenties at most, with high cheekbones accentuating flawless ebony skin. His curly, gelled Afro reached the top of his ears. He wore a coral necklace and form-fitting black tee-shirt. The photo could have been ripped from an *Ebony* magazine. He
mugged directly into the camera lens while he flashed the Peace sign. The photo screamed 'ladies' man.'

Been there, done that, too.

The last photo was a grainy close-up of a Missouri driver's license. An intimidating, rough-looking black man with a sloping forehead and angry expression dominated the screen. His full cheeks and long face covered most of the sky-blue backdrop. The typed information at the left indicated Tyrone Sparks was six feet six, weighed 280 pounds, and was thirty-two years old. He looked like a bouncer outside a seedy nightclub or an angry leg breaker for the mob.

I nodded at this photo. This dude fit the bill of scary-looking bogeyman. But the others? Lonnie Washington, Earl Mooney, and Benny Blades didn't look like criminal masterminds or diabolical members of anything, let alone a major counterfeiting ring. I'd seen my share of hardcore antisocial personalities and psychotics in the state mental health system. They didn't fit that mold, either. But, as a social worker, I'd be the first to admit looks can be deceiving. I replayed the photos on my DVR over and over again, trying to pry my way into the souls of the four alleged criminals. I got nowhere. The pictures perplexed me. They say a picture's worth a thousand words. It seemed like I'd need a million to understand what motivated these men to become criminals.

I don't like disconnects and didn't need a mirror to know I was frowning. Containment. Cutting off heads. Counterfeiting. What was going on with Maynard, his friend from the crapper, and these four alleged criminals?

Good guys one, bad guys nothing.

I recalled my early days providing therapy in a state-funded drug program. It was amazing how often the conspiratorial whispers from one junkie on parole to another made it to my ears while I sat minding my own business in a stall. It made for lively group sessions and life lessons.

We already cut off the head.

Think about what's still out there. The big top is the key.

When I drifted off to a restless sleep well past midnight, I knew two things for certain: the full force of the civilized world was about to crash land on Lonnie Washington's slight frame; and tomorrow was destined to be yet another lousy day.

$ $ $

It took immense effort to get out of bed and dress every morning. To complete even the most mundane activities required an iron will. The way I felt this morning, nothing on earth could get me moving. All I wanted to do was pull the covers over my head and pretend the outside world had evaporated away, *poof*, into thin air.

Instead, I drove to the Missouri Botanical Garden with a small bouquet of white roses.

Kris had been buried back east, in her native Bronx. But for whatever crazy reason, I needed a place, a piece of ground to claim, to feel a connection to her. So I'd adopted a secluded spot in the English Woodland Garden. She liked to walk the Garden, and we often sat on the same shaded bench to get out of the sun and talk. Friends and family of Joyce Duane, a social worker I'd known who had also died too soon, donated money for the memorial bench. Now it sat weathered and often unused. Today was no different.

I walked past the bench and followed the stepping stones down to where a small stream cut through a wooded wonderland of giant Hostas plants, ferns, flowering ground cover, and lush green bushes, hidden under a dense canopy of mature shade trees. The damp ground smelled of cypress mulch while the fresh scent of wintergreen filled the air.

Standing at the edge of the brook, I watched the water swirl and cascade over rocks and around roots, heading down toward a small pond in the distance. One by one, I peeled the flowers from the bouquet and tossed them into the stream, watching them spin and dance on the surface and move on.

"I miss you," I whispered.

I stood there for I don't know how long, as birds twittered and chirped and delicate-fingered ferns dipped and swayed in the breeze. Time hadn't healed the pain; but still there was a serenity about our spot that afforded me comfort and refuge. I sighed, turned to head back to sit on our bench, and then froze.

Wearing that parrot green sports coat, Detective Baker stood quietly near the bench, watching. He was stalking me, just like last year. He threw the ubiquitous toothpick to the ground.

"Figured you'd be here," Baker said.

"You followed me."

"Hard to believe it's been a year today."

"Time flies when you're having fun," I replied.

I made it to the bench and sat down. Baker folded himself in two and lowered his bulk beside me.

"Never had the pleasure of meeting her, but I came to know she was a special lady. I'm sorry, Cool Breeze." Then: "For what I said yesterday, too."

"Look, if you're here about—"

"Please take the case."

His voice was thick with desperation.

"Why?"

His coal eyes hardened for a moment. "I can't tell you."

"Sorry. Not good enough."

In one fluid motion, another toothpick materialized in his mouth. "He needs an experienced professional to talk to. He needs you."

"Bullshit. The city's crawling with therapists."

We sat in silence. A couple pushing a stroller walked by. The shadow of a plane passed over us.

"Who does he get when I say no again."

I thought I saw the faint birth of a smile. "Some pimply-faced counselor from the Entitlement Generation who don' know shit 'bout the real world but think he or she do 'cause they sat in a stuffy classroom and shit out term papers, or maybe he'll get Sister Thomas with her cross and rosary beads. Both ways, he shuts down and probably kills hisself."

"Sister Thomas, how old is she now?"

"Cake I saw last month had a hundred and sixty candles on it. Set off the smoke detectors, I hear."

Baker rolled the toothpick between his teeth and waited.

I sighed, leaned back against the bench and stared up through the trees to the pale gray beyond. No sign from above. *Do I continue this way?*

"Why me? You know as well as I do that no one can prevent him from going ape-shit in a place like city jail."

"You've seen it all. You've been there. You're smart, hard to intimidate, and think fast on your feet. You remind me in some ways," Baker added, "of me."

"Nice try, but don't bullshit a bullshitter. Cut to the chase or I'm walking."

Baker's jaw tensed. "I'm tryin' to stop a crime here."

"Are you saying he's innocent?"

"No. Like I said, he a counterfeiter all right, but if this case isn't handled just right, a lot more bad shit is gonna happen."

"But you can't tell me. Why?"

"I just can't, that's why."

The garden suddenly seemed desecrated and I felt it, or me, spinning. I closed my eyes to shut out Baker and all things Baker—the murder, being framed, held prisoner, and almost killed.

"Cool Breeze, I'm not askin', I'm beggin'. Please don't walk away from this. I need you."

"Tyrone Sparks aside, the rest of these guys look like they'd have a hard time organizing a poker game. Benny Blades looks like a ladies' man and Earl Mooney looks like he belongs in a hospice program. He'd have needed a rocket powered wheelchair to flee the scene of a highly organized police sting. Give me a break."

Baker's eyes widened. "See? That's why I need you. You see through that kind of shit."

I stood up and looked down at Baker. "One thing. You tell me what crime you're trying to prevent or I walk."

Baker remained silent; his brow furrowed, his eyes pained.

I turned and walked away. Ten yards, fifteen, twenty—

"Wait!"

I stopped and turned. He was right behind me.

"Good to see you got some fight left in you," he said, working his toothpick. "I got no proof. The wrong ears hear this, I'm suspended. We—I—need help to find hard evidence. I gotta find out how much the big fish know before I can say more. It's for your own good, mine, and the little brother's."

"We?"

"Slip of the tongue. Dude like Maynard got his own Secret Service protection." His voice lowered: "I think the little brother's talents are the hidden prize."

"Does 'the big top is the key' make any sense in your cop world?"

"Not a lick."

This time I believed him.

"Why?" Baker asked.

I shook my head. "It's not important for now."

"I'm a homicide dick. I can't get directly involved in the case."

"Not without drawing attention to yourself."

He didn't respond.

"Surely you have friends in the department who can help behind the scenes."

I watched his calculating smile spread. "That's another reason I need you."

This could only mean one thing. "Tony?"

My best friend Tony Martin, a Ph.D. psychologist who does police ride-a-longs in the city, had been my mentor when I began my career in the state mental health system ten years ago. Back then he worked in his own thriving private practice and a reputation as one of the best marital therapists in the Midwest. In our professional circle he was known simply as *The Voice.* His silky smooth elocution always reminded me of a white James Earl Jones. Women routinely turned their heads at the sound of his mellifluous voice, but it was a woman—a client—and Tony's colossal lapse in judgment that led to a few frenzied minutes of taboo behavior that cost him his practice and nearly his wife and daughters. He aches to end his three-year exile with the police "knuckle-draggers," as he calls them, and return to private practice.

"The Voice wants to be back in business," Baker said.

"Which is precisely why he won't jeopardize his job."

I know people on licensing and insurance boards."

The web he was spinning perplexed me. "All this for a classmate you knew a long time ago? I don't buy it."

"Don't make me get on my knees."

"You still haven't told me what crime you're trying to prevent."

Baker rolled that damn toothpick around in his mouth and stared at me.

I walked away. "Do not follow me again. Do not call."

"I think Maynard intends to kill the little brother, but I can't prove it—yet. I need someone I can trust, talking with him on the inside."

"Why would Maynard risk killing someone you say is suicidal?"

Baker turned pensive. "Maybe we find out together."

"What else about this case aren't you telling me?" I realized how stupid the question was once it left my lips.

Baker rolled the toothpick to the other side of his mouth. "If the Man throws the book at Lonnie, the brothers in the hood ain't gonna like it one bit. Could be riotin,' lootin,' random mayhem and shit. Lonnie goes down, it gonna go bad for the city."

"Why? What makes him different from any other poor minority criminal in prison?"

"You wouldn't believe me even if I could tell you. You gotta learn that on your own. Take the case and you'll find out."

"You're being too enigmatic, Detective."

"Best I can do. You a smart guy," he said, glancing back at the bench, the stream, then up through the branches at the cloudy sky. "Sometimes too smart for your own good."

I thought of the secure confines of my couch, the varied names of my burgeoning fears, and of Lonnie's shell-shocked mug shot. The sadness in his eyes said it all. *I feel your pain, brother.*

"Baker, you're a bastard."

"It won't take up much of your time," he insisted.

The referral kiss of death. "I've heard that before."

I remembered the 2006 baseball Cardinals and the *USA Today* headline the day before the World Series began that read, "DETROIT IN THREE."

And when Buster Douglas knocked Mike Tyson on his ass.

I thought of a hundred-to-one longshot horse winning by a nose at Fairmount Park.

What are the odds of a regular Joe beating City Hall?

I thought of Maynard's cryptic words to his co-conspirator.

My id said: *Don't do it; he's offering nothing but more trouble and pain.* My ego said: *Maybe you can help this man, and maybe about now you need a jolt from a lightning rod.*

Baker waited patiently while my internal battle raged.

"I'll see him today, but I make no promise to stay on the case when it all goes to hell, and it will. I walk away any time I feel like it. No questions asked."

"Hot damn! I knew you'd do it. I will let the jail know to expect you. You won't regret it, my man."

"I already do."

"I know you the man for this, Cool Breeze."

Counterfeit

"That makes one of us."

I left the soothing English Garden ready to be fitted for my lightning rod.

Next stop, Gateway City Jail.

THE END OF THE LINE

Rain dripped from the concrete fangs of two massive lions standing guard at the Gateway City Jail. I hurried up the steps between the imposing Doric columns. What a dinosaur. The new county jail is a spa compared to this.

After passing through the metal detector screening line, I walked down a cold, shadowy hallway that smelled of old building, institutional cleaning fluids, and stale city air. Dust motes shone and drifted like dying fireflies in the slivers of light slanting through the high, narrow windows. The closer I came to the visitation area for the special lock-down unit, the smell changed to fear and the windows disappeared.

This is the end of the line.

Last year I was nearly an inmate here.

I checked in at the guard station, received a guest badge and a litany of guidelines from a beefy guard who rattled off a long list of visitation no-no's in rapid fire monotone. Heightened security and greater restrictions applied in lock-down, the area reserved for the most dangerous or self-destructive prisoners. No Plexiglas partition separated prisoners here during visits with their attorneys, counselors, or priests, and the guards confiscated my keys and wallet and change, even pen and paper, until my time ended. Then they ushered me into a cramped room with lime green cinder block walls, a water-damaged drop ceiling, and harsh fluorescent lighting. A scarred and battered gunmetal gray steel table stood bolted to a steel plate in the middle of the floor. The smell of mold and sweat filled the room.

"You have thirty minutes," the guard said before the door slammed shut with a heavy metallic thud.

Counterfeit

The end of the line.

It wasn't until I turned to sit at the table to wait that I noticed Lonnie Washington. He seemed fragile, small, like he had folded into himself like an Origami bird. He said nothing. Didn't even look up, but instead stared with blank eyes into the middle distance. Two of him could have fit in his orange prison jumpsuit. His wrist chains were hooked to a thick bolt in the tabletop while leg irons secured him to a steel plate welded to the floor.

I took the chair across the table from him, closer to the door.

His eyes remained vacant and fixed on some point in the corner of the floor. His straight, slender fingers and hands appeared tattooed on both sides, and the artistry looked jailhouse or amateurish at best.

He had whipping boy written all over him.

"I'm Dr. Mitchell Adams, a social worker in private practice. It's good to meet you, Lonnie. Detective JoJo Baker thought it might help if you had someone to talk with on a regular basis in here. What do you think?"

No response.

He didn't acknowledge my presence or move a muscle. His lifeless, dark eyes never wavered. I couldn't tell if he'd heard me.

"Detective Baker is concerned you might have a hard time adjusting and thinks I can help you deal with this place."

Nothing.

"He also told me you're having thoughts of killing yourself. Is that true?"

Still no response.

I tried five minutes of silence and we sat like two strangers waiting on the same bench for a bus. *Waiting for Godot*. Waiting for something.

But there was nothing. I sat quietly for five or ten more minutes until suddenly his right hand shot up and the eerie, ghost-like rattle of his chains filled the tiny room. Startled, I recoiled, feeling foolish once I realized the shackles permitted him to raise his hand mere inches above the table. Oblivious to my reaction, his hand quickly moved back and forth in the air, his eyes still fixed on the corner. At times his hand returned to the tabletop, seemed to grab some imaginary thing and continue its movements in the air. After five minutes of this, all movements ceased as quickly as they'd begun and the gloomy silence returned.

"What did you just do, Lonnie?"

Nothing.

"I know you can hear me. Talking helps pass the time."

Zippo.

Silence ruled again until the hand made similar motions in the air, eventually returning to rest on the scarred table. Those slender fingers trembled at times.

"JoJo said you attended school together."

Nothing.

"When I first met him, JoJo scared the hell out of me, but after I came to know him I consider him a friend, of sorts." *The things I'll say to start a conversation.*

When our time ended, I said, "It's been nice meeting you, Lonnie. I'll come back tomorrow to see how you're doing. Is there anything you want or anyone you'd like me to call?"

Counterfeit

More nothing.

The guard unlocked the door and escorted me out.

My next five visits passed in much the same way. The vacant staring persisted. The hand movements increased in frequency and for some reason I attributed a sense of urgency to them, but not one sound or word passed his lips.

While I struggled for days to find an in-road to Lonnie's trust, the case against him was proceeding full steam ahead. Evidence had been impounded and was being analyzed, motions were being filed, neighbors interviewed. Maynard made more tough, reassuring statements to the press as he continued to build the city's case against Lonnie. The media took hold of each new development and ran with it like a dog that had finally caught up to a car. People on the street were interviewed, claiming to have seen the three fugitives in various parts of the city and country, asking about a reward, while a few brave or foolhardy souls questioned the veracity of Maynard's facts. Baker hounded me daily for reports on my "progress" with Lonnie.

$ $ $

On day seven Lonnie showed a fresh sign of life, a slow trickle of blood weaved its way toward his brow from his closely cropped Afro.

"Lonnie, you're bleeding," I said, removing a handkerchief from my back pocket. "Let me get that for you—"

His body went rigid as his lifeless eyes turned fearful. They instantly tracked to the door, which burst open and a guard the size and demeanor of a defensive lineman lunged forward.

"Sir, you were instructed never to pass the prisoner contraband of any kind," the muscular guard warned. The badge on his massive chest read Sergeant Donnell Collins.

I held the white cloth up for him. "Fine, but this man is bleeding and can't raise a hand to his face. Get him a bandage or let me wipe the blood before it reaches his eye."

Sgt. Collins wore latex gloves and inspected the handkerchief closely. "You'd be amazed at the resourcefulness of prisoners, especially this one. He could use this to hang himself, choke a guard, conceal a weapon, or jamb a door. I must account for your safety too, he could be HIV positive. You get this back when you leave."

Collins stared down at me, most likely taking me for a weak, bleeding-heart softie from the suburbs in a swell gray sports coat and matching twill pants.

I am, however, more than the sum of my parts. *Or at least I used to be.*

I returned his glare. "I know you have rules. We all do. One of mine is to help people when I can. He's helpless and scared. Attend to his wound or I will."

Collins inspected Lonnie's head. "He's got a small cut in his scalp. Superficial. Head wounds tend to bleed a lot." He used my handkerchief to wipe up the trail of blood and apply pressure.

"We'll take him to the infirmary and give him a lollipop when you're done." He raised the bloody rag. "This will be disposed of. You have twenty minutes left. I'm watching."

As Sgt. Collins left and silence returned to the cold Spartan room, I heard the white fluorescent tubes above us buzz steadily like a concealed nest of provoked hornets.

I sat back down across from Lonnie. "You certainly reacted quickly to my breach of prison etiquette, didn't you?"

Another silence lasted so long I heard each second tick away on my watch. The room was warm, and I felt myself start to nod off.

"What's Detective Baker look like?" Lonnie asked, looking at me for the first time.

Finally.

"Good. There is someone inside. He's six foot four, more muscular than Sgt. Collins, has a nasty scar around his left eye socket and loves to chew toothpicks like they were the fingertips of bad men. He often wears a parrot green sports coat and his big bald head has a waxy shine to it. What broke your silence?"

He shrugged. "I don't know. You were kind. You stood up for me, and yourself. Does he have a lady friend and, if so, what's her name?"

"Simone. She was an exotic dancer when they met. Give me a tough one."

He raised an eyebrow. "How'd he get that scar?"

"Fighting off a gang of drug dealers who'd attacked Simone in the middle of the night. They chained him to a tree on the east side. I can recite the gory details, but I'd rather not."

"Impressive, but that doesn't mean I should talk to you."

"I've been known to help the occasional person in trouble."

"You feel guilty. You're repaying some kind of civic debt to JoJo. You have my permission to walk away right now with a clear conscience."

I sensed no emotion behind his statement, just opinion.

"Look, you're in about the last place a man would want to be—
"

"You don't know me," Lonnie interrupted. "You come here asking personal questions like I'm some sort of pet sociology or abnormal psych project." He assessed me from head to toe. "What's the worst thing that ever happened to you, your Beemer break down in the 'hood at night?"

I looked him in the eyes. "I'd been a ladies' man most of my adult life. Never even wanted to get serious. But then I let someone get close and fell in love. A deranged client of mine murdered her and then went after me. I should be dead."

Some days I think he succeeded.

"Detective Baker almost pinned the murder on me. It's how we met."

Awkward silence and then recognition spread across his face. "I remember that. The police arrested the killer about the time the Gateway University scandal broke. You passed up book and movie offers?"

I nodded. "I want my private life to remain that way."

He sat for some time in silent contemplation. "Your last new client was the delusional killer."

"Very perceptive," I said. "And I'm only sitting here today, on this side of the table, because Detective Baker and I figured out the truth. I also think he figured out that we need each other."

He smiled wanly. "You know what they say I did, right?"

Was he saying this for shock value? "Yes."

He didn't proclaim his innocence. Rather, he stared at me, seemingly lost in thought. "I like your substance. I apologize for the Beemer comment, that was out of line."

Lonnie's eyes tracked to the door again. Without moving a muscle, he said, "Guard at the door." Then, in a whisper: "My work is over. No one can save me. I'm as good as dead."

I asked him what he meant but all he said was, "Would you check on my momma? LaKeesha Washington, she lives off Grand, on Hebert." He rattled off the street number as the door swung open.

"I'll see her today—" I answered as two heavy-set armed guards surrounded him. They began to unshackle him as Sgt. Collins escorted me from the room. "—And I'll see you the same time tomorrow."

For a fleeting instant a vestige of life fluttered in his eyes. "You mean it."

As I left the room, a guard barked at Lonnie to drag his bony ass to the infirmary for his Band-Aid and lollipop. After the guards unhooked his leg irons from the bolt in the table, Lonnie rose awkwardly and nearly fell twice as he hobbled toward the door. Then I noticed the disability Baker spoke of.

Walking in shackles can't be easy, but doing it while walking on your ankle and being dragged along by a couple of larger guards at their unshackled pace is damn near impossible. The sight of his deformed club foot made me wince.

Scott L. Miller

A DARK NETHERWORLD

I drove north on Grand Avenue past the lush Gateway University campus and its many contemporary buildings of higher learning, beyond the fabulous Fox Theatre and Powell Symphony Hall. It was late afternoon on a fine spring day made for soaking up the sunshine. I had the top down and an old Jimmie Spheeris CD playing. A couple eye blinks later, I crossed over to the dark side of the moon. Manicured landscapes disappeared and, in their place, empty weed-filled lots vied for prominence with abandoned and boarded-up buildings spray painted with gang tags. Inhabited homes, some tidy with yards fenced off as if the owners were trying to hold back the steady march of decay, barely outnumbered the decrepit remains people once called home. I passed a chop suey joint, a tavern, a church, and two quick loan stores. The number of cars on the road decreased. A vendor sold trinkets and jewelry from the hood of his old beater parked on an empty lot. The number of cars on the road decreased. Small clusters of people loitered or milled about outside what appeared to be the area's only open business establishment, a yellow mini-mart/liquor store, while some pedaled bikes or waited for busses. An old Bondo-primed Riveria with tinted windows sped past me and cruised with abandon through a series of red lights.

I passed Grand and Dodier, where Stan the Man Musial patrolled the outfield in old Sportsman's Park fifty years ago, which later was renamed the first Busch Stadium. Ni building remained, those there was a baseball field. Too many vacant buildings and businesses from a bygone era now reduced to empty shells with broken windows and buckled parking lots overrun by weeds and glass. Before National Bridge

Avenue and Fairground Park, I made a left off Grand onto Hebert Street, where some of the mostly brick bungalows sat vacant and dilapidated, one next to another, block after block. Every so often the detritus of a burned-out shell of a house stood in an empty lot like a desiccated skeleton. Postage stamp yards revealed bare spots interrupted by crabgrass, broken glass, and discarded fast-food wrappers. Hebert Street looked to be one of the worst maintained streets in a badly blighted neighborhood.

If Lonnie Washington was printing money like there was no tomorrow, he certainly didn't seem to be spending it on his mother.

LaKeesha's small brick and wood A-frame appeared almost as bleak and Godforsaken as the jail. Shortly after I'd parked my Solstice at the curb, two young boys on the street began fighting and throwing chunks of broken bricks at each other from the scattered rubble of what I

assume used to be a house next door. In the interests of peace (and my cherry red Solstice), I called the boys over and gave them each five dollars to watch my car while I spoke with Mrs. Washington. The smaller one named Ty had a wry smile while DeAndre was taller, darker, and carried more meat on his frame. They grabbed the bills and took their positions.

I peered up at the house and noted that the brick facade needed tuck pointing. Warped wooden steps leading to the front porch were nearly void of paint and one stair was missing altogether. The screen door nearly fell off when I rapped on it, it hung suspended by the strength of two screws, silver duct tape, and a prayer. A short, hefty black woman opened the door a crack. She grimaced, her tongue protruded, she repeatedly smacked and puckered and pursed her lips, while her eyes blinked rapidly. The involuntary and purposeless movements persisted as her fingers moved clumsily up and down the door jamb while she struggled not to move.

"You the po-lice?"

"No ma'm. Are you Mrs. Washington?"

Her nod became a grimace as her tongue shot out like a snake smelling the air. Her lower lip jutted as her head bobbed and weaved. "You with the television peoples?"

I introduced myself. "No, I met Lonnie for the first time last week. I'm a social worker trying to help him. He asked me to check on you and see how you're holding up through all this."

"You a white man in this neighborhood knockin' on my door … and you ain't the po-lice or a reporter?" Her tongue stuck out again and her head bobbed like a turtle's. She seemed confused. "What you say you are again?"

I tried another tact. "I'm a social worker and I talk with Lonnie five days a week about his problems. May we talk for a few minutes?"

Behind me, near my car, the two boys resumed yelling and fighting. This time
the smaller Ty had brought reinforcements—a scrawny German shepherd now joined in the fray, barking and baring his fangs at DeAndre, the gradually building tension in the street appeared to transfer to LaKeesha.

She smacked her lips and the trembling increased. Her expression softened, but then her tongue protruded, her lips smacked, and her head resumed bobbing. She looked in all directions as if for guidance. She seemed to be having an internal dialogue with herself or someone else. She said, "Oh my, I don' know what to do, Skinny. I can't talk with no one unless I check with Lonnie first." When she at last stood still for a brief moment, I noticed she had a lazy right eye. She blinked her eyes, bobbed her head, and looked at me. "Sorry Mister, but I gots to go. His only problem is he shouldn't be in no jail!"

She slammed the door so hard in my face that the screw holding the lower screen hinge bounced onto the porch landing, rolled between the weathered and warped planks, and disappeared into the dark netherworld below.

The same could happen to Lonnie.

His mother was clearly borderline mentally challenged. Her socially inappropriate, bizarre gyrations, movements that would lead the average person on the street to assume she was wildly psychotic didn't faze me in the least. I'd seen the symptoms hundreds of times. But if I didn't want Lonnie to fall between the cracks, I needed answers, and it appeared I wouldn't be getting any today from LaKeesha. *Who is Skinny?*

I turned back to the car and realized the boys had run off, oblivious to their duty, the shepherd chasing DeAndre with Ty bringing up the rear, giggling and happily bashing a dead stick against a row of gnarly tree trunks.

It was time to go to work on the answer man.

Scott L. Miller

BREAD AND CIRCUSES

Never underestimate the power of food. For the rest of my jail visits, I schlepped doughnuts and bear claws and Starbuck's coffee to the guards every morning to grease the wheels, maybe curry a modicum of favor for Lonnie. I learned that Sergeant Donnell Collins had once been a middle linebacker on the Kansas City Chief's practice squad until he blew out a knee ten years ago. He was nicknamed The Truth. The other guards deferred to him. The Truth settled all disputes at his level.

I also became acquainted on a lesser level with the other guards who regularly trolled for doughnuts. There was Smilin' Henry who loved to tell bad jokes, Big Daddy Dwight who had eight kids and a fifty-six inch chest shaped like an oak wine barrel, Rain Man Marty who rarely talked and looked like he'd done too many drugs in his twenties, and the crew cut twins Wilbur the Truck and Zack the Train Johnson who enjoyed hunting, tattoos, and heavy metal music. I got the impression most of the guards had endured their share of hard times and could have landed on the other side of the bars, given a simple twist of fate here or there.

I like to think the sweets bought me a little more time to connect with Lonnie, because I needed every minute of it. I was not allowed to pass him anything tangible, only the meager comfort of words and my time. I imagine, for a man in his position, that didn't seem like much.

His prison file read like a rubber-stamped version of the classic disadvantaged black criminal, with three glaring exceptions, but the telling part came in what it didn't contain. It said Lonnie had been born to a mentally retarded woman with a history of drug abuse and psychiatric illness; father unknown, no other family; the state took custody at birth and he'd spent time in, and ran away from, over ten different foster homes; he was diagnosed with attention deficit disorder as a child and was non-compliant with his medications; workers and practicum students in various residential facilities that warehoused him between foster homes labeled him a loner, an antisocial personality with borderline traits who probably abused small animals and set fires when young, though there was no documentation of it. The reports portrayed adult Lonnie as uncooperative during interviews and intentionally inconsistent with his responses to MMPIs and various psychological and personality tests. He reportedly had negligible insight and judgment, poor impulse control, was manipulative, displayed a blatant disregard for authority (again, with no corroboration), and was deemed a chronic, recalcitrant criminal, dangerous to others, with poor rehabilitation potential. About the deviations: he received a perfect G.E.D. score at age fifteen while in a foster home and, based on his IQ, could have passed the Mensa test in his sleep. He had an uninterrupted work record since age eighteen, at times working two and three jobs; and the file listed no prior crimes against people or property as a juvenile or adult, no drug possession or sales charges, not even a jaywalking or traffic ticket. Felony mass counterfeiting was his first known first brush with the law, if you don't count the runaways from foster homes.

On Monday his right hand shot up in the air again.

"What's with the hand movements? Are you drawing?"

"Force of habit. If I'm a model prisoner, I'm allowed thirty minutes a day to draw. Unsupervised access to pens, pencils, paints, even charcoals, isn't allowed in the special security section—because they're potential weapons." He seemed to look past me, beyond the cinder block walls. "I get the urge to draw something, my hand goes up." He finished his imaginary picture.

"Drawing is an escape, a release for you."

"I did it most every waking hour in the real world." He looked down at his fingers. "They

seem to have a mind of their own in here."

It reminded me of the pacing behavior of a big cat in a zoo.

I nodded at his slender hands. "Are those tattoos?"

"You're not the first person to think that." He turned over his green and black stained hands for my inspection. "These are the permanent inks from my trade."

"The counterfeiting?"

He held my gaze, his eyes hardening. "I worked in a printing business for ten years." He turned away from me and shut down for the rest of our allotted time.

Smilin' Henry escorted me out of the room. He thanked me for the doughnuts and said, "Hey Doc, what costs less, beer nuts or deer nuts?"

"I don't know, Henry."

"Has to be deer nuts, 'cause they're under a buck." He slapped me on the back and grinned. "See ya next time, Doc."

$ $ $

On Tuesday I asked Lonnie if he'd seen or spoken to Detective Baker since his arrest.

He briefly averted his eyes to the door. Body language of looking for the exit meant he didn't want to answer. "Why would I?"

I sensed him withdraw from me again.

Counterfeit

"Your welfare seems important to him. When did you know each other?"

He shrugged, as if to shake off my question. "Don't remember. It was in another world. When we were kids."

"You certainly made an impression on him." I leaned back in my uncomfortable metal chair and studied him. "He's concerned that you're planning to kill yourself. Does he have a reason to worry?"

He didn't answer. He wouldn't look me in the eye.

"You told me the other day that you're already a dead man. Why'd you say that?"

He ignored me and this time Rain Man Marty silently walked me out, his beady eyes shifting nervously in all directions. Marty didn't answer my questions about Lonnie, either.

$ $ $

"I read up on counterfeiting last night," I told Lonnie on Wednesday. "It's said to be the world's *second* oldest profession— seventh century BC saw the advent of currency, and a hundred years later the first counterfeiters appeared."

He nodded. "European countries would draw and quarter counterfeiters or burn them at the stake. The Netherlands boiled them in oil. In the Coliseum the Roman emperors ordered them fed to the lions to entertain the masses, part of their Bread and Circuses..." His voice trailed off.

Was he thinking of his future?

"I learned that the two big counterfeiting booms in the US occurred when paper money appeared."

"In the American colonies around 1650 and especially during the Civil War, when half of the money script was fake," Lonnie interjected.

"Abraham Lincoln enacted a law creating the Secret Service to fight counterfeiting."

"On the very day he was assassinated," he answered. "Early US counterfeiters were hanged and the first bills bore the warning, 'Tis death to counterfeit.' To this day, it remains a capital offense in China, Vietnam, and most of the Middle East."

"You know a lot about counterfeiting," I said, as an outside commotion in the hallway flared. Frenzied screams and shouts, the quick shuffling of feet, and a telltale thud against the cinder block wall. An eerie silence followed.

Ears tuned to the hallway, he listened for movement that never came. He swallowed once and whispered, "I like to read."

"What about the Superdollar. Do you think it's an urban myth?"

In the world of counterfeiting, speculation about the Superdollar was akin to talk of the Holy Grail. In the seventies, the US allegedly sold a large printing press to Iran exactly like the ones our Treasury uses. Rumor is that North Korea now has it and is mass producing copies of US currency so perfect you'd need an electron microscope to tell the fakes from the real thing.

He squirmed in his seat while a brief, wistful look filled his face. Was that a flash of thinly concealed excitement beneath his apathetic façade? "I wouldn't know."

During my doctoral practicum in a state-funded drug and alcohol program, junkies would wax poetic while describing their drug of choice in group sessions. Lonnie showed the same contact high about counterfeiting. A brief display, but one he recognized and curbed.

"When counterfeiting peaked again in the early nineties, the Treasury redesigned our paper currency in 1996—"

"Increasing jail time and fines for forgers," he said. Stopping himself, he waggled a slender green-black finger at me. "We're done today."

He's a smart, patient man. Part of the skill set needed in his profession.

On my way out I followed in Big Daddy Dwight's immense shadow.

"He's so small and frail, Dwight. How is he managing in here?"

He turned back to me. "He hasn't talked to you about his time?" He read the answer from my look and said, "It happens with a first timer. Some worry they'll flip out, others think talking about the inside with a visitor makes them relive it instead of forgetting it and focusing on the outside for half an hour. I'm only allowed to say that prisoner Washington is doing his time here. You're welcome to make an appointment with the Superintendent to discuss it further, if you'd like."

I held out my hands. "What harm could it do to answer? Is this standard guard-speak for all inmates, or just this one?"

He ignored me and resumed walking. We turned a few corners and were back at the guard station. "Here we are, Doc. You may collect your belongings on your way out. Have a blessed day."

So much for cutting corners.

That night Baker called me at home and said, "Get two beers from the fridge and go to the front door."

He sat sprawled in one of the chairs on my landing, batting at a persistent fly,. "Summer gonna take over soon and make people crazy. People kill each other more when it gets hot. It'll soon be the start of my busy season."

I sat down and passed him a Rolling Rock. "What the hell am I doing with Lonnie?"

He twisted off the green cap. "You goin' all Sartre on me, Cool Breeze?"

"Don't be a smart-ass. How can I possibly help this guy?"

"You earn his trust yet?"

"No. He's talking, but only admits he knows a lot about counterfeiting."

"He must like you if you got him talkin' already."

"You say you haven't seen him for years. How do you know what he's like now?"

Baker drained the rest of his beer and burped. "Got another?"

"No. You're not telling me everything, and I'm getting tired of the games. I quit."

"You can't!"

"Watch me."

I saw the panic in his eyes. "What you find out about him so far?"

"He's genius-level smart and extremely controlled, he won't discuss suicide and he's a pro at hiding his feelings. My gut tells me he's hopeless and fearful for his life, but that he accepts his fate as if it's some sort of penance. I expected someone different. His first brush with the law comes this late in life and it's high stakes counterfeiting? Why? The only positive human connection he admits having is with his mentally challenged mother. Like you, he's not telling me everything."

Baker nodded. "No minor arrests, nothing, then at thirty-nine he hits the big-time for counterfeiting. Don't you think that's strange?"

"Are you saying he's innocent, that he was set up?"

"No, he's a counterfeiter, like I told you from the jump. I'm saying we up to our eyeballs in strange here and the little brother needs all the help he can get."

"Why does he say he's a dead man? Why would someone want to kill him?" I asked, handing him another beer.

Baker twisted the cap and stared at me like I was being obtuse. "Why do people kill? The answer's old as man, Breeze. Think about it."

We sat in silence until he said, "Four hundred seventy-five US bills weigh one pound. One pound of the little brother's bills is worth $47,500 and twenty-five million dollars weighs over 526 pounds. His share, assuming they split it equally, weighed more than he did. Millions in cash, unlike jewels, is heavy to lug around and easier to spot. This batch is hot and heat leaves a trail." He leaned back and drank half the beer.

"Maynard said the police recovered ninety-five percent of it, so why would anyone want to kill him for counterfeit money he doesn't have?"

He stared at me with that 'you-know-why' look again. "Lonnie removed all twenty-five million from the basement the night *before* the raid. They closed up shop and the little brother was about to burn the two flawed test sheets when that old cop came calling. Those two sheets the only hard evidence they got on him."

"You said you haven't talked to him. I quit."

The unmovable force that is Baker grabbed my arm and stopped me in my tracks.

"I got a lot of birdies flyin' out there, Breeze, and this is bigger than that scandal you helped us break last year."

"Helped *you* break?"

"You know what I mean," he said, exasperated.

"Then I'm definitely out." I looked at my arm he held and then back at him. "Let…me…go."

His vice grip tightened. "The little brother needs you. I need you. If I gave you the whole story, lives would be ruined and a lot of good undone. You have to trust me—learn it on your own and you'll understand. Nothing and no one is as you suspect in this cluster fuckin' melodrama; it's all upside down and inside out."

"Why do you need Tony's help if you have all these birdies out there? Answer that or I'm gone with the wind."

That smug smirk resurfaced. "Read this." He handed me Xeroxed pieces of paper that described in bare bones narrative the capture of Lonnie Washington, including a detailed written and pictorial inventory of the impounded counterfeiting equipment, money, weapons, and drugs. The officer in charge at the scene was none other than Joseph Moreno, the city police chief. Assistant Chief Rhymes, and officers Carter, Malvern, and Downey were other cops listed as present. Exactly as Maynard described on camera, it curtly described a coordinated police raid on an illegal counterfeiting operation.

"So?"

Baker pointed at the sheets. "You see the name Dan Quinn anywhere?"

I shook my head. "Doesn't this happen all the time—the higher ups take credit for the collar? Like in the movies when the FBI swoops in to trump the local fuzz?"

Baker took the paper from me and returned it to his jacket pocket. "One of my birdies saw the bust go down. He said Quinn was the only cop there."

"How reliable is your feathered friend?"

Baker lowered his eyes briefly. "He's a chippy. He smokes crack when he can get it, or some weed. He on the payroll, but he's always been solid with me."

I rolled my eyes. "I quit," and got up to go inside.

Baker relented. "The little brother told his court-appointed that Quinn was the only cop on the scene. You said it yourself—if this were a coordinated police sting, how could an old man, on oxygen, with one foot in the grave, escape through one of the two exits in the building against five experienced, fully-armed cops? Dan Quinn is a fat old Irish beat cop with nineteen years' service; he drinks and eats while marking off the days to his twenty and out. He couldn't catch a one-legged pickpocket in a closet."

"So what does Quinn have to say about it?"

Baker tensed. "He's into the wind. Never clocked out that shift and there's been no answer on his home phone. Missed his next shift and didn't call in. Chief Mofka ordered the building super to let them into Quinn's apartment. No evidence of foul play, but it looked like he'd packed in a hurry. Wife left him years ago. No kids, no siblings."

I thought back to the report. "What do officers Carter, Malvern, and Downey say about Quinn?"

Baker deftly peeled off the beer label in one whole piece. "That he was never

there."

"And Tony fits into this how?"

A toothpick slid into the side of Baker's mouth. "I never knew Quinn, but a birdie told me when his wife left him it affected his work and the brass forced him into counseling—"

"Enter Tony."

He touched the tip of his nose. "Back when he was a hotshot headshrinker like you in private practice. My sources dried up. I can't ask The Voice about him 'cause I'm a homicide dick and he wouldn't tell me shit anyway because of confidentiality. You his best friend so maybe you can connive some way to help us find Quinn, or at least what happened to him. You got the gift, man. I seen you in action."

"Who's playing whom now?"

Baker rose and patted his breast pocket. "Don't mention the report, not even to The Voice. If word got out, I'd lose my badge. You got me over a barrel and I need your help."

I told Baker the conversation I'd overheard in the bathroom stall before the press conference, what the man who sounded like Maynard had said and the other man's responses. By the time I'd finished, his muscles were coiled like springs. "I think we're onto something," I said.

"It all fits. But we got no proof, even if you were sure it was Maynard."

I didn't quit. I still thought about it, but Lonnie remained an intriguing enigma. What is his *work* and why isn't it complete? My comfortable—and safe—sofa beckoned, but unknown forces drew me to see whether Lonnie could complete his life's work from the twisted rubble of his foiled master plan.

He and Baker had blazed a twisting path for me. I decided to see where it led.

FAIR IS FOUL

On Thursday LaKeesha Washington silently invited me in, and I followed as she trudged up fourteen rickety steps to her one-bedroom loft. The living room looked like it hadn't seen a fresh coat of paint since the Carter administration and, even though it was five in the afternoon on a sunny day, inside was nearly dark as a cave. She directed me to one of two threadbare paisley print chairs with armrests. I removed old National Enquirers from the cushion and sat down. A shot chair spring stabbed me in the back.

LaKeesha stared at me with her one good eye while the lazy one drifted off somewhere over my left shoulder. She smacked her lips as her tongue periodically shot from her mouth. Her head bobbed up and down as before. A siren whooped below as an ambulance sped down the street.

"Thanks for inviting me in, Mrs. Washington."

"It's LaKeesha. I ain't never been married. Sorry about the chair," she said. "The one here just as bad. So, how's my baby Boo?"

For the next fifteen minutes I put a positive spin on how he looked and said that he was keeping his spirits up. I kept his remarks about being a dead man to myself and that he doesn't want her to visit him in jail, at least for now. "Lonnie wants me to tell you not to worry about him and that he's more concerned about you. He wants me to check in on you from time to time to make sure you're okay."

"When can I see him?"

"Lonnie said he'd like to wait until the case isn't so high profile on television and

you can come visit him without being pestered by reporters."

Counterfeit

She seemed to understand as she repeatedly tried and failed to smooth the creases in her polyester slacks with crooked fingers. I read it as an anxiety tell. She finally raised her head and said, "That sounds like my Boo." Then, in a rueful voice, "After all I put him through, too." She squinted and audibly smacked her lips.

The darkened room was stuffy, but two gray plastic box fans circulated the closed air. "What do you mean?"

"Boo didn't tell you? I was no fit momma for that child. I was fifteen—drinkin' and smokin', runnin' the streets. Didn't have a lick of common sense and still don't have much. One night I got drunk and high … with someone I looked up to. I don't remember havin' sex … but I must've because seven months later my little Boo came into the world." A cloud passed over her round face as she continued, "The DFS peoples took him right after he was born. I had no clue how to take care of myself, much less a premie with a twisted-up club foot. Boo been in and out of foster homes, some of them treated him shameful. You know what helped him survive, Mister? His drawings. That boy took to art like a duck to water, I swear." Crayons, pencils, markers, charcoal, oils, watercolors. He can draw anything he put his mind to. Paint a portrait or shade a sketch of anything or anybody. He sure didn't get that from me; I can't even draw a straight line."

LaKeesha's rickety front door banged open, and the muffled sounds of voices and laughter on the landing preceded the steady clog of wooden heels on hardwood slowly making their way upstairs. Three women appeared, lugging armfuls of groceries into the tiny kitchen. They wore brightly colored, traditional dashiki dresses with layers upon layers of jangling gold and silver costume jewelry. One was stocky, one was hippy, while the one in the center was much older, tiny, rail thin, and wore a bright purple turban.

The lady in the picture next to Earl.

"You better not be the press," the little woman said, with a hint of steel in her deep voice. She glared at me, a hand on her hip. She reminded me a little of the late Lena Horne.

"Excuse me, Mister," LaKeesha said meekly, rising, looking as if she were in trouble. She motioned for the women to join her in the kitchen.

A few minutes later, the three women returned and the petite one sat in LaKeesha's chair eying me warily. The other two stood, flanking their leader, like devoted acolytes. LaKeesha remained in the kitchen, and I heard cabinet doors open and close, the rustling of grocery bags, and the slow clunk of cans being stacked on the counter.

"We're going to talk while LaKeesha puts away her groceries," said the diminutive lady in the middle. "My name is Yolanda. Everyone calls me Skinny Yolanda or just plain Skinny. I got the biggest mouth in the city and take shit from no one." Inclining her head to the right, she said, "This is Tyra—" She pointed a bony finger over her left shoulder, saying, "—and Shirley. That poor woman in the kitchen has been through hell her entire life. We need to be sure you're on her side. How do we know The Man ain't using you to get to Lonnie?"

She glared at me, crossed her arms, and swayed a few times from side to side as her friends seconded her sentiment with a chorus of "Mm-hmms."

"Ladies, I'm Dr. Mitchell Adams, a social worker in private practice. LaKeesha may have chosen to tell you I have a connection with Lonnie, but I cannot disclose anything to you without his permission. He has asked me to check on his mother from time to time and give her updates about him. That's why I'm here. Do you have a problem with that?"

Yolanda didn't uncross her folded arms. "If you're appointed by the court, then you workin' for The Man. That makes you no friend to Lonnie or us."

I explained my lack of fee.

"Huh." Yolanda was speechless, but only momentarily. "You have some sort of identification?"

I gave her one of my business cards.

She handed it back to me. "Anyone can have these made."

I produced my driver's license, holding my thumb over my address. She compared my face to the photo.

"Your card said you have a Ph.D. in Social Work and your own private practice in Clayton, why are you seeing Lonnie for free?"

"Detective Baker, St. Louis City Homicide asked me," I said

"Little JoJo called you?"

"Yes, ma'am."

She mulled this over and raised an eyebrow. She seemed to soften at the mention of Baker's name. "I see. Lonnie didn't tell me you'd be paying a visit to his mother, so he must have some trust in you." She cast a furtive look at the young, hourglass-shaped woman on her right. "But trust put him where he is and turned the others into fugitives. He has more faith in people than I ever will. I will go along with this, even though it's against my better judgment. If I find out The Man is using you against Lonnie and the others, I will personally whup your ass up and down this block in front of God and everyone." A pause, then: "And listen here, you think JoJo Baker is some kind of badass? I can put him across my knee on a whim, so don't even think about crossing me, honey." Skinny shook her head from side to side as her tiny frame swayed in the chair.

Her friends seconded the sentiment with a chorus of amens and hallelujahs.

"Does LaKeesha understand the charges her son faces?"

"She doesn't completely grasp the concept. She knows it's bad but thinks he's been accused of stealing money at work. She knows he's innocent of that because he's always been an honest, hard-working man."

She reclined in her seat and her intensity level dialed down a notch. "Now that we've dispensed with the pleasantries, let me tell you how Lonnie Washington entered this world. If you're going to help him, you need to know how this world has treated him. Before that, I must tell you about LaKeesha."

I sat forward in my chair. Finally, just maybe, I might get somewhere.

"LaKeesha was born dirt poor and mentally challenged. Her mother was a prostitute and her father unknown. Mother sure did like her heroin, though." Skinny pronounced it the old-fashioned St. Louis city street way, 'herr-rhine.'

"LaKeesha's attendance in Special School was spotty, given the lack of structure at home. At twelve, she had to fend off the parade of men who passed in and out of her mother's wayward life. She ran away from home countless times. When things got bad, she stayed with us. At fifteen we got her a job bussing tables in a pool hall on the north side. One night she started feeling sick and screamed at the top of her lungs, 'My cooter hurts!' The hall went quiet as LaKeesha dropped to her knees and shouted, 'Sweet Jesus, I been shot! I'm dyin'!' All the badass men stood there, mouths open like they'd seen a ghost. They thought she was havin' a seizure or the St. Vitus Dance. When her water broke, I ordered two big strapping bucks to lift her onto their table. No one, not even LaKeesha, knew she was pregnant. She's always been a plus-sized girl." Yolanda smiled and added, "Earl took one look at the table and said to his friend, "Let's call it a draw," and passed out. I delivered little Lonnie right on the green felt. We wouldn't have let her drink malt liquor and smoke weed if we had known." Yolanda smiled and added, "Earl woke up, saw the mess on the table, told his friend 'Let's call it a draw,' and passed out again. I dragged his bony ass onto another table and attended to mother and child until the EMTs arrived."

"So over the years you and Earl became her de facto aunt and uncle?"

A dark cloud seemed to settle over her weathered face, "The one and the same scrawny, infamous little Negro. That was before Earl bought the printing shop. He was a butcher in his thirties when Lonnie made his surprise entrance into the world. We've had our knock-down drag-outs, but I can't stay mad at that crazy old man for long. We've been together forty years."

"Was there a father figure in Lonnie's life?"

Tyra and Shirley looked at Yolanda who appraised me again.

"Family Services took baby Lonnie into custody straight from the hospital. I was full of piss and vinegar about it at the time, but LaKeesha was mentally retarded, fifteen, and living in a converted closet behind the pool hall. We didn't have room for LaKeesha and a newborn in our little house, according to DFS." Her jaw muscles tensed. "She didn't know who the baby daddy was."

I started to say something, reconsidered, and let her continue.

"That boy's club foot twisted in and down at almost a ninety-degree angle. He had manipulations, castings, and his first surgery at age three months. A post-operative infection and pneumonia nearly killed him twice. His caseworker called him a failure-to-thrive baby. He underwent an Achilles tenotomy surgery and had to wear some contraption called a Denis Browne Bar splint twenty-three hours a day for three months and then twelve hours a day until he was four. The structure in those foster homes was inconsistent, so if he resisted wearing the brace long enough, he eventually got his way. The more time he spent out of it, the more he

reverted to walking on his ankle or side of his foot, and the more permanent his disability became.

The two other women tsk tsked and shook their heads as if bemoaning the same sad story for the first time.

"He was bullied and beaten in most of the group and foster homes because he was a small, shy child with a deformity that made him different. He learned to keep his feelings to himself and his mouth shut. He turned inward and lost himself in books, falling in love with art because of his special gift. He loved the Renaissance and knows the works of all the artists in the period. He'd sit for hours in the Art Museum and sketch paintings. He avoided the delinquents in the group homes as best he could, but when the abuse became unbearable he'd run away, sometimes to the museum. The police always brought him back and the bullying resumed. Lonnie made himself into the smart young man he is today."

And a felony counterfeiter.

I heard a glass jar fall and break on the kitchen floor, followed by idle muttering.

"Does LaKeesha need help in there?"

Skinny Yolanda grinned. "I'm sure she does, but that's one of her jobs. She does everything slow, that's the way she is. We looked after her all the years he was in foster care. This is part of the routine Lonnie devised for her, and it works. She had to quit drinking and smoking and develop a healthier lifestyle to earn this house. This is a palace compared to what she grew up in."

"Did Lonnie have any history of legal problems before this arrest?"

"No."

"What happened to him after the foster homes?"

"When he turned seventeen, the state system didn't know what to do with him, so they found LaKeesha HUD housing, a caseworker to help manage her affairs, and reunited them. For the next four years he worked two jobs. At twenty-one he moved into his own place because he believes every able adult should be self-sufficient. He saw her daily, made certain there was healthy food in her pantry and that her bills were paid on time."

LaKeesha appeared at the arched doorway and announced, "Yolanda, my chores are done, and I cleaned up the mess on the floor. I'm finna to take my nap now." She turned to me, her lips smacking and tongue protruding. "It was nice meetin' you Dr. Mitchell, and thanks for telling me about my baby Boo."

"Nice meeting you. Lonnie wants me to see you once a week. May I visit you this time next week?"

"Okay," she answered, turning and padding slowly down the hallway in worn yellow hospital-issue footies.

Skinny Yolanda smiled in LaKeesha's direction and turned back to me, "Right on schedule. She has the mind of a child, but with guidance she does what she can. With Lonnie gone again, we'll look after our little sister."

"How long has she had Tardive dyskinesia?"

"Years. The clinic doctors misdiagnosed her as being mentally ill. Her condition is irreversible."

Long-term use of antipsychotic neuroleptic medications causes the neurological disorder knows as Tardive dyskinesia, characterized by repetitive, involuntary, and purposeless movements. She will likely die before her time due to TD. LaKeesha was a classic example of incompetent health care. Sadly, she was not alone.

"She's lucky to have friends like you three."

"We more than friends," blurted Tyra, the hippy hourglass figure in orange standing to the right of Yolanda.

Skinny Yolanda shot Tyra a surreptitious dirty look. "Lonnie may trust you, but I'm a mangy old dog who's been kicked one too many times."

More than friends.

"Yolanda is with Earl, Tyra is Benny's lady friend, and Shirley may be Mrs. Sparks. I smiled at the ladies and said, "I commend you for looking after LaKeesha."

The larger ladies, eager to respond, deferred to Yolanda like they were muzzled and tethered to a leash. The stern look on Skinny Yolanda's face said I'd learn no more tonight.

Counterfeit

"Is that your red sports car parked on the street?" asked the plump Shirley to Skinny's left.

I nodded.

Skinny Yolanda smirked. "If you don't want to see it on blocks missing tires, a stereo and what not, I wouldn't leave it alone much longer."

"I hired DeAndre and Ty to watch my car."

The ladies exchanged glances and giggled, which soon escalated into full-out laughter and knee-slapping. Shirley's belly shook like a bowl of green Jell-O under her bright dashiki. Skinny pointed at me while struggling to compose herself. "Little Ty can jimmy a car in under a minute, and I do believe DeAndre's even faster."

In the rapidly advancing twilight, I heard glass breaking and the throbbing, reverberating bass of Blaupunkt speakers from a passing car in the street below. Some of the wind went out of my sails thinking about the safety of my car.

"You mentioned a structured routine. Lonnie asked me to see his mother this time every

week. I told him I would." I repeated my earlier question. "Is that going to be a problem?"

Skinny stared at me, unblinking. The tiny woman, hard as bone, said, "Why are you

doing this?"

That was a question for which I had no complete answer.

"Baker asked me for a favor, and I like Lonnie."

I could tell Skinny didn't believe me. "Give me your hands."

Confused, I held them out. She leaned forward, so close I felt her breath on my face. Strong, bony fingers turned my hands over while her relentless, unblinking gaze assessed me. Her dry palms felt like sandpaper and her fingers like talons digging into my skin. Tyra and Shirley closed their eyes and swayed behind Skinny, who muttered strange words under her breath. I heard Mambo, Loas and Petros more than once, but the rest was unintelligible.

"You don't work with your hands as much as you should, boy." She closed her eyes and swayed rhythmically. She began mumbling to herself as sorrow filled her lined face. "Doubt is your brother, and a great shadow shrouds you. But your light is strong so follow it. You are here for the right reasons, you just don't know them yet." Her penciled-on eyebrows knitted together while a look of anguish spread across her leathery face. Spasms racked her slight body as she said, "He will change you, and you will betray him. One of you will die and one will be reviled."

Skinny Yolanda opened her yellowed eyes, exhausted. Tyra and Shirley gently laid their hands on her shoulders.

I retracted my hands, fighting the urge to wipe them on my slacks.

If this was a test, I think I just failed. I was prepared to be shown the door.

Yolanda stood up straight as a post. "The dark days are upon us, and we will all be challenged. I will tell the neighborhood brothers that you and your shiny car are off limits, at Lonnie's request. They in turn will pass the word to the gangs, but I warn you that does not guarantee your safety. Maintain your business arrangement with DeAndre and Ty," she said with a wry smile, "the responsibility will do them good."

Counterfeit

"Sounds like Lonnie's will carries great weight in the neighborhood."

The smile evaporated and the callousness returned to her voice. "You may be book smart, but here you are a babe in the woods. The truth you seek is found in the lives of those on the streets. Open your eyes and ears to this abandoned world. We are a largely forgotten people, but many in number and strength. Your world should never forget that, boy. Listen to the spoken and unspoken words of those you meet on your journey. Talk with the beggar in the street, do not look the other way and pretend he does not exist. Experience the world as he does. Only then will you learn the truth instead of what you expect to find." She nodded toward the door. "Remember my warning. Leave us."

I had a strange feeling I was Macbeth exiting the lair of The Weird Sisters, portending the future with a touch of their hands. I recalled the play's ending.

Fair is foul, and foul is fair.

My couch called to me, like a true friend. Baker's hands were tied and he wouldn't say why. What have I gotten myself into?

I returned home and Googled those chanted words. *Great.* I'd just had a Haitian voodoo priestess warn me that the arcane truth about a crippled counterfeiter waited for me somewhere on the streets in the 'hood—and that one of us will die.

How I longed to speak with Kris, draw strength from her. In bed, wide-awake, I looked to the sky but clouds hid the stars. I closed my eyes, imagined her next to me, listening, suggesting. Her words cut in and out like a blocked radio signal and disappeared. Had the light gone out? I longed for my best friend and lover so much I feared I'd split in two.

I'd caught brief flashes of the old me. Taking the hard road, doing the right thing. If I was the one to die, at least we'd be reunited.

BOOK TWO: TRUTH ON THE STREETS

What is done out of love always takes place
between good and evil.
Friedrich Nietzsche

Scott L. Miller

TO BE HONEST

When Kris wrestled with a problem, she'd bake some elaborately sinful treat or cook a gourmet meal foreign to her. Taking a step back to do something new freed up her mind.

Tonight I made my first pizza from scratch. While the aromas of sliced garlic, fresh basil and feta cheese mingled in my kitchen, I read archived articles about the fairy-tale famous Maynard family. Great-grandfather and grandfather were resolute men of iron and steel with little education who built their companies from the bottom, transforming them into industry leaders in steel and shipping. John Maynard Senior was the first to attend college, graduating with a law degree and earning a reputation as the most feared prosecuting attorney east of the Mississippi. His wife Catherine, a former beauty queen, stood as sole heiress to her father's beer empire. Business connections convinced Senior to make a run for the Senate. He won and served five terms. With a formidable power base established, he ran for president, won again, and served two terms. By the time Junior was born, the Maynard name contained power and old money in a state renowned for it. Born on the fourth of July, news of the delivery spread like word of an army returning victorious from the battlefield. Junior rode home from the hospital in a Bentley and grew up at Dogwood Farms, nine hundred acres of lush blue-green rolling hills where stallions covered brood mares and thoroughbreds trained to be stakes winners. Junior had national name recognition from his White House years. His pedigree, good looks, and charm garnered him the moniker *Golden Boy*.

I ended by reading recent news articles. The *St. Louis Post-Dispatch* dubbed Junior a "PARAGON OF VIRTUE," the *New York*

Counterfeit

Times labeled him a "CRIME CRUSADER," and in the article "THE FUTURE KING?" the *Wall Street Journal* asked when, not if, the first-born to the throne of one of the nation's most powerful and successful businesses would parlay "his business connections, his family's political legacy, and his brilliant legal mind" into another two-term Maynard presidency. In a country without royalty, he was indeed The Boy King.

Enough Camelot.

Back to the streets. Where to start? Do I wander aimlessly down the streets of the north city corridor with a lantern like Diogenes looking for an honest man? Do I squeeze Baker again for information he won't give? Do I press Tony about a former client of his who may be missing and somehow involved in a doctored police report and, if so, how do I broach the subject? The oven timer dinged and, instead of heralding a brilliant and insightful idea, I salivated. I pulled the pizza out of the oven, poured a glass of beer, and decided to invite Debbie Macklin to lunch. Our paths had crossed for years, and we'd always been more alike than I care to admit—competitive, driven, opinionated, cynical, and full of ourselves. We'd had a falling out last year after a schizophrenic client of mine made the news when he was severely beaten and left for dead outside a Jefferson County "massage parlor" that served as a front of prostitution. I convinced her to do a timely piece on massage parlors versus licensed massage therapy businesses. My ulterior motive was to exert enough legal pressure and public outrage over his attack to shut the parlor down.

Sensing a media opportunity, she scheduled the filming of my slot to overlap with the with the interview of the massage parlor boss, a pimp named DeLuca. Emotions ran high in the studio and I lost my cool. She got what she wanted. Ratings soared for days as the heated exchange and my right punch to the pimp's jaw were replayed three days running. The massage parlor wasn't shut down, but it was driven out of Jefferson County and my client eventually recovered. After Kris's murder, she'd knocked on my door with condolences and a giant fruit basket. A few weeks later, she asked me out, in a nice way, and I declined, in a nice way.

Debbie's crew was filming something out in West County the next morning, so I met her at the 54th Street Grill in Chesterfield Valley. She walked through the door twenty minutes late wearing an oversized red cashmere sweater and white stonewashed jeans with matching red tennis shoes. Since her elfin feet were never on camera, she wore tennies for comfort. As she sat, I caught a generous splash of *Euphoria* perfume. Her blonde hair was pulled back in a ponytail held in place with a matching red band. A misbehaving bang occasionally fell in front of her slender face, which she'd brush back with a quick flick of her hand.

"Sorry I'm late. We had to do thirteen takes at Chesterfield City Hall with one of our state representatives. She kept us waiting, and then insisted on getting her rant just right about Missouri's illegal immigration problem. That issue's older than Benghazi. Move on to a new topic. I'd love to check the citizenship status of the kitchen workers in her husband's restaurant and the gardeners on their estate. Hopefully, the piece will remain in the can. I thought we'd moved on to more important topics since the last election, but, after all, this is Missourah."

Still the same Deb, yearning to land a national news gig on a bigger, brighter stage.

She noticed me looking at her oversized sweater. The temperature gauge on my dashboard had read 84.

"I'm always cold, sue me."

"That's because you have no meat on your bones."

Our bright-eyed young waitress introduced herself as Tiffany and took our order. Debbie asked for a garden salad with fat free balsamic vinaigrette on the side and water with a lemon wedge while I chose a blackened Cajun burger and a second Corona. Tiffany happily bounced toward the kitchen.

"It's good to see you again, Mitch. I hope you're doing as well as you look." She sat leaning forward, smiling, her voice flush with anticipation. "I've missed you at the station."

Oh, no. She's trying too hard. She thinks this is a date.

"I always choose you when I watch the news. I saw you question John Maynard the other day. What do you know about him, off the record?"

She stiffened and blotted her ruby red lips with a napkin. "'Off the record,' that's my line. What's your interest in Maynard?"

"Curiosity, he's a local personality from a famous family. He's about to try a big case. His star is rising."

Her eyes narrowed to suspicious slits. "I'm here for this?"

She quickly painted me in a corner. I held her stare and leaned forward. "To be honest, I also wanted to see you."

Never trust anyone who starts a sentence that way, Deb.

Perky Tiffany arrived with my charred burger and Debbie's hamster food, then sped away to her next table. I saw older patrons begin to take notice of Debbie, the local news personality. A few simply looked over while several young men ogled her.

"That's more like it." Her smile returned. "Okay, Maynard. He's brilliant in court and waits for the perfect time to go for the jugular. I've met him off camera and he's the real deal, articulate, charming, and witty. He's a patriot and a family man. His lofty pedigree and ruggedly handsome good looks don't hurt, either."

"And 'off camera' means?"

She nibbled a lettuce tip and her eyes gleamed. "After a shoot with Missouri politicians in Jeff City, I was invited to a party that lasted into the next morning. One with lots of drinking and loose lips. For me, those soirees are like blood in the water to a shark. John was there and the movers and shakers kept talking about how they want him to make a run for the vacant senate seat in the fall."

"That would be exciting," I said, trying my best to mirror her intensity level without overselling it. I sipped my beer. "He sounds like someone I'd like to meet."

She blotted her lips again and sat evaluating me. Is she sizing me up, trying to figure out my angle? She smiled. "I think that can be arranged. Be my escort to a private campaign party at the Haller estate and you can meet him this Saturday night."

She handed me a card with her home address and phone number already on the back. "It's formal. The station owner has a reserved table. Don't worry, you aren't obligated to make a contribution."

I hid my surprise. "I'm always ready for an excuse to get my tux out of mothballs."

"Great. Pick me up at seven. Drinks at eight. My building has a doorman. Park out front and have Maurice call up for me." She looked at her watch. "Damn, I wish I had more time, but I have to meet my crew to turn a live shot for five."

As she got up, she squeezed my shoulder and whispered, "I'm glad you called." I caught a much stronger whiff of her perfume.

Counterfeit

Déjà vu all over again. We all have our uses, and Type-A Debbie and I had been down this road before. I took some of her uneaten lettuce and placed it on what remained of my burger while she rushed to her silver Jeep Cherokee, climbed in, and drove away like she'd just robbed the place. Her personalized plates read: 4 4ALL.

Tiffany ambled by and placed the bill on our table with a bubbly 'Thank You for coming!' She spelled her name in large loopy letters, the i dotted with a big heart. A smiley face decorated the bottom of the bill. I smiled and hoped the world would never take that away from her and that no man would use her the way I planned to use Debbie.

SUMMER ON THE NORTH SIDE

The truth is to be found in the lives of those on the streets. That's what Skinny had told me.

I'd made plenty of home visits in the city years ago when I worked for the state and was well aware of the Department of Justice statistics that mental health workers who make home visits are six times more likely to be victims of non-fatal, violent crimes than the general population.

If the truth is to be found in the lives of those on the streets, I headed back to the north corridor in search of it.

Not knowing where to start, I returned to Hebert Street to confer with my diminutive, neophyte employees DeAndre and Ty. I found DeAndre up a tree, lighting firecrackers and tossing them at a set of plastic toy soldiers he'd arranged in the dirt below. The remains of a model tank in the center of the green infantrymen lay melting in flames, a casualty of model glue and a lighter, a small plume of smoke billowing out of its sunken turret from a well-placed cherry bomb. Nearby, Ty launched bottle rocket after bottle rocket into the vacant lot next to LaKeesha's building.

They had a plan and were sticking to it until all their ammo was gone. *I hire only the very best.*

I parked a safe distance from the tree, thankful the snarling German shepherd was nowhere in sight.

As I walked toward DeAndre's tree an exploding firecracker sent a bazooka-wielding soldier tumbling end over end down a slope. "Nice shot," I said.

DeAndre scrambled down from his bomber's perch while Ty dashed across the street toward me, yelling, "Want us to watch your car again, Dr. Mitch?"

The older DeAndre shouted as he jumped from the lowest branch. "Ten dollars this time, each."

I reached for my wallet. "I have a deal for you."

DeAndre said, "We hear you a social worker. You gonna put LaKeesha in a nursing home?"

It's a hard-to-kill stereotype promulgated by television. Locking the elderly and disabled in nursing homes and taking babies away from their parents is de rigueur for social workers on the boob tube.

I waved two ten-dollar bills in the air. "Nope, I'm trying to help her son. You guys know Lonnie?"

Ty started to answer but DeAndre silenced him with a slap on top of the head. The older boy said, "He rich. Ever'body in the neighborhood know him."

"There's a ten for each of you—if you watch my car *and* give me the name of a grown-up nearby who will talk to me about Lonnie."

Ty began to blurt his response when DeAndre punched him hard on the arm, "Wait your turn, chump." DeAndre ignored Ty's grimace of pain and turned back to me. "Next block over, the house on the corner, dude name of Terrell Barnett live there, goes by T-Bone. He cool. He knows Lonnie. Maybe he talk to you. Gimme my money, please."

"Here you go. What about you, Ty?"

The smaller, younger Ty scratched his head and dropped his remaining bottle rockets. Picking them up awkwardly, he pointed down Hebert. "See that house with the green door at the end of the block? Old

Miss Givens live there. The doorbell works, but you gotta wait." He paused to nod his head and grin. "She move real slow."

"You're the man, Ty. Here you go." I handed him his ten.

My hyperactive little minions ran off to continue their pyrotechnic fun, once again
oblivious to my shiny red Solstice.

T-Bone or old Miss Givens? I flipped a coin and it landed tails for T-Bone.

Terrell Barnett lived on Sullivan Avenue off Grand, in a small run-down brick bungalow with a full front porch and no swing. Bars protected the windows and both shades were drawn and discolored by the sun. Flattened Pampers cardboard boxes taped to the inside of the front windows blocked any view of the front room. There was no doorbell so I knocked. Nothing. I banged louder on the door. Still nothing. I tried one final time, fitting my hand between the steel bars and rapping on a glass pane.

I heard shuffling inside and a minute later the door opened enough for coal-colored eyes with muddy scleras to peer at me. The unmistakable pungent aroma of marijuana wafted my way while muffled rap music beat rhythmically from a back room. The person behind the door didn't move or say a word.

"Sorry to disturb you, Mr. Barnett. My name's Mitchell Adams. I'm talking to people in your neighborhood today—"

"You a census taker? I'm the only one livin' here, tha's all I gotta tell you." He started to close the door.

"I'm not with the census bureau, T-Bone. I'm talking to people in the neighborhood about Lonnie Washington. Have you—"

Counterfeit

The droopy red slits widened, the door slammed shut, and the chain behind the door slid open in its track.

The weathered door creaked open and a huge young tattooed black male built like a refrigerator stepped onto the porch. He wore a tight-fitting wife-beater T-shirt and baggy L.A.

Lakers sweats. He'd put on dark shades against the bright sun. The end of a roach dangled in a hemostat held between two meaty fingers.

Frowning, he stared down at me. "Why you want to know?"

"I'm here to learn how he is viewed in the community—"

"They should throw away the key on that uppity nigger," he interrupted again. "Best thang you can do is let him burn in hell."

"What'd he do to make you feel that way?"

T-Bone took a drag, sucking the smoke deep into his lungs. He exhaled. "He tole me to stop chasin' the dragon. Here I been his momma's neighbor more than a year, watchin' out for her, even cut her fucking grass once or twice but tha's not good enough." He shook his head, saying, "Here we all suppose to be brothers in the 'hood. Not him. My man Deuce got plans for a nightclub with a mosh pit where the waitresses are pole dancers dressed in sports uniforms. Tha's an idea waitin' to pop, man. He even found a building near the Loop with me as bouncer and he just need the start-up capital, but that little gimp turn him down. My homey Cornelius finna to open a bar once he out of rehab but will the little big man with all the green help him? Hell, no. He *too good* now he hit da prime time. Probably spent it all on hos and blow. I'm glad the po-po nabbed his scrawny ass. You want more, talk to the brothers hangin' at the mini-mart." He shook his head and added, "Wish I knew where Mooney and the rest are so I could collect the reward. You see that gimpy cocksucker, tell him T-Bone hopes his black ass getting a good workout in there. Get the fuck off my porch."

Terrell Barnett slid inside and slammed the door. I wondered what Skinny thought of T-Bone.

I was relieved T-Bone slammed the door instead of slamming me.

I doubled back to Hebert and rang the bell next to the splintered green door of old Miss Givens' narrow brick bungalow. Ty was right, it took some time before a frail, elderly black lady pushing a walker opened the door. She smiled warmly and said good morning.

"Good morning, Miss Givens."

"And how do you know my name, young man?" Kind eyes alert, smiling.

"Little Ty down the street suggested I speak with you." I pointed just as DeAndre lighted and aimed the last bottle rocket at Ty, now running for his life in the vacant lot, giggling all the while.

She shook her gray head but couldn't prevent a smirk from showing. "Those boys are so chock full of life. I wish they could give me some of that energy. Well, why did that little devil direct you to me, sir?"

I handed her one of my cards. "My name is Mitchell Adams and I'm a social worker. I've been talking to people in the neighborhood about Lonnie Washington."

Her owl-shaped eyes beamed under penciled-in eyebrows at the mention of his name. "My name is Coretta Mae Givens and you are most certainly welcome in my humble home, Mr. Adams. I just put on a pot of water, would you like some tea?"

"If it's not too much trouble, thank you."

Counterfeit

She led me into a small but clean living room with a cloth sofa and two matching chairs to complete the grouping. The room contained no television, but a small radio on a table played soft classical music next to an open copy of Upton Sinclair's *The Jungle*. Also on the round table sat a three-tiered aluminum tray of petit fours, M&Ms, and hard candies. A glass of hot tea on a white lace doily next to today's paper completed her set-up. I sunk into a comfy chair holding a

faux china teacup adorned with cherry blossoms while the pleasing aromas of orange Pekoe and cinnamon drifted to my nose.

Miss Givens set her walker aside and carefully sat down. On the wall behind her chair was a small, plain crucifix made of ironwood. "Why are you inquiring about Mr. Washington?"

"I am an advocate for Lonnie, I am not working for the police. I want to better understand how he is perceived in the community. This is an informal gathering of information and you are under no obligation to speak with me. Nothing you say will be connected to you in any way or revealed to Lonnie."

T-Bone hadn't given me the chance to present my entire dynamite opening spiel, but I'm sure it wouldn't have mattered.

Miss Givens was so tiny that when she settled into her chair she nearly disappeared. "If the charges are true, what he has done is illegal, Mr. Adams, and for that society is obliged to punish him. From what I hear on the radio, the great Chief Prosecutor Maynard himself intends to do so with impunity. I choose not to own a television, I find they waste time on trivialities, so I listen to select radio stations and read the classics to keep my mind sharp. I'm aware that Lonnie has become quite the center of controversy around the neighborhood, and I fear this contentiousness is merely beginning."

She spooned sugar in her cup and swirled it once. "Let me tell you a story, if you will indulge a feeble old woman.

"Please," I said with a smile. I took a sip and waited.

"There once was an idealistic young girl who devoted her early years to teaching grade school in the inner city. She found love late in life, so she and her husband were never blessed with children. He became sick, she quit her career at fifty to take care of him at home, then eight years later he was called to heaven with the bone cancer. It's a horrible and painful way to die, Mr. Adams, and I wish it on no one. She spent the next quarter century volunteering at her church, in food kitchens for the homeless, and grade schools. She missed her husband so much, and watched helplessly as her final extended family members slowly died, leaving her alone with her memories, which she still has intact, glory be to God. Alone, on a fixed income, she opened her home to the needy, served hot meals and coffee to the homeless in winter and sandwiches and lemonade in the summer. She listened to them and tried to give each person a ray of hope, even when there seemed none. Last year she was beset by health problems that consumed every penny of her disposable income.

"Then months ago, unbeknownst to her, her landlord stopped paying the mortgage on the building even though she always paid her rent on time, but it was she who found herself on the street with no place to stay. She was so downhearted and full of despair she prayed God would take her so she could be reunited with her beloved Ike. The first month, she stayed with various families of church friends while hopelessness festered inside like that same corrosive bone cancer that killed her husband. Her depression hit bottom when she had to apply for welfare after a lifetime of work. She felt destined to waste away in a nursing home among strangers and die alone of a broken heart in a drab room that smelled of fear, but at the end of the next month a miracle occurred."

Miss Givens slowly reached into the drawer next to her and removed a cardboard box. She removed a fancy red ribbon with a deliberateness and reverence reserved for religious rituals. She picked up the only item in the box with great care, a neatly folded piece of stationery, before she spoke again.

"A plain manila package with no return address arrived for her via currier at the home of a church friend. Inside it were the keys and title to the home she had been forced to vacate by

court order. Big red block letters stamped on the title announced, 'PAID IN FULL.' The

package included this handwritten letter in the most beautiful, flowing, and elegant script."

She handed me the letter, which read:

Dearest Mrs. Coretta Mae Givens,

You don't know me, but I recently learned of you. You have worked hard your entire life and served the homeless for many years and now late in life find yourself in a similar situation through no fault of your own. I know if I was there, you would say those less fortunate souls you fed and comforted gave you much more in return than you could ever give them. Years ago, you helped someone very dear to me who was down on her luck. That is why this package has come to you. You will always be a teacher and a mender of damaged hearts. Please start anew by mending yours.

LW

P.S. The title is authentic and advance payments of one thousand dollars each have been placed in your new accounts at Laclede Gas and Ameren Electric. I encourage you to verify the accuracy of this letter by calling City Hall records department at (314) 555-2500. Welcome home!

I handed back the keepsake, and she took it and placed it back in the box like it was a treasure. Then she continued, "She sat down, tried to compose herself and said another prayer before she dialed that number. The lady at City Hall promptly confirmed the title's authenticity and in the most matter-of-fact voice told her to have a nice day."

Coretta tried to compose herself but lost the emotional battle. "I moved back here that same day!" A tear surfaced on her cheek as her voice cracked.

"Did you ever learn who bought the house or sent you the package?"

She shook her head. "No, sir. I encountered nothing but dead ends every step of the way. If someone at City Hall or the revenue office knew the identity of my anonymous benefactor, they weren't telling me.

There was no paper trail for me to follow. It must be Lonnie Washington. The initials on the letter are LW."

Coretta silently offered me a piece of hard candy. "I have a sweet tooth. It's my vice, I must admit."

The letter she'd shown me was not written by Lonnie. I'd seen samples of his handwriting in his prison file and this was definitely not his. I declined the treat. "Thousands of people share the same initials, Miss Givens, his mother being one among many."

"Yes, but who else could it be?"

"Have you ever met Lonnie?"

"No, but the writer acknowledged that and said I had helped someone dear to him. I helped feed LaKeesha for years before the state finally returned him to her. I drove her to church and taught her basic math skills and how to balance a checkbook. She is a kind-hearted and simple soul, though easily influenced by others."

Coretta unwrapped a hard candy and resumed, "I haven't lost all my marbles yet, Mr.

Adams, though I'm sure that day is fast approaching. The retired teacher in me knows that Paris exists and is in France even though I have never been there. I also know in my soul that the Lord Jesus Christ is my savior even though I have no empirical evidence He ever existed. And I know in my heart that the man named Lonnie Washington who sits in jail accused of counterfeiting, armed robbery, and attempted murder is my angel of mercy even though I have no proof he is nothing more than a common criminal." She popped the sweet in her mouth and smiled at me, her lined face filled with peaceful certainty.

First came Skinny's claim that Lonnie devised (and by inference, funded) a structured schedule for his mother to earn her home, provided she take self-responsibility and maintain certain standards, and now this.

I must have paused too long or she read doubt in my face, for she said, "If you're not convinced, talk to Shondra McKinney."

Coretta sucked on the candy in her mouth and started to pull herself out of the chair, "It's closing in on noon. If you will excuse me, I have to make sandwiches for my lunch crowd."

Before I left, I helped this tiny angel of mercy make twenty ham and turkey sandwiches and I lugged in two gallon jugs of sun tea from her rickety back porch. The day she quit volunteering would probably be the day she died. She gave me Shondra's address, which was several blocks farther north off Grand, and a sandwich for the road.

By the time I walked to my neglected but undisturbed Solstice, I had almost finished my sandwich. Ty came racing by on a rusty old bike way too big for him and yelled, "What she servin'?"

I told him. He turned and shouted, "Ham and turkey, DeAndre!"

I ran some errands downtown. By the time I backtracked to the mini-mart to talk to the men loitering outside in the shade, it was twilight. Mention of Lonnie's name started mouths flapping. A young black man who'd requested money from Lonnie to start an escort service said, "He didn't give me no fuckin' reason. I don't do drugs but I don't want to flip no greasy spoon burgers for a livin' neither. No minimum wage shit, you hear?" Several other men there who'd asked Lonnie for seed money for their schemes and were rejected either waved me away or spit on the ground. Most wouldn't even mention his name. To them I was a bad memory of their failings.

Counterfeit

"How did you learn about him coming into money?" I looked around, wishing someone would answer. The smell of weed appeared in the air as bottles popped and beer cans whooshed open.

The wannabe escort service manager spoke in a voice like he'd swallowed sandpaper. I noticed a healed tracheostomy scar. "The pretty boy got to drinkin' one night and bragged about the four of them printing more money than he'd ever seen in his lifetime. He said they look exactly like the real thing, too. Next morning the whole damn neighborhood knew."

The group around me steadily grew. A short thin black man stepped forward. "I don't know the man, but from what I hear he didn't hurt no one. The po-lice always come down hard on us black folks." Another man nodded and said, "Friend of mine know him, says he ain't got it in him to hurt anybody. He thinks Maynard and the po-lice wanna make an example of him, crack down hard on the brother, frame him, cuz he gonna run for the Senate." A group of young white men left the mart with six-packs in hand, walking to their cars, and paused to listen to the discussion. A young white man wearing a cut-off football shirt and his hair in a ponytail stepped forward, raising his voice. "He got caught counterfeiting. He's guilty. They should throw the book at him." His large white buddy gripped a brown paper bag in his muscular forearms and nodded, adding, "If he shot that pregnant woman, he should fuckin' get the death penalty." The fervor in his eyes dared anyone to challenge him. That touched off a wave of finger pointing and name calling between the factions.

Night had fallen now and my pleas for cooler heads and 'innocent until proven guilty' were drowned out by the sheer number of escalating claims of racism from both sides. The bodies went into motion, twisting and revolving like the eye of a hurricane. For every person that left the scene, two more took their place. When the spewed epithets turned personal, men began to posture and jockey for position, pushing back against one another. Darkness now blanketed us in the testosterone-thick scrum, while the wannabe escort king with the coarse voice slammed into me and yelled, "Who the fuck are you, Snowball? You started this. I'm gonna stop it. I'm gettin' my gun." The pushing and shoving intensified, a punch was thrown, a man to my right assumed a defensive posture with a jagged stick in hand, and somewhere behind me a beer bottle broke. The sides divided along racial lines like squares in a Civil War battle.

Hot town, summer on the north side.

I fought my way out of the swirling pile of bodies and ran to my car As I drove away, I called 911 and reported the disturbance outside the mini-mart. I kept within sight of the melee and three units with sirens flashing responded in minutes as the wannabe escort king exited his car, holding a piece at his side. Seeing the cruisers, he wisely climbed back inside his car and drove away. The cops dispersed the mob with a quick show of force, making no arrests. No one left the scene with any apparent injuries.

Good job, guys. I owe you one.

Talk of Lonnie and the men in hiding consumed the Metro area this summer. Colleges and universities debated the circumstance of Lonnie's arrest on the St. Louis community. Some blacks speculated he was a victim, he'd never get a fair trial, and that he may have been set up. Whites held on to their faith in the system. Racial tensions broadened the divide between black and white. People made comparisons to the OJ case.

Counterfeit

The streets weren't giving up their secrets so easily.

Scott L. Miller

THE GOOSE THAT LAYS THE

GOLDEN EGGS

"Your mom is hanging in there; adhering to the routine you arranged."

Lonnie raised an eyebrow at my last statement but remained silent.

"She asked how you're holding up, and I said you were doing fine," I said while I looked at his face. "Was I wrong?"

He sported a fresh strawberry below his left eye, the lid swollen and bruised. "Keep telling her that."

"How'd you get the shiner?"

Minutes passed. His arm shot up and sketched a picture in his mind's eye. "They moved me into general population and rescinded my art privileges. My new Samoan cellmate welcomed me with a nice Hawaiian punch."

"Baker tells me you're suicidal. Is he right?"

"Wouldn't you be in a place like this?"

"I asked you a question."

"It doesn't matter what I think."

"It matters to your family and friends."

"That doesn't change the fact they'll keep me in gen pop."

I used all my tricks, but he sidestepped questions related to danger to self and why he'd been relocated.

I told him about Skinny, Tyra, Shirley, and the men outside the mini-mart. "I also met Coretta Mae Givens, a delightful neighbor who lives on your mother's street. She thinks the world of you even though you've never met. She's convinced you bought her house to repay past kindnesses to LaKeesha."

He held his deadpan look. "She's confused. How could I do afford that on my salary?"

"She showed me a confirmation letter. It said someone bought her home and placed it in her name. Someone with the initials LW."

He sat still as stone, eyes fixed on the scarred table top.

"I met another neighbor, T-Bone, who said you refused to bankroll a scheme of his buddy's, some business venture about a mosh pit with pole dancers."

"He's a junkie and a dealer. Stay away from him. He's dangerous."

"Others said the neighborhood knew about the counterfeiting from—"

Anguish spread across his swollen face as he raised his voice to silence me. "What does it matter? I'm here."

"A man at the mart said the bills are perfect—"

He rattled his chains. "People say and do crazy things when it's hot and they're drunk or high or angry. You should know that. You shouldn't be hanging around the neighborhood, especially at night."

"Lonnie, I'm not saying I want to bail, but I don't know what good I'm doing. If you're not suicidal and don't want help to cope with jail, why should we keep meeting?"

He lowered his head and his breath seemed to leave his frail body. In time he said, "I want you to be there when I meet with my momma before they convict and transfer me to a federal institution. I hope you can help us come to grips with it, especially her."

I nodded. "We'll work on that. Anything else?"

"Yeah. Make sure the world knows what happens here and what you learn."

My attempts for him to elaborate were met with stony silence as our time ticked away.

$ $ $

That afternoon I drove my friend Tony Martin across the muddy Mississippi on Highway 67 to Fast Eddie's BonAir in Alton, Illinois, to meet one of his banking contacts. Fast Eddie's is one of the busiest, adults only, restaurant/bars in the metropolitan area, selling massive quantities of cold beer and cheap food. The busy walls are filled floor-to-ceiling with off-beat, double-entendre street signs and glowing neon signs. It's a good place to people watch, the time I took Kris here we watched a raucous group of leather biker dudes and chicks yuk it up next to a table of nuns. Tony had arranged the meeting before the rush hour crowd so we'd have a booth and relative quiet.

Tony spotted Milton Peebles hunkered down alone in a corner booth swigging from a frosty mug of beer with a half-empty pitcher sitting in the center of the table. "Beware, a little of this old coot goes a long way. He may have gone off the deep end after his wife died last year, but he knows banking and finance shit inside and out."

We sat down and Tony introduced us.

"You're late," he said, staring hard at me. "I had to order this one. On you."

The old man pointed a bony, gnarled finger at me. "You're here for that boy on the news, the Schwartze counterfeiter, aren't you? Rules don't apply to those people," Peebles said, shaking his head and glaring at me like I'd just run over his dog.

Counterfeit

"Behave," Tony cautioned.

Peebles dismissed the warning with a wave of his hand.

I met his steely gaze. "Tony tells me you're the man to see when it comes to the economy and banking."

Peebles leaned back and puffed out his sunken chest in our secluded corner booth. He was a tall, slender man whose stooped shoulders were noticeable even while seated.

"There are twelve regional Federal Reserve Banks in the country. I served a term on the Board of Directors at the St. Louis branch. Sixty years in the banking business, my wife dies, and they force me out. Yeah, your friend's right. I'm the man."

I leaned forward. "Forget about the boy in custody. I know Nixon did away with the gold standard in 1971, so what's the negative impact on our economy, on anyone for that matter, if someone were to circulate *perfect, undetectable* counterfeit US hundred-dollar bills?"

Peebles looked like I'd just forced him to suck a lemon. "That's never been done before. These clowns just think they created perfect fakes, but they can't replicate the paper. Didn't you see the news? Their fakes were spotted and the police imprisoned one of them right away. Seventy-five percent of all counterfeit bills are confiscated long before they hit the street. Fake money is like a flaming hot potato, whoever has it last is the victim because they're shit out of luck for the money. The cops are called in, the Feds canvas the area with all their manpower, and the crooks are caught, just like your boy. Even with the most advanced, high-tech copier—"

"Humor me," I interrupted. "Perfect duplicates. Let's say someone with extraordinary talent, patience and the will to create exact duplicate metal plates of the 1996 US hundred-dollar bill also obtained access to the patented government rag paper and authentic color-shifting ink used by the Treasury Department. And let's say the same person worked for a printing company that owned a large printing press. Hypothetically speaking, what's the effect on our economy if this were to happen?"

Peebles refilled and then took a long pull on his mug. The amber foam rested on his white handlebar mustache while he thought. His blotchy red nose twitched and he blinked so much he reminded me of a myopic, six-foot rabbit. After some thought he said, "I recall there was some type of robbery at the DC branch last year that was described as attempted." A trace of wonder registered in his voice as he added, "*If* your boy got a hold of that paper and ink and *if* he created perfect forgeries, it would be the most perfect crime in the history of man. In fact, I'm not even sure it would be a crime."

"Why?"

"Counterfeiting is a crime only if the bills can be identified as non-legal tender. Only the counterfeiter would know a crime's been committed. In your hypothetical fantasy world, if the forger is not caught and he spreads his duplicate bills, the market is flooded with excess cash that the banking community has deemed authentic. In a primitive, all-cash economy, this would dramatically dilute the value of money, but modern economies operate mainly on bank-issued credit, not cash. In essence the forger becomes his own operating branch of the Treasury Department. He prints money when he needs it."

"Does the government take a hit on the bogus money?" I asked.

Peebles laughed so loud it triggered a vicious coughing jag and he doubled over. Tony and I waited for him to stop wheezing and regain control.

Counterfeit

"You naïve young man. Of course not, Uncle Sam has doesn't need to seek a profit on its own currency. The Fed is the source of the currency. Treasury simply recycles what the Fed has previously issued. The Treasury recaptures the money it spends through taxes and the sale of its securities."

"So there's no effect at all from the funny money?" Tony asked.

Peebles motioned for our waitress to bring another pitcher of his sour ale and glared at Tony. "Did I say that? No, I didn't. Interest owed the public by the Treasury from the fake bills must ultimately be covered by increased taxes. That's a wash for the public as a whole, but not for those who pay more in taxes than they receive in interest payments. Bottom line is the public takes a slight hit on fake notes in approximate proportion to the taxes they pay."

"So the net effect is a marginal private redistribution of wealth," I said. "Like Robin Hood stealing from the rich."

Peebles clucked his tongue. "If you romanticize this boy, you're a bigger fool than I thought."

What I remembered of the Robin Hood legend is that he embodied the societal standards of the time, being generous and courteous, especially to women and caregivers, while opposing the stingy rich.

I thought of Coretta's story. "Depends on what he did with the money."

"Spin it any way you want, he's still a thief," Peebles sniffed. "He couldn't have created perfect fakes. The odds are astronomical." The way his voice trailed off lent the impression he was re-evaluating that part.

Peebles waved his bony hand in the air as if he were dismissing me, then leered at our nubile, green-eyed waitress when she asked if we wanted another round. She rolled her eyes as she left.

"Forget about eight-hundred-year-old tales, back to your boy. You put it crudely, but from an economic perspective you're essentially correct. Some redistribution of wealth would occur, based on the amount." He raised his mug, gulping as if the drink were air. "How much counterfeit money did he print?" his voice rising, reminding me of the conspirators I'd overheard in the bathroom.

"Twenty-five, maybe thirty million, tops."

Peebles emitted a low guffaw and I thought he might start choking again. "Chickenfeed. There's at least 1.6 trillion in real currency circulating in the states at any given time. That's not enough to cause a blip on their radar screen." He suddenly flashed a crooked smile of delight and added, "Even so, your porch monkey will never again see the light of day as a free man."

Tony started to react but I stopped him with a hand on his arm.

"Why do you say that? I read that counterfeiting in Missouri carries a maximum sentence of twenty-five years and a hundred thousand dollar fine," I said.

"The very idea of counterfeiting undermines the basis of our economy and threatens government authority. Have you seen the downtown Federal Reserve Bank on Locust Street? It was designed to connote a solid foundation, stability, and strength. It's a huge, impenetrable concrete armored tank with thick steel bars that secure the windows on the first two floors and tight armed security inside its bomb-proof walls. The fountains and flowers in the plaza don't even begin to soften the intended architectural mood. Your boy will face twenty-five years average jail time, plus fifteen years for circulation; and the judge has free rein to dispense more time unless he cooperates, by handing over his accomplices."

Peebles drained the dark fluid from his sweaty mug and smacked his thin, chapped lips. He'd finished off the first pitcher and was into the second by now. "Even if he created perfect duplicates, he's been apprehended with the goods and tools of his trade. The Secret Service will grill him, use any psychological tool they can, promise him the best deal if he gives up his friends and the shooter. They will tell him he's not the one they really want and convince him the others are the big fish. This ploy will work because there is no honor among thieves. They will get inside his head. They will constantly remind him of the coldest truth, that he will lose his freedom and his family, unless he gives them exactly what they want. If he doesn't, the government will prove to the masses this boy is dangerous and should remain behind bars. Those in power trample any upstart anarchist. They will make an example of him to restore order from chaos and keep the lower classes in their place. *His kind* does not get money for nothing—"

"Unlike the wealthy," I interrupted. "For the masses, it's strictly Bread and Circuses."

He squinted, making a sour face. "—especially a Schwartze counterfeiter." He stared at me for some time and said, "Bread and Circuses. It's been a while since I heard that phrase. To update the analogy, it's fast food and football now. For St. Louis, maybe baseball. It worked for the emperor then and works for the rich now."

"That's one way to look at it. Another is that it was a harbinger for the fall of the Roman Empire." I thought of the Occupy Wall Street movement and whether it's a precursor of future upheaval. Have citizens of our aging democracy conceded the protest or will there be one cataclysmic rebalancing? Time will tell, but I certainly didn't want to talk politics with Peebles.

"Mr. Peebles, I can't thank you enough for your insights and expert opinion on complex issues that we know so little about. I am sorry to hear of your wife's death."

Peebles poured the last dregs from the pitcher into his mug as the bitterness wafted over from across the table. "The bastards said I'd become an embarrassment to them and if I didn't resign, that I no longer fit their mold and if I didn't resign, they'd fire me. I hired a good Jew shyster and took them for all I could."

Tony shook his head while I said, "More power to you, sir. Is there anything else you can tell us about what this boy is up against?"

"Even if this Schwartze made perfect copies, and I don't believe it for one minute, but if he did, the government will find experts willing to testify that they can tell the difference between his bills and the real McCoy."

"Why?"

"Because he's the goose that lays the golden eggs. Every major organized criminal on the planet would kill to enslave him and force him to churn out money. If by some miracle he created perfect copies, I feel sorry for the poor bastard. It would be better for him if he was simply a run-of-the-mill crook and mediocre counterfeiter."

I recalled the fable and how it ended for the goose. "Why?"

"He's gotta have the worst luck of all time. He must be quite the artist. To create perfection and have it taken away, along with the rest of your freedom, must be the worst feeling in the world. You better pray the reason his eyes are brown is that he's full of shit."

"Why's that?"

"Why, why, why? Use your head. What do the rich and powerful want? More money and power, of course. One fortune is never enough if you can obtain a second by subterfuge or force. Breaking the Ten Commandments is all part of a day's work to them, especially when it comes to 'Thou shalt not steal' or 'thou shalt not covet' thy neighbor's wife or possessions. If the right amount of money can lead to enough power, then 'thou shalt not kill' isn't so taboo anymore. Why work to earn your next fortune if you can steal it? It's all about love of money, and money begets power." Peebles smiled. "That's why I feel sorry for your poor bastard."

Tony slid out of the booth and walked to the door.

I was ready for some fresh air myself. The stale beer smell now cloying, I motioned the server over, paid for the pitcher and ordered him ten jumbo twenty-nine cent shrimp, a Big Elwood on a Stick and a side of cole slaw. I left him my business card. "Call me if you think of anything else, Mr. Peebles. There are better ways to deal with your wife's death than by crawling inside a beer keg. You and my client have something in common, you're in prisons of your own making. Here's your receipt for the food when they call your number—eat up, it looks like you could use the nutrition."

"You're trying to help a dead man," he said, peering over his mug.

Peebles' echo of Lonnie's earlier remark raised a shiver along my spine.

"I know but eat the food anyway."

He waved a gnarled hand at me in exasperation as I turned and headed for the door.

I left the old curmudgeon alone in the dark corner booth to chew on shrimp, a grilled beef kabob, and my words. Free beer and the secondary gain of speaking his peculiar brand of schadenfreude at the downward spiral of another man's life wasn't enough for him to talk smack about the establishment with a total stranger if his wife was still alive. But she wasn't, and I knew how alone and angry he feels. There was more to his story.

What concerned me most were his comments about murder. When I agreed to take this case, I worried that I might end up holding a lightning rod in a thunderstorm, but now the storm had escalated into a war between a boy king and alleged evil villains, replete with prophets, a voodoo priestess, and consequences of Biblical proportions that may include the killing of four people to help elevate the Golden Boy onto the throne.

I told Baker I'd walk away from this whenever I felt everything going to hell. Was now the time?

On the drive back to Missouri, I told Tony about the discrepancy between Lonnie's story of his arrest and the official version Maynard reported on air. I mentioned that in Lonnie's account, Dan Quinn was the cop at the scene. I didn't mention anything about Baker.

"I know the cop," Tony said in a matter-of-fact tone.

"Is it standard procedure for the arresting officer not to be mentioned at the scene?"

"How do you know he wasn't?"

Counterfeit

I had to back pedal fast. "Maynard announced it was a coordinated, sophisticated police effort. Lonnie swears Quinn made the collar alone, that no other cops were at the scene."

"You believe everything this counterfeiter says? You've always been the skeptic, the empirical evidence guy. Besides, when Maynard spins it that way he can claim more of the credit," Tony answered, but a slight frown formed on his brow. He grew pensive.

I'd planted the seed.

I thought about Lonnie and Peebles and self-made prisons. I thought of the couch that no longer offered solace.

A smart man would walk away, but I had a formal benefit to attend, a trust to betray, and a prospective senator to meet.

Scott L. Miller

MODERN LIFE OF RILEY

At seven sharp, my Solstice idled in front of Debbie's building while Maurice the burly doorman buzzed her apartment. Thirty minutes later, she made her entrance wearing a white floor length silk evening dress with a halter neckline, secured in front by an o-shaped circle of rhinestones gathered at the bodice with shirring down the front. At the center of the o was bare skin. As she turned toward Maurice to escort her to my waiting car, the back of the dress revealed thick criss-crossed straps across her bare back, with a V-shape plunge just above her buttocks.

The pirouette appeared to be for my benefit. The dress flattered her thin body, and I smiled in admiration.

I tipped Maurice after he closed the passenger door.

"You approve?" she asked, her dangly crystal earrings sparkling in the light.

"Brava. Kudos to the silkworms who gave their all."

She appeared briefly confused. "You look very handsome. You look like you were made for that tux. Is that a rental?"

She'd forgotten my comment from the other day. "Nope, I actually own two. This classic black and one with a white jacket that makes me look like a waiter."

"A very handsome waiter," she said and rested her hand on my arm.

The Haller estate encompassed pristine rolling hills in Chesterfield, an affluent west county suburb of St. Louis. It included two lakes, numerous arched bridges that traversed a meandering creek, a stable and a steeplechase course. Old man Haller, a multi-millionaire from his days in the railroad industry, had hosted lavish political fundraisers for over forty years, including events for John Maynard, Sr., until one spring day last year when, in his nineties and in failing health, he sat down under a weeping willow tree near one of his lakes and shot a bullet through his brain. His family vowed to continue the fundraising tradition, were they setting their sights on Maynard, Junior?

Debbie flashed her press pass and invitation for two and we gained admittance after a brief security search. Most of the affluent guests mingled under the gilded archways of a beautiful loggia, the high-domed ceilings painted with sunny blue Mediterranean landscapes or bustling European inspired market scenes. I grabbed a glass of surprisingly good Champagne from a passing server (who wore a white tux) while Debbie opted for spring water with lemon. We toured the living space that included a three-story great room complete with works of Picasso and Rodin while a string ensemble played a light and airy version of Vivaldi's *The Four Seasons*.

Beyond the great room was an elevator that no doubt used to transport old man Haller to and from his master bedroom suite. I noticed an empty podium at the far end of the loggia and thought of past men on the senatorial and presidential trail who'd stood at that spot making tough statements and bold promises and of all the whispered backroom conversations that must have happened in those shadowy alcoves. Debbie and I were two of the youngest people in attendance, save for the servants. White and gray hair, no hair, diamonds and rubies, furs and facelifts met us every way we turned. I caught a glimpse of the mayor of St. Louis chatting up a former Missouri senator when Debbie poked me in the ribs.

"See that guy over there," she said pointing briefly to a short thin man wearing a form- fitting dark blue power suit and sporting a prematurely receding crew cut. He stood very erect and seemed stiff and precise in his movements. His clean-shaven face and bright blue eyes constantly darted about the room absorbing every nuance and detail. "That's Paul Fallon, Maynard's right hand man."

As if on cue, Fallon spotted Debbie and quickly strode our way, hand extended.

"Glad you could make it, Miss Macklin," Fallon said, his unsmiling face the antithesis of his words. Debbie introduced me and we shook hands. His handshake was firm but his fingers damp. I thought I detected a brief glimmer of recognition in those keen eyes when he heard my name.

He kept his focus on Debbie, and for that I was thankful.

"Mr. Maynard and the dignitaries present won't have face time for you tonight and, of course, remember you are not here as a member of the press. Enjoy the energy and excitement of the evening." He nodded as if to include me. "Dr. Adams."

The tightly-wound little man spoke with clipped and precise words. He turned on his heels and strode away, talking non-stop into his Bluetooth. He seemed self-assured and calculating,

Just as he had in the bathroom at City Hall.

I ate Tiger shrimp in a delicate ginger sauce and end-cut prime rib from a Noritake crystal plate while Debbie nibbled on a carrot stick and broccoli stems. I wondered how she was able to keep standing erect and imagined her eating a pint of ice cream alone in a midnight-darkened kitchen. I gazed beyond the draped bunting while two stately white swans glided along the glass top of a clear lake as large koi of all colors slowly swirled below. The sun began to set and the lower horizon turned sanguine. I grabbed a second glass of the bubbly, feeling the beginnings of a warm glow in my belly.

A modern-day life of Riley.

The string quartet switched to a light, up-tempo version of *Happy Days Are Here Again.* That and the flashing lights cued the guests to their seats. A pudgy balding man in his fifties, old man Haller's eldest son, trudged to the podium. He acknowledged and thanked the mayor, two former mayors, various state senators, and representatives and other key officials for attending the first party fundraiser for the vacant senate seat. Uncomfortable with public speaking, he reminisced briefly about his father's love of business and politics. When he said his dad was surely here in spirit smiling down on them tonight, the crowd applauded and lifted their glasses in a toast. He thanked Paul Fallon for providing tonight's security, pointed to some of the several strapping young men in solid dark coats standing along the walls and at the main entrance, and then turned over the microphone to the mayor of St. Louis.

Current and former elected officials gave emotional and truncated party speeches, little more than preaching to the choir, but each speaker urged everyone to open their checkbooks tonight for the party. Two politicians received polite applause when they announced their intent to seek the nomination. Other speakers mentioned John Maynard and whether he planned to throw his hat into the ring. The two who'd announced shot furtive glances at Maynard's table.

Maynard was one of the last speakers and appeared reluctant to walk to the dais, long enough for Fallon to be seen prodding him forward. On the way he stopped to shake hands and receive pats on the back. Heads turned and glasses rose as he flashed his trademark smile. "I wish to thank those of you who want to hear another announcement. Your support and confidence mean a great deal to me, and I know some of you want me to begin following in my father's footsteps tonight, but I have a major trial to prepare for and a city to clean up. With that in mind, I must disappoint you tonight, but as my dad used to say, 'Never say never.'

A muffled buzz spread through the attendees, who looked blindsided by the news.

"I want to thank the Haller Foundation for hosting this event." Looking at the tables of local businessmen, he raised his glass. "I praise you captains of industry … you are the true

visionaries, the men who form the backbone that makes this the greatest country in the world. Thank you for the jobs you create. With your support, our party will surely win the senate seat next fall. Gentlemen, give each other a round of applause!"

While he spoke I watched him and those listening nearby. They waited on his every word. He turned their disappointment over not running into joy with his mini pep rally. The buzz in the air was for the party but also for him. He had national name recognition and brains and looks, but tonight he'd turned them down. I wondered how long it would be before 'never say never' turned into 'if not now, when?'

As the applause for him continued, one thought kept coming to mind: John Maynard Junior looks tipsy.

I asked Debbie if she saw it, too.

She rolled her eyes. "It's a fundraiser and he's schmoozing, working the movers and shakers. He had a drink in his hand at the podium, but I hear he limits himself to one." She lowered her voice to a whisper and said, "I've heard he has what's called a flushing response, if he has more than one alcoholic drink he gets physically ill. After one drink he switches to water with a slice of lime. He can never abuse alcohol. Don't be such a skeptic, Mitch."

I've read about the alcohol flushing reaction caused by the diminished ability of a person's body to break down alcohol, the telltale red face or blotches caused by excess dilation of the capillaries. Because roughly half of Pacific Rim Asians have the condition, it's often called the Asian Glow. The condition is much rarer in the rest of the world. There is research that says people with the condition are much less likely to be alcoholics. I let it go at that.

For the next hour we mingled with supporters. I watched Debbie work the crowd, trying to absorb it all. At one point she was so engrossed in a conversation she actually nibbled a bite
of prime rib from my plate.

The horror!

Shortly after that, four local sports celebrities cornered us and proselytized their Evangelical agenda. Two, wearing wedding bands, ended their spiel by hitting on Debbie. Throughout the evening many older men asked what I did for a living, which usually brought the conversation to a screeching halt. One stoop-shouldered octogenarian simply walked away shaking his head.

After the clean-cut Christian Crusaders renounced us to search for fresh converts and conquests, Maynard appeared, handsome in his tailored tux and flashing a lot of teeth. He thanked Debbie for attending. He was shorter than I imagined. He'd already extended his hand to me as Debbie said, "Chief Prosecutor Maynard, Dr. Mitchell Adams is a—
"

He took an extra step, so close I could feel his breath. His unblinking eyes fixed on mine. "I know all about Dr. Adams and his fine work."

He knew I was seeing Lonnie.

I smelled gin on his breath, saw no blotches on his face or neck, and noted the scotch in his cut crystal glass. "And I'm learning more about you every day," I said, "from the arrest coverage, of course."

"You were in the audience on the steps at City Hall when the news first went public," he said coyly, waiting for my reaction.

How could he possibly know that? Did he also know I'd been a fly on the wall in the bathroom?

"You either have an outstanding memory or a very observant staff." Or every speaking event is taped by your security force.

"Fortunately I have both." A confident grin formed on one side of his face.

And those eyes, do you even have eyelids?

"It sounds as if this case is impinging on your career plans."

"On the contrary," his eyes studying my face, he said, "I anticipate every possible turn in each case and use them to my benefit. I take surprises out of the equation. That's why I always win."

I handed him a personal check. "I had hoped my contribution would go toward your election campaign, but it seems the party and I will have to make do without you again this year."

He looked at the check. "This is most generous. I don't know what to say, other than thank you."

"You didn't see that one coming, did you? You can't predict every twist life throws at you. Such as: three of the four men remain at large and trials can be delayed ad nauseum."

"Justice will be served, and on time. Life remains on course."

"For you, perhaps. Not for the little black man."

He raised an eyebrow and lowered his voice. "Should we pity him? Does a less-than-happy childhood excuse criminal behavior? He had his chance for the American Dream but chose a darker path."

"Not everyone had the opportunity to grow up on Dogwood Farms."

"He made poor decisions. He'd hurt anyone for money."

Maynard briefly acknowledged a silver-haired dowager with a wink and smile as she passed.

I glanced at Debbie, her mouth open in stunned surprise.

"There's a lot of that going on. I'm sure it will all come to light."

At last he blinked. He started to respond when Paul Fallon congenially called his name and stepped between us. Behind Fallon loomed two unsmiling security men, their attention now on me.

"Am I about to get the bum's rush? I can make quite the scene here."

"Be our guest," Maynard said. "You think it's all about you—"

Fallon interrupted Maynard and said, "John, the mayor has a favor to ask before he leaves for another pressing engagement."

Maynard flashed his winning smile a final time as he walked away. He handed my check to Fallon.

Fallon gently guided me away from listening ears and said in sotto voce, "You made quite the news splash about this time last year, Dr. Adams. Keeping your cool in such a life-threatening situation must have been great publicity for your business. Now *that* limelight's faded," he spread his arms, looking about the great room and loggia. "You're here. Looking for another run as a feature on tomorrow's six o'clock news."

I mirrored his tone. "You can spin bullshit until the cows come home. It's still bullshit."

The stiff-backed Fallon fixed his smarmy smile on me. "Like last year, you're involved with yet another dangerous man."

"You have a very distinctive voice, Mr. Fallon. Has anyone ever told you that?"

Fallon's smile was part sneer. "Of course. Be careful, Dr. Adams. Don't let your client drag you down into his hellish world. It's a long road back, and if anyone should know about those long lonely roads, it's you."

He hadn't picked up on the voice comment.

He leaned close and whispered in a voice dripping with velvet menace, "We don't want anything else to end unhappily for you."

"If I didn't know your boss was such a law-abiding citizen, I might take that as a threat. Your concern is touching, but I'm adept at spotting wolves in sheep clothing. You are right about one thing, I am enmeshed with another dangerous man."

He took a step forward. "One day you're going to find yourself in a situation you can't talk your way out of."

"It happens to all of us sooner or later, doesn't it? C'est la vie."

He turned on his heels and left. One buff young security man wearing shades and a stone face lingered, my apparent shadow the rest of the evening.

Debbie walked up to me, puzzled, placing a hand on my arm. "I thought you and John had never met?"

"First time tonight."

"He certainly knows you."

"Deb, I see Lonnie Washington in therapy."

I watched as the pieces fell into place in her mind. She put a hand to her mouth. "The counterfeiter who shot the pregnant security guard?"

"I'm not convinced he shot or robbed anyone."

"Why on earth would you see someone like him?" she asked, eyes wide, dumbfounded.

"Helping people is what I do."

"He's an amoral criminal, for God's sake."

"He may be."

She folded her arms, her movements stiffening. "This is why you asked me out in the first place, isn't it? This was all about you and your work. You used me, you bastard."

She threw her water in my face and stormed out.

By that time, Maynard and Fallon were high and dry, safe on the other side of the mansion. But the mayor, politicians, celebrities, captains of industry, and every blue hair and bald head turned and looked down on me as I pinched the lemony water from my eyes, combed back my sopping hair with my hands, and tried in vain to slough the water from my tux. The beefy security guy stepped forward, his meat hook of an arm reaching out.

And I was worried I wouldn't get the chance to cause a scene.

ONE PERSON AT A TIME

The next day I returned to the North Side and knocked on the door of Shondra McKinney, and a middle-aged, light-skinned African-American lady answered. She had a wide face and nose, almond-shaped eyes. A thin streak of bright white hair interrupted the left side of her closely cropped Afro. She was of average build and wore no jewelry. Her blue jeans and bright yellow top had a somewhat baggy Wal-Mart quality, but they were clean, as were her comfortable-looking white Converse tennis shoes. She was guarded at first, but at mention of Coretta's name she readily invited me inside. The small living room was furnished in Spartan fashion but painted bright and cheery.

"Etta Mae said you might drop by. After meeting Lonnie, do you think he is capable of shooting a pregnant guard and committing armed robbery?"

"I believe most people have the capacity for much worse, if desperate enough. I've seen too much of in my work, I've seen too much of what man is capable of. If Lonnie is the counterfeiter people say he is, my answer is a resounding yes."

"Then you don't know him very well."

"You're right. I don't, but I'm learning."

Shondra made a quick sign of the cross.

"I am a foster mom. That is what I am. My husband Jimmie and I were foster parents over twenty years. After completing a tour in Afghanistan last year, he returned home changed. He'd wake up crying, sullen and distant from horrible nightmares. A pint of Jack sometimes helped him sleep, he said. He saw a counselor at the VA for his drinking and post-traumatic

Stress but he still struggled. One cold winter night he said he was going to the store for coffee but went missing for hours."

Her jaw tensed and her fingers curled into fists. "Then at two in the morning, I thought the gas furnace had exploded. Turned out Jimmie's truck was … was right here." She pointed at the space between us. "He crashed through the front wall, snow and ice blowing through the house."

"I am so sorry, Mrs. McKinney."

She wiped her eyes and nodded. "They say he died instantly. He was drunk. Thank God our little angels were all in bed. The next day I woke with this shock of white in my hair."

A horn blared in front of the house.

Her mood instantly changed. "Come with me and I'll show you something precious."

We walked down a homemade handicapped ramp to the front yard where a battered white-and-blue Call-A-Ride van sat parked. The driver, a stocky black man with a smiling round face, operated the wheelchair lift that contained a white teenaged male with severe hydrocephalus. At the same time, the side doors opened and a chubby white Down's syndrome girl and a tall, skinny black boy with no arms raced to Shondra's side. Looks of delight filled the two smiling faces. Shondra introduced me to Kathy and Dimitri, then to Andrew in the wheelchair, calling them her babies. Kathy gave me a hug and wanted a kiss. Shondra wheeled Andrew up the ramp into the house while Kathy and Dimitri ran inside ahead of us.

Shondra turned the television on low for Dimitri and asked Andrew if he had to use the bathroom. When he nodded, she wheeled him down the hallway. She called over her shoulder to the others not to eat more than two cookies with their milk before dinner.

Dimitri, who looked about fifteen, turned to me and said, "I know why you're here."

He gives me a good answer and I'll put him on the payroll with Ty and DeAndre.

"Why am I here?"

"Because you want to learn about that man in jail. Here's all you need to know—he's a hero."

"Why do you say that?"

"Most rich people care only about things—if they have five cars, they need six; if they have a plane, they want a yacht. That man didn't know us, but Kate and Andy and I would've lost our home if not for him. My birth parents didn't want me no arms. Same shit, different day with Kate and Andy. Miss Shondra and Mr. Jimmie put a roof over my head and loved me for who I am." He said with a voice calm as a glassy pond, "You better not hurt him or I'll be really mad."

"I'm trying to help him. Maybe Miss Shondra's the hero here," I said.

He looked at me. "Why can't they both be?"

"You've got a point, but I can think of a third hero in the story."

"Who's that?"

"You. A grounded young man who's overcome adversity and has the wisdom to realize what matters is definitely a hero in my book."

We heard Shondra return from the hallway bathroom as Dimitri whispered, "Miss Shondra and that man are my heroes."

Counterfeit

She sat down and sighed. "Where was I? Neighbors took us in that night as Family Services worked on finding emergency housing for us. Every dime of what money we had went

for the kids or into the house and, since you're a social worker, you know no one's ever gotten rich being a foster parent.

"The same morning, a tow truck winched out Jimmie's truck and a work crew arrived to remove all the debris after the police, EMTs and insurance people did their jobs. I hadn't contacted the workers. I was still in shock. They just rode in, right through the fog I was lost in back then. I assumed our homeowners' insurance must have sent them. After the clean-up, a construction crew of nine men and women pulled up and began installing a replacement wall, door, and storm windows. They rewired, insulated, and dry walled, primed and painted. They replaced the destroyed carpeting and delivered this used furniture. Then they began on the outside work, installing vinyl siding to the front of the house and new guttering and downspouts. The last thing they installed was that steel safety barricade in front of our yard along the bend in the road to help prevent an accident like this from happening again."

"You're a licensed foster home. Was Family Services behind the work?"

"I kept asking the crew, and each time they insisted they didn't know who hired them, that the money was paid up front. As they completed the job and drove away, the foreman handed me a sealed envelope." Shondra opened a tiny drawer in the end table next to her and passed me a handwritten note which read:

Dearest Mrs. McKinney,

The poor people in our neighborhood like to say, 'What goes around, comes around,' but Justice is indeed blind, her scales are tipped, and her visits to us are infrequent. You are, and have been, a source of strength and comfort to me. You gave me hope when you held me to your heart and said you loved me. I didn't believe you at first, I couldn't, that was survival instinct on my part, but in time you taught me not to hate myself and gave me the courage to face my lot in life. Your home was an oasis for me and many others. One day I asked why you took in kids and you said, "I'm changing the world one person at a time." I will never forget you and Jimmie, may his soul rest in peace. If not for you I would have committed suicide by cop years ago. You urged me to make the best of my abilities. I tried, I really did, and I hope you won't judge me too harshly. I'm trying to change my world one person at a time.

You tore down the walls I'd constructed around myself, I wish I'd been able to keep them down. In return for your love I give you a wall. May you keep the home fires burning for future lost souls and discarded innocents. I got the better end of the deal by far.

Counterfeit

It was the same elegant calligraphic script as Coretta's letter. Not by Lonnie Washington's hand, and I didn't know what to make of these letters.

I looked up and Shondra's eyes were red, a tissue in her hands.

"My benefactor left no paper trail. Many years ago, Family Services placed a teenager with us who didn't speak a word for weeks. He wouldn't even look us in the eye. He'd run away from countless foster homes. Bullies beat him because he was small and weak. I eventually came to realize there was something different about him. He never was much of a talker, but when he spoke, he had something worth saying. He was so attuned to learning the right way to do things, no matter how small. School came easy to him, he could read something once and remember it, but his passion was painting on canvas.

"The teenager I knew for two years back then never raised a fist in anger or uttered a harsh word. I realize that was a long time ago and an ocean of water has passed under the bridge. Has he changed? Did the world harden him so? Is it me or has the world gone mad, Dr. Adams?"

"You're not mad, Mrs. McKinney, but I'm not sure about the rest of the world."

Back at the car, my phone rang. It was a 911 call from Detective Baker. Ty and DeAndre were nowhere in sight.

He was in a heated argument with someone on his end of the line when I returned his call. I heard him say he was going to use somebody's head for a soccer ball if they didn't deliver as promised. I heard a woman in the background weeping. He said, "There's been another arrest. I'll be over for the six o'clock news." Before I could ask who, he'd hung up.

$ $ $

I made an early dinner of grilled chicken quesadillas with sharp cheddar cheese, ripe avocado, Arkansas tomatoes, lettuce, lime salsa and fresh cilantro on flour tortillas. I washed them down with a dark Negra Modelo in a frosty mug. I felt a good kind of tired tonight, after my first work out and three-mile run in I don't know how long.

This had been my life of Riley before Kris' murder.

Maybe I was tired of rotting on the couch.

Or I'd licked my wounds long enough.

Maybe it was the fear of Skinny's prophecy.

Or the thinly veiled threats from Fallon.

The dishes were soaking in the sink when Baker showed up with a grim look and a twelve-pack. We sat down again on my front porch.

"They caught the big man," he said, popping open a can.

Tyrone Sparks, with the sloping forehead and menacing stare. "He was the muscle of the group, right?"

He made a face and handed me a beer. "They took him down a block from home. I'm not surprised, but I hoped it wouldn't happen."

"You're a homicide cop and you're disappointed a felon's off the streets?"

He ignored my statement. "Worst thing is they separatin' him and the little brother in jail."

"How do you know?"

He wiped his Fu Manchu and crushed the can with two fingers. "A little birdie told me."

"Is the birdie named Skinny?"

He ignored me again and looked at his watch. We went inside. "Your groupie's about to come on. Got any chips?"

Counterfeit

I offered Baker the sofa while I rummaged for a half-full bag of lime chips in the pantry and a Bitter lemon for myself.

The credits for some popular show about a beautiful but tormented crime-fighting eighteen-year old orphan with supernatural and time-traveling powers were rapidly scrolling down the screen as I sat down. That could happen.

Then Debbie Macklin's big hair filled the screen while she announced a breaking Channel Four news story. "Channel Four is pleased to be the first station to air the capture of a second alleged member of the St. Louis counterfeiting gang. City police safely and quickly apprehended this dangerous man, and the exclusive amateur video you are about to see was taken by a private citizen during the tense police action. If you have young children near the TV at home, you may not wish to have them watch what we are about to show…."

The screen bounced and jiggled while the cameraman tried to narrate the action in clipped, excited phrases as he jogged to keep pace. Figures quickly darted in and out of the camera's visual field, momentarily lost while running behind parked trucks and buildings. Six or seven cops entered and left the screen at various times during the intense foot chase until the large subject was surrounded in the middle of Cote Brilliant Street. Two cops aimed pistols at the man and fired point blank. The large man staggered like Frankenstein from the Taser charges until finally collapsing. A brief but rough take-down allowed the cameraman time to focus in on the rigid face of Tyrone Sparks lying on his stomach, blood flowing from his mouth to the pavement, his head tilted to the right and wrists secured behind his back in zip ties with a cop kneeling on his back. Then the hand-held camera bounced wildly, showed nothing but a dull gray sky, and the screen went black.

Debbie's face briefly returned to fill the screen until a mug shot of an unsmiling Tyrone Sparks appeared. Coal dark eyes glared at the camera and the side shot displayed his prominent forehead. Debbie's voice-over intoned: "Tyrone Sparks was taken into custody after resisting arrest near his north city home. A warrant had been issued for his arrest concerning his possible involvement in the alleged counterfeiting ring based out of Brother-Hood Printers, a printing press on the north side where Mr. Sparks is employed. The Secret Service and city police are questioning him about his role in the alleged crime and hope he can provide information leading to the apprehension of the other employees. As you can see from the graphic video, Mr. Sparks attempted to flee, ignoring officers' commands to stop. He required two separate shots from electric Taser stun guns before the large and unusually strong man could be safely subdued."

The screen cut to previously shown pictures as Debbie continued, "Now the search intensifies for these men—Earl Mooney and Benny Blades. Investigators have been working around the clock to find that one break in the case that will lead to the other employees of the printing company who appear to have gone into hiding after the arrest of Lonnie Washington. Chief Prosecutor John Maynard, Jr., had this to say about today's news…"

Baker belched as if on cue as the screen cut to the chiseled face of Maynard, seemingly at home with a bank of microphones in his face. He smiled and said, "I am excited about our police force taking yet another extremely dangerous criminal off the streets and confident the apprehension of Mr. Sparks will lead to more information and arrests. I want to thank our brave policemen and women who work long hours to keep the public safe from people like this known felon. We have shut down their operation and are systematically flushing out and capturing these dangerous criminals. You have my word, this is not over. It's only a matter of time before justice is served."

Then the screen returned to the same pictures of Benny Blades and Earl Mooney as Debbie's voice-over said, "Once again, these are the known remaining counterfeiters. If anyone in our viewing area sees these men, do not initiate contact but call the police immediately at the number on the bottom of the screen. There is a twenty-five thousand dollar reward for useful information leading to their arrest."

Debbie's wispy body and big hair returned to the screen as she wrapped up the main story. "For more on the sinister and shadowy world of counterfeiting, be sure to watch the first of my two-part special that airs tomorrow at 6pm."

Baker said, "Got any dip to go with these?"

I shut off the TV, looked at him in silence and remained seated.

"Dip helps my crime fightin' skills. Huntin' down bad guys is hard work. Salsa'll do in a pinch."

I returned with the leftover quesadilla mixture, much to Baker's surprise, who said, "Now it's a party."

"Why are they sequestering Lonnie from Tyrone if they're both in general population?"

He popped open another cold one and took a long pull. "So the big man can't protect the little brother. They tryin' to get into their heads and play one against the other. Somebody's
orchestratin' a master plan and pullin' strings."

"I think Maynard plans to steal Lonnie's money and kill him."

Baker whistled. "Don' say that aloud again, Cool Breeze. You got no proof and you're wrong."

"You think so? Could it be the Secret Service?"

"The Secret Service has ultimate jurisdiction over counterfeitin' cases, but works with the local law. SS are the main interrogators and will offer deals and use psychological ploys to get Lonnie or Tyrone to rat the others in exchange for a lighter sentence and the hope of eventual freedom. Maynard convincin' the judge to house Lonnie and have the trial here isn't unusual. City and some county jails house federal prisoners all the time 'cause the feds pay the jails to do it. I'd be shocked if the SS ain't playin' by the rules."

"Why do the names of the police chief and his top assistant suddenly show up on the arrest report and not Dan Quinn? It has to be Maynard and his men making a deal. He has his greedy, unblinking blue eyes on Lonnie's money."

Baker nodded and worked his toothpick. "Keep that to yourself, too. I know he's not after the little brother's money, but I can't tell you why." He looked at the chip loaded with chicken and avocado in his hands. "Damn, this shit ain't half-bad for white people food."

"Beats Power bars and a pee jar. Would Tyrone ever roll over on Lonnie?"

Baker popped his fifth can. "They tight, known each other for years. I don' think he would, but the SS is savvy. They'll use his family against him."

"Why did I think you'd say that?"

He played dumb and tossed me a beer. "My birdies tell me shit, but they not everywhere and don' know everythin'." His tone sobered as he leaned forward, "This is gonna hit him hard. He may be ready to open up now. You need to get him to talk and talk soon."

Counterfeit

I told Baker about the letters and mysterious help Coretta and Shondra received.

He ignored it, waving it away with a giant hand. "Get him talking before it's too late."

$ $ $

"I heard about Tyrone. I'm sorry."

Lonnie lapsed into a prolonged silence. I feared I'd already lost him today.

He looked thinner since our last meeting and I noticed a new development—a tic danced below his left eye, among other fresh bruises and strawberries.

For minutes the tic was his only sign of life.

Then he broke the silence: "I have to watch my back in here all the time."

"What's it like?"

His slight shoulders sagged. "Imagine being in a place where you can trust no one, where the only face you might rely on is a visitor and the only voice you might count on is the one you hear during your ten-minute phone call. Imagine a place where someone is always after you or trying to take something important from you. You're being watched all the time, and not necessarily by the guards. All the while you have to watch everyone else. You're in an environment that is not always violent, but forever hostile. I worry most in the areas in the areas where the cameras don't reach. You have to sleep with one eye open all the time, you're always vulnerable, never able to rest or relax. You constantly walk a tightrope and everyone waits for you to fall. You're trapped in a place where you long for just one moment of solace. That's what it's like," he said as his gaze hardened.

"You mentioned the guards. How do they treat you?"

He looked at the door behind me. "Some are decent, others dehumanize or demonize me, but the overall feeling is one of utter disdain, in their words and looks. They are

trained to demoralize. Today Zack Johnson gloated about Tyrone's arrest while his brother Wilbur told me, 'don't get your hopes up, that big buck won't ever get a chance to protect you in here.'"

I motioned to his eye. "Your stress is increasing. How can I help?"

"You can't. I'm handling it the best I can."

He nodded slowly. "The guards make certain bad news spreads quickly. Anything that demoralizes prisoners is viewed as an effective means to exert control. They made sure I watched the news today. They called Tyrone an extremely dangerous man, painted a picture that he was an out-of-control mad dog."

"Did he not do three years for assault?"

He assessed me with cool, calculating eyes. "He did."

I looked at him, awaited more.

"You met his wife Shirley at my momma's. Six years ago, Shirley was his girlfriend and they went to dance at a club after dinner to celebrate their engagement. A drunk made a pass at her, which she politely rejected. When they left, the drunk and two of his buddies followed them to the parking lot with broken beer bottles. Tyrone wanted to drive away, but they attacked and it got ugly. He had to hurt all three to protect Shirley. I'm sure he'd do it again if he had to. Turned out one of the drunk's buddies was connected to a local, high-powered lawyer who mopped the floor with Tyrone's court appointed one. He may look scary, but he's a teddy bear long as no one messes with Shirley or their kids. The judge sent him away for three years in what was a clear case of self-defense. That's the complete story of his conviction, but the news didn't report that, did they?"

"No, they did not."

His head bowed toward the metal table and for the first time, he looked defeated. "I warned him to resist the temptation of visiting Shirley and the kids in case we ever had to retreat to our hideouts. They staked out his home, of course. His family is like air to him. He felt he had to see them."

This was his first oblique admission of felony involvement.

"They will try to break him, but he doesn't know where the others are. I fear they will threaten to make life even more difficult for Shirley and the kids. Who knows what a man will say or do when pushed to the extreme?" The tic quivered as if in response to his own question.

"Has the interrogation been rough?"

"The local police are cupcakes compared to the Secret Service. They're smarter and the intimidation is subtle but much more psychological. They've offered a lighter sentence, the hope of freedom and seeing my family again, if I give up Earl. They say Earl's old and dying anyway, which is mostly true. If I don't, I'm gone for life. It's a Hobson's choice."

"Why do they want him so?"

"For his mind. I had the talent, but he was my mentor. He's probably one of the last true artisans of the craft. They plan to make certain his knowledge is never passed down. Sixty-five years ago, a sage old man descended from slaves and one-eighth Indian, Cletus Jackson, had no sons of his own. He noticed Earl's talents and took him under his wing, grooming him as an apprentice engraver. Like his daddy before him and his granddaddy before that. The last act of a master counterfeiter is to find and train a prodigy to continue the craft and, no, I did not pass on my knowledge."

I wondered about that. "Do they beat you during the interrogations?"

He shook his head, but the tic remained. "The local cop threaten to hand me to the white supremacists or the Mexican prison gang since the pregnant guard I supposedly shot is Mexican-American. Another enjoys tripping me when I'm shackled because I have horrible balance from my club foot. That cut in my scalp you saw when I first spoke to you. He stuck his foot out, The SS will say things like 'I wonder who will take care of your mother if you go away for the rest of your life,' or 'your mother lives all alone in a bad neighborhood, it'd be a shame for her if Tyrone makes the deal with us instead of you, so tell us where the others are.' I'm used to threats and beatings, but forever is a long time. I'm only human." He shook his head and a look of determination returned to him. "I'm going to stay strong and see my work finished."

Plans for the future, bleak though it may be. "You never were suicidal, were you?"

His right hand moved automatically in the air as he drew another imaginary picture. He'd been doing less air drawing this week. A smirk crossed his face briefly.

The habitual motion struck me again as profoundly sad, reminding me of a panther pacing his cage perimeter, reduced to an automaton.

"You want to see your work completed. What do you mean?"

"They want me on constant edge and that's where I am. Food, water, cigarettes and protection are the four basic staples in here.

Cigarettes, even though I don't smoke, and my three squares buy me protection for now."

"You didn't answer my question."

"I know."

"You're not eating?"

He nodded.

"What does 'protection for now' mean?"

"Remember what I told you the first time we met?"

"Yes."

"The writing's on the wall," he said with an edge in his voice.

"Is there someone I can talk to—your court-appointed lawyer, the superintendant, Sgt. Collins?"

He looked to the door. "There are things you do and things you don't do in a place like this. There's an unspoken code. I've seen inmates cross the line and it always comes back to bite them. You don't rat on another inmate and you never call out a guard. You do your time and don't make waves." He whispered, "I have friends. Everything I set out to do remains in motion."

"May I share information you tell me with your old friend from school, if I deem it crucial to your well-being?"

He nodded. "Promise you won't tell Momma what it's like in here. Tell her I'm doing fine."

"I will, but she needs to see you. I know you don't want her to see you like this, but you two need to meet soon, before things deteriorate. If convicted, they'll transfer you to a federal prison farther away and it'll be harder for your mother to visit."

He looked at me and whispered, "There won't be a trial."

Sgt. Collins knocked and walked into the room to say our time was up.

"What are you saying?" I said.

Lonnie stared at the cold, pock-marked concrete block wall with a look of complete despair and turned away from me.

Who would make sure there is no trial?

$ $ $

Leaving the jail, a souped-up black Cadillac Fleetwood screeched to a halt in front of me

and the driver window powered down to reveal the scarred face of Detective Baker. He wagged a finger at me. "Get in. We gonna take a little ride."

The shabby interior smelled of stale sweat, fast food, and pork rinds. Juice and soda cans and Power bar wrappers littered the front matt and back seat. A pair of fuzzy yellow dice hung from the rear view mirror and the barrel of a shotgun protruded from under the bench seat.

He revved the engine. "I'm worried about the little brother, Cool Breeze. My snitches inside are spooked. They clammed up tight as a virgin's legs on prom night. What'd he tell you?"

My training and code of ethics caused me to backpedal from that often asked question. I remembered Skinny's fear that I was workin' for The Man. A crazy idea hit me—could Baker be working for The Man?

He's a homicide dick who's holding out on me. He's using me to prevent another crime, or so he says. Had he somehow conned me all this time? Had I forgotten the manipulation and threats from last year?

"What he and I talk about is confidential. You know that, JoJo."

He glared at me a long time while he drove by feel. The more the car steered itself toward oncoming traffic the more anxious I grew and the more he stared at me with something like hate in those black eyes. His massive hands squeezed the steering wheel with such force I swear I heard it crack. At last he said, "'Fraid you'd say somethin' like that."

He slammed the undercover car to a screeching stop in the left traffic lane as the cars behind veered and quickly jockeyed around us to avoid a pileup. He ignored the glares, horns, and upturned fingers from passing motorists. He slid over on the bench seat so close the ubiquitous toothpick in his mouth stabbed my cheek and I smelled pork rinds on his breath.

"You and me about his only friends now. Fuck confidentiality. You gonna tell me what I want to know. What did he … tell you?"

"I'm beginning to believe he is a modern day Robin Hood."

"You not understand the question?"

"Loud and clear. Skinny told me before this was over I would either die or betray Lonnie and be vilified. I want to prove her wrong."

He backed away, surprised. "She grab your hands?"

I nodded. "And chanted strange names. Is she a voodoo priestess?"

I imagined a tiny doll of me in Skinny's raspy hand and a needle in the other if I disappointed her.

He didn't answer. He looked grim, lost in thought. I assumed he was weighing the possible outcomes in his head. "Damn. Here's the only deal you gonna get. I tell you something if you tell me everything the little brother has said about the case."

"How do I know I can trust you?"

"You don'. Why would I be working this on my own time if I wasn't on the little brother's side? Your nervous Nellies take a leap of faith seeing you. Now's your turn to jump."

I closed my eyes. "Only if you go first."

His eyes narrowed as if to challenge but he said, "You were half right. People want him dead when he's no longer of value, but they're not looking for his money."

"They want the three outstanding shares because Lonnie's share has already been spent, or is in the process of being spent."

He whistled, looking surprised at me. "Babe Sleuth just called his shot."

This time my eyes narrowed. "The bills are perfect duplicates, aren't they?"

"Proof's in the puddin'. Word is that every bill of the little brother's share has passed for real."

"How do you know?"

He shook his head. "My turn. What did the little brother tell you?"

I had a decision to make. Lonnie had given verbal consent to disclose privileged information to Baker if I deem it critical to his survival. "Tyrone's arrest hurt him deeply. He opened up about life on the inside, how the Secret Service plays mind games, offering a lighter sentence if he gives up his co-conspirators. It's strange. He admits to a role in the crime but denies philanthropy. Prisoners are beating him, not the guards. He's trading food and cigarettes for protection. He's lost weight and the intense stress has produced a facial tic. He's got a target on his back, is convinced his days are numbered unless he gives the SS

Earl and Benny. He says the guards make him watch every news show about the case, especially Tyrone's arrest."

Baker perked up at that. "That can help us. Keep him talking about the case."

We were still stopped in the left lane of traffic with no emergency flashers on. "What am I supposed to be looking for?"

"Dunno, and that bothers me. When I have to react to what comes next it usually means I'm too late. The little brother is smart, and we may need his eyes and ears to help us to
find evidence we can use."

"He's preoccupied with death. Is there any way he can be sequestered from general population for his own safety?"

"Last thing I heard before my birdies quit singing was that his court-appointed attorney made the request but the super nixed it. Two men have the super's ear—the Police Chief and Maynard."

Baker slid back behind the wheel and negotiated a quick, illegal U-turn.

"That reminds me, I met Maynard at a party. He already knew I'd been seeing Lonnie in jail. Same goes for Fallon. It seems I make Maynard's guard dog nervous. He fired a verbal warning shot that night. Now I'm convinced it was Maynard talking to Fallon in the mens' room."

For the first time he looked truly surprised. "You never cease to amaze. He and that little pit bull terrier Fallon just put you at the top of their shit list."

"They made veiled threats, all deniable."

He smiled and slapped the wheel. "You been busy, Cool Breeze. I owe you. Usin' your street cred, usin' your contacts," he looked at me and said, "Looks like you grew your pair back, so maybe we even."

"I've met amazing, kind people in Lonnie's neighborhood, and some I hope to never see again. On both sides of the law."

Baker had circled back to the front steps of Gateway city jail. "Don't jaywalk; don't spit on the sidewalk. Watch yo' ass, because every past and present aspect of your life is now being investigated by Maynard's staff. Your family, friends and associates too. They'll use shovels, anal probes, whatever it takes."

Now that I had my cojones back, I wanted to keep them. Sitting back and waiting for the next bad event to happen wasn't my style.

THE THINGS WE DO FOR LOVE

Tony and I had finished stretching and were taking shots before our one-on-one basketball game. He was taller, stronger, and heavier, but ten years older and my quickness and shooting usually made the difference in a half-court game. The tradition began years ago when Tony had his practice, when one of us needed to blow off steam or ask for a second set of ears regarding a difficult case.

The playground was deserted and I'd intentionally been quiet the entire time, swishing and banking jumpers. Tony eventually said, "So, what's on your mind?"

"Dan Quinn. He's missing."

"Three days now, I hear," he said, as he dribbled around the key and took a shot.

I jumped to grab his rebound. "Officially missing. He ever do something like this before—be a no-show, no-call at work for days?"

"I wouldn't know," he said, with sudden cautiousness.

I dribbled around his flank and made a hook shot in the lane that he tried to block. "Huh. Maybe he stumbled into the wrong crime scene at the wrong time."

"Being a cop is dangerous work."

"My hunch is he's already dead or running for his life."

He glared at me, grabbed the ball, and drove the lane like a bull, pushing me backward with his bulk to make an easy lay-up.

"You have anything to back this up, other than one of your famous hunches?"

I palmed the ball at the top of the key and told him everything I knew, without mentioning Debbie.

He listened then said, "You're certain it was Maynard and Fallon in the crapper? Whispered voices are much harder for witnesses to identify correctly. More often than not it turns out they were mistaken."

"I've heard them since then. I'm sure."

He frowned. "But Maynard told the world on TV almost all the money was impounded at the scene."

"I think he was lying. Quinn would know that for certain, wouldn't he?"

"You don't have any proof and you're placing too much trust in the word of a counterfeiter. That could land you in deep shit, grasshopper."

"Alleged counterfeiter."

"Yeah, okay," he said, smirking at my rebuttal. "Quinn's probably on a bender or got lucky in a bar."

It was my turn to grin. "Lucky enough to jeopardize his twenty-and-out pension? He must have alcoholic amnesia or he hooked up with one hell of a woman."

"Your theory involves a lot of lies and people—Maynard, his key staff, and a mole in the Secret Service."

Not necessarily the last part.

I nodded. "You're right, but a lot of money can turn smart people stupid. People have done worse for far less."

I drove past him and swished a fade-away baseline jumper just over his outstretched arm.

"Shit!" he shouted after swatting nothing but air.

He really thought he'd blocked that one.

Counterfeit

I felt the start of a sweat on my brow, while I found a rhythm on the court. "I know cops, especially lonely and middle-aged ones, sometimes eat their guns. Could he be sprawled in a cheap motel or cabin decomposing somewhere?"

Something I said seemed to make him pause and think. The belly of his t-shirt was saturated with sweat and he stood palming the ball in his hand. "I'll look at his file. I doubt it'll help, and that's all I'll do."

With that, he powered down the lane again and pulled up for a shot in the paint. I leapt and blocked the ball, diving to the asphalt for possession before he could use his superior strength and position against me. He cursed again when I came up with the ball, slamming hard and fouling me out of frustration. "You fast little fucker. You skinned the shit out of your knee, you crazy sonofabitch."

"Thanks. Whatever you find … I need it tonight."

"You're going to hell for this, you know."

"I won't be alone. We all know how the road is paved."

He was mouth breathing as he put a hand on my back to check me. "I can't believe you took this no-win, pro bono case. What good can come from it?"

The question on everyone's mind. "I took it for all the wrong reasons. I took it for myself." At least pro bono means 'for good' in Latin, and I already I felt the whole mess had done me some good. At least I was off the couch.

We left the court bloodied and completed our tradition by eating lunch at Uncle Bill's Pancake House. The fact that we'd moved seamlessly from warming up to our most intense physical play ever wasn't lost on either of us.

$ $ $

When I met with Lonnie, his left eyelid was closed, red, and swollen. That didn't faze the tic, which quivered and twitched unevenly. His jaw was bruised and his eyes betrayed the same hardened, glazed over quality as his mug shot. He leaned as close to me as his shackles allowed and I smelled the same unwashed fear and desperation I'd smelled the first time I entered this end-of-the-road place.

I sat down. "This was never about the money, was it?"

Five minutes passed until he shook his head. "I did it for love."

"Earl?"

He whispered, "He's been living on borrowed time."

I waited for him to continue.

He coughed into his shackled palm as best he could, keeping his head bowed for some time. His narrow shoulders sagged like a collapsed tent while he leaned forward and said in a conspiratorial hush, "You've seen his picture. He's eighty-three years old and needs an operation. Insurance calls it experimental even though hundreds have been done successfully. No hospital will let him through their doors without fifty grand up front. He's borrowed against his business, double mortgaged his house, has payments on the press. No bank would extend him another loan in this economy with his credit history. It was this or kiss Skinny farewell and die."

"Would you do it all over again?"

"In a heartbeat."

"Who shot the lady guard?"

He wetted his cracked lips and stared at the battered and scratched tabletop. "I don't know. Earl hired local talent. Their leader had worked as a Treasury guard in the past and knew when and where the building was most vulnerable. They posed as security guards at shift change and their plan to substitute inferior quality paper and ink drums for the authentic supplies went smoothly until they reached the final security checkpoint. What the ex-guard didn't know was that building security had been tightened the day before due to a recent rash of office computer thefts. All truck and car payloads leaving the building were subjected to multiple mandatory searches. The lady guard was clever, she discovered the hidden paper and ink. She drew her gun, but one of the robbers shot her. The crew narrowly escaped to claim their cut and deliver the goods. Earl told me everything went smoothly." He coughed.

"Why'd he lie?"

"He knew I wouldn't have completed the plates if I'd known an innocent was hurt. The prosecutor will claim I'm only saying this because I was caught and anything I have to say about it now would fall on deaf ears. I'm ready to be judged on my actions once they're known. I'm confident you'll put them in their proper context, but you're still missing pieces."

"How do you know the details of the robbery if Earl kept them from you?"

Regret crept into his face as he weighed his answer. "You're a smart man. I talk to people. I listen to them and ask questions. Like you." He coughed again.

He's a midget version of Baker.

"You're being intentionally vague."

"You'll find that answer when you think about this later. It will mean more to you that way. I have complete trust in you now."

His eyes shifted to the door behind me, and I heard the guard coming in.

"One last question. When did you first learn about the lady guard being shot?"

The door opened and the massive Johnson twins entered.

He doubled over and suffered through a lengthy coughing fit. He winced as he tried and failed to press his fingers to his brow, clearly in pain, his breathing suddenly labored. Thick gobs of fresh red blood colored his ink-stained palms. He managed to say, "The day I was arrested."

I shouted to the guards, "This man needs to go to the infirmary now. He's coughing up blood and bleeding internally."

The Johnson twins stood dumbfounded until Sergeant Collins appeared at the door. He nodded for the twins to unchain and escort him to the infirmary. He told them to hurry, and this time I sensed compassion in his voice. As Lonnie left he turned to me. "Tell Momma I'm fine." Collins and I watched the three men leave.

"What the hell is going on in here, Donnell? He's scared of his own shadow and people are beating the shit out of him."

He stared at me self-consciously as we stood by the visitation table.

"Well, aren't you going to answer me?"

He stared transfixed at the tabletop as if he were debating how to respond. Quickly looking around, he took me by the arm and directed me away from the stuffy room. "This is a prison, Dr. Adams. As you can see, this prisoner is a physical runt and runts get picked on, have their food taken by force, and are easy targets for larger, more aggressive inmates. A well-planned assault can be over in seconds. Runts get bullied on the outside, too."

"They don't get killed, Donnell. Do you watch him at all, or do the guards conveniently look the other way when instructed?"

His face hardened and his eyes narrowed. "You're out of line, Doc. We can't watch them all the time."

He's right. Keep your emotions in check. I took a breath. "You mean the other prisoners or the guards?"

Donnell whispered, "Both. Now shut up, Doc. You've gone too far."

"Is he abiding by the rules? Is he getting into fights?"

Sergeant Collins looked uncomfortable again as he glanced back into the empty room. He'd found his voice again and spoke with more force. "I can't share that information with you, Doc. The prisoner will tell you that if he wishes."

Why is this guy nervous and acting strange?

"We're both straight shooters. What's the harm in telling me about his time in here? He's lost weight, he's depressed and scared out of his mind, Donnell. He's my client and I think someone is systematically breaking him with the intent to ultimately kill him."

He opened his mouth to answer and abruptly stopped. He said, "He's doing his part and we're doing ours. This job is hard. The men in here are hard. Enough said. As for the rest, I can't say. Good luck, Doc."

I think he'd come to like or at least respect Lonnie, on some level.

What was Collins trying to say without saying it?

$ $ $

There was no time to waste. I sought out Dennis Hanover, Lonnie's court-appointed attorney. Thin and nearly devoid of shoulders, he was dressed in an oversized three-piece brown suit designed for winter not summer, a thin black tie, and black penny loafers. He sported a bowl-cut hairdo with a patchy light brown mustache and long matching sideburns. He looked like a teenager but had to be at least in his mid-twenties to get through law school. I wouldn't be surprised if he still lived with his parents and took the bus to work. He lugged a ratty maroon accordion file folder, and his movements were jerky and awkward.

I introduced myself and shook his hand. His handshake was wet and limp. He said to call him Denny. I told him that Lonnie was just rushed to the infirmary. "He's being beaten. What are you going to do about it?"

He pushed out his next words with short, crisp, quick bursts. "I asked that he be isolated for his own protection. Kendall denied it. My hands are tied."

"He's a punching bag in there, Denny. They're going to kill him if you don't do something."

He fumbled for words. "You can't talk to me that way. It *is* a prison you know," he sniffed, "and he's a felony counterfeiter."

"Man up, Denny. You're obligated to provide him with the best legal representation you can. You're his attorney and you've already tried and convicted him?"

He shrugged and sniffed again. "They caught him red-handed, for Christ's sake."

"How many prisoners do you have on your caseload, Denny?"

He shifted his weight from one foot to the other. "Over a hundred, give or take a dozen at any time."

"He's suicidal, Denny. That gets him out of general population and back into special security."

"It could, but I never heard him talk about killing himself."

"You're not trained to recognize the signs and symptoms, Denny. Call whoever you need to. Get him back there. Do it now."

He scowled like I'd just ruined his day. "I'll need a notarized, written report from you attesting he's a danger to himself. I'll give it to the super and he'll decide."

"You'll have it on your desk in twenty minutes. Give me your fax."

We exchanged business cards and I told him to call me as soon as he made it happen. I dictated a psychological assessment into my cell phone, called my trusty service and told them I needed a stat note transcribed and sent to Denny's fax. At the front desk, I also completed an affidavit, which was then notarized, attesting that Lonnie Washington verbalized a plan to kill himself in our session. My efficient service had my report on Denny's desk in fifteen minutes. At best my assessment was a stretch and at worst a bald lie that theoretically could cost me my license.

Scott L. Miller

THE BUCK STOPS HERE

That afternoon I slipped quietly into the shadowy back corner of a Channel Four studio to watch the filming of Debbie's counterfeiting series. The busy crew recognized me and assumed Deb had invited me.

The segment began with a close-up of dapper Debbie sitting erect in a chair. She wore a gray jacket, matching skirt, and a white puffy blouse, but still looked too skinny to throw a shadow. Her hair was pulled back from her cheeks, and, once the make-up artist had completed her last-second touch-ups, she donned her serious investigative news reporter face.

"Good evening, we start off part one of Channel Four's special on the world of counterfeiting with agent Stan Winston, a veteran anti-counterfeiting expert with the St. Louis branch of the Secret Service, who has closely examined many of the recent hundred-dollar bills Lonnie Washington allegedly mass-produced earlier this year. Thanks for being here with us tonight, Stan."

In his early forties, Stan was fit and lean, with the wiry look of a runner or tennis player. He had short curly black hair and bushy eyebrows, and was dressed in a conservative dark suit and red tie. He was tanned, and he fiddled with his wire-framed glasses before he spoke. "I'm happy to be here, Miss Macklin," he said, though his body language indicated otherwise.

"What insights can you share with us about the quality of these counterfeit bills?"

Agent Wilson nodded and cleared his throat. "The counterfeiters we're dealing with here attempted the impossible, to replicate the exact process and standards used daily by our Treasury

Department to mass produce hundred-dollar bills. They engraved two knock-off master metal

plates, stole a large amount of authentic government paper and ink, and used a large printing press. However, they made mistakes in the production process with ink distribution. Considerable talent is needed to blend the exact amounts of ink, water and pressure to duplicate the look of real money. That requires months of practice. They likely didn't want to waste precious paper on trial runs and their greed led to their capture. Their bills are detectable by anyone accustomed to handling money." He held up a large cardboard display on the edge of a desk that contained enlargements of two separate one-hundred-dollar bills, but the board slipped from his hands and fell to the studio floor.

"Cut!" the director yelled. "Just reposition the board and we'll edit."

"Sorry," Stan said.

When the scene was reset, the red light reappeared.

"If your camera will zoom in, I will point out the most glaring differences."

He used a laser pointer to start with the bill on the left. "This is an enhancement of the front of a current legal tender US one-hundred dollar bill." He focused on the portrait and continued, "As you can see, the detail that goes into the hundred-dollar bill is a true work of art. The crown of Benjamin Franklin's head is comprised of numerous fine lines running parallel across the forehead and angling down both sides, just below a receding hairline with the hair combed straight back. Note the clear, sharp boundaries that separate the head from the background. Note the serene and somewhat bemused look on Franklin's face. Up close, the lines in his coat are like curved roads of plowed fields on hillsides and his hair gives the appearance of rolling waves. The way the portrait was etched into the master plate also lends the appearance that a light is shining on parts of the forehead, cheek, and chin, as they are significantly lighter. This chiaroscuro effect is intentional, to make the job of the counterfeiter as difficult as possible."

Next he aimed his laser at the portrait of the bill on the right. "This is a blow-up of a bill seized in the recent St. Louis police raid. The differences are noticeable to the naked eye—the details lack sharpness and clarity, they merge into one another, there are blurry areas with no shades of light and dark in the forehead, cheek, or chin regions and no sense that a light is shining on Benjamin Franklin's portrait. These bills are noticeably darker than authentic currency because the counterfeiters burned the plates too long. The arc light burner uses high-intensity light to burn the negatives onto the metal plate. The light burns away a thin layer of the plate beneath and is supposed to leave only the lines of the negative intact and raised. It is, essentially, a stamp in metal carved by light and then cleaned in chemical washes. They burned away too much of the master plate, forcing too much ink onto the bills, and that is why these fakes are too dark. Similar flaws exist on the backs of the bills, also related to the plate-burning process. They lacked the necessary skills and patience to make their counterfeits passable."

Debbie said, "These bills are greatly enlarged for our viewers, Stan. Are these differences readily detectable at regular size?"

"I'll let you be the judge of that, Miss Macklin."

He held up two life-sized hundred-dollar bills for Debbie's inspection as the camera zoomed in on the money and her manicured nails.

After a brief moment Debbie picked one and said, "This one is much darker and must be the counterfeit one."

Stan smiled. "That's right, but there's better news. We now have an easier, quicker and
foolproof way to detect and weed out the remainder of the fake bills from circulation."

"What's that, Stan?"

"When held under a black light, the embedded security strip in a legal tender US hundred-dollar bill glows faint red or pink. These counterfeits glow a bright blue."

Debbie looked confused. "If the counterfeiters stole real government paper, why are their strips blue?"

"All denominations greater than two-dollar bills have security strips embedded in them. The counterfeiters unknowingly stole a large lot of five-dollar rag paper and printed hundred-dollar bills on five-dollar paper sheets.

"Fascinating," Debbie said, looking both impressed and pensive for the camera.

"The starch pens used by businesses to detect counterfeits are useless against these bills because they are printed on authentic paper which has high starch content and the pens contain starch. This black light test, however, is one hundred percent accurate and I recommend all businesses obtain a black light to check every hundred-dollar bill they receive."

She nodded. "Where can businesses obtain black lights?"

"Black lights, also called UV-A lights, are available at local hardware stores, on-line, or may be obtained at cost by contacting our office at the number listed on your screen. Anyone found in possession of these counterfeits with intent to distribute will be thoroughly questioned and the bill will be confiscated. The outstanding fakes are now essentially worthless to the counterfeiters because they can no longer be safely passed."

Debbie repeated the number on the screen then said, "Thank you, agent Winston, for keeping the Channel Four viewing public up to speed on the latest happenings in this fascinating
story that has captured the attention of the entire St. Louis metropolitan area."

"You're welcome, Miss Macklin."

The camera returned to a close-up of Debbie who said, "Experts are now calling this case the most infamous crime in St. Louis history, far outdistancing the five million stolen last year from an ATM repository by armed robbers who were quickly captured. Experts also anticipate the eventual counterfeiting trial will become the most notorious court case in St. Louis history.

"Stayed tuned tomorrow night when Channel Four takes you on a private tour of the Washington, DC Bureau of Engraving and Printing where you will see authentic hundred-dollar bills being printed, cut, and stacked. Plus you will also hear the incredible story of a reformed counterfeiter who served fifteen years in federal prison who now uses his special knowledge to teach the Secret Service how to identify and catch counterfeiters. Stay tuned to Channel Four, the only station with the latest updates on this fascinating case."

Stan Winston's account added another twist. I refused to believe Lonnie had used the wrong paper—he was too smart for that. Had Winston been turned or had Lonnie conned me? I recalled the prophesy of Milton Peebles about the Golden Goose. If he was right it opens a whole new Pandora's Box.

I hoped Peebles' eyes were brown and that *he* was the one full of shit, but I remembered them as black and beady and keen as a laser.

I left the shadows of the studio door before Debbie noticed.

I waited in more shadows on a park bench reading a novel for thirty minutes until Winston emerged from the studio lugging a suitcase and walking to his car. I'd chosen an empty bench next to a non-descript dark blue sedan with a bubble-top on the dash, thinking it looked like the kind of car a Secret Service agent would drive. I looked up casually and rose to make it obvious I was waiting for him.

"I'm Bill Dolan," I said, extending my hand which he shook, "You did a good job in there. Your work must be fascinating. It's incredible how sophisticated the Secret Service has to be to keep ahead of the bad guys."

His look turned skeptical. "Are you a reporter?"

I laughed. "God, no. Nothing like that. I'm the son of the station manager. Is your test really foolproof?"

He shifted his weight. "Why do you ask?"

"I received two hundred-dollar bills yesterday and one of them looked funny."

He looked down at his shoes briefly, then back at me. "Do you have them with you?"

I nodded.

A perturbed look crossed his face and he glanced at his watch.

"Do you remember where you obtained the suspect bill?"

"I can do better," I said, "I know who gave it to me and where to find him."

He said, "Come over to the bench with me."

He quickly extracted tools and vials from his briefcase while I laid two bills on the bench between us. He donned gloves to handle the bills, he snapped and smelled them, inspecting them closely through a jeweler's loupe. Then he subjected areas of the paper and ink to various tests.

"They both look real to me. There's no excess ink spillage. One last test and we're done," he said, reaching into the case and grabbing a small, hand-held device.

"Is that the black light you mentioned inside?"

"Uh-huh," he said in a bored, clinical tone. "I can already tell you what we'll find.
They'll glow red." And, sure enough, the thin strips in both bills glowed pink in the daylight.

"Good news. Your bills are real, you get them back," he said, sounding disappointed.

"Thanks. I'm curious, do you run all the tests yourself, or do you delegate them to subordinates?"

"Why?"

I gave an exaggerated shrug. "No reason. My favorite shows are the CSI ones, and I'm fascinated by the techniques you guys know."

He paused. "The simple tests—weighing, measuring, checking for prints, and black-lighting—were done by underlings. I like to be hands-on, so I conducted the chemical and quality tests."

If I pressed him for more, red flags would start flying in his head.

Counterfeit

He looked at his watch and said, "Gotta go." He tossed his briefcase in the back of the sedan and sped away, trying his best not to sneak looks at me but failing.

One of the bills had come from my bank this morning. The other came to my home yesterday in an envelope with no return address. The note inside it simply said: *One of 250,000.* Same handwriting as before, but no signature, no LW.

The crisp new bills looked identical to me.

I told myself this didn't prove anything because I didn't know for certain the origin of the second bill. But I stood there alone in the parking lot wondering whether agent Wilson or a lab rat in his office had been turned, and to what degree.

Scott L. Miller

CHANGE IN THE WEATHER

That night I drove down Hebert Street and sensed something different, something wrong. Thunderclouds were building in the distance and the air felt charged, volatile. A growing throng of young and middle-aged black men had gathered on the street, the line stretching from Fairground Park, tracking my every move as I parked in front of LaKeesha's brick and frame house. Some of the men I recognized from the scrum at the mini-mart. Instead of running up to negotiate their next pay raise, DeAndre and Ty quickly pedaled away from my car, casting furtive looks over their shoulders. It was too late to drive forward or backward as the mob of bodies had already surrounded my car.

Oh, shit.

I didn't see Skinny Yolanda over the heads of the mob along the street, but she broke through their ranks and approached my Solstice under a full head of steam, her square jaw set and those oval obsidian eyes fixed on me.

When I got out of the car she slapped me hard across the face and struck my head and shoulders with closed fists. She lunged forward at me while I backpedaled. I couldn't understand her guttural screams, she was that out of control. Her sole focus was on attacking me. Her long nails clawed at my face, she kicked, spat, and bit me. The silent mob of gawking onlookers had doubled by this time but made no effort to intervene. Icy stares met me from all sides.

I reacted instinctively. I wrapped my arms around her thin, twisting, fighting ones and took her to the ground as gently as I could. Still, we hit the bare dirt near the buckled sidewalk hard. The mob encircled us during my take down, I assumed to lend her aid, but they held their ground once they saw she was unhurt. We wrestled and I held onto her until she at last stopped hitting, biting, and scratching. Her heart rate and breathing at last normalized from sheer fatigue as she said, "You did it! You did it! You led them to him, you bastard!" She repeated the last two words softly to herself as if chanting a mantra.

Then the crying started and all the fury left her. She went limp and sagged in my arms like a wounded bird with a broken heart.

That made me feel worse than when she was hitting me. It dawned on me what happened and how they had played me.

She sat on the crabgrass, one thin leg folded under her, her back to me, and sobbed. I released my grip and she said, "They found him. Lonnie told me you were different from the others. He's a good judge of character. I wanted so much to hope again. I knew I shouldn't have trusted you. My readings are never wrong."

He needs an operation...

Lonnie had confided in me about the lung surgery and now they have Earl Mooney.

Sgt. Collins had tried to warn me with his eyes, but by then it was too late. He knew.

They'd been doing more than watching.

Her anguish transferred to me. Any response by me would be trite or stupid. Sometimes it's best to keep your mouth shut and take your lumps.

The clouds had thickened overhead and lightning flashed above the black stone faces looking down on me, judging.

Skinny turned to me and grabbed my palms like she had done in LaKeesha's living room. She began to sway and arched her neck so far backward I saw only the whites of her eyes. We were locked as one when she said, "Evil is coming for you on swift and silent wings. Run fast or it will destroy you. Evil cannot hide its nature forever for that is its underbelly. To survive, you must be re-born from fire. To live, the spirit must cross over. Go now, boy. Talk to her."

She fell backward into a trance-like state. I caught her and gently placed her on the ground before her head hit the sidewalk. Shirley and Tyra nodded to several men who silently carried her to LaKeesha's house. The men made it clear they did not want me to follow. DeAndre and Ty walked their bikes away from me without a word.

$ $ $

I needed to talk to a friendly face. I dialed Tony, but he didn't pick up. I tried Marilyn, another therapist in my practice, but my call went straight to voice mail. I even tried Baker's number, and when he didn't answer, it hit me. I'd become a circle of one since Kris' murder, isolating myself from friends and co-workers. Though the sky looked ready to open up, I drove south to talk to Kris. I had a half-hour at the Botanical Garden before closing time.

I walked past couples and families with strollers hurrying to the parking lot to beat the rain. The temperature had dropped and gusty winds swirled since I'd left Hebert street. Once inside the English garden, the canopy of the mature shade trees muffled the howling wind. Our spot was vacant, for anyone with common sense had already left. I sat down on the Joyce Duane bench. In front of me, the small meandering stream gently burbled. This time no birds whistled songs in the trees, they'd all taken cover.

Counterfeit

I felt the first rain drops land on my arm and said, "I let a client down today, hon. He put his trust in me and now a sick old man will die in a jail infirmary because of me."

An ear-piercing clap of thunder rolled above me and the rain intensified.

"They used me. I never saw it coming. How can I face him again, face his mother? I'm lost. I don't know what good I'm doing. They'll never let him see the light of day again as a free man."

A crack as loud as cannon fire made me jump. I looked up to see a massive branch splinter away from the trunk of a tall wide tree and plummet toward me, snapping smaller branches and scattering leaves in its path. I had no time to react. Just before it fell through the canopy and crushed my skull, the branch caught and lodged in the fork of another tree. The gaping hole that had suddenly punched through the tree canopy allowed the downpour to soak my clothes and run into my eyes. It was not cleansing. I shuddered, but didn't move.

I turned back to the stream and said, "I wish you were here. I need someone to talk to, to help me figure out what to do." I sat there waiting when two chipmunks appeared along the stream, followed by a thin red fox. The fox had them trapped. All three stood frozen as the rain beat down. The predator inched forward, when suddenly one chipmunk charged. The fox quickly broke the chipmunk's neck, but by then the other had raced to the safety of its nearby hole in the ground. The emaciated fox trotted the way it had come, head held high to balance its prey in his narrow jaws.

I heard a snap. Above, the heavy branch groaned and dropped another foot closer before snagging again. A horn blared and I saw weak lights flashing through the storm. An angry security guard in a golf cart yelled, "What're you trying to do, get yourself killed?"

"I'm trying to figure out which chipmunk I am and how to attack a fox."

He stared at me, mouth open. "Get in, before you get killed!"

I climbed in the cart, and the guard steered the golf cart down the path. Behind us, the jagged branch crashed through the last tree, gouging a deep hole in the soaked ground in front of our bench.

It took the entire cart ride in horizontal rain, and then some, to convince the guard I wasn't nuts. It wasn't easy.

$ $ $

Once home I ran five miles on the treadmill and showered. It helped. Some.

Baker called and said, "You heard?"

I rubbed my jaw. "Skinny hit me with the news."

"Sweet Jesus. Still got your pair?"

"Yeah, but my pride took a beating."

"The world don' give a shit about that. I'm on my way." He hung up, sounding sad and angry.

The credits for the latest hit reality show about two teams of has-been celebrities doing whatever it takes to be the first to find all the bizarre and kinky items on their scavenger list were rolling as Detective Baker and I sat down on my leather sofa.

And they say the Golden Age of television is over.

Baker brought a twelve-pack and a bag of spicy pork rinds.

I thanked him for the beer. "How'd you sneak pork rinds past the subdivision gates?"

"Told 'em I was the Mexican pool man."

"Smart thinking. I have real food, if you don't mind leftover barbecue."

His ears perked up. "Pork steaks or ribs?" Grilled pork steaks smothered in Sweet Baby Ray's home-made barbecue sauce ruled summers in St. Louis. I was more of a rib man.

"Both, and brats."

"Gimme some cold pork steaks with hot sauce," Baker said, devouring a pork rind while he twisted the cap off a beer. "Protein helps crime fightin', too. Hurry back, your stalker's about to come on."

From the kitchen I told him about Stan Winston's filmed segment with Deb, his take on the bills, and my test of him.

I heard the first notes of the energetic, pulsing Channel Four theme music, carried two plates and habanera sauce, and set them on tray tables in the living room. I sat down just as a close-up of Debbie Macklin's thin face filled the screen. She stood in front of City Hospital near the Gateway jail, an animated and serious look on her peaches-and-cream complexion. She turned toward the hospital ER entrance just as an ambulance crew wheeled in a stretcher carrying a cachectic-looking, elderly black man hooked up to IV drips, chest tubes, and an oxygen non-rebreather mask.

Debbie turned back to the camera and announced, "Channel Four is the only news station with this exclusive live feed on the latest breaking developments concerning the local gang of counterfeiters. We have been closely monitoring this case and we learned that a third counterfeiter has just been apprehended, possibly their ringleader and financial kingpin. Earl Mooney—" as the camera cut to the earlier photograph of him smiling for the camera while holding his portable oxygen device at his side, hugging the woman I now know as Skinny

Yolanda, "—was captured without incident, under the alias of 'John Goode,' at a hospital in the Dallas-Fort Worth area, with SWAT back-up. More on this breaking story is sure to follow. Chief Prosecutor Maynard Jr. had this to say about the latest arrest."

The screen cut to a close-up of Maynard in front of another podium, flashing those perfectly capped teeth. "Today marks another triumph for good over evil. I can't say enough about our city police, working in conjunction with the Secret Service and their Texas counterparts. We located and arrested Earl Mooney, the leader of the counterfeiters, who fled the state to elude justice." Maynard paused, unblinking, staring into the camera. "I want to comment now on the escalating tension in the city as a result of these arrests. If these men were white, Asian, or Hispanic, the weight of the law would come down equally on them. Instead of dwelling on the skin color of these criminals, these isolated pockets of unrest and anger should be grateful the integrity of their currency remains intact." Maynard paused to point a finger at the camera. "If you are in possession of a counterfeit bill, it will be confiscated and you will be thoroughly questioned. You will be a victim of fraud.

"Only one armed and dangerous counterfeiter remains at large and he is Benny Blades." The screen cut to the same close-up of a smiling Benny giving the peace sign to the camera, looking every bit the ladies' man in his tight black T-shirt. Maynard stared intensely into the camera and said, "The reward on this man's head remains in place. We will find where he's hiding and arrest him. It's only a matter of time."

Debbie Macklin returned to the screen. "Channel Four now turns to a new consultant, Dr. Howard Davies, a clinical forensic psychologist in private practice who has been frequently called as an expert witness in several high-profile local trials. Dr. Davies, is this case dividing the city along racial lines?"

Baker reached for the remote, but I grabbed it away from him.

"Hired gun" Howard's wide body filled the screen, his porcine belly hanging over his belt and his trademark off-the-rack suit from Sears wrinkled as ever. Howard supplemented his considerable income by serving as an expert witness at trials, if the price was right. He adjusted his glasses and when he spoke his salt-and-pepper mustache went into motion in tandem with his chins.

"Debbie, in certain sections of the metropolitan area, I think it has. I've noticed that the longer this manhunt drags on, the tougher and more authoritarian the language of the Chief Prosecutor becomes. Some people are questioning whether Mr. Maynard would be using hot button phrases like, 'dangerous gang of criminals' and "triumph of good over evil" if these alleged counterfeiters were white. The overwhelming majority of whites interviewed have no issue with Mr. Maynard's tough talk or the police procedures used against these alleged counterfeiters. He is as advertised, tough on crime, in their opinion. The prosecutor and police chief are the two major symbols of authority, of law and order in this city.

"Some African-Americans view the police as an organization controlled by whites and perceive that the police detain and arrest a greater percentage of African-Americans. The case has sparked renewed interest in social issues such as the disparity of jailed African-Americans compared to whites and the absence of competent legal counsel to low-income people. Recent questions have been raised in the community by those who are not convinced these men pose any real danger to the public. A few in the community are raising questions of whether these men posed any real danger to the public. I see parallels that mimic the OJ Simpson investigation and trial in Los Angeles—people rushing to judgment before the trial, increasing gun sales, fear of potential riots, tension in the streets and universities, and colleges debating the civil aspects of the upcoming trial. The prudent course is to give the alleged counterfeiters and Mr. Maynard the benefit of the doubt until all the facts are known. Everyone is innocent until proven guilty. The trial will reveal all."

I wish I had that kind of faith in our judicial system. Life would be so much easier wearing blinders.

The camera moved from his chins to Debbie's narrow as an arrow face. Their size
differential was so great she could have been a moon orbiting planet Howard.

"Thank you for your insights, Dr. Davies. And now, here's Dan Jenkins with other area news…"

I clicked off the television and noticed Baker had eaten the pork steaks, half the bag of rinds and drained another beer. The big man could put it away.

"Ain't life a bitch," he said as his eyes swung toward me and he reached for another bottle.

"They—somebody, the city cops or the SS—eavesdropped on my sessions with Lonnie. I'm sure of it. Lonnie confided to me about Earl's experimental operation and the very next day they catch him. It's too coincidental—they simply checked the few hospital registers that perform the specialized surgery and used his age and physical description to locate him."

Baker sat up, all ears. "That visit room is monitored visually and with a guard posted outside the door. Listening in occurs when family and friends visit to make sure nobody planning an escape; warning signs are posted in all family visiting rooms and next to the phones. If someone listens in on a privileged doctor/prisoner or attorney/prisoner conversation, that's a violation of the little brother's rights of privacy and they risk losing the case and their careers. Never heard it done in all my years on the force, but there's a first time for everythin'. You got proof?"

I shook my head slowly.

"Shit," Baker said, sitting back down. "Golden Boy already claimin' it was good old-fashioned police work that led to the collar. My only hope is to find Quinn, but I hit a dead end. He ain't using credit cards and his social security number hasn't registered anywhere. He either in a hidey-hole or planted in pieces six feet under."

He noticed the cuts and scratches on my face and neck. For the first time tonight he smiled. "Cut yourself shaving?"

"I think you knew damn well what happened five minutes after the fact."

"Powerful things come in small packages."

"Does she think she's a voodoo priestess?"

Baker raised an eyebrow and opened another beer. "You a non-believer in religion, Cool Breeze?"

"Voodoo's a religion?"

Baker nodded, his eyes glassy and full of fatigue. "With many faces. Slaves on plantations in the Indies sometimes used slow-actin' poisons when their masters beat them and treated them like animals. Since Whitey back then didn't understand shit about the culture and showed no desire to learn, rumor spread that witchcraft, curses or supernatural powers were at work. Voodoo went underground to survive. Skinny isn't a witch doctor or voodoo priestess, but she has a connection to the beings that rule the spirit world, called the loa. She communicates with them. Sometimes the signals are strong, other times not. She not gonna poison you or lay bad juju on you, but people in the 'hood pay close attention to her readings."

"Speaking of the neighborhood, I'm persona non grata there now. I'm flying east Saturday morning and plan to be back first thing Monday to see Lonnie."

This time Baker looked confused.

"If Skinny has the spirit world covered, I'm going back to where this drama began, in the world of the living."

TRAFFIC ACCIDENTS, HOUSE FIRES, PUPPY MILLS, AND METH LAB BUSTS

The morning after my exile from the streets of north St. Louis, I completed a five-mile run and worked out with weights. In the evening, I went to dinner and a movie with two co-workers. I was home by eleven for my early morning flight out of Lambert.

Frantic pounding on my door woke me three hours later. I had a flashback to Detectives Baker and LeMaster and the horror of Kris's murder last year. Through the peephole I spotted a slender-as-a-thread person with big hair smoking a cigarette and hugging herself as if she were cold or, more likely, stressed.

I opened the door for Debbie and she immediately began pacing the length of my living room, puffing away, head down, lost in thought. She wore a classic full-length black evening dress and a pearl necklace. She carried her high heels in one hand. Her face was red and puffy; her make-up streaked from crying.

"Sorry if I woke you. I have to talk to somebody."

"It's okay. I didn't know you smoked."

At two in the morning I am a master of insight.

She shrugged. "It's yet another way to keep my weight down for the camera, sucking over fifty legal carcinogens into my lungs." A pause, then: "For my so-called career." Shaking, she turned toward me and said, "I'm such a fool. You were right all along."

"You're no fool. Come on, sit before you fall down. Let me get you some water with lemon."

She shook her head. "Stoli, or Grey Goose, if you have it. Or a dirty Bombay Sapphire or Beefeater martini, straight up and chilled. You can throw a lemon wedge in or, better yet, some big fat salty olives." Her large green eyes a tad out of focus, she smiled crookedly and said, "Yum!"

"How much have you had?"

"Not enough."

When I returned with our drinks, she slowly rocked back and forth in a chair, looking for an ashtray. I handed her a small plate since I don't own one.

"I don't stock vodka. This is Tanqueray, straight up, freezer-chilled, with two bleu cheese stuffed olives. I also brought water with lemon."

"Thanks." She took the martini and sipped like a dainty bird at first. When it met her approval, she took a healthy pull.

"He invited me to an ultra-exclusive soiree tonight at the Ritz-Carlton in Clayton. He said it was his way to thank the station for our coverage of the counterfeiting story." She took another swig and laughed.

First a nibble of prime rib, now gin and olives. *What's next, a pie-eating contest?*

"Maynard?"

She nodded. "The little rat bastard Fallon orchestrated the entire evening. A stretch limo dropped me off and the chauffeur told me a penthouse suite had been reserved for me if I wished to stay the night. Security escorted me to one of the posh corporate banquet rooms on the second floor. I danced, drank and flirted. I worked the room sniffing stories. Since this began, I've been invited to yacht parties, this year's Super Bowl, and private island resorts in Hawaii and the Caribbean. Big-time money. Big-time players. A really big shoe!" she said, giggling at her own impression of Ed Sullivan.

"Since what began?" I asked.

She paused to take a gulp and gin splashed on her dress. "I … uh … I haven't been exactly ... up front. Before the party at the Haller estate, Fallon promised me exclusives to all breaking events in the case."

"Why? What was in it for them?" I asked, having a pretty good idea.

"Same thing I said," slurring her s's. She hiccupped and added, "He said I'd find out later. Why look a gift horse in the mouth, right? So I agreed.

"Anyway, it was late and I had a buzz, so I took the offer of the suite. Fallon and a security man escorted me to a penthouse. Maynard reserves the entire eighteenth floor of the Ritz for his major St. Louis events. When the elevator doors opened, Fallon rode back down alone but not before he said to enjoy myself and flashed that warped little smile of his. *He knew.* The hunky security guy walked me to my suite and I saw one of the business fat cats from the party enter a room with his hand on the ass of a stunningly hot babe young enough to be his granddaughter. A waiter followed wheeling a room service cart with champagne into their suite."

I wondered about the accuracy of her story, given her state. "What happened next?"

"The suite was gorgeous and big as a house. Panoramic view of the Arch and downtown.
Marble columns, fireplaces. Fully-stocked fridge, wet bar, all-night room service. Mirrors above a giant circular bed, green Italian marble walk-in shower and four-seat Jacuzzi—"

"Cut to the chase already. I'm not going to buy the place."

She put a finger to her lips as if to shush me, lost her balance and nearly fell off the chair. "It's my story, and I'm going to tell it my way. I almost sold my soul for it, so let me be."

I closed my heavy eyelids briefly and let her continue.

"Beyond the master bedroom was a dark-paneled room that housed a fax, copier, and several flat screen televisions mounted to the wall, turned to the latest stock market trends and news."

She chugged the dregs of her martini. "I'm gonna need another one of these babies to get through the rest."

"Here you go," I said. She didn't notice that I'd handed her the water tumbler. "Then what happened?"

"I'd just showered and was naked when I heard the click of a key card open the door to my suite. I held a robe to my chest as Maynard walked in, suit coat off. He was smiling. He began to unbutton his shirt. He *expected* me to be there, waiting. He put the do-not-disturb sign on the outer knob, closed the door, and finished unbuttoning his shirt."

She made a face at her glass. "This one's not as good as the first."

"They never are. Go on."

She shrugged. "He said he was happy to see I'd made myself comfortable and asked how I liked the suite." She took another drink and said, "Then he tossed his shirt onto a high-back chair. The guy *is* really ripped. Wow."

"Stick to the facts, oh ripped one."

She made a face at me, not understanding. Then the light-bulb clicked. "Very funny. I asked him what he thought he was doing in my room. He walked to the wet bar and poured himself three fingers of Glenfiddich. He wasn't I-don't-have-a-fucking-clue-what-I'm-doing drunk, but he was drunk. I looked for those skin blotches you talked about and saw none. He walked up close and said, 'Do you want to keep reporting traffic accidents, house fires, Midwest puppy mills, and meth lab busts the rest of your career?' I shook my head, terrified, and dying to get dressed. He grinned and said, 'This is politics, babe. How far do you want to go?' I stood there not knowing what to say. Then I asked what was going on in the suite next door and he said, 'Keeping key constituents happy.'"

She took a sip of water and exhaled deeply. "He walked closer while I backed away, the Terri-cloth robe the only thing between us. I was scared shitless. I reminded him he just announced he wasn't running for the senate and he answered, 'After I clear this case, I may feel differently. I can throw my hat in the ring late. With my name recognition I'd win in a landslide.'"

"Did he put his hands on you?"

"No. He didn't solicit sex or speak directly about having sex. Everything was implied, but he expected to fuck me. That was his quid pro quo. I told him I was getting sick and backed into the bathroom and got dressed. I demanded he call security to drive me home. He apologized for Paul's 'honest mistake' with the suites but didn't offer another. While he phoned security, he went through my purse before he let me leave."

"Probably checking for a tape recorder or microphone," I said.

"As I left, I heard him dial a number on his cell and whisper, 'Je suis encore dans une

blonde humeur. Envoyer la tall Russe.'"

"Sorry, I didn't take French."

She smiled, albeit crookedly. "Well I did. My high school French finally paid off. He said, 'I'm still in a blonde mood. Send up the tall Russian.'"

"Did he threaten you in any way? Did he terminate your arrangement?"

She waved her now empty glass in my face, wanting more. "To the contrary, he acted like nothing had happened. He was cool as the gin you're about to pour. He said he wants me there when he announces his candidacy."

This time I made a stiff drink for me and water for her, wondering about her story. "Do you have any proof other than your word against his?"

She shook her head sadly and her eyes had difficulty focusing. The rocking resumed. Hiccups caused her thin body to jerk.

"I'm such an idiot," she said, slurring her words. "And to think I was furious at you for using me to get close to him." She slapped the back of my shoulder like we were long-lost pals and said, "Iconic, isn't it?"

"Iconic, indeed. A limo drove you home. How did you get here?"

"I drove the silver Jeep, you silly man. Hi ho, Silver!" she said, ala the Lone Ranger and promptly fell off the chair.

"No more driving and no more booze for you."

Even though my townhouse had three bedrooms, the second housed my office and the third my library. I hid her car keys, carried her into the master bedroom and placed her on my king-sized bed. As I did, she opened her eyes and ran a hand through my hair.

"God, you're gorgeous. Can I tell you a secret? I've always had a thing for you." She fumbled to undo the buttons on my shirt and when that failed she slid the straps of the black evening dress off her alabaster shoulders, revealing pert, firm breasts with large nipples. "Fuck me, fuck me now," she said into my ear.

"I think you've had enough excitement for one night."

"Fuck me. I want you inside me," she moaned, softer.

"I think we'd both regret it in the morning," I answered as I covered her slender legs with a blanket and placed the lemon water on the night table.

That seemed to sober her. "You're still in love with her, aren't you? Admit it," she said, hurt bleeding into her voice. When I didn't answer, she said, "God damn you," softly as she turned her head away.

"I'm going to let that slide because you're drunk. Good night," I said and turned off the light but kept the ceiling fan running. Besides, I'd used her plenty this week.

She stared with unfocused eyes in the direction of the revolving blades. "No mirrors. Tha's good, you silly man you. No more booze for you. And no sex," she said as she hiccupped again, closed her eyes, curled into a tight ball, and closed her eyes.

I turned the night light on in the master bath while my erection and I retreated to the couch. The younger me would have acted differently.

That was the first time I'd gotten close to a woman in a year. Kris has an inner *je ne sais quoi* that enhanced her physical beauty and made her the total package. Someone like her is a rare find.

Several times in the middle of the night I heard the bed springs squeak followed by the padding of elfin feet as she went to vomit. I held her hair back each time as she emptied her stomach contents. The last time, I caught her surreptitiously sticking her finger down her throat as she sat on the white ceramic tile, hugging the porcelain throne. When she finished, I cleaned her face with a cold washrag and had her take small sips of water.

She seemed steadier. I asked, "How long have you been purging?"

She brushed tousled hair from her face. "Since I moved from the production booth to in front of the camera," she exhaled and added, "Two years now, give or take."

"Do you want to stop?"

She sat with her legs folded under her bottom next to the toilet. She said nothing, looking pale and gaunt, and then she began to weep. I held her until she'd calmed enough to answer. "I don't want to live this way. No job is worth this."

For what remained of the dawn, we talked about her childhood, her parents, her body image, treatment options, and doctors and therapists who specialize in eating disorders. Then her thoughts returned to what had transpired in the Ritz penthouse.

"I screwed up. I allowed myself to get caught up in the Maynard mystique, the promise of the national spotlight. I thought I'd been accepted into an elite group. I'm so stupid."

"No you're not. You were recruited by a master manipulator."

"I lost sight of my journalistic creed: to be objective, seek the truth, and provide a fair and comprehensive account of newsworthy events and issues in the community. I'm supposed to act independently, serve the public trust with thoroughness and honesty, because an enlightened public is the forerunner of justice and democracy." She looked up at me, tears shining in her eyes. "You probably think I'm lying, but I really believe in the creed."

"I know. I've fallen from grace before," thinking of how I met Kris. "It means we're human."

She wasn't done. "My job is to avoid conflicts of interest, remain free of associations that might compromise my integrity or damage my credibility. But I failed. I drank the Maynard Kool-Aid, deluding myself into thinking I could remain objective."

You're not alone. Some news channels sold out long ago.

I brushed back another stray bang. "That's enough self-abuse. Do you always dump on yourself when you're drunk?"

She smiled sadly and gave almost a faint chuckle. "Calorie guilt."

Low self-esteem behind the professional façade.

"You're right. New plan: I want to expose the bastard for what he is, but I don't know how."

I thought of Maynard's security entourage. She's in over her head. It's way too risky for her.

"Don't even think about it. You'd be the disgruntled, former employee in a case of 'He said, She said.' He could turn the tables and claim you made advances toward him, accuse you of professional misconduct, or say that you sacrificed integrity to advance your career."

Her tiny frame sagged inward. "What am I supposed to do, nothing?"

"Journalists are supposed to avoid undercover or covert methods of information gathering, right?"

"Yes, unless traditional methods fail and the information is vital to the public knowledge or well-being."

I smiled. "I'm not a journalist. I've done undercover work before. Are you privy to anything, past or future, we could possibly use against him?"

She sat thinking, then perked up. "You'd give me the exclusive, right?"

I nodded. "That's the Debbie I know. Welcome back."

Leaning her arm son the toilet seat, she said, "I had a hunch Fallon wasn't giving me unfettered access to Maynard's schedule, so I copied his personal appointment calendar for this month and I was right, it didn't match." She fished a crumpled and torn piece of paper from her purse and handed it to me.

Hardly damning evidence, for I imagined there were times when even Fallon couldn't reach the Golden Boy.

"It's a start," I said. "Lay low. If you want out, tell Maynard, but do not go back with the idea to dig up dirt on him. His security team will have you under the microscope. They'll catch you and you'll be up shit creek."

"I know."

I don't know how far Maynard was willing to go to protect his turf, but I have an idea.

It was now eight a.m. and I served orange juice and toast, which she kept down. I had a plane to catch in two hours.

I thought about my night out, my dinner and movie with friends, and it seemed like it happened weeks ago. *So much for a break from the case.*

The bell rang as I walked her to the front door.

Baker stood dressed in his trademark black, gold earring in his left lobe, bald head reflecting the early morning sun as he calmly looked at us.

She walked up to me, stood on tip-toes to peck me on the cheek and said, "Thanks for last night. Call me." Her formal black evening dress was wrinkled and her big hair was helter-skelter.

She eyeballed Baker from head to toe, leered, and said, "Mandingo. Woof!"

Baker laughed and said in his baritone voice, "Fuckin' A, girl. Mandingo the porn star, not the slave."

We watched her stagger silently to her silver Jeep like an extra in a zombie movie, holding her black stiletto heels in one hand.

"Damn, you not only grew 'em back, but anorexic Barbie could barely walk to her ride, Cool Breeze. My man!" He smiled, his gold front tooth gleaming.

"It's not like that."

"Shit," Baker said skeptically.

I grabbed an overnight bag and said, "Maynard tried to fuck her after a party last night. When she refused, he called security for a hooker. Others were provided to major party contributors."

He perked up. "He force her? We got any physical evidence? Eyewitnesses?"

I shook my head. "They were both drunk. No witnesses." I didn't mention the quasi-deal Maynard had forged with her earlier. "Any luck finding Quinn?"

"Nada. Old Irish still into the wind, or worse. You workin' on The Voice?"

I nodded. "She also said Maynard plans to wrap up the trial quickly and is considering a late run for the senate."

"He can't control the speed of a major trial."

"I know, and that's scary. Maybe Lonnie's right. There isn't going to be a trial because Maynard has a more permanent solution in mind."

His hands balled into fists. A vein beat visibly on his temple as he weighed possibilities.

"I have a plane to catch."

He looked surprised. "You bailin' on me, Cool Breeze?"

"I'll be back in time to meet with Lonnie first thing Monday, if he still wants to see me. The only witness we have is over seven hundred miles away."

MONEY FOR NOTHING

I flew into Dulles International and rented a red convertible Mustang GT. I've got a soft spot for convertibles and don't quite understand why anyone would drive with a roof over their head if they had a choice. The weather was resort-like. I lowered the roof and soaked up the sun.

Virginia wasn't that far, but the freeway grind gave me plenty of time to dwell on Skinny's powers and predictions. By the time I got into the District and reached the D.C. library near the Mall, they remained an enigma, so I filed them away for the time being and prepared to take my next step.

I'd scanned old *Post-Dispatch* issues last week and found no references to the armed robbery at the Bureau of Engraving and Printing in D.C. eight months ago. In his first press interview, Maynard claimed Lonnie and/or the others had shot and nearly killed a pregnant security guard in their daring getaway. So I reviewed the archives of the *Washington Post, Examiner, Times-Herald, The Hill, City Paper,* and *Business Journal* and none mentioned a robbery or shootout at BEP. I found a few back-page articles warning area businesses to be on the lookout for a possible increase in counterfeit bill trafficking. Generic warnings with no specifics. I wondered if this was how the Treasury and Secret Service usually operate and whether this was the first major theft of paper and ink.

I did a reverse Google name and address search for the guard and entered it into my rental's GPS. The Skyline Towers apartment complex had no skyline or towers worth mentioning. Drab pitted odes to concrete stood cramped together like dominoes hastily spray painted every color in the spectrum. Drying laundry and bed sheets hung from tiny patios behind many tenements while potted plants, bikes, barbecue grills, and lawn chairs filled the others. The warm air smelled of bus exhaust and fast food. Several windows were broken or boarded up. A culturally diverse mix passed me in the dark hallway to the elevator, while the cries and laughter of young children behind first floor open windows floated to me.

On the sixth floor I pressed the doorbell marked Rachel Sanchez and immediately heard a stampede of many feet rushing the door. Four little Latino boys greeted me, jumping up and down, talking all at once, while behind them a very pregnant woman holding a toddler warily assessed me from the kitchen. The woman walked to the door and offered a neutral smile. She was Mexican-American, young, petite, and pretty, her short black hair tucked under a Redskins cap. She wore a sleeveless green camouflage tank top with white shorts and flip-flops.

After I introduced myself and offered my card, she prompted the kids to play outside. It didn't take much. She offered me a seat at her kitchen table and said, "This one's ready for her nap. Let me put Angela in her crib. Have a seat." She turned down a short hallway with worn brown carpeting and pictures of the boys lining the walls. I sat waiting in front of an old dinged oak table in the tiny kitchen, wondering how Lonnie was. The worn linoleum floor under my feet was sparkling clean and harvest-gold colored. The appliances were lime green and, like the floor, probably original items after this pitted concrete cookie cutter slid down the truck chutes sometime in the seventies.

Rachel returned and said, "She's out like a light. Would you care for some tea or coffee?"

I declined her polite offer.

Counterfeit

"Why is a social worker from St. Louis knocking on my door in Virginia?"

"I'm providing therapy to a man who is suspected of being one of the four who shot you and robbed the Bureau of Engraving and Printing last year. I want to get a complete picture of my client and something about this case tells me I should talk to you."

"This couldn't be done over the phone?"

"I sometimes prefer to a face-to-face dialogue."

Rachel arched an eyebrow. "This is quite a long home visit you're making. I'm not sure how I can help. I admire your dedication, though." She seemed nervous and added, "I'm that way with my kids."

The boys looked the same approximate age. "Are they all yours?"

She laughed and rolled her eyes. "Technically no. In reality, yes. Angela and one of the boys are mine. The other three are my sister's." A wistful look crossed her pretty brown face as she continued, "Teresa has some inner demons and an uncanny ability to hook up with the wrong man. She left her boys with me last year to get away for the weekend with her boyfriend. She hasn't returned. Every so often she calls, promises to stop by or send money, but never does. It's not the first time this's happened, either. Anyway, I feel like they're my kids, too. I've been a single mom to them since my boyfriend left after the shooting." Her shoulders sagged a bit as she confessed, "I guess I share my sister's defective man-picking gene."

I leaned closer to her. "If you'll pardon me saying this, I anticipated you having an infant, not a toddler, and didn't expect you to be pregnant."

She looked confused and stiffened, her defenses rising. "What do you mean?"

"The robbery occurred eight months ago. I heard that you were quite pregnant when shot, that you and baby barely survived. You look like you're due any day now…"

She looked perplexed and more than a little spooked. "Who said I nearly died?" She make a quick sign of the cross, extended her slender right arm and pointed to small circular scars, one on the inside of her lower forearm and one on the outer. "The bullet went clean through and through the fleshy part of my shooting arm. I never lost strength or range of motion because of it. The worst part came after, a mild infection, but oral antibiotics took care of that in a week."

"Your lives didn't hang in the balance?"

She chuckled nervously. "No, but don't get me wrong, I was scared out of my mind at the time. Getting shot burns like hell. I looked down and saw my blood oozing out on the pavement. I was sure the next sound I heard would be the kill shot, but luckily it never came. I'd just learned I was pregnant the week before and went into shock worrying about the baby. Paramedics rushed us to the hospital, we were treated and stabilized, and went home the next day."

She wasn't showing the day someone shot her.

"Had you told anyone you were pregnant?"

"Not until I got to the hospital. I told the doctors, of course."

"Was there a barrage of bullets during the robbery?"

Rachel laughed again. "Where did you get your information from? One bullet was fired, the one that passed through my forearm. I was new on the job and didn't follow protocol. I drew my weapon on a man who already had a gun trained on me, the driver shot the gun from my hand and sped away. Michael," she said, rubbing her belly, "and I are lucky to be here."

"I agree. What do you mean about protocol?"

"If heavily armed criminals try to steal counterfeiting supplies, the Treasury manual instructs workers to avoid a shootout on the crowded premises. We are to defuse the situation by allowing the would-be robbers to slowly progress through the gate system, after signaling electronically for police and SWAT backup. SWAT provides the shock and awe before the getaway car hits the street, in a long, secluded section of the garage. My bosses had informed us earlier in the day that computer equipment had been stolen recently from offices and to be on the lookout for bulky electronic theft, to search all vehicles capable of hiding larger items. Their truck had already cleared every checkpoint when it came to me and usually I just wave everyone through, but that week was different. I was the lone guard at the last search stop. My partner had gone to use the can when their truck rolled up and," she added sheepishly, "I know all the tricks about hiding things—or people—in trucks. The flatbed of their truck looked odd when it came my way, so I kept the guardrail down to have a closer look. After I moved packing crates out of the way, I could tell the flatbed had a false bottom. I immediately thought these might be the computer thieves, but when I saw their cargo, I panicked and drew my weapon before calling for back-up. I made a rookie mistake. I heard a bang and fell to the ground bleeding while the truck laid serious rubber and crashed through the gate. A guard at the checkpoint before mine thought the gunshot was an engine backfire. I radioed for police and SWAT, sure the robbers would be caught in minutes. If my partner had been there or the guard at the other checkpoint before mine had reacted faster to the gunshot, they would've been."

"How many men were involved in the robbery?"

Rachel sipped her tea. "Four black males, probably thirty to forty years old, maybe younger. All average builds, they stayed inside the dark truck and used forged I.D. badges and knock-off uniforms to pass through the checkpoints. The truck windows were tinted, they wore sunglasses, and it was dark. They were smart. They switched vehicles a few miles away." A wry look crossed her face as she continued, "The only prints lifted from the abandoned truck were on the driver's side door, from guards at the last two checkpoints, and mine from the search. We all testified to touching the van, but I bet someone's still watching us because the Treasury brass insists it was an inside job. Anyway, the truck used in the heist had been stolen earlier that day and the plates on it lifted from another vehicle. They vanished into the night with ink and paper."

I showed her headshot photos of Lonnie Washington, Earl Mooney, Benny Blades, and Tyrone Sparks. "Were any of these men in the truck that night?"

I watched her big brown eyes take time to study each of the photos. She immediately ruled out Earl because of his age and Tyrone for his large size. Focusing on the other two, she blushed a little and said, "It was dark. This one," pointing at Benny's picture, "is too young and good-looking, I would have remembered him, and the other," pointing at Lonnie, "looks too small and sickly. The trigger man had a definite hardness or calculation to him. He was a pro. I'm not a hundred percent certain, but I'm almost sure these last two weren't there either."

"Is there anything else you remember about the men in the stolen truck—tattoos, birthmarks, earrings, a certain way they talked, what they wore, gold chains, facial tics, something dangling from the rear-view mirror, or any peculiar mannerisms?"

She paused. "No. I've replayed it so many times in my mind."

"There's something else, isn't there? What?"

I waited. She fidgeted with her nails and bit her lip.

"Two weeks, maybe a month after the shooting, a man called me at home. He asked if I'd recovered from my injuries, how much work I'd missed, how much pain I'd had. He sounded pleasant enough, but I didn't know him and he wouldn't tell me his name. I thought he was from Treasury. I hung up on him."

"Why did you think that?"

"I don't know. Maybe to keep tabs on me. Call me paranoid, but I wouldn't be surprised if all of us on duty that night weren't under close observation for months. They gave me two weeks paid leave, then made me burn what little sick time I'd accrued. After that came unpaid leave while the in-house investigation dragged on. We heard rumors of disciplinary action coming down for all the guards at the checkpoints, but they doled out slaps on the wrists to the men with seniority and fired me because of my 'unacceptable crisis response.' I was their fall guy. I had no job, five mouths to feed and another on the way."

"Then what happened?" I said, having a pretty good idea.

"The mystery man called again. He apologized for my firing, urged me to be patient, and hung up."

A frightened look came over her face and she said, "Oh, my God. You didn't call me, did you? Your voice isn't the same."

"No. What do you remember about the voices?"

Rachel chewed on an unpainted nail while she thought. "The first was polite, soft-spoken. He sounded truly sorry about my injury. He was in a hurry, like he didn't have much time to talk. He sounded African-American. Are you working with them?"

It sounds like I am.

The silence while I thought things through seemed to frighten her.

She crossed her arms and stared at me hard. "Why are you really here?"

I repeated the purpose of my trip.

She leaned forward. "You know about the money, don't you?" she whispered, as if sharing a big secret.

"You received a package in the mail with a letter that had no return address," I said. It wasn't a question.

She stared long and hard, trying to figure me out. "Will you excuse me a minute?"

I nodded.

She walked down the hallway again and returned with a shoebox in her hands. She sat across the table from me. "How did you know I received a letter?"

"You're not the first."

She removed the lid, extracted a .38, and pointed it at my chest.

I did my best to focus on her eyes and not the gun. I failed miserably.

Void of emotion, she said, "You're a stranger. You come here unannounced asking all sorts of questions. You know about the letter. I don't know your intentions, but extortion crosses my mind. I have to think about my kids." She briefly glanced at the .38 and added, "I feel more comfortable now."

"That makes one of us," I said, drawn to the blue steel barrel. *Please don't have another unacceptable crisis response now.*

"Why do you think I received a package?"

"Others have who helped my client."

Her eyes narrowed. "I didn't help him," she said, her voice full of challenge. "I drew my piece on four robbers."

"But you, your unborn baby, and your kids suffered collateral damage. You were innocents hurt by the actions of others. My hunch is he feels culpable and wants to right the wrong the only way he can. I'm here to learn as much as I can about my client. I am not here to blow the whistle on you."

She sat thinking for some time.

My eyes now developed a mind of their own, glued to the gun in her hand.

She tucked it into the waistband of her shorts and pulled out a folded letter from the shoebox. "Two weeks after the second man called, a package came in the mail. Inside it were six documents and this handwritten note."

She handed me the letter, in the now familiar and elegant calligraphic script, which said:

Dear Rachel Sanchez,

I grieved at word of your shooting and its impact on your family and job. Please accept these humble gifts as small retribution for what you endured. I have also arranged a standing interview for you with a local company, McMahon Securities at 555-3535. A position is waiting for you there, with better salary and benefits, when you're ready. Imagine how much better the world would be if every child had a guardian angel such as you. Please accept the enclosed trust funds in the names of the five children in your care. The sixth fund will activate upon birth and a legal name. I made this last account slightly larger because no one should be shot at before they're even born. The annuities reach maturity when each child turns eighteen. Continue doing your great deeds, the world is a better place with you in it.

LW

Her face flushed with excitement and anticipation. "It's your client, isn't it?"

"I can't prove it, nor is he taking credit for it, but I think so."

Her brow furrowed in anger. "Then this money…"

"Ultimately came from the government paper and ink that a second group of men shot you to steal."

Rachel sat there staring at the box in front of her. I assumed her thoughts were taking her back eight months in time, her boggled mind fast-forwarding to the present.

"He's accomplished what no other known counterfeiter in history has been able to do, create exact duplicate hundred-dollar bills. I assume your kids' trust funds are in that box, paid for with money he printed, bills that passed every bank test with flying colors. The money used to purchase these college funds can never be traced back to you, or him for that matter."

I explained Milton Peebles' take on the negligible economic impact to society as a result of the bills.

Her brow furrowed, "It's still wrong, he didn't earn it. He made a ton of money for nothing."

I nodded. "That's one way to look at it. Here's another, and I'm not saying my way is correct. He's been honing and perfecting his ability to engrave master plates for ten hours a day, 360 days a year for twenty-two years, logging a total of 79,200 work hours. Assuming the stolen paper produced twenty-five million in hundred-dollar bills and they split it four ways, that leaves his take at six and a quarter million. Divide hours worked into that and you get a 'wage' of just under seventy-nine dollars an hour, for abilities only a handful of craftsmen in the world possess. His share doesn't include equipment costs to print, cut, and count this large sum of money, nor does it take into account what they paid the other men who robbed the US Treasury. So the $79 an hour figure is grossly inflated. A great amount of talent, patience, perseverance, and time went into this."

"That still doesn't make it right. He knew he was committing a felony," Rachel sniffed.

That's the only argument I don't have a counter for.

"No, it doesn't. You have choices here, important ones. You don't have to cash in the trust funds. You can destroy them if you believe the money is tainted. You can also refuse the job interview."

Rachel looked down. "I started at McMahon about a month ago. Better pay, regular hours, and the people there are nice." She spread her arms and continued, "After Treasury fired me I had no money to pay the bills and was about to lose our home. Now by the time my lease expires I hope to be able to get a larger apartment in a safer neighborhood."

I wondered how Lonnie could be so connected to pull strings in a legitimate security job in D.C. until an idea came to me that didn't involve cold hard cash.

She seemed overwhelmed by the news I'd brought, it took some time for her to regain her voice. "A better job and trust funds for the kids' college? This is too much. LW doesn't even know me. I'm not anyone special."

I raised the note in my hand. "LW thinks otherwise."

Her tone softened. "What's he like?"

I described him physically as best as I could, then said, "I know he loves his mother and family. He has a soft spot in his heart for children and those who care for them. I know he places great importance on the values of education and work. He abhors violence and has a highly developed sense of right and wrong, although you and others may not agree. That's okay. He lost himself in his studies and art to escape the chaos of his early life. I believe he honed his special talents in order to change the world the best way he knew how, after life painted him into a corner. He makes no excuses for his actions and accepts his punishment. I don't believe he spent a dime of the counterfeit money on himself."

Her brown eyes grew even bigger. "What should I do about the trust funds?"

"What you think is right. I think you made up your mind when you pulled that gun on me. You can do a lot of good for six lives you love deeply. My advice is: think about the choices and listen to your heart."

I left Rachel to her thoughts and had the rest of the day to kill before my flight home. I spent part of it touring the US Senate building, one of our largest remaining repositories of fear, graft, scandal, and self-serving stagnation. With this being an election year, attack ads were already starting to pollute the landscape, newspapers, and radio waves with their rants. I rode the Metro between the monuments and other tourist attractions, wishing St. Louis had built similar efficient mass transit along the major highways.

The final stop of my weekend trip was the Bureau of Engraving and Printing. I strode between the rock solid, imposing Doric columns of the massive building at 14th and C Streets and observed government employees printing millions of dollars in rapid but controlled assembly-line fashion. It was a piece of cake to imagine Lonnie working there as a well-paid government employee.

I viewed the tools he must have used that others have for the last 125 years to make our

currency—the gravers, the high carbon steel burnishers and the hand-held glass. I watched the craftsmen print the 32-note sheets, then cut, count, and bundle them into usable currency. Everything my tour group heard concerning the processes of plate engraving and money-printing Lonnie had already shared with me in greater detail. I left with a smile on my face because I could have given the tour. Later, I found literature about BEP job openings and learned that designers earn 190 grand a year, master and sculptural engravers can reach up to 155K and plate makers make 130 grand. The top salary is over $91 dollars an hour.

It would have been the perfect legitimate job for him.

TIGER FOOD

Back in my own bed that night, sleep came in fitful pockets. I dreamt I was at work, somewhere in an unfamiliar office. My boss entered in shadows and accused me of stealing. I started to argue when two men entered the room, one little, one big. The little one nodded to the big man, who punched me in the stomach and dragged me from the room. My boss said, "Take him to Bruno in the basement. Have him start with pliers and a box cutter. Nobody fleeces millions from the Mafia." As I struggled into the lighted hallway against the much stronger man, my boss was Maynard, the little man Fallon, and the big man Fallon's beefy security man with the reflective sunglasses.

The next morning I went to the jail to see if I still had a client.

Lonnie barely moved during the session. He did not sketch or draw any imaginary thing in the air today, his arms were still as stones. The grim look on his face said it all.

"I'm sorry about Earl," I said.

He nodded, the faraway look that I first saw in his mug shot had returned to his eyes. "It's just like him to use the alias Johnny B. Goode. He knew Chuck Berry. The guards gloated when they told me of his capture. One said all my friends would be here soon, but that I'd never see them again, except maybe in passing at court."

He kept a close eye on the door during our visits and today was no exception. I casually reached under the battered steel table with my right hand and felt blindly along the underside of the table as I spoke. He looked at me with a quizzical eye but quickly understood and resumed his role as lookout.

Counterfeit

"I took a weekend trip to DC and toured the Bureau of Engraving and Printing."

My fingers immediately connected with something hard and smooth and round—probably calcified, dried up gum—and then continued to feel along the criss-crossed metal frame that held the top in place.

Nothing there.

"You don't say. You didn't tour any monuments or have lunch with brother Obama," he said, playing along in a weary, indifferent voice.

My hand found nothing unusual on my side so I reached farther toward his.

"I must have missed him. He's a little busy with hearings, scandals, and the latest mess in the Middle East with Syria and Egypt."

"The world's changed over the last decade. Terrorists abroad want to kill us while home-grown robber barons kill the middle class. The system has tied his hands. It's probably why his hair is turning gray. Have you read *The Time Machine*?"

"Sure. I love that classic."

"I'm a Morlock caught not serving the Eloi. Most all of us will soon be Morlocks if events hold the course they are on."

"I hope you and H. G. Wells are wrong about that."

No sign from him that anyone was near the door.

"The Morlocks don't realize the power we possess."

"Back to my BEP tour, I watched engravers and printers make currency. Had you ever considered working there? They make good incomes."

He flashed a wry smile. "Over the years, I placed applications with the Bureau fourteen separate times."

When he said that, my fingers wrapped around what I was searching for.

It's here!

"No kidding," I said, trying to sound nonchalant.

It took some doing but I finally pried and pulled it loose.

He watched the door, his tic fluttering. "I met or exceeded every requirement from a professional, trade, artistic, and knowledge standpoint. I had an unbroken work record as an adult, half of it in the printing and engraving fields, but they wouldn't interview me. I'm pretty sure they thought I was a security risk due to my chaotic childhood. Can you believe that?" His wry smile returned while he eyeballed the door. "I wouldn't be here if they'd hired me, but I don't blame them. I chose my path."

I showed him the tiny box. His eyes goggled but then quickly returned their attention to the door while I slipped it in my pocket. His facial muscles tensed with anger for the first time as the tic intensified.

"I bet they wish they'd hired you now."

"As long as the Eloi are served, what do they care?"

His shackles clinked softly together while he raised a thumb to signal the coast remained clear. He took a deep breath, trying to calm himself. "I didn't see this coming," he said, his sad brown eyes darting to the bug in my pocket. "I'm sorry for what Skinny did. You get beat down long enough, it's easy to think the world's against you."

"That's human nature," I said. "I met a nice young person on my trip who received a special gift and isn't sure they deserve it or want to use it."

I thought I sensed hurt in that downcast face before he masked it. "I don't know what you're talking about."

I leaned in closer and whispered, "You didn't rob the BEP. You can't control the actions of others. Even God doesn't do that."

"I still don't know what you're talking about. What can I possibly do from a prison cell?"

"You're right. I guess we don't have much else to talk about anymore, do we?"

At least not anything we want overheard.

He shifted his slight frame in the chair. "Would you check on my Momma?" He glanced down again at my pocket. "She has a package for me and I'd like to know what it contains. Can you do that? Maybe you can tell Simone's friend about it, too." *Meaning Baker.*

"If that's what you want."

He nodded. "I'm all alone in here and I'm being hunted."

"What about DH?" Denny Hanover, the court-appointed public defender.

He thought about it and shook his head. "Simone's friend first."

I was about to leave when he said, "The guards made sure I saw the Channel Four news segments on counterfeiting."

"I watched the first one," I said, waiting for him to continue.

"They glowed red," he whispered proudly.

Shocked by his admission, I held two fingers to my mouth to remind him that the walls have ears.

"I don't care anymore. They're never going to let me out of here, except in a body bag. I will prove mine glowed red."

I stretched out my legs, thinking of the bill that came in the mail. "Okay. I'm listening."

The tic forced his lids to quiver awkwardly. "I can't right now. I understand if you believe what you saw on the news, everyone else does, but after I'm gone, you will believe."

"Why would a Secret Service agent lie in front of a television camera?"

"There's about eighteen and a half million reasons."

"It's a simple test, to wave a light over a bill and check the color."

"They made me watch the segment," he reminded, with an edge in his voice. "My answer remains the same. Did he perform the test in front of the camera?"

I thought about it. "No."

"Would've been dramatic visual proof for the audience, don't you think?"

I told him about my encounter with agent Wilson. "He claims he farmed out the basic tests to lab workers. It could be him or someone in the lab. Why the charade?"

"I created fear and uncertainty among the Eloi. The first purpose is to comfort businesses that the fakes have been or will be quickly removed from circulation. The second and more sinister motive sets the stage for plausible deniability."

"What do you mean?"

"They will soon claim all the fakes have been removed from circulation and burned. The public quickly forgets they were ever there and returns to watching the Kardashians and Duck Dynasty. Everyone receives kudos for a job well done and the Chief Prosecutor earns another bump in his approval ratings."

Counterfeit

He put his fingertips as close to his mouth as possible and quickly opened his hand. "Poof! Like magic, the eighteen and a half million appears as tax-free legitimate money in someone's pocket shortly after Earl, Tyrone, Benny, and yours truly are silenced or put away forever."

I recalled the prophetic warnings of Milton Peebles. "We have to do something."

He closed his eyes in a futile effort to halt the tic. "The forces behind this think they have left no evidence of wrongdoing or even impropriety, that their chain of command has successfully quarantined the blame to us and they have. The power players must feel confident they are far enough removed to avoid any blow back." He allowed himself the slightest of smirks while he whispered, "The Eloi have a surprise coming."

Was he starting to crumble under all the pressure? Was he losing his grip on reality? Everyone has a breaking point. I know that all too well.

Through pursed lips he said, "Earl chose me. I failed to pass on his teaching and more than a century of arcane knowledge will soon scatter in the wind. I'm the last of a dying breed. I looked forward to the challenges of the new hundred-dollar bill due out this year. It will have holographic images generated by micro lenses embedded in the paper's matrix." His eyes shifted to the door and the advancing guard.

"I'll let you know about the package."

I started to leave the city jail as inconspicuously and nonchalantly as a man could with something in his pocket that could incriminate City Hall. Every face I passed seemed an extension of

Maynard's and I felt trapped back in my dream of the night before. I half-expected to walk headlong into the muscular man with the sunglasses who'd drag me to Bruno. Or worse, to Maynard. My heart raced like it never had on my safe, comfortable sofa.

I made it to my car without incident and sped away.

$ $ $

The phone rang while I finished my strength training workout in the basement. It was Baker. "Turn on the idiot box. News comin' on in a couple minutes. You want to see this." He sounded like somebody had just run over his dog, then backed over it again just to make sure it was dead.

"Now what?"

His sad tone switched to anger. "Long story. I hope to be there in twenty. It's gettin' dicey here. If I'm a no show, don't trust anybody connected to the police, not even The Voice. I think you're okay for now, but be safe and don't use your cell. 'You-know-who' is on a crusade, and he be cuttin' a wide swath. This is way beyond a cluster fuck. This is turnin' into wrath-of- God shit."

In the background, I heard the crash of splintering wood and frenzied, angry shouts. Before I could say another word, Baker said, "Gotta go. Follow the bags, Cool Breeze. You'll know what to—"

Loud noise filled my ear, like the phone hit the floor on his end. The line went dead.

Follow what bags?

I stripped, toweled off, and changed clothes. I grabbed a Bitter Lemon, stretched my calf muscles, and did isometric exercises, while I tried to imagine what was happening.

Counterfeit

I watched and recorded the news as Debbie Macklin's serious anchorwoman face filled

the screen. "Good evening, viewers," she said. "Our lead story is another Channel Four exclusive. We have breaking news on the day's incredible and shocking feature story. Earlier today, Benny Blades, the last of the known counterfeiting suspects, was spotted by an off-duty patrolman leaving the south city apartment of a female acquaintance. The officer called for backup and followed the suspect by car into the St. Louis Zoo parking lot, where Mr. Blades entered the grounds wearing a bulky dark windbreaker and carrying a leather attaché case."

The screen cut quickly from the familiar Glamour Shots Photo of a grinning Benny making the peace sign to an aerial video of police and SWAT members squatting behind the cover of police cars, guns drawn, focused on an area beyond the perimeter of the camera lens. "Assuming the suspect was armed and possibly carrying an explosive device in a highly public area, SWAT, in a coordinated effort with city police and zoo security, initiated an emergency evacuation. As the police net closed around him, the suspect panicked near the bird cage and fired warning shots into the air to incite a public stampede. The suspect ran south toward the zoo exit near Hampton and found it sealed off by authorities. He sprinted to the Herpetarium where he made an unsuccessful attempt to take hostages, eventually fleeing the building. He ran into the zoo railroad tunnel where a tense police standoff ensued. After negotiations broke down, police fired tear gas canisters. The suspect came out firing at officers and fell into the tiger pit at Big Cat Country where he was mauled by the alpha male tiger. The suspect was later confirmed dead upon arrival at Barnes Hospital."

She held a hand to the Bluetooth in her ear and said, "Reports just in confirm the suspect had strapped an explosive device to his waist. The motive for bringing a bomb to the St. Louis Zoo is unknown at this time." The screen quickly shifted from an EMT crew wheeling a covered body on a gurney, to teams of forensic investigators laying out colored markers and gathering evidence into bags near the mouth of the zoo railroad tunnel, to Big Cat Country, and to policemen interviewing witnesses. Then the scene shifted to a row of parked cars along the north entrance on Government Drive. In the background I noticed the same burly security man in a business suit and sunglasses heft two large orange duffels from an old, green Chevy Nova and throw them in the trunk of a dark late-model SUV. I almost missed it as the bags were on camera a few fleeting seconds. Only after replaying the scene did I notice the rear of the SUV temporarily lower from the weight of the bags. The duffels had large, faded logos of the Green Bay Packers football team on one side. From the brutish manner in which the agent manhandled the duffels, I doubted that either bag contained a bomb. He slammed the rear SUV door shut and two other security men stood to attention to guard the SUV. I froze the frame on the back of the SUV with the men standing guard just before the man in sunglasses blocked the camera view. I scribbled a note.

Heavy duffel bags. I thought again of Milton Peebles and his warning. Thou shalt not steal. That commandment is right up there with thou shalt nor murder and thou shalt not bear false witness against thy neighbor. It looks like Maynard's going for a trifecta.

The screen ultimately returned to Debbie Macklin who said, "Officers Malvern, Downey, and Carter were first responders at the scene, followed by Assistant Chief Rhymes. Channel Four will interview them as more on this incredible hostage shooting unfolds. Chief Prosecutor John Maynard was briefly at the scene but offered a terse no comment before being called away. Channel Four will interrupt your late-night programming to bring updates on this incredible story when they occur. I think there's more here than meets the eye. And now here's Dan with more local news."

I was likely the only viewer who believed her penultimate sentence was improvised and the only listener who detected the subtle shift in her attitude toward the Golden Boy.

The same three officers who claimed to collar Lonnie at the printing company, replacing Quinn and filing their own reports, now showed up at the zoo. The only one apparently not present at the Zoo was Police Chief Joseph Moreno, the man who wants to use drones to help fight crime in St. Louis city.

More troubling was the fact that Detective Baker was a no show. Did the ominous sound of splintering wood mean I'm left to fight Maynard by myself?

I heeded part of Baker's warning.

The rest I didn't.

At noon the next day I called my friend Tony at his work desk in the city police department. I called from a public phone. "I need you to run a plate, your eyes only."

Loud crunching filled my ear and a defiant Tony said, "Oh no. Get Baker to do it."

"I can't find him or I would."

"No way. Last year you asked me to run one and the shit hit the fan."

"What the hell are you eating?"

"Double-decker ham and Swiss on rye with my secret ingredient—a liberal bed of hot barbecue Old Vienna ruffled potato chips in both layers."

"That'll make it easier for me to mop the court with you in our next one-on-one game."

"In your dreams, slick."

"Tony, this is really big, more important than last year and besides, your involvement ends with running the plate, just like last year. If any shit flies, it'll land on me."

I heard him sip something from a straw, the sucking sound meant he'd reached the bottom. "Are you okay? Why are you calling from—?"

"I know where I am," I interrupted, aware that cop phones have caller ID and their walls
have ears.

"Shut the front door! You think someone's following you. This is about the case you're working. I'm in. When do you need it?"

"Sooner the better. After you run it, don't call me on my cell, home, or office. I'll call back when I can."

"Gimme," he mumbled between bites and crunches.

I read him the plate number. "Have you seen Baker? I think something's happened to him."

He smacked his lips. "Haven't heard anything, but I never see him much anyway. I'll ask around, discreetly."

"What about the other favor I asked our friend?"

"You're barking up the wrong tree; I won't violate HIPPA. I do that and the board will never give me back my license."

Counterfeit

We fell silent until he said, "Hey, Marilyn and the gang just got back from camping. Remember that time in fourth grade when our parents took us to that secluded trail cabin where that pack of wild dogs chased us into the Black River and you nearly drowned? We stayed in that rundown cabin isolated from the fishing and hiking trails and nearly burned down the screened-in patio trying to cook hotdogs on the grill. Remember how much grief we caught for that?"

I had no idea what he was talking about because I'd only known him ten years. "Yeah," I said, playing along, "I was grounded for two weeks and your old man tanned your hide. Where was that again?"

"I don't remember, but Lester and Anna went with us."

I had to go with the flow. "Those were good times. I still see Anna every now and then and she always asks how you're doing."

He filled the awkward silence by saying, "Sorry I can't help you, buddy. You'll have to figure out how to save the day some other way."

"I understand. Give my love to Cindy and the girls."

I hung up, not wanting to linger too long in the waiting room on the ninth floor at St. Luke's Hospital, just in case.

When I reached my laptop, I pulled up a map and a list of Missouri camping and recreational areas and eventually found what I was looking for. Lesterville and Annapolis, Missouri were tiny towns south of St. Louis on the Black River with cottages and recreational facilities. A phrase he'd used earlier also seemed a bit hokey and slightly emphasized, so I Googled it and a website for *Secluded Trail Cabins* appeared on screen, located between Lesterville and Annapolis. I printed directions and left another, more urgent message for Baker to call.

Would an old Irish cop riding out the last days before his retirement prove to be the missing link that topples Maynard, and is he hiding out in a cabin in the Missouri woods?

THE PRIMROSE PATH

My throat was dry when I arrived at the jail for my next scheduled meeting with Lonnie. If the police are aware their bug is missing, they know who took it. Would I be taken into custody? I hadn't heard from Baker since his rushed call and what sounded like his door being broken down. Does it all end here? I was mentally prepared to be arrested. I had my attorney on speed dial.

Today was the day we planned to meet with his mother and I didn't want to break my word. I had talked with Lonnie about the meeting in earlier sessions, helped him process his feelings, ways to say them, and the toughest part, how to end the visit. LaKeesha's mental limitations made her prep work more difficult and her behavior under stress less predictable.

Skinny, Shirley, and Tyra escorted LaKeesha to the city jail and remained in the outer waiting area. LaKeesha was dressed in her Sunday best, a white and yellow flowered dress, her hair had been straightened and jelled. She wore a matching box hat with a sheer veil. Her white vinyl purse matched her shoes. I caught a whiff of bath soap and baby powder as she entered the visitation room. Signs reminded all that visitor conversations are monitored.

She stood for a moment with her mouth open, appearing shocked by her son's appearance. The involuntarily movements increased as she settled stiffly into the metal chair, clearly uncomfortable in this grim environment. Her head swayed from side to side, her tongue darted out of her mouth, her own facial tic danced while she waited for her only child to speak.

I sat behind in the shadows, off to LaKeesha's right, with a clear view of their faces.

He kept his gaze on his mother, fighting his facial tic with a stiff upper lip. "It's good to see you, Momma."

Her mouth trembled and her eyes widened when his iron shackles rattled and she whispered under her breath, "Oh, my Boo. You look so thin and tired." She held on white-knuckled to the purse in her lap with both hands like it was an anchor. Her eyes darted around the room anxiously. "How do the po-lice treat you in here?"

I sensed his anxiety level ratchet up in tandem with hers.

"Prison guards watch over and supervise us, Momma. Not the police."

"Remember to breathe, both of you," I whispered.

"Then how come they so many po-lice in the building?"

He made a concerted effort not to move his hands and rattle his chains. "They bring people to and from the jail. They also have other police business here."

She nodded. "Do the guards treat you right?"

"For the most part, Momma. They do."

"How's the food?"

"You know me, I never really took much pleasure from food. I only eat enough to fuel my body."

She pointed a shaky finger at me. "Dr. Mitch here been real good to me. He visits every week to say how you doin' and he checks on me. He a good man and he cares about you."

"He is. Like the Eddie Green song goes, 'A good man is hard to find, you always get the other kind,'" he looked at me and nodded.

I smiled. "Back at you."

Counterfeit

She gripped her purse tighter. "Amen to that." She struggled to say her next words, stopping and starting repeatedly, the Tardive Dyskinesia getting the best of her.

"Wha … what … gonna happen … to you, my Boo?"

"I don't know. Life has always been hard for us. We've had to have thick skins to make it this far. We've survived drive-bys shootings and robbers and gangs. Sooner or later it's everyone's time. If they convict me, they will want to keep me in jail for fifteen years."

The purse in her hands began to tremble. "I told myself to be strong when I saw you. Dr. Mitch helped me get ready for this, but I can't help thinkin' this is my fault. I wasn't a fit momma to you. All those foster homes and strangers, no regular place to call home and feel safe, no steady friends. I'm so sorry, Boo." A tear weaved a crooked path down her cheek.

He reached out a hand as far as he could toward LaKeesha. "I alone am responsible for this, not you. I'm proud of you—you got sober and straight, learned how to read, and manage your checkbook. You are able to take care of yourself now and your home. You've always been here for me as an adult. Like you, I did the best that I could. I tried to make a difference in my own way."

She took hold of his hand and squeezed hard. "Coretta sends you her love. She told me to tell you Shondra is praying for you, too. Others too, I forget all the names." She made a sour face as her tongue darted out in spasms, "I hear such talk, what some hateful people say should happen to you." She broke down, her body racked by spasms. I signaled Sgt. Collins who stood watching near the door the entire time.

"That's life, Momma. You can't please everybody. You can only control your own actions and do the best you can."

A somber Sgt. Collins and stoic Rain Man Marty entered the room. I'd briefed them that this was likely the only meeting between Lonnie and his mother. Neither seemed surprised, which heightened my sense of foreboding.

Sgt. Collins gently lifted her purse from her lap and handed it to Marty. He held the handbag in front of his chest like it carried a virus from the CDC, surprise and confusion replacing his perpetually vacant stare. Collins freed Lonnie from his chains and stepped back. Lonnie looked up at the behemoth guard who simply nodded. He hugged his mother and they clung to each other. For the duration of their embrace, the tics stopped.

She softly repeated the words, "My Boo," in a trembling voice.

"I always loved you, even when I didn't know you. You gave me life. You're an amazing, strong woman. Remember that, Momma."

She'd remained strong longer than I'd expected. Our prep work had helped. I nodded silent thanks to Donnell for his breach of protocol.

Neither wanted to break the embrace. I gently intervened or we'd still be there.

"I love you, Momma," he said, the tic quivering. He passed his hand over his heart. "You're always here."

She reached for him again as Marty gently took her elbow, but she caught nothing but air. "I'll see you again, my baby Boo!"

I squeezed his shoulder.

Too softly for her to hear, he whispered, "See you on the other side, Momma." A tear trickled down his cheek.

Counterfeit

After Rain Man Marty escorted LaKeesha from the room, Collins searched Lonnie, re-attached the leg and wrist irons, then left the room again. Lonnie turned to me and whispered, "They made me watch the news about Benny. I told you I'm a dead man."

"I'm sorry about Benny," I said, frustrated I was apologizing so much.

"Like me, he despised guns. He'd never hold one, much less shoot it at people. And as for carrying a bomb?" A smile bloomed on his face.

"Am I missing something?"

"I know why Bennie drove to the zoo and what he carried."

I waited.

"He used to live for his ladies, he wined and dined them, took them clubbing. He has … had a friend who works two part-time jobs, one in retail at Saks Fifth Avenue on Lindbergh and one at the zoo. He was meeting his friend at the zoo with cash—no gun, no bomb—because the store was closed. He'd already bought a ring and wanted to surprise Tyra with a sable coat. He was about to propose to her before…."

I heard the chirp of Sgt. Collins's walkie-talkie as he re-entered the room. He said, "Mitch, I cut you some slack earlier, but we have to return Lonnie to his cell."

I'll be damned. *He called him by his given name.*

Lonnie leaned forward. "Remember, I saw what you saw. Did you know Benny was a big Packers fan?"

I recalled the footage and nodded. "And I once had an old green Chevy Nova."

"You are observant."

"Time's up, Doc," Collins intervened. "Step away from the prisoner, please."

Lonnie nodded. "Watch your back."

"You too. I plan on seeing you again."

"From one side or the other, you will hear from me. Thanks for everything you've done."

"You're very welcome. Until we meet again."

We shook hands and I hugged him, shackles and all.

Sgt. Collins released the leg shackles from the bolt in the floor and followed as Lonnie limped and shuffled away, dragging his ruined right foot. His chains still clanked down the musty hallway long after I'd lost sight of them. The sound reminded me of a ghost shambling through the murky shadows of a dark haunted house searching for his body.

By this time, LaKeesha and her friends had already departed.

I felt a sudden tug of envy. If this was goodbye, as Lonnie fears, at least he'd been able to express his feeling to his mother one more time. The last time I'd seen Kris, we'd had a fight and she left angry, walking away from me and shaking her head. The next place I saw her was the morgue. There were so many things I wanted to say, to take back, but I never got the chance.

The envy turned into a feeling of accomplishment, small maybe, but important for the three of us.

$ $ $

Halfway home, my pager vibrated when I reached the Highway 40 Galleria Mall exit. I hoped it was Baker, but caller ID said *Gateway Jail*. Denny Hanover, the young court-appointed attorney, called to say that Superintendent Kendall had rejected my appeal to return Lonnie to special security.

Counterfeit

"The man's suicidal. He can't do that."

"The super didn't believe you. He said there were no other reports from guards or ancillary staff corroborating your testimony and no self-destructive behavior observed from the prisoner. He thinks you fabricated the story."

As if he listened to our conversations.

"What was your response, Denny?"

He sniffed again. "I told him he better be right about this."

"Your concern for Lonnie is overwhelming."

He guffawed in exasperation. "Hey, I didn't have to call. I'm doing you a favor. I'm also calling to say your 'suicidal' client just started a prison fight with another inmate. He came in second. If he wasn't depressed, he should be now. Thought you might like to know." Click.

By the time I headed back east and parked at Gateway city jail, a heavy rain pounded
steadily from a bloated slate colored sky and thunder rolled. No breeze stirred as the downpour beat hard and loud on the convertible top, sloughing off the windshield in sheets. The few umbrella-toting pedestrians moved quicker with each lightning flash. I was drenched long before I walked inside.

Sgt. Collins granted me a second visit with Lonnie, no questions asked. The look on his face was as bleak as the weather.

Lonnie held his now unshackled hands in his lap. His head was bowed in a vacant stare, as if he'd seen too much or his body had shut down. He didn't acknowledge my presence or return my greeting. A nasty strawberry knot loomed under his blackened left eye, threatening to close it. Occasional jerking movements seized control of his body. The facial tic was constant. He ignored my questions about his eye and his well-being.

"It'll be soon."

"What do you mean?" I said, knowing the answer.

At last he lifted his emotionless face to meet mine. He raised his slender hands above the table top. The thumbs and index fingers had been twisted and fractured, splinted, and bound in heavy white gauze, with traces of blood seeping through the outer layers. "My drawing and engraving days are over."

I felt sick to my stomach. "What happened?"

Wheezing, he said, "The Aryan brothers had left me alone during my stay ... until a couple hours ago. Three jumped me. They took a ball peen hammer to my right thumb and index finger while the others held me down. They bent and twisted them until the bones snapped." He fell silent. He looked up, exhausted. "I lost count how many times. I passed in and out of consciousness. They stomped on them for good measure. After that, they started on my left hand, just to be sure.

I clenched my fists and forced myself to sit still in the chair.

"I woke up in the infirmary. An orderly I know said he saw a Good Wood hand the hammer to Zack Johnson after they'd finished."

"Good Wood?"

"It's one of many prison terms I've learned here. It's a 'stand-up' white guy who brutalizes other prisoners for privileges or favors."

"I have to stop this."

He lowered his head to the table. "I never expected to be captured. Dr. Adams, I welcome my fate because of what happened to my friends." He paused to wet his cracked and swollen lips, raising his sad eyes to mine. "Help me find Benny's share. He broke the basic rules of counterfeiting: never tell anyone you're printing, never pass it where you live, and never spend too much in one place." He suffered another coughing fit and doubled over in pain.

I started to talk but he waved me off. "They're right on schedule. There won't be a trial. The good times pass in an eye blink, the rest is pain and suffering. Don't worry about me. I need to settle my account with The Man."

"What can I do?"

He locked his eyes onto mine, seeming to find more resolve. "Paint my life with a broader brush than the sharp tip of a violent, antisocial felon. Remember, no matter what you hear about my death, I was murdered. I did not kill myself, nor will I try to escape. I have harmed no one here, nor will I hurt anyone. Between you and Skinny, I know you'll make sure

Momma understands. They will have to kill me in cold blood or have another prisoner do it."

I never felt so impotent with a client before. "There must be something I can do."

He looked at me. "*Tell* my story. It won't be easy. Many won't believe you. I can help with that. I wish I'd met you when I was young. Maybe my life would have turned out differently."

"I feel like I've done nothing to help you, and this sounds too much like goodbye."

The tic beat along with his heart. "Word getting out sealed my fate."

We passed the next few minutes in silence.

"Did you know there's a patron saint for social workers?" he asked.

I nodded my head. "Saint Louise de Marillac. Born in France near the end of the sixteenth century. With St. Vincent DePaul, she founded the Daughters of Charity. Do you have a patron saint?"

"There isn't one for counterfeiters or forgers. There is a saint for thieves, St. Dismas, but I don't consider myself a thief, so I adopted St. Eligius of seventh century France. He's the patron saint of metal smiths. He was master of the mint in Paris and built the basilica of St. Paul. He was generous to the poor, ransomed slaves, and was known for his hard work and honesty. He foresaw the date of his own death."

I didn't like the last part.

"I didn't know you were a religious man."

"I enjoy the allegories and messages in the writings and scriptures of all religions, but that's as far as it goes. I believe God created the world and that nature is a part of God, but God lets the world play itself out in random fashion. I do believe in an afterlife where your spirit is

reunited with everyone you've ever loved. If you haven't loved, your soul wanders the earth. I believe heaven and hell are constructs of men because both exist here on earth."

"Maybe God intervened by giving you the abilities you have."

"Had," he said wistfully.

"Some of the help some people received occurred after your arrest—many of them intricate, detailed, and time-consuming business matters—and could never have been managed behind bars without significant help."

"Who says I helped anybody but myself?" Lonnie said quietly, wincing.

"You're still a bad liar. I know about the letters, Lonnie. Many good, noble people were rewarded for their St. Eligius-like behavior. He would have been proud."

He looked into my eyes. "Does the name Michael Anthony ring a bell?"

It's vaguely familiar.

He smiled. "If you're a fan of old television shows, you may remember him as a man with a silky voice, the secretary to John Beresford Tipton, the semi-retired industrialist on—"

"The Millionaire," I said. "Each week Mr. Anthony handed out one million tax-free dollars to a person thought to be worthy by the philanthropist. I remember seeing the occasional rerun when I was a kid. I liked the message of the show, but I don't think it enjoyed a long run."

He whispered, "Help me. I'd love to have Mr. Anthony acquire Benny's share, but that's asking too much. I have an idea about the bags. You'll hear from me soon."

Don't wait too long, Lonnie. I want to help while you're alive.

"You've met some of my more vocal detractors. They say I enjoyed playing God, that I

thought I was Don Corleone in The Godfather. I agonized over many of these decisions. Six million doesn't go far with all the need out there. People kept coming to me after my share was spoken for. I had to turn so many away." He winced in pain again. "I changed my little piece of the world, at least for a time. I helped caring people help those in need. They did, and continue to do, the real work."

He seemed about to pass out. I got up to get Sgt. Collins but he said, "No. I will ask things of you … difficult, dangerous tasks. You're under no obligation to accept them. You got me this far and that's what

I needed. You're a good friend. Thanks, Mitch." He raised his head, determination on his face, and yelled, "Guard! We're done here." Then he looked back at me. "Please go. I don't want them to see me break down. The tic is bad enough."

As Collins walked stepped through the doorway, I said, "What tic?"

He grinned at me one last time and, for a moment it stopped.

I gave him the peace sign and smiled, but it felt like goodbye.

Smilin' Henry walked me out and the look on my face told him this wasn't the time for a corny joke.

$ $ $

The super kept me waiting an hour. James Kendall looked to be in his late fifties, balding, shaped like a bowling pin, with a salt-and-pepper colored crew cut and black-framed glasses. Broken blood vessels crisscrossed his bulbous nose. He wore a conservative black suit, white shirt, and black-and red-striped tie. He looked like a man from an earlier decade or, maybe just old before his time. There was something about him.

I sat in front of his imposing desk, aware that the room was specifically designed for his chair to be elevated from the visitor ones, like a judge's bench. "Who ordered guard Zack Johnson to arm three prisoners and turn a blind eye when they further crippled my suicidal client?"

His lined, ruddy face remained stoic. "You don't mince words."

"I do when the situation warrants."

He picked up his phone and called his secretary. "Mr. Price, produce guard Zack Johnson in my office in five minutes and bring in the file for prisoner #6011304." Kendall turned back to me. "These are serious accusations, Dr. Adams. I trust you have proof other than the word of an antisocial prisoner."

Mr. Price, an elderly black man I'd spent the last hour chatting with in the outer office, entered with a manila folder and handed it to Kendall. As Price was leaving, a knock sounded on the door frame and Zack Johnson walked in and saw me sitting. He stood six and a half feet tall and weighed close to three hundred pounds. On the right side of his thick corded neck the sharp angles of a green and red tattoo poked above his shirt collar. His closely cropped brown beard showed a tint of red in the light. From his belt dangled a set of keys with an eight-ball keychain. Johnson stood at attention facing Kendall. The super did not offer him a seat.

"Tell me about the recent incident involving prisoner Lonnie Washington," Kendall said while he read the report in front of him.

Johnson stared straight ahead. "At 14:30 hours, there was a disturbance in an off-camera area near the showers. I arrived first on the scene—inmate Washington was lying on the floor with a shank nearby and convict Hayes standing over him. I questioned those present and determined that Washington had attacked Hayes with the shank. Hayes overpowered him, breaking fingers in the process of defending himself. Convict Hayes remains in solitary with all privileges suspended, pending your decision on his punishment."

"That's what the incident report says," Kendall said, looking down at me for the first time since the entrance of the guard. "Do you have any evidence that anything other than this transpired, Dr. Adams?"

"Why would he attack Hayes?"

Johnson looked at the superintendent who nodded for him to answer. "For a blo—, for sexual favors, sir. Hayes and other witnesses gave the same story."

"What did Lonnie Washington say happened?" I asked.

"That three men attacked him without provocation."

"Lonnie Washington is a hundred-pound cripple," I said. "What about Hayes?"

The super referred to the file. "Hayes is six feet, two hundred pounds, and thirty-one years old. I know where you're going with this. Guard Johnson has already told you Hayes was threatened with a deadly weapon."

"How do you explain the multiple fractures to his left hand?"

Johnson looked for and received the Kendall's silent approval. "After the first struggle, Washington grabbed the knife with his left hand and Hayes defended himself again with equal force." He added defensively, "There are multiple witnesses."

"Prisoners breaking their own code of silence. How convenient for you. Why trust them over Lonnie Washington?"

Kendall didn't allow the guard to answer. "I'm going to ask you once more, Dr. Adams. Do you have evidence that anything other than this transpired?"

"Three Aryan brothers jumped him, held him down, and mangled his fingers to bloody
stumps so he could never draw again. They used a ball peen hammer given them by this man—" I pointed my finger at the huge guard, "— Zack Johnson."

The guard glared at me, but Kendall intervened. "What is your proof?"

"Other prisoners saw Hayes return the hammer to Johnson."

"You claim Hayes was seen handing the hammer back. That implies someone saw guard Johnson handing it to the convict. Do you have one witness who will step forward?"

I refused to go down that road with him.

Kendall allowed a smirk to form on his lumpy face. "Give me a name and we will conduct a thorough investigation."

"How do you explain, in this life and death struggle, that only his thumbs and index fingers were crushed beyond repair?"

"I don't have to explain it. It happened. Eyewitness reports say Hayes repeatedly stomped on Washington's hands to disarm him. There was no claim of a hammer, not even by Washington, until hours later."

I noticed Johnson doing a slow boil so I turned to him. "You did a shitty job keeping Lonnie safe today." Raising my voice, I said, "Who ordered you to look the other way for five minutes?"

His crimson face turned to me, his meat hook hands balled into fists. He took a step toward me.

"Enough!" Kendall yelled. "These men have extremely difficult, stressful jobs. We house

hundreds of violent men here—murderers, rapists, pedophiles, delusional psychotics, violent paranoid schizophrenics, and aggressive antisocial personalities—men with no qualms about attacking someone just for looking at them the wrong way. The weak are preyed upon. An attack can start and end in a heartbeat. The surveillance cameras give us an eye in the sky for most of the grounds, but there are blind spots and the prisoners know them. The guards cannot cover the blind spots all the time. You are treading on thin ice here, Dr. Adams. Are you claiming there is a conspiracy here?"

"If Hayes acted in self-defense, why does he remain in solitary?"

"For fighting, using excessive force, for not calling the guards. Take your pick," Kendall said.

I noticed Johnson's jaw muscles tighten and Kendall must have too, because he quickly ordered him back to the cell block.

Once we were alone I said, "Why wasn't Lonnie placed back in special security? I signed an affidavit. He's suicidal."

"That decision rests with me," Kendall answered, "and there is no corroborating evidence to support your opinion."

"*I am* the expert on this subject. Not you, not the guards or kitchen help."

He stared down at me in silence, unwavering.

"It's almost as if you've been listening to our privileged conversations."

That got a reaction, albeit brief.

"Are you insinuating—"

"I found a bug hidden under the tabletop in our confidential visitation room."

Kendall leaned forward, wetting his thin lips. "May I see it?"

"Not a chance. If anything happens to me, the news goes straight to the media."

A tiny smile appeared on his face. "How very convenient for *you*. You admit stealing a transmitter from the jail. If you did, there may be legal consequences. Why should I believe this latest claim, especially after reading your testimony that your client is suicidal?"

"Lonnie didn't want me to speak with you and doesn't know I'm here, but my profession mandates I speak on his behalf. He is convinced someone will murder him before his case goes to trial, and if that happens I'm holding you responsible."

"It doesn't sound like the talk of a suicidal man. That last part I won't dignify with an answer."

"Then sequester him for his own safety. He cannot defend himself."

He sat rubbing his lined brow, his patience waning. "I believe you've been led down the primrose path by a very clever and manipulative sociopath in prisoner Washington. You are not the first to be duped by an intelligent con man. You won't be the last."

I smiled up at him. "You have an answer for everything today, Superintendent. What about tomorrow, or the next day?"

He shifted his bulk uneasily in his leather Captain's chair, the springs squawking. "Why the smug expression, Dr. Adams?"

"I unearth secrets for a living. Too many players are involved for this to remain buried. I want you to know that."

"If you're thinking mistrial, you are sadly mistaken. How much longer do you wish to play this game?"

I flashed a smile again. "I know you lied about the bug."

He stood still for a ten count, then guffawed and folded his pudgy arms across his stomach, the sleeves of his suit riding up his forearms.

"I never said it was a transmitter. I said I found a bug. You knew the type of bug I found because you knew it was there all along. The day before Earl Mooney was captured, Lonnie confided in me about an operation Earl needed to prolong his life. A handful of hospitals in the country perform the specialty procedure. The next day I received a gloating call from someone much higher up the political/legal food chain than you, thanking me for my help in the investigation. You're working for his boss. Earl Mooney was arrested with the help of illegally obtained information from your jail."

This time Kendall smiled. "Prove it."

The fat bastard called all my bluffs. My initial nagging feeling when I entered this office vanished when I thought of Maynard. "I saw you at the Haller estate chatting up Maynard and Fallon. You looked like old buddies or accomplices."

"And you wear your drinks well. I take it you didn't get any that night?"

Very funny.

"What I got was a lot of information that will come back to haunt you."

"I didn't see your entrance, but you know how to make an exit. If it's attention you seek, you certainly were the buzz the rest of the evening." He made a tsk tsk sound and couldn't resist piling on. "Last year and now this. Not everything is a conspiracy, Dr. Adams, but there are no hard feelings. If I were in your position, I'd probably employ the same tactic. Don't worry, no one's going to challenge the veracity of your affidavit. What you have is smoke and innuendo. I'm a Superintendent of Corrections and Maynard is a symbol of law and order. Of course I'd be there."

"You sound defensive."

"You've hooked your wagon to another dangerous sociopath who's on an obvious self-destructive path here."

"That sounds like your master has already handed you your next job—murder Lonnie Washington. Prove me wrong. Keep him alive. Place Lonnie in special security to make sure no harm comes to him.

He's completely defenseless in here and must be isolated. He deserves his day in court. Fail to do that and I'll hire a lawyer that eats attorneys like Denny Hanover for breakfast; one who'll have state review boards lining up to perform colonoscopies on you and your jail. How long do you think you and your cronies would last in a place like this?"

He stood up stiffly and looked at his Rolex. "You're fishing expedition ends here. I'm late for a meeting." He buzzed Mr. Price to escort me from the premises.

"Tell your masters I'm not going anywhere."

If looks could kill, jails wouldn't need a death row.

Like a judge, he exited first.

I couldn't see Sister Thomas or a newbie fresh out of school standing up to Kendall and his masters, but what real good had I done?

I walked down the long dark tunnel with Mr. Price toward the light of the exit door, despairing for Lonnie. It felt like the light up ahead was a speeding train. I considered ways to let the world know what was happening to Lonnie.

By the time I trudged to the parking lot, the rain and clouds had scudded away and left the kind of muggy, sunny day St. Louis is famous for. The streets glistened as if all the dirt and garbage had flushed down into the city sewers. Up ahead, an ear-piercing alarm blared. I noticed a growing crowd in the parking area in front of the jail. Twenty people had encircled a car while others slowed to gawk at the commotion. They'd surrounded my little red Solstice—all four tires and the convertible top had been slashed to shreds; the windshield, side windows, headlights and taillights completely smashed. A black mini-crowbar and ice pick lay on the curb.

I ran up and asked if there were any witnesses but nobody stepped forward. Soon an older patrolman pushed through the crowd and said, "Buddy, this your car?"

I nodded. "I've been inside the jail a few hours on business." I pointed at the tools on the grass. "Have you found the culprit yet?"

"Nah, I don't see a body attached to them," he said in a matter-of-fact tone. "You got any ideas?" He looked around the lot. "No other vehicles were targeted. Looks like you pissed off the wrong person."

Rain must have still been pouring during the smash job because an inch of water covered the front floor mats. I shut off the alarm. "I've been doing a lot of that lately."

The cop looked to be in his sixties, with a pockmarked face and beer belly. He absent-mindedly pushed his cap back with a pudgy thumb and pointed back at the jail, "You be careful, keep pissing people off and you'll wind up in there. Now you're peeing on my charcoal. Call for a tow or I'll have to write you a ticket. All this broken glass poses a safety hazard to the other vehicles. Gotta move the car to sweep up this mess."

I got out my cell. "A prison guard named Zack Johnson probably did this during the last thirty minutes. He's six and a half feet tall and weighs three hundred pounds, has a reddish-brown beard, and red and green tats on his neck." I shouted, "Did anyone see this man?"

No one said a word.

In broad daylight, in front of Gateway jail, with all these cops coming and going through the main entrance nearby and nobody saw anything.

The patrolman looked at me calmly. "Tell you what, I'll have the lab boys check the weapons for prints. If his prints are there, he and I will speak. If they come back clean, see if you can get him to confess.

Here's my card. Good luck without a witness. Chalk it up to bad karma. That's why you have insurance, sir. Make the call."

The light at the end of the tunnel had been a train, Zack-the-Train Johnson.

"To protect and to serve, huh? Who do you serve?"

"The law, the status quo, my wife, and my boss—but not in that order. Call for the tow or I'll have it impounded." This time he raised his voice, shouting, "Show's over people. Move along."

It's not the first time I've had a car vandalized in a work-related conflict, but I hope it's the last. I made the call and checked with security at the front desk, asking them to look at the tape from the outdoor camera thirty minutes ago. They said the storm had temporarily knocked out a number of cameras, including the two monitoring the front lots. I also noticed my garage opener was gone.

I'd violated the unspoken prison code Lonnie mentioned. I couldn't stop them if they meant to kill him, so I'd lashed out with threats of my own.

Low clouds on the horizon had turned from crimson to indigo by the time I pulled in my driveway with a white rental Mustang GT and parked in the garage. I found my spare garage door opener and changed the code. Just in case. My eyes hurt and my belly growled after a long, shitty day.

Cutting off the head. A transmitter used for privileged conversations? An altered police report? Lonnie's assault. My car vandalized. Plausible deniability. Missing perfect duplicates of millions of dollars? Were Peebles' warnings turning prophetic?

Fighting City Hall seemed like child's play compared to taking on the Golden Boy.

Scott L. Miller

EVERYONE ENDS UP BLIND

Before I could close the garage door and shut out the world for the night, a car horn blared. Baker in his black Fleetwood, passenger door open.

"Get in," he ordered.

He didn't answer when I asked why.

He revved the powerful engine once I closed the door and we raced back toward Highway 40. His only movements were tiny hand corrections on the wheel while mirrored

sunglasses concealed his eyes in the approaching darkness.

"What the hell happened the last time we were on the phone?"

Baker's toothpick gently bobbed up and down while he maintained a cool facade. It was his one tell, the only yardstick that his internal emotions were running high. "Let's say the Secret Service and I didn't see eye-to-eye on things. They made it clear they didn't appreciate a city homicide dick pokin' around a counterfeitin' case. Let's leave it at that."

"How'd they find out?"

"Don't matter now." He sounded defeated.

I glanced at the road and noticed just how fast this souped-up ghetto car was racing east without the bubble light on. "Can you at least tell me where are we going?"

The toothpick bobbed again. He sat still but for a pulsating vein on the right side of his shiny bald skull. "You been there once before. No more talking. I'm in no mood."

Baker was a force of nature, and I learned a year ago not to fight it. We drove in silence until he cut across the two left traffic lanes and took the north exit onto Fourteenth Street. He parked next to a fire hydrant and said, "Out."

On the sidewalk, I looked up at the building and said, "Oh, no." Why did I spar with Kendall?

"'Fraid so, Breezy."

Walking into the city morgue, feeling the bite of the cold air, waiting for the attendant to present the body, everything took place in slow motion.

"It's no longer just a funny money case," Baker said, still wearing the shades. "Now I'm on the job."

The color of Lonnie's skin was otherworldly, his eye sockets were buried by the swollen flesh from a brutal beating. His nose was broken in two places. He finally looked at rest but I knew his spirit wasn't.

"Who did this? When?"

"Couple hours ago … by a new arrival busted for dealin' drugs. Nigger outweighed him by two hundred pounds. Said the little brother tried to force him to suck his Johnson."

"With two useless mangled hands. That's the same story Kendall fed me after three men jumped Lonnie earlier today and broke his fingers."

He nodded. "It was an execution, a sadistic one." Baker raised the sheet again to reveal Lonnie's club foot. It had been broken and twisted backward. "My pigeons are all singin' now that the little brother's dead. It started near the john. Nigger beat him to a pulp and stuffed his head in a crapper. Said he was launderin' the little brother."

"What happened to his killer?"

"The Man got him in isolation."

"Kendall," I said, sarcastically.

I looked away, feeling crushed and sick to my stomach.

Baker snapped a toothpick in two with his teeth and inserted a fresh one. "Makes sense this time. Lotta righteous brothers in lockup wanna even the score. I can't wait to interview the fat piece of shit. Some penny-ante dirt bag name of Terrell Burnett." He saw the look on my face and stopped.

I recalled the wife-beater t-shirt, the Lakers' sweats, the hemostat, and the scowl behind the sunglasses. "I met him. He lives one street over from LaKeesha and goes by the name of T-Bone. He likes pot with his Wheaties for breakfast and hated Lonnie for not bankrolling a buddy's lame business scheme. Terrell hoped to be a bouncer at a sports bar with pole dancers, I think."

"The attack was planned. The Aryan skinheads served as lookout when it went down. Gonna have to be a closed casket."

"Let's get out of here," I said, walking to the door. Needing fresh air, I walk outside and sat on the front steps while Baker said he'd be a minute. The moon was fat in the sky, low on the horizon. The city was peaceful, asleep early tonight.

He came out carrying two large Styrofoam cups, handing one to me. I could smell what it was.

"Does his mother know?"

He shook his head.

"She'll have to be told, and soon."

He nodded. "Skinny on her way."

Another toothpick snapped. This one he didn't replace. "I'm gonna lean on him hard. He gonna tell me who he made the deal with. This was murder for hire."

"Lonnie will be front-page news by morning."

He snarled, "Think your bony little blonde pin cushion gonna tell the viewers 'xactly how the little brother was murdered?"

I let the sexual reference slide. "For Maynard, this effectively ends the counterfeiting story, other than the trials of Earl and Tyrone. We're not going to let that happen."

He didn't acknowledge my remark. We sat in silence—me thinking, Baker fuming.

Shaking his head, he said, "I can't believe a brother does this to another brother. 'Specially a crippled one. But the sad truth is it happens all the time." Baker pulled off the lid to his coffee cup and groaned. "Us brothers got a long way to go."

"Mankind has a long way to go. Technology advances outstrip our emotional intelligence. If an eye for an eye continues, everyone ends up blind."

Baker raised an eyebrow. "That pretty profound for a social worker. You make that up?"

"I don't remember the exact quote, but no. Gandhi did."

"Hmm. He the little bald, toga-wearing dude in India who also said if he had access to enough guns he'd a used 'em on the British instead of taking the non-violent path?"

"The one and the same."

"Go figure," Baker said. "Life's a bitch. He musta been from a 'hood, too."

"One of the worst ones. He fought them the best way he knew how, given the resources he had."

"Like Martin Luther King," Baker said.

"The eye for an eye cycle has to stop somewhere. Might as well be with us."

"Maybe you right, Cool Breeze, but I don' think so tonight."

"When did you first meet Lonnie again?"

Baker paused behind those dark shades while he watched an unmarked make a right at the intersection. "I told you. In school. I noticed a light on in a locker and opened the door to see this poor little dude inside, trussed up on one of those rusty metal coat hooks like a side of beef, calmly doing his homework like it was just another day, a pocket flashlight hangin' from his mouth. At the time it was one of the saddest things I ever saw. I lifted him off the hook and got the bullies off his back. We became tight, but less than a year later he ran away from his foster home and never returned to school."

"Huh," I said.

We sat in more silence until Baker said, "Drink up."

"You know damn well I don't drink coffee."

Baker stared me down. "You almos' always try my patience, Cool Breeze, but today be extra shitty. Don' make me mad. Drink the damn coffee."

It was the strongest Irish coffee I've ever had.

Baker lifted his sixteen-ounce Styrofoam cup to the night sky and said, "To the little brother, no one fuckin' with you anymore up there. You always kept it real."

We took another pull and I raised my cup. "To a modern-day Robin Hood, defender of the weak against the strong, the deck was stacked against you from birth, yet you did a lot for many good people."

Baker smiled. "My man, Cool Breeze. You found the truth on the streets on your own. It means more that way, don' it?" He produced a dented metal flask from his black leather jacket and refilled our cups. The alcohol warmed my empty stomach, and Baker hoisted his cup again. "To the little brother who helped Cool Breeze get his balls back."

The more we drank the more the hard liquor burned my insides. I had the beginnings of a buzz when another blast from my recent past made his dramatic entrance.

I tensed immediately and thought I saw Baker straighten up ever so slightly at the sight of him.

He was nattily dressed in a three-piece suit that matched his short salt-and-pepper hair. He'd traded the glasses for contacts and entered the room with a cock-of-the-walk bounce to his step that belied his diminutive stature. Last year I'd known him as Detective Francis LeMaster, Baker's former partner in city homicide. He was now Assistant Police Chief LeMaster. In addition to Baker and Kris' killer, he'd been the other major player in my nightmares from last year.

Ignoring me, LeMaster told Baker, "You're off the case and you damn well know why. Hand over your badge and gun; you're suspended until further notice. I can't have my officers going rogue. If I hear one word from any of my sources that you're still working this case or in any way aiding or abetting this one here," he warned, pointing a manicured finger at me, "The chief will know and you will be directing traffic for the rest of your days. Is that clear?"

"Yassir, boss," Baker said, snapping to mock attention. He lifted his cup as if for another toast.

LeMaster ignored the taunt and turned to me. "You stay out of this. You've used up your nine lives here."

"My client's dead. I'm off the case." I thought: *What else is there you don't want me looking into?"*

"Badge and gun," he said, facing Baker again.

He handed over both in one fluid motion.

LeMaster left us on the steps, his polished Florsheim heels clicking loudly on the concrete.

"Little big man's gone corporate," Baker said.

"Do you think he's part of all this?"

"Dunno. He just got promoted. Not yet part of their inner circle, so probably not."

"What'd you do to piss him off?"

He weighed his answer. "Combination of things. Convincing you to take the case, enlisting help on the inside for the little brother to survive, helping his family."

"Why did the Secret Service break down your door?"

"To search my crib. I didn't feel like it, warrant or not. I may face an obstruction charge."

"What were they looking for?" I said, waiting for an answer that never came.

When he remained quiet, I asked, "What are you going to do?"

"Go home and pick up another piece. Then do whatever I can to settle the score. I just came into a lotta free time and so did you."

Lonnie said he would ask things of me, difficult things, but he never had the chance.

I recalled Maynard's personal calendar Debbie had copied.

"Remember what I said about Gandhi? That we might as well be the ones to stop the cycle of violence?"

Baker nodded.

"I have another idea."

$ $ $

Counterfeit

In bed that night I flashed back to my first trip to the morgue a year ago. Baker and LeMaster had escorted me there in the hope I could identify a Jane Doe. I half-expected the corpse to be that of Lisa Carter, a client of mine who was a no-show for an appointment, but the shock of seeing Kristin's destroyed face on the slab threw me into an emotional blackout. While the detectives searched for evidence to convict me, I didn't have time to grieve because I was fighting for my life. I desperately tried to hold on to her image and raged when I lost a little sense memory of her with each passing day. How fleeting and fragile life is and that how much can be taken away in an instant. Her killer framed me, forcing me to either give up or catch him. I got lucky. None of us is the same person we were a year ago. We evolve, adapt, and shed our old skins to hopefully become better versions of ourselves.

I fought last year and look what it got me. What did I tell Peebles about prisons?

I could exist off the practice, avoid tough clients, and stay on the couch. I could do webcam therapy. I could move to another office, mail my life in, wrap myself up in layers of dead skin until I could feel no more.

The black envelope promised danger.

Lonnie died for what he believed in.

He asked me to tell the world his story.

I had a decision to make that would define me.

FLASH DRIVE

My idea made perfect sense the more we drank and toasted Lonnie, flushed with hard liquor and anger and bent on retribution, but in the sober light of a new day it all looked like so much Swiss cheese.

Still, doing something is better than nothing.

My curiosity mingled with anxiety.

And sometimes curiosity gets a cat killed.

The mail in my box from yesterday did nothing to calm my fears.

A plain brown manila folder with a letter containing three colored business-size envelopes had been stuffed into my mailbox. It bore no return address and the stylized calligraphic letter inside read:

Dear Mitchell,

If you're reading this, you know I'm dead. Whatever version Maynard releases to the press, know this: I was murdered in cold blood. I've moved on to a better place, but my story needs a final chapter. You deduced the existence of Mr. Anthony on your own, and that means others can as well. He is completely untraceable to me and loyal to a fault. My final wishes will be carried to their fitting conclusion, as long as Mr. Anthony remains undisturbed.

The green envelope contains a modest reimbursement for your counsel and the friendship you offered. I know you see gratis clients but that didn't seem right, so I based the amount on a sliding scale therapy rate for local not-for-profit agencies of twenty-five dollars an hour since I was technically indigent. I allocated my entire share to others more worthy than I and Mr. Anthony has the accounting records to prove it. I realize this amount is far below your normal hourly wage, but I thought it was a fair compromise. If it was all about the money, you wouldn't have seen me at all and ventured out of your comfort zone for a stranger. You helped

Counterfeit

me stay sane in an insane place, but as the weeks passed, I think in some small way I helped you get your drive back. I saw the fire return to your eyes as time went by. You have a difficult job, but you probably hear that all the time. I wish you the best.

The red envelope is to be used at your discretion and contains, among other items, fifty of my counterfeit US one-hundred-dollar bills. When we first met, I warned you that I wasn't a pet sociology project of yours. Consider this a sociology test if you will. Have special agent Wilson inspect the bill with the small white paper clip attached to it. Tell him you received this bill at a venue that would be impossible to trace, perhaps from a cashier at a local casino, and you're concerned about its authenticity. I sensed skepticism when we discussed this earlier, although you were kind enough to reserve judgment after the news segment.

Once the bill passes the scrutiny of the St. Louis Secret Service office (and it will), you may be tempted to think this is a legal tender US bill I planted among my counterfeits. That will be the party line of the experts. Have them vet all fifty bills if you wish. That is why I've attached the dated photograph. The truth should never be a casualty.

Beware the black envelope. Hide it in the safest place you know. It is dangerous and I cannot in good faith ask you to act directly on what is inside. If Benny's murder is a prelude to the confirmation of my worst fears, and if by some twist of fate you or the proper authorities can locate those who possess his duffel bags, this will seal their guilt. Wouldn't that be something!

If this plays out the way I believe it will, and if you are able to successfully use the last two envelopes, this time I think you should consider a book or movie deal.

I'm sorry that so much information was withheld from you. Painted into the same corner, I'd do it all over again, but at least now you know why.

Good luck and watch your back.

LW

P.S. Mr. Anthony sent you the lone bill. I hope you had it checked. It was also one of mine.

Not knowing what else to do, I opened the black envelope. A brief note explained the flash drive. I inserted it in my computer to make sure it contained what the note promised and the I taped it to the top of one of the blades of my bedroom ceiling fan. Then I picked up Maynard's personal schedule that Debbie had pilfered from his office and began following him.

The first day, the Golden Boy was surrounded by beefy security staff who limoed him to every daytime destination while Fallon clung like a sycophant and hovered like a mosquito. He had lunch with his trophy wife Barbara, the Mayor, and Fallon downtown at Tony's on Market Street. By day's end, I worried that my sporty rental Mustang GT may be too conspicuous, so I stayed farther back. Maynard attended meetings in the city and county, leaving his office four different times, but all I could do was watch him enter and exit buildings. After his last scheduled meeting that night, security drove him to his gated community home, leaving me on the wrong side of the bars, parked alone in the dark with my mind numb from one of the longest, most boring days in memory. I left Maynard's locked gates and traded the flashier white Mustang for my parents' non-descript blue Toyota Camry LE. Sensible Dad, a tenured professor of accounting, kept asking me why I had to trade cars in the middle of the night, while Mom, a retired school teacher who still pined over selling my great aunt's '67 Corvette when I was young, happily grabbed the keys.

"It's a long story, Dad."

"I'm sure he has a good reason," Mom told him, hanging the Mustang keys by the door, smiling. "We're going for a ride in the country tomorrow to put that pretty white horse through its paces."

Mom picked up on my anxiety level when I left but didn't ask questions. She was the intuitive one and knew I'd talk when I could, deftly balancing a mother's trust with a mother's worry.

I drove home in their car and invited Tony over for a drink. I'd studied the bug earlier and Googled it. It seemed to be a compact transmitter only, with no built-in recording feature or miniaturized cassette tape.

I showed it to him.

"Where'd you get this?" he said, slowly turning it over in one hairy hand.

"Taped under the table where I meet—met with Lonnie. The same room where he met with his attorney."

"Slap my ass and call me Susan!" He did a double take. "No shit?"

"Is there any way to track where this came from, Suzie?"

He took a gulp of beer while he thought. "A friend in vice occasionally shows off some of her spy toys to me. I believe it's a newer transmitter, but there's no way to find where it came from or who planted it because your prints are probably the only ones on it now. There's another problem."

My hopes sank. "Which is …"

"There are more sophisticated models to listen in on even whispered conversations from greater distances and the drop ceiling in that moldy room is the perfect place to conceal it, even a miniature camera if they wanted." He tossed it back to me. "Somebody has to be listening for this little baby to be effective. If you had the tapes of your privileged conversations or testimony from the person eavesdropping, you'd have something."

No wonder Kendall was so smug, but I still imagined a cop sitting in another room with his feet up, eating doughnuts while he listened. My gut told me this is how they found Earl, but I had no proof. Any hope for a mistrial with the bug now seemed like a mirage on a distant road. Kendall was right, the cops would continue to claim they used good old fashioned, honest police work to capture Earl.

"Who's his court-appointed?"

The guy was so non-descript I had to pause. "Young kid named Hanover."

He rolled his eyes. "He's fresh out of school. Wouldn't be surprised if they cherry-picked him."

He looked around the living room. "Shit on a shingle, I just thought of something." He whispered conspiratorially, "What about here?" He made crawly motions with his fingers.

I shrugged.

He drained his beer. "Jumping Jesus Christ, you're in deep shit again, Mitch. Too deep, buddy. You gotta let this one go."

"He may have been a counterfeiter, but he didn't deserve to be murdered. I think—"

Tony shushed me by putting his finger to his mouth.

He wrote on a piece of paper and handed it to me. "Will bring over my vice friend with detector equipment tomorrow night—only way to be sure." He winked and smiled, "She looks up to me."

"Don't be stupid enough to venture down that road again."

Counterfeit

He waved away my admonition with a hairy hand. "Strictly platonic—but she does have a great rack."

He badgered me with more scribbled questions until the process grew tiresome and I kicked out my paranoid friend and went to bed.

I dreaded my second mind- and butt-numbing day of undercover work. I tried to think what would Baker do, and put together a bag for the car. Eight years of college and I borrowed my parents' Camry and stuck a pee jar in the front passenger seat.

Scott L. Miller

BLACK POWER AIRLINES

My phone rang at four in the morning, saving me from another dream round of mob torture from Bruno and his pliers.

A deep voice said, "Scored a hit with your tip from The Voice. Meet me outside in twenty. It'll be dawn by the time we get there. Dress in green and brown. Camouflage gear even better, if you got." The line went dead in my hand by the time my fuzzy brain realized it was Baker.

When I was a kid my parents would take me fishing. Back then, I owned a cheap knife in a camouflage sheath that I kept in my tackle box, both long gone. That made up my entire camouflage period. I dressed in the dark quickly, putting on khaki-colored pants, an old green-and-brown checkerboard shirt, and tennis shoes. I thought of Lonnie, LaKeesha, Skinny, and all the others I'd come to care about, hoping Dan Quinn would start the dominoes falling all the way to the Boy King himself.

Baker's sleek black Fleetwood appeared silently out of the thick pre-dawn fog like a drone gliding through clouds. I climbed inside.

"Knew you were the only one who could get The Voice to deliver. Good job, Cool Breeze." He seemed alert and rested, like now was mid-day for him.

"You said we'll be there by dawn. How, by helicopter?"

He grinned and placed a bubble light on the roof of his Fleetwood. "Black power, my man. Got some modifications under the hood and StreetBlaze with 100 Octane and ethanol. Buckle up and enjoy the ride."

We had already left my subdivision in the rear view. "It must be a hundred miles from here—"

"More like one twenty from your door," he said, a toothpick resting in the corner of his mouth.

My look remained skeptical.

"Have I ever lied to you?"

I held the look on him.

"I mean about the big stuff." He read the doubting look on my face. "I may have floated some white lies about the little brother being suicidal to get you here, but you know how big this is. Plus you got your stones back, you can't put a price on those babies. I figure we even."

We were already on the I-270 south ramp racing toward I-55 South. The few cars and trucks on the lonely fog covered interstate ahead seemed to be standing still as we flew past. At times Baker had to steer adroitly to avoid ramming slower vehicles as they materialized like icebergs out of the ground fog.

In my own foggy haste to get ready I'd forgotten something. "I have to pee."

He put on his best formal white person voice, saying, "You should have thought about that before we left the house, son." In the dark he tossed something in my lap. "Here, put your tip in the pee jar. Miss and you're cleaning it up."

By the light of the dashboard I made out an old Mason jar. "You're kidding."

"This black night train ain't stopping till we reach Deliverance country, Breezy."

I wondered if he ever cleaned the jar, weighing whether I could hold it until we arrived. The Caddy flew over a dip in the road and answered my question. I hesitated, unscrewed the top, and unzipped.

As if reading my mind he said, "I wash it out regular—drink my Gatorade and Power Shakes out of it at lunch." His deep voice softly chuckled in the dark.

"You almost a real, badass private dick now, Cool Breeze."

After I finished, we talked about the hushed conversation I'd overheard in the men's room between Maynard and Fallon. It seemed so long ago it felt like a dream.

"With what we've learned, Maynard hatched a plan to steal the outstanding counterfeit money when I overheard them in the john. If they were high quality—"

"Which they are," Baker interjected.

"I think Maynard was referring to Lonnie when he said, 'We already cut off the head.' He knew Lonnie was the talent behind the operation and Earl his mentor. Plus, they didn't have the money then, so they created the illusion that the lion's share had already been recovered."

Baker faced me, nodding agreement, as the blue light from the dashboard illuminated his skull from below. The serpentine scar on his left side seemed to slither toward me from what appeared to be a sunken eye socket caused by the eerie light from below.

"Fallon bought into the idea and spoke of containment—"

"Politico-criminal speak for damage control," he interjected.

"And that includes a multitude of crimes, false press reports…."

"Falsely linking the little brother and the others to guns, drugs, the robbery, and shooting the pregnant guard—"

"Bugging privileged conversations…"

"Brutalizing and puttin' a contract out on the little brother to save time on a trial."

Counterfeit

"And the coup de grace, altering the police report of the arrest."

"Replacing Quinn on the report with heavy hitters a bad sign. We pissin' up the good ole boys' rope."

"And we still don't know what 'the Big Top' means," I said.

I sat in silence for a while, staring at the murky road ahead, thinking of the possibilities. We'd already been burning up Highway 67 for some time, the speedometer past one-thirty, the engine not close to red-line. "What do you think we'll find when we get there?"

His toothpick bobbed and he flicked his brights once when a doe in a strand of trees near the highway took a first tentative step to cross the road. Luckily, she thought better of it until we passed. He exhaled. "Not sure. I put out feelers, called in favors, and spread his photo around the area. A smart cop be hard to find when he decides to go underground. Guess we about to find out how smart he is. My birdies tell me he grew a beard since he went into the wind."

"I hope he's underground by choice," I said, settling back to rest my eyes.

Thirty minutes later, a series of kidney-busting bumps and stomach-churning dips jarred me awake, while we hurtled over winding, rock-strewn back roads, gravel loudly pinging against the car undercarriage like hailstones.

He flicked off the headlights and slowed the car to a crawl before cresting a small rise. As dawn's first light broke the eastern sky to our left, he pulled off road and coasted to a silent stop under a thick grove of elms and maples.

"Right on time, Sleepin' Beauty. Thanks for choosing Black Power Airlines. Return your seats and tray tables to their upright positions or your ass be walkin' back," he announced as he finished a Power Bar, crumbs falling from his bushy Fu Manchu. "You want?" he said, offering me one.

"I'm stuffed. I'd just made eggs Benedict and French toast when you called."

He laughed.

I rubbed the sleep from my eyes. "You drove so fast I feel like we just traveled back in time."

"We did. Looks like 1930 here in Crackerville, Missouri. Back when men were men and sheep were nervous." He pulled the trunk release as his face turned serious. "Let's get ready."

He was all business as he donned a Kevlar vest and tossed one to me. He checked a .9 mm Glock and tucked it in his belt. An ankle holster and .22 went on next and he placed a hunting blade in the narrow of his back.

"Ever shoot at a person before?"

"Went duck and pheasant hunting with my dad when I was a teenager. That count?"

He made a face. "Here," he said, tossing me a heavy pair of binoculars. "You be our eyes then. Stay behind me at all times. Don't do anything stupid. When I start to walk, don't make a sound and step in my footsteps. Follow my lead and directions, always."

In the distance a rooster crowed.

"We don't know what we walkin' into. We do know he don't want to be found. Man feels trapped, he defend himself just like an animal. I'm breakin' all the rules with you being here. You swear to do exactly what I tell you, no questions asked?"

I nodded. The rooster crowed a second time. I noticed Baker dressed in his trademark black outfit and my nerves got the better of me. "Why did I have to wear brown and green?"

"Because I be a black Ninja warrior and look damn good in black. Take some deep breaths, you'll be fine long as you do what I say."

He completed his arsenal by grabbing a sawed-off shotgun. "Let's roll," he said, striding up the rise.

Just me and us chickens, I thought.

The uppermost tip of the sun peaked over the eastern horizon, turning the clouds crimson as we began to crawl on our bellies to the crest of the hill. Ahead of us I saw the outline of a small wooden building, little more than a camping shack, with several large boulders on the sloping hillside.

"Tell me what you see."

I squinted through the binocs I carried around my neck, focusing them. "The ground slopes down about 200 yards to a small wooden yellow A-frame. The slope levels out past the shack for about ten yards down toward the Black River. The side nearest the river sits on tall stilts, the side closer to us rests on shorter timber, and there's open space beneath the shack. The entrance includes a tiny front porch that looks ready to fall down. The roof is warped with moss-covered shingles. A small window AC unit is in the front window, left of the entrance. That must be the bedroom."

"Good and thorough, you must be a little OCD. Lemme scan the grounds."

After some time he handed the binocs back. "We goin' in. Slow. Keep me between you and the cabin at all times. I do this," he said, raising his right arm from the elbow perpendicular to the ground, "that means stop immediately. You cool? Take some deep breaths."

I nodded, cool as that crowing rooster.

"I almost forgot," he said, handing me something small. "Spare car key. Hold on to it. Something happens to me, hightail it outta here and call 911. There's a loaded .38 in the

glove box. Safety's off. There's a bullet in the chamber. Just point and shoot to kill."

"That's comforting, thanks." If I wasn't anxious before, I was now.

We started silently down the hill, the going very slow, keeping off the gravel. Fifty feet from the porch, his right hand shot up and I nearly walked into him. He pointed out a trip wire running between two boulders. We gingerly stepped over it and forged ahead, even slower, like sitting ducks out in the open. My mind screamed for Baker to hurry.

He located another wire at the base of the dilapidated stairs as we finally stood pressed up against the wall under the bedroom window. He crab-walked into the space below the cabin and located a trap door. He pushed on it gently but it didn't budge. Baker returned without a sound and motioned that we'd move in quickly, hoping to surprise and disarm a sleeping Dan Quinn.

The window above us had been left open to let in the cool night air. Suddenly I heard movement inside and tugged hard on Baker's tight black shirt just before he stepped onto the second stair. Floorboards creaked inside and we heard a man urinating and farting. More heavy, slow movements followed until we heard a plate and silverware tossed into what sounded like a sink. A loud belch broke the short silence. The sun had risen from the eastern sky but visibility remained poor due to ground fog rolling off the river. Next we heard running water and what sounded like a shower curtain being drawn.

Baker whispered, "We're goin' in. Don't assume he's in the shower. He could have made us. Could be a trick. I will clear each room first. Stay behind me and make sure you step over the trip wire."

As soon as his weight landed on the second stair, it creaked loudly, as did several others
on our way up. The screen door was latched from the inside, but he quickly cut the mesh with his knife, reached in, and flipped the eye-hook. He swept the tiny front room with his shotgun then cleared the kitchen, with me his shadow. A steaming cup of coffee and a lit cigarette sat wedged in the groove of a plastic ashtray on the small rustic wooden kitchen table. Outside the rooster crowed for the third time. He quickly swept the cramped bedroom and breathed a little easier, but only for a moment. The lone person inside *was* in the shower, and now whistling. He motioned for me to back away as he crept forward.

Raising the shotgun, he flung the curtain open and shouted, "Freeze, Quinn!"

A short pudgy naked man with soap in what was left of his white hair raised his arms in a defensive posture. Shaking and trapped, he pleaded, "At least let me get dressed. Then make it quick, one in the head."

He kept the shotgun trained on Quinn. "Shit, if I was here to kill you, Irish, you already be dead."

"Can I dry off and get dressed then?"

"Where's your firepower, Quinn?"

"I haven't told a soul, I swear. Tell them I'm keeping my part of the deal."

He aimed the shotgun at Quinn's balls, which he cupped with trembling pink hands. "The piece, Dan. I see it ain't in the shower. You gotta have one nearby."

"It's in the kitchen," he said too quickly. "Can I at least get my bath towel?"

"You're lying to me, Quinn," Baker said in a sing-song voice, grinning.

I saw the towel behind me on a small bed cluttered with piles of clothes and went to it. Underneath was a .357 Magnum. I held the gun up for Baker to see.

"Who's that guy?" Quinn said, noticing me for the first time.

"Another friend who wants to see you stay alive."

"And talking," I added, handing Baker the Magnum.

Quinn was so red he looked on the verge of a heart attack. "Well, friends, how about I get dressed now?"

"You not gonna lie to me twice, Irish. Where the rest of your firepower? All of it."

He sighed. "There's a deer rifle, shotgun and night-vision goggles under the bed and a .38 in the drawer to the right of the sink."

Baker nodded to me. I found exactly what Quinn said I would.

"I'm freezing wet here, friend," saying the last word sarcastically.

"I see by your shrinkage, Irish." Baker glanced at the rumpled clothes on the bed and told me, "Shake out the towel, that pair of tighty-whities, and the red flannel shirt. They free of weapons, toss them to him. That all he gets for now."

I did so. Quinn quickly and self-consciously dried off and dressed in the clothes Baker allowed.

"Are pants and shoes too much to ask for?" he said.

"Don' want you gettin' any ideas 'bout making a run for it."

"Okay," Quinn said, "You still think I'm holding back a weapon from you?"

"I would," Baker answered immediately. "Now we gonna walk into that raggedy ass kitchen and you gonna answer some questions."

I pulled up three wobbly pine chairs.

"We gonna sit and have our morning coffee like civilized folk," Baker said, pouring himself a cup. "Good to find you above ground, Irish," Baker said, the shotgun across his lap, hand on the trigger guard.

Partially clothed and still alive, Quinn seemed to draw on new found courage and said, "Who's this guy again?"

"I'm Dr. Mitchell Adams, social worker in private practice. I met regularly with Lonnie Washington in jail before he was executed."

He stared at me hard. "You got one less client. I wish I'd never stumbled into that shop. Forget about him. Go back to your practice and thank your lucky stars you can."

Baker grimaced when he tasted the coffee and said, "Who you think sent us to off you?"

Quinn resumed squirming. "Look, I'm glad I was wrong about you. No offense, but if you found me, they can too. I gotta get outta here. Now."

"That's cool, Irish. We let you go, after you tell us everything you know about the bust, why you abandoned your job, and what got you holed up here in Hooterville with an arsenal of weapons and trip wires."

He shook his head, the wattle under his chin jiggling, his face pink as the morning sky had been. "How do you boys know you weren't followed?"

"Look," I said, "the sooner you talk to us, the quicker you're out of here. Were you the lone cop who busted Lonnie Washington at Brother-Hood Printers?"

He hesitated, then finally nodded his head.

"Is that a yes?" I said, sterner this time.

"Yes, yes. I got a tip from some men on the street. They looked like tweakers. I thought it was bogus, sounded like one of them had a beef with an employee. There were no prior incidents or calls about the business or owner. Three black males were working the main floor when I entered. They seemed decent enough, but I could tell my presence spooked them. They were hiding something." He turned to Baker and said, "You been a cop long as I have, you get a sixth sense for this or you get dead."

"You were the only officer at the scene," Baker said.

"Isn't that what 'lone cop' means, friend?"

"Then what," I said.

He turned back to me. "I heard a noise in the basement and asked one of the men to walk with me to the lower level. Soon as my back was turned, they scattered like church mice, even the old owner with his oxygen tank. I drew my weapon, went downstairs, and found Washington preparing to burn something in a drum. He did not obey my command to stop, but his Bic wouldn't light by the time I reached him. I cuffed him to the radiator and called for back-up. He didn't resist but he didn't answer my questions, either. I emptied the contents of the drum on a table and found two sheets of imperfect hundred-dollar bills."

That matches Lonnie's account.

"Who came as back-up?" I said.

Counterfeit

"Carter, Malvern, and Downey. I figured, no big deal, I collared a small-time counterfeiter before his crappy product hit the street. It happens that way seventy percent of the time. I wrote my report, but before my shift ended I got a call telling me not to bother, that this was my lucky day and I should consider myself retired a year early with full pension and benefits effective immediately. I was to turn in my gun and badge and encouraged to spend the rest of my days fishing and hunting. I thought it was a joke, my buddies know I've been counting down the days to retirement. I checked with HR and found out it was legit."

"Who told you this?" I said.

"I'm getting to that. Let me tell it my way, dammit. Two things happened—one made me curious and the other scared the hell out of me. I tried to turn in the report on the final arrest of my career but the desk refused it, saying the other officers had already submitted reports. Then I watched the evening news and heard almost all of it had been recovered. I knew I was up a creek without a paddle then—"

"Why?" we both asked at the same time.

"I searched that building from top to bottom and there was no money in it, other than smaller bills in the cash register and the two flawed practice sheets downstairs. Also, the Chief and his second-in-command were never there."

"Did you find guns at the scene?" I asked.

"Not a one."

"Drugs?"

"No."

"Who called you?"

He didn't answer.

"We will protect you if you testify," Baker interjected. "I can get the Secret Service—"

He shook his head. "I think they got to one of them. You don't know who to trust any more than I do. This isn't just my life; he made threats to my ex-wife. I know most guys hate their exes. The divorce was my fault. I want her back."

"Who called you? Who are the players? Tell us and this man will mobilize an army to keep you safe," I said, pointing to Baker.

Quinn sat slumped, staring beyond his spare tire, picking at his patchy beard with chewed fingernails.

Baker and I made eye contact. He looked optimistic.

"I don't know you," Quinn said to me before turning to Baker, "but I know about him."

"What you think you know, Irish?"

"You're a homicide dick with a good conviction record. You're old school, but not my school. You also aren't above bending or breaking the rules to get what you want."

"That something else we got in common, Irish."

He considered that for some time. "I want immunity from prosecution. I want new identities and two safe houses for me and my ex." He hesitated. She can't stand the sight of me right now. I want details about the deep cover, and I want it in writing. Give us immediate protection and I'll tell you what you want to know."

"*One* safe house, Irish. Two costs too much and is harder to defend. It's either hide out against the forces huntin' you until the trial or take your chances under the same roof with the ex."

He thought about it for a long time. "Okay, one house."

"You'll testify?"

Counterfeit

"I'll testify."

"You got a deal," Baker said. "I'll put it in motion." He pulled out his cell.

We have our witness. At last we were going to hear the names Maynard and Fallon, the police chief, and others. I leaned forward and asked, "Who are the players, Officer Quinn?"

He leaned back and when he opened his mouth a spray of warm liquid hit my face,

stinging my eyes. Glass shards rained down on the wooden planking while Quinn shook and twitched in his chair, falling face first in a heap in front of me. Something crashed through a second window, raining more glass down on us and then it exploded at the base of the wall near Baker, hurtling him head first into the iron stove and setting the drapes ablaze. I collapsed to the floor, stunned and disoriented, my ears ringing from the blast. The flash fire turned the wood cabin into a tinderbox, a solid wall of flames blocked the exit. Baker lay motionless while the cabin filled with the stench of gasoline smoke, choking us both. Lungs burning, I dragged him into the bedroom while another concussive device rocked the kitchen floor. The flames followed us into the tiny bedroom, licking at our heels. I crawled to the dresser and tried to slide it with all my strength, but its feet were stuck in the uneven floorboards. I climbed to my knees, the dense black smoke engulfing me, stinging my eyes as I fumbled blindly for the dresser. I hit it hard with my chin and nearly knocked myself out. Flames danced as they devoured the sheets, clothes, and the old mattress behind us, spreading ever closer. Consuming everything, the hungry beast roared and raged, licking at my feet, ready to devour us. I fumbled for the top edge of the dresser and pushed it over. I tugged on the weathered brass latch to the trap door, but it was frozen shut. Our only hope gone! I groped for Baker's knife and pried under the latch with its tip. Pain shot up my ankle and I screamed as I popped the latch free from the trap door. I pulled a dazed Baker through the square opening by the collar of his leather jacket. My pants caught fire when I crawled out and landed on top of him.

I lay there panting and coughing as Baker slowly began to come around, both of us taking in better air. Red embers slowly dropped through the spaces of the floorboards above us. It felt like we'd landed under the grate of a giant barbecue pit. We had to make a run for the woods near the river.

"We gotta go back and get him," I shouted over the roar of the inferno.

Baker finished a coughing jag. "He was dead before he hit the floor. Took two rounds from a rifle with a silencer. One in the neck, one in the head." He pulled at my collar. "The shooter's still out there. We can't stay here."

"We reach the woods by the river, maybe we can lose him there. The smoke will give us
some cover. You good to run?"

He nodded.

We crab-walked out from under the fiery shack and ran together, I expected to feel a bullet in my back and, sure enough, I felt searing pain. We kept running until we made it into the woods and caught our breath behind cover within view of the cabin. I went to my knees, the pain worsening, terrified I'd been badly wounded when Baker spun me around, hunting knife in hand, and dug a large smoldering ember from the back of my shirt. It must have landed on my back during our escape. We watched the cabin collapse to the ground and heard a third explosion. Quinn's propane barbecue tank exploded, twisting and dovetailing in the air like a missile. It landed in the shallow waters of the Black River, where it rotated slowly like a smoking dreidel.

Baker's eyebrows had been singed off in the fire. He had a head laceration and a large ugly knot on the right side of his bald skull.

Once he regained his wind he said, "We circle back through these woods and see if we can come up behind these sons of bitches. We no match for a high-powered rifle."

We trudged through a moderately dense thicket, making as little noise as we could, but still making plenty. We had to hump two miles until we exited the woods not far from Baker's Fleetwood, which appeared untouched. He grabbed the spare gun in the glove compartment and handed it to me while we retraced our pre-dawn steps. Over the crest of the hill a small number of people stood gawking, drawn by the explosions, near the burning pile of wood and twisted metal that used to be Quinn's cabin.

They looked to be fellow campers and fishermen.

"Did anyone see a car or SUV speed away from here, or anything else suspicious, just before the fire?" I asked the small gathering.

A skinny man in a Bass Pro Shop baseball cap turned to us and shook his head. "We called the local fire department. They're all volunteers, so it'll be awhile. Hope that wasn't your cabin." He looked at us closer and added, "If you boys were in there, you're lucky to be alive."

My thoughts returned to Quinn.

"Time to boogie," Baker said.

"What about Quinn?"

"He still dead. You drive. I'm seeing two of everything."

"You probably have a concussion. You need a neurologic workup."

"No, but I could use a Red Bull. Take me back to the 'hood. I'll show you where to drop me off."

"What about your shotgun and fingerprints? They're in the wreckage."

"It ain't registered, but my prints are. That fire was so hot, with all that soot and gas accelerant, the chances are slim any prints remain in that rubble. Besides, a rifle killed Irish, not shotgun pellets."

Before leaving, he closely inspected under the car and hood for anything out of the ordinary—a bomb, tracking device, tampered brake lines and the like—and pronounced it clean.

I produced a Dictaphone from my pocket and listened to the conversation I'd taped with Quinn. Someone high up the police food chain had told Quinn he was officially retired but we never heard who made the threats, oblique or direct, to his ex-wife. We knew Malvern, Carter,

Downey, the Police Chief, and assistant chief Rhymes were involved on some level, but we still had no proof.

Baker slumped in the passenger seat, the dazed look returned to his face, as he noticed the recorder. "Thanks for havin' my six, Cool Breeze. You still think quick on your feet, like last year. I won't forget it."

I made sure Baker didn't fall asleep on our return to St. Louis and dropped him and the

Fleetwood off where he wanted. He'd be out of commission, and I told him to see a doctor, knowing that would fall on deaf ears. By then it was noon and I took a cab home.

After a long cold shower bath and treating the burn on my back as best I could, I wolfed down lunch with four aspirin. I wanted to climb into bed, but our informant was dead and we had a small window to identify the missing money before it vanished forever.

I'd never seen a person die in front of me before, much less have their blood and brain matter speckle my face. I scrubbed myself red in the shower while the image of Quinn falling forward replayed in my mind. Baker and I almost suffered a worse death. I made a mental note to seek out Quinn's ex-wife after this was over to tell her his final thoughts were of her. I hoped Lonnie's vision of heaven was right, so Quinn would eventually be reunited with her.

I gathered Maynard's crumpled schedule, bottles of water, and my pee jar. I had to find the bags.

ON THE RUN

I'd missed the second morning of tailing Maynard, but noticed tonight was a late one on his private calendar. His first evening engagement came at a downtown convention center as the keynote speaker to a Christian family group. The last cryptic notation on his calendar that night, the only one written in his hand, intrigued me. It read:

"Jack Murphy, 1810 Penthouse, 23:30, the Ritz-Clayton, Your Wildest Dreams, Marte/Gisselle, 3K."

Even his handwriting was creepy.

Who's Jack Murphy? The Ritz Hotel in Clayton has eighteen floors, is Maynard meeting three people at 11:30? Is 3K three thousand dollars? What's 'Your Wildest Dreams?'

From across the street I watched the Maynard convoy pull into the center's underground parking garage and his entourage enter the building. The marquee flashed tonight's topic: the role of faith in the political arena. He'd be occupied for the next two to three hours, so I decided to grab dinner at a nearby St. Louis Bread Company. Sliding into a booth with my order, I watched other couples mingle in the crowded restaurant and thought of Kris. Would I ever stop missing her? I opened the book I'd brought with me but kept reading the same line over and over, so I put it down.

I imagined following up on Lonnie's idea to pursue a book or movie deal. He'd be the star and it could be called *Modern Day Robin Hood* or *A Good Man.* Don Cheadle could play Lonnie, though he's getting a bit long in the tooth for the role. Idris Elba could go bald and play Detective Baker. Jon Hamm, a St. Louis native, could play

Maynard. Sofia Vergara could be Kris, in flashbacks. As for me, I guess it depends on how all this ends, because I can't see me right now. The book cover also remains blurry. I'd need much more than quick thinking and clever words to come out of this one with anything close to a happy ending. I speed dialed Baker's cell. The recorded opening of the Shaft theme song filled my ear, followed by his one-word command: "Speak." Beep.

"You okay? Call me."

I had to do something. I had to find the ending.

What would Baker do? Anything he could, legal or otherwise.

Back in my parent's Camry, I took a chance and dialed the front desk at the Ritz and said, "This is Rex Smith, Jack Murphy's assistant, calling to confirm Mr. Murphy's reservation this evening. I see he's due to arrive at eleven thirty tonight, and the room number is 1810."

After a brief silence the female clerk returned to the line and confirmed the reservation and room number. No questions asked and in a silky, refined British accent she even told me to have a lovely evening.

I drove to the Ritz and parked along the street under a curving line of small trees a block from the hotel. Any closer would have meant valet parking. Since I was early, I reacquainted myself with the opulent main floor lobby—brown marble walls and dark polished wood glistened everywhere the eye turned; the expansive open floor plan contained black Steinway grand pianos, immense gas fireplaces, several bars, a high-end gift shop, Grill Room, a Cigar club, and plush multicolored carpeting in a bright, almost modernistic pattern. The men's room sparkled with green marble walls and classic black accents. Light jazz music played discreetly in a back corner of the ground floor.

Kris and I had stayed at the Ritz one night after a wedding. We made love in front of a marble fireplace and then watched the downtown Fourth of July fireworks from the balcony.

I climbed the extra-wide twisting staircase to the second floor. Here were huge meeting, reception, and board rooms each capable of holding several hundred guests. Some sat vacant while others were in use. In each were giant round wooden tables brimming with tall cut floral displays, ornate crystal chandeliers suspended from twelve-foot-high ceilings, and the latest electronic and overhead A-V equipment. Subdued oil paintings of hunting dogs on point, bucolic landscapes, and wealthy women posing with privileged children lined the hallway walls along the second floor. Easels stood in front of two board rooms bearing the words 'Maynard Party,' so I huffed it down the staircase and bought a gin and tonic.

I settled into a plush, over-sized armchair with an unobtrusive view of the entrance within easy earshot of the front desk. I read my book while I waited for the Golden Boy to make his entrance. Well-dressed older couples milled in and out of The Grill or Cigar Club. I worried my casual dress would make me stick out, but after eleven, younger people in polo shirts or Cardinals attire began to trickle into the bars. I overheard the Cards had just defeated the visiting Cubs. I sipped my drink and cracked opened a Robert B. Parker book, keeping half an eye on the front glass doors. Tough guy Spenser had just won a funny verbal sparring session with the latest bad guy, a prelude to an inevitable physical confrontation, when a sleek black limo discharged the Golden Boy right on time. A young security man wearing sunglasses exited with him. The body builder was the same lead security dog for Maynard I'd seen shadowing him before. The same one that escorted me out the door at old man Haller's estate. The same one who'd hoisted the heavy duffel bags into the dark SUV.

Jack Murphy must already be in room 1810 waiting for the others. Is he another high roller Maynard supporter? Is he tied to the plan to steal the counterfeit money or is he a phantom?

I pulled the bill of my Cardinals cap down to conceal my face as he briefly lingered at the front desk to pick up his key. The desk clerk, the same distinguished lady that sounded like she was from across the pond said, "Good to see you again, sir. Have a most pleasant stay, Mr. Murphy."

Mr. Murphy! Pieces of the puzzle instantly began falling into place. It was the last thing I wanted to hear, but it confirmed my worst and most sordid suspicions. Maynard and his security man abruptly turned and walked straight toward me. I held the book in front of my face and lowered my head.

Please don't recognize me. I'm not tough-guy Spenser.

They turned right, in the direction of the guest elevators. I exhaled in relief.

Before they reached the elevator Maynard said, "Might as well wet your whistle, Mr. Dodd. My guests are late, as usual." The big bodyguard silently veered off into the bar across from the elevators. Maynard took the elevator alone. There was no display above the elevator to indicate which floor Maynard punched, but I already knew.

Mr. Dodd nursed a beer with half an eye on the hallway near the elevators. Every so often he checked his watch and looked at the revolving glass entry door. I waited ten minutes, then kept my back to Dodd as best I could and joined others walking to the elevators. The hand-polished cherry wood interior shined and smelled of rich pungent oils. I rode to seventeen and climbed the stairs, with a good idea who the guests were now.

I caught a break on the penthouse floor. Room 1810 was at the end of a wide hallway that contained an alcove with a window and two oversized floral print colonial chairs. I sat waiting in one of the chairs with my Spenser book and drink. After midnight the elevator doors whooshed open and discharged two leggy young women with long flowing hair—a blonde and a redhead—wearing fur coats and black fuck-me pumps with stiletto heels. Oblivious to their surroundings, chatting away and oblivious to their surroundings, they spoke about a guy named Alfonse.

They hadn't noticed me at the far end of the wide hallway. I stood, moved around the corner wall, and peered out with a perfect view of room 1810. As they approached, the blonde appeared drunk or high, wobbly on her heels. She started to knock on the door to 1808 when the redhead whispered, "Gisselle, you idiot, the cash cow is over here. With any luck, he'll be drunk and pass out quickly, like before. Be wary of this one. He likes to choke."

The redhead whom I assumed was Marte quietly knocked on the door to room 1810 and struck a sexy Vogue pose against the door jamb after she poked Gisselle in the ribs as a reminder not to slouch.

John Maynard, Jr., a.k.a. Jack Murphy, opened the door and made a quick, desultory sweep of the hallway. He didn't see me behind the wall. He was shirtless, revealing a well-toned abdomen for a man his age, and wore a red-striped business tie wrapped around his forehead like a makeshift sweatband. He held a drink in his hand. "I love it when you girls come together. Let's see if we can make that can happen at least once more tonight. Apres vous." The Golden Boy opened the door wide enough for them to enter as he fondled and pinched their asses. The girls giggled and shimmied in feigned delight as he slowly closed the door.

VIPs gone wild. I'd recorded the call girls' hallway conversation and Maynard even smiled for my camera phone.

When in doubt, go with your gut. I was feeling pretty cocky that my early diagnosis was right on the money, and then—

The elevator doors at the other end of the hall whooshed open again, and Mr. Dodd, stood glaring at me with my cell phone at the door to Maynard's suite. He drew a gun from his speed holster and sprinted toward me. Blocked from the lone elevator, I ran down the hallway away from Dodd. All the doors I came to were to other hotel suites. I heard Dodd gaining on me, when I spotted the red exit sign above the last door on the right. In my panic I'd forgotten about the stairwell I'd taken up from the seventeenth floor.

I pushed open the heavy fire door and flew down the steps, nearly falling as my shoes slipped on the sharp edge of a step. Even the stairwells in the Ritz were wide and clean, with fresh beige paint on the walls, and thick metal hand railings. I opened some space between us as I negotiated the turns and steps faster than my larger, more muscle-bound pursuer. I resisted the urge to look back because it could slow me down or cause me to stumble. I had to shake this guy on my own. Safety in numbers wouldn't help—he'd simply call hotel security and Clayton PD, and have me arrested. He'd claim I assaulted or threatened Maynard and that'll be the end of me. I couldn't take that chance.

Racing down the steps to the fourteenth floor, I wondered whether I should exit and try to lose him or risk getting an elevator, but figured I didn't have enough time. I kept sprinting down the steps and nearly stumbled several more times. It sounded like the young security guard was a little farther behind me now, or at least I hoped so. As I raced down the ninth, eighth, and seventh floor stairwells I heard his breathing echo in the confined space. Was he tiring? I hadn't seen a fire alarm during my mad dash or I'd have pulled it. Between the third and second floors I heard a *pffit!* and sparks exploded from the metal railing near my hand. My left hand suddenly burned. He'd attached a silencer and the bullet had ricocheted off the metal rail and my hand. I rocketed down the stairs, hitting the door marked LOBBY hard with my shoulder and winced as sharp pains shot up and down my left arm. The fire door banged against the inner wall, and I darted and weaved around a startled elderly couple standing near the exit by the registration desk. Blood dripped from my hand onto my slacks.

Sprinting past the perplexed clerk with the British accent, out through the main entrance and into the cool night, I looked behind me for the first time. My pursuer bowled over the confused elderly man and raced after me, his gun concealed again. I ran along the cobblestone and circular brick entrance in the opposite direction of my car, sped past two bewildered valets, and punched a quick number in my cell phone while I ran. I darted around the corner of the building, as Dodd took aim again. Damn! Maybe I should have yelled "Fire!" in the lobby. Too late now.

I kept running and tripped over concealed wiring for the hotel floodlights illuminating the blue and white Ritz sign and fell face first into a hedge of rose bushes. Scratched and bleeding, I bounced up and bolted down the street, past a row of closed businesses, and careened into a shadowy alleyway behind them. I whispered a few quick words into the phone as loudly as I dared, and sprinted farther down the darkened alley only to discover it dead-ended in a tall concrete wall with no exit. I'd run myself into a corner. The only way out was the same way in. I yanked on every back door used for deliveries. All locked. Halfway down the dark alley sat a wide stack of packing crates, five feet high and partly illuminated by an overhead light. I pulled a ridiculously lightweight stick of thin pine from one of the packing crates and kept running to the end of the alley where, on the left, in almost total darkness, stood a Dumpster. I scrambled behind it, breathing hard, and listened. The sole light to my left came from a dim streetlamp fifty feet away, partially blocked by trees and another building. I hoped my shadow couldn't be seen to my right.

I heard footfalls running down the street I'd been on and prayed they'd pass the alley entrance, but they skidded to an abrupt stop. Mr. Dodd walked slowly down the deserted back alley, methodically testing each locked door I'd just tried. By the time he tested the last door, his shadow had grown to monstrous proportions. I held my breath and peeked out from behind the Dumpster to see Dodd screwing the cylindrical silencer back on his gun. A smug smile crossed his face. He hadn't uttered a word during the chase, his detached professional calm a sharp contrast to my abject terror. He would reach my hiding hole in seconds. My heart thudded in my ears as I flashed back to last year's crime scene photos of Kris. So much for the grand book idea. Would I meet my end next to a Dumpster just like Kris? If I was, I wasn't about to go down without a fight. I squeezed my flimsy stick and, just as I was about to make my stand, a spotlight flooded the mouth of the alley. A voice called out over a loudspeaker, "You sir, there in the alley. Over here."

Dodd stopped with his back to the police cruiser. He discretely removed the silencer, reholstered his gun, and walked toward them. Two uniformed Clayton police officers stood next to their vehicle. I couldn't make out their muffled conversation, but in the brilliance of the floodlight, I saw Dodd glance back at the Dumpster and crack his sick smile. The three seemed to be having a light conversation. Their body language indicating it was about to end. Dodd knew if I was hiding behind the Dumpster, I was trapped and, once he appeased the cops, he'd return to finish me.

I decided to give up and take my chances with the Clayton police. It might not go well, but it'd be better than a bullet between the eyes. I stood against the grimy Dumpster when a sudden noise to my right startled me. The back door nearest me rattled open. A kitchen worker smoking a cigarette and overloaded with garbage bags trudged with stooped shoulders toward the Dumpster. I sprinted past the kitchen worker toward the closing door as the diminutive Mexican worker called out, "Hey man, you can't go in there."

"Watch me," I said, barely catching the steel door before it closed.

While I ran, Dodd faced me, the only one who noticed me race through the door. The appalling smile returned. He seemed perfectly willing to resume his pursuit later, which frightened me even more. Maynard's men planned to handle this loose end on their own.

I sped through a maze of industrial dishwashers and ovens, tall stainless steel bread racks and various food supplies. I juked past the late-night, three-man cleaning crew, darted between tables stacked with inverted chairs, and ran out the front door without looking back. After turning a corner and running for blocks, I forced myself to slow to a walk. I found my bearings and took a circuitous route back to the nondescript Camry, avoiding the streets and business lights as best I could. I looked over my shoulder frequently for Mr. Dodd or a dark SUV.

Counterfeit

Back in the car, I felt the sting of blood in my eye and throbbing in my hand. I pulled thorns from my scalp and found a rag from the Camry's back seat to wrap the base of my thumb. The bullet had hit the fleshy area between my left thumb and index finger. The shot from the stairwell above must have missed my skull by inches.

I'll never ask, 'Where's a cop when you need one?' again. The cruiser had responded to my 911 cell phone call just in time.

Glad his men were probably searching the area for my red Solstice, I drove the Camry to an ATM and withdrew the maximum my bank allowed in a day. They'd be staking out my townhouse, so I couldn't go home. I knew not to check into a hotel with plastic because my location could be tracked the instant I used my cards. Soon enough they'll discover I used a credit card to rent the white Mustang. I had to get it back from my parents.

Who could I turn to? Tony and Baker would be under surveillance. I thought of the seven therapists in my practice, especially Marilyn, the one with the most seniority, but the connection was too obvious and I didn't want to put them in danger.

I had to find someone with no known connection to me. Many caring people in the city sympathetic to Lonnie's cause would gladly hide me on his behalf, but Lonnie's enemies also lived among them. Maynard and his team wanted me and that video. I had to trust someone and involve an innocent. The only idea I had was a crazy one.

I snuck in the back door to my parents' home like I'd occasionally done in high school, woke my startled parents, and returned their Camry for my rental Mustang GT. I borrowed all the cash they had. Mom gave me some bandages and Betadine and, God bless her, made me a sandwich. I told them not to worry even though I knew they would, and not to believe the news reports if my name was mentioned. I told them I was helping someone, and would explain everything soon. I apologized for the blood in their car. I said I loved them, hugged them longer than normal, and drove to Lambert's long-term airport parking. I parked the Mustang in a remote end of the lot, took a shuttle bus, and used cash to check into a nondescript motel near the airport.

I showered, soaked my bloody shirt and shorts with soapy water in the sink, and hung them to dry. I disinfected my wounds—my hand had stopped bleeding but would need stitches, and the burn on my back stung. I ordered room service steak and potatoes and washed down four more aspirin with two beers. I fell asleep with the television on, nothing on the news re-runs about me. In my dreams, Quinn's warm blood and brains kept splattering onto my face. Only this time the side of my face was missing and the cabin floor rose up to hit me. I heard Fallon's voice in the background saying, "you won't be able to talk your way out of this one."

MOUTH OF THE LION

I slept past noon until a car backfire startled me awake. I called Tony's cell from my drab and musty greenish brown hotel room on a prepaid cell phone. I ached in places I didn't know I had muscles and chewed more aspirin.

"Fuck me sideways, what hornet's nest from hell did you step on? Where are you? I hope you're holed up in Hitler's bunker somewhere planning to hibernate."

"What have you heard?"

"There's an APB out for your arrest. Judge Reinhold rubberstamped search warrants for your townhouse and office. You should've seen Marilyn when they arrived at the office this morning. She turned into a protective mama grizzly with your files. They arrested her for obstruction of justice. I went to post her bail and they put me in a room and grilled me. After all the chest thumping and posturing, they let us go but I'd bet money they're tailing me and listening in on my phone calls. They wouldn't say why they're looking for you. Judas Priest, they've interviewed your parents, canvassed your neighborhood, and knocked on every door in your subdivision. I used the spare key you gave me to your place and you won't like this—they turned everything inside out looking for something. Your computer's gone, your office files ransacked. They have a real hard on for you, Slick. Just like last year, only worse. What's going on?"

I worried about the flash drive taped to my bedroom ceiling fan and hoped they didn't know exactly what they were looking for. "The less you know the better. Hopefully we'll have a beer and laugh about it soon."

"Let me know what I can do. Don't get killed. I used to live vicariously through you, until last year. It looks like the old Mitch is back. Stay one step ahead of these bastards."

It was too late for room service breakfast, so I carb loaded with pasta, mashed potatoes, and bread. My clothes were still wet and wrinkled so I stayed put and turned on Channel Four.

I caught the tail end of a news flash announcing Maynard's eleventh-hour plan to run for the vacant Missouri senate seat. Mere mention of this caused several candidates to drop out and shift allegiances to the Golden Boy.

I called Baker's cell and got his voice mail again.

When in Rome … I dialed the one man who seemed to fit the bill. For the second time in a year, my life was in the hands of a moody, unpredictable, volatile personality with poor impulse-control.

When my clothes were dry enough, I bought a Hard Rock Cafe shirt and a Rams cap. We met at midnight in the bar of another nearby airport hotel. I chose a dark corner booth facing the entrance. This time I was the first one there when a stooped-over figure in a London Fog trench coat sat opposite me and removed his Fedora.

"Mr. Bread and Circuses. This had better be good," Milton Peebles said, a sour look on his face. "I drove a helluva long way and I'm not supposed to drive at night. You're lucky I'm an old man who can't sleep."

"I don't feel so lucky right now," I said, ordering him a Guinness.

I described Lonnie's execution, how he'd spent his share of the counterfeit money, and the run for my life from Dodd. I played my trump card, the video of Maynard with the hookers.

"I have duplicates, so if anything happens to me they will be sent to diverse people in the media, police, Treasury Department, and Secret Service."

Peebles took a long pull from his frosty mug. Sensing my anxiety, he said, "Relax, I'm not going to call the cops. Your entire story, while entertaining and not out of the realm of possibility, still hinges on whether your boy's bills can pass the scrutiny of an expert."

"You brought what I asked?"

He smiled. "You're going to be sorry."

I withdrew two crisp hundred-dollar bills from my wallet and placed them on the table in front of Peebles. "Let's do a double-blind test. I obtained one of these bills from my bank early this week and the other was made by Lonnie. You're the expert, you decide." I leaned back and sipped my diet Coke.

Peebles leaned closer and his eyes widened in anticipation, holding his breath briefly, like a lover awaiting a kiss or an addict his fix. He raised a bushy eyebrow as he reached deep into a coat pocket and withdrew a jeweler's loupe among other tools. He held both bills to the light, inspecting the watermarks and security strips, then scrutinized the fine lines of both Benjamin Franklin portraits. After he fished tiny colored vials from his coat pocket and subjected both bills to various chemical tests, he felt them, crumpled them, snapped the bills, tried to peel them apart, he studied the color of the ink on both bills and examined the detail on both backs.

His Guinness sat untouched for thirty minutes until he said, "These are both real. You've been conned."

Still? "You can't have it both ways, Peebles. Lonnie created one of these."

"He duped you into believing he created perfect duplicates because deep down something inside you wants to believe him. How do you know one of these is the dead Schwartze's handiwork?"

"Answer my question and I'll show you proof. Which is fake?"

"You've been conned," he said, looking at me like I was the one child left behind at school. "They're both the real deal."

"Pick one anyway, just for fun."

He frowned, studied the bills, still undecided. After a minute he picked one.

I pulled out part of the contents from the red envelope, photographs, and arranged them on the table between us. He used the loupe to compare what he now saw to the bills themselves. He went back and forth at least ten times, making odd grunting and clucking sounds.

He looked up at me, incredulous, shaking his head. "I'll be damned. The little Schwartze did it. I can't tell them apart." He leaned back in the booth. "I wish I could have shaken his hand and bought him a drink."

I pointed to the photos. "The first one is Lonnie and Earl standing in front of the printing press with a freshly printed thirty-two bill sheet of Benjamins. In the next one he's pointing to a serial number on a bill." I picked up the one Peebles thought was authentic. "*This* bill. The pictures were dated and timed, with a copy of that day's *Post-Dispatch* in the foreground as further proof. The others showed enhanced detail of the bill, still uncut, and surrounded by other bills of equal high quality.

He drained his mug. "I need another."

I flagged the waitress and ordered for us. "Why would Agent Winston go on record in front of millions and say the fakes were poor quality? Is he in bed with Maynard?"

"I have an idea about that," he said, sipping his next beer. "There were two practice sheets found at the scene, right? Imperfect ones?"

I nodded.

"If Winston only had access to bills from the two test sheets, that would explain it. Too much ink blurred the detail and made it appear lines are missing, darkening the bill's color. His critique is correct except for the black light. The Schwa—Lonnie's bill clearly glows light red, which means Winston is involved—unless he delegated some of the work."

"I talked to Winston. He did."

"Sloppy on his part. Just so you know, Maynard's goons will hunt and destroy you and that video, now that he's thrown his hat into the political ring. Power is a drug. He craves his next fix and it has to be larger than the one before."

"Lonnie said they removed all twenty-five mil from the basement the night before the arrest."

Nearly salivating, he held up Lonnie's bill and said, "If he made a quarter million of these beauties...."

"He gave away his six and a half million, which leaves eighteen mil give or take. I know who took at least some of the money the day the police murdered Benny, but I don't know where it is now or who has it."

He drained his second mug. "Let's say everything you claim about Maynard is true. You will never link him to Lonnie's death. How are you going to tarnish his silver spoon?"

I sat nursing my diet Coke, feeling helpless. "He knows the money's counterfeit and, even though the bills have passed inspection so far, he'll want to legitimize them, get the counterfeits into bank circulation so they can never be traced back to him. He told me at the party he anticipates every possible outcome in advance and eliminates them. He wants no doubt to remain about the money. He will launder the bills as soon as he can. "

Peebles leaned back and smiled. "There you go, you have the entire weekend until nine Monday morning to find the money and connect it to him.

"I can use the tape against him, threaten to go public. I could ruin his reputation if he runs for office."

For the first time tonight I heard the old man laugh. "He wants to avoid that, and

contacting him centers you in his cross hairs. If somehow you survived and went public with the tape, it would be a bump in the road, but it might not derail him."

"Are you kidding," I said, raising my voice. "This ruins Maynard."

His crooked grin held a smug swagger. "Listen to this advice from a hardened realist. His phalanx of spin doctors and media experts have already worked out multiple scenarios to deflect the blow, they will claim and create proof that you doctored the camera to satisfy your own need for attention, the hookers will conveniently disappear, his loving and doting family will stand by their man, his supporters will rally around him, and *he* will be portrayed as the victim while you will be subjected to a brutal smear campaign that rivals The Inquisition. You will be lucky if you're merely discredited. And here's the rub—his approval ratings may actually rise." He slapped the table to emphasize his point.

Talking with Peebles reminded me of being in psychoanalysis, of your core being probed with a cold blunt instrument, cracked open, and inspected for flaws. Peebles would have made a good teacher, if anyone survived the class. He spoke his mind, forced you to survey a situation from all angles, shared useful information, and delighted telling you when you were full of shit.

"I could see this happening a hundred years ago, or maybe when the Mafia wielded more influence, but these days—"

"Trust me, it's worse since Citizen's United. Look at the Peabody Coal decision here in town. Look at CEO salaries. Precious few uber-rich corporate leaders get there without breaking spines and crushing basic human rights along the way, and now the Supreme Court has ruled corporations are people. Money governs now, son. Not *We the People.*"

Peebles leaned back and hooked his thumbs under his black suspenders. "A few years back, a man ran for office and lost. He received forty percent of the votes. No big deal. Happens all the time, right? Before the election, a jury found him guilty of six-figure embezzling. Against his counsel's advice this convicted felon still ran, even though he couldn't take office if elected. He was a dead man running. Yet hundreds of thousands of voters pushed their asses out of their Barcaloungers on a cold rainy day and voted for him, solely because of his party affiliation. Stupid votes count the same as informed ones and stupid is influenced by spin. Spin is now backed by unlimited money. Let's just say Maynard could weather this storm and win."

"People should know the type of person Maynard is before they vote."

Peebles stared at me like I was that kid who missed the bus again. "They should also be able to point to the US on a world map, know the difference between the Declaration of Independence and the Constitution, and speak basic grammar correctly, but that's not as fun as watching reality TV, is it?"

He was right about one thing. I must de-personalize this, become calculating and cold. What move would he make next? That much money is heavy. He's got it. How can I link him to it?

"I think we're more alike than you care to admit, Mr. Peebles. I can be a cynical realist with the best of them while you sit here railing against the establishment with an energy and passion reserved for that of a closet idealist or an Occupy Wall Street member. You have a big axe to grind."

"Perhaps. Let me tell you something that might surprise you. In the year 2000, twenty-nine members of an elite band of 541 people were accused of spousal abuse, seven were arrested for fraud, nineteen accused of writing bad checks, an amazing 117 had bankrupted at least two businesses, three had been arrested for assault, eight for shoplifting, fourteen were arrested on drug-related charges and a staggering (no pun intended) 84 were stopped for drunk driving but all were released after claiming immunity. One guess what group this is."

"The United States Congress."

Peebles smacked his thin chapped lips together. "You're smarter than you look. Those numbers are from 2000 but they don't vary much from year to year. Congress *is* a crime wave, son. To think that they will pass sweeping healthcare reform or give a flying fart about the everyday working man and woman is akin to thinking Bill Clinton is a poster boy for monogamy. Maynard will fit right in."

Great. Will Peebles sell me out to Maynard next?

"So, you're saying if the system is broken, don't fix it?"

Peebles motioned to the bartender for another Guinness. "You have enough to do before Monday and I'm too damn old. If you want to die, keep leading with your emotions. You're tilting at windmills while Maynard's goons close their nets around you. If what you say is true, you may have a day or two before you end up alongside your counterfeiters."

I was betting my life on the word of a dead counterfeiter and a package that an unknown confederate sent me. I can't survive on the run much longer. Someone would silence me one way or another.

"Now that you know these bills are the real deal, I think you want to influence how this plays out. Give me someone I can turn to who'll offer protection during a fair investigation."

Peebles sipped his Guinness and wiped his dry, weathered lips on a dingy sleeve. The familiar brown foam clung to his white mustache as it had at Fast Eddie's. His nose twitched again and he stared at me for what seemed an eternity.

Raising Lonnie's bill to the light, he said, "Such craftsmanship. It takes a lot to impress me. Remember this, anyone can kill anyone. If Maynard wants you dead, he will have someone kill you and soon."

He took something small from his shirt pocket. My now-rumpled business card that I'd given him at Fast Eddie's. He quickly scribbled something on it.

"Some say that as a man ages, he becomes more conservative in his thinking and world view. I'm an exception. After my wife died, I felt sorry for myself and mad at the world. I got drunk one night, staggered out to my car, and passed out behind the wheel before I ever turned on the engine. A cop woke me and gave me a DWI because the keys were in the ignition. The cop showed no mercy and neither did the prosecutor. I didn't have congressional immunity to wave in their fat little piggy faces. That's why they kicked me off the Board. I've never told another soul that, except Betty when I visit her grave at Mount Carmel."

"They were wrong."

Peebles scoffed. "Right, wrong, what difference does it make? It's done. You bleeding hearts have an overinflated sense of social justice. You are right about one thing, though, I want to see how this plays out." He fondled Lonnie's bill and stared at it. "I can't believe what I'm holding. This is a real treasure. Hold on to it. For what it's worth, I hope they don't kill you."

"That's very bleeding heart of you."

He handed the card back to me. "Mark DeFrane is a straight arrow at the St. Louis branch
of the Secret Service. He'll listen and won't kowtow to Maynard, his daddy, or their attorneys. He took a bullet meant for Maynard, Sr. when he was president. Saved the old bastard's life. Maynard owes him, not the other way around. You convince DeFrane, and you just might make it through this. After your time in the spotlight last year, Maynard's team will twist everything and claim it's all about you. I bet you a real C-note. If he doesn't have you killed, his legal team will try to ruin you. Either way, he moves up the food chain to the senate."

I thought of Skinny's prophecy. One will be reviled.

"I'll take that bet," and we shook on it.

Counterfeit

Peebles rubbed his gnarled hands together and grinned. "I almost hope you stick it to The Man. Good luck Sonny Boy, you will need it."

I pocketed my card, thanked him, paid our tab, and left the bar. I wore the Rams cap low to cover my eyes and kept to the shadows on the walk back to my motel.

I'd convinced the ultimate skeptic that Lonnie's bills were dead ringers. Now I had to hope Peebles' eyes and mind were sharp enough and that Lonnie hadn't somehow conned us both.

I used the prepaid cell again before I went to bed that night. DeFrane was noncommittal about my claims, but wanted to meet. He promised nothing more. I confirmed what I now suspected, learned that 'The Big Top,' is code for the Secret Service. So who was their mole? That, among other things, kept me tossing the rest of the night. I may have to stick my head into the mouth of the lion tomorrow.

I WALK THE LINE

I checked out of my hotel room the next morning and drove Highway 70 downtown. I didn't notice the big black SUV following me until I was halfway to the city. I saw the plate number and knew. After changing speeds and lanes so many times I figured I'd get pulled over for reckless driving, it always returned in my rear view, maintaining a steady safe distance. It shadowed me all the way into downtown and mirrored every turn I made. Its tinted windows rendered the passengers invisible, but I had a pretty good idea. I fumbled for my regular cell and made a quick call. No need to use the prepaid. It was showdown time.

If only I knew—

When I stopped at a red light in the city, the SUV slammed hard into the rear of my car. My forehead struck the steering wheel, snapping my neck back violently. I saw stars and sparks. The force of the impact caused the trunk lid to fly open, instantly shielding the SUV from my vision in the rear-view mirror. I checked the side mirrors and saw no men with guns rushing toward me. I was disoriented, my vision fuzzy. The crunching shriek of metal on metal returned and for a second I thought I was diving deep in a submarine. I felt the world moving again and realized my rental was being pushed into the intersection by the heavier vehicle. I floored the brake pedal but the car moved inexorably forward. The smell of burning rubber and smoke filled the cabin. I threw my shoulder into the damaged door but it wouldn't open. To my right an eighteen-wheeler barreled down on me from the cross street doing at least forty. I sat directly in the truck's path now as it bore straight at me, its horn blaring at ear-splitting level. I floored the accelerator but nothing happened, my back bumper apparently entangled in the front grill of the

SUV. I rocked the car back and forth from reverse to forward, watching helplessly as the huge chrome grill of the eighteen-wheeler grew in size as it neared. Suddenly the Mustang tore free and I rocketed forward into the intersection against the red light. I was too late. The truck pulverized the right rear quarter panel and spun my car 270 degrees. Hubcaps rolled down the street and the side windows exploded, showering me with glass shards. I held on to the wheel, my head impacting the driver window so hard my ears rang. I fought to straighten the car, sideswiped a Yellow Cab and nearly blacked out. I regained control and steered away from the cars stopped behind the taxi as the driver cursed and shook his fist at me. I floored the pedal while the dark SUV remained blocked on the other side of the intersection by cars and trucks splayed in all directions. Behind me a distant siren began to wail.

The Mustang wobbled west on Market Street on two flat tires as fast as it could. Black smoke billowed from the engine and by the time I turned onto 10th Street I was running on rims and had no control of the rear wheel drive. The oil light winked on. The smoking car jumped a curb and crashed to a stop against a fire hydrant in front of the Thomas F. Eagleton US Courthouse building, home of the St. Louis branch of the Secret Service. The relentless black SUV sped toward me, its red dash light spinning and siren wailing. The cabin filled with smoke. I had to get out of there. I reached for my cell phone with the Maynard tape but it was gone. *Damn!* The crash must have knocked it off the passenger seat. A burning wire smell filled the air. I groped blindly with both hands, cutting them on glass shards until I finally found it wedged between the passenger seat and my briefcase.

I pulled it free and juked past an armed guard stationed outside. I sprinted up the two sets of five steps and ran toward the curved glass entrance. I lost all hope when I saw the line inside the lobby.

Beyond the oval main foyer stood four armed guards stationed at a security checkpoint near a walk-through metal detector, where all visitors stood waiting to be screened. The guards were already converging on the entrance; a short, thin one had his weapon drawn at his side while the dark SUV screeched to an abrupt stop alongside my smoking car.

I should have seen this coming. I'm running into a US courthouse like a lunatic. I'll be detained and Dodd, as head of Maynard's Secret Service detail, will arrest me. *I'd come so close.*

Then the strangest thing happened—

The thin man with the drawn gun opened the door for me, and I ran inside with my arms up, then placed my hands behind my head. I called out my name and that of DeFrane, ready to comply with orders to lay face down on the floor.

Instead he said, "Follow me."

We passed the checkpoint without going through the metal detector and jogged along beautiful, polished Terrazzo floors to the stainless-steel elevators. As the doors closed I saw Mr. Dodd and his partner, short and stocky with wing-nut ears, try to bully their way through the checkpoint only to be detained by three security men. The thin man quickly and thoroughly frisked me.

We rode in silence to the eleventh floor, which was nothing like the lobby. I followed the thin man down a narrow Spartan hallway with bare white walls and dark blue industrial carpeting. We made a quick left and a right to the end of the hallway. A simple wooden sign read US Secret Service next to a plain brown door. We entered a very small waiting area with a table and two chairs under a picture of President Obama and Janet Napolitano, the current Secretary of Homeland Security and head of the Secret Service. Behind a Plexiglas partition sat a smiling young secretary the thin man called Denise, who immediately buzzed us through the inner door.

The thin man knocked softly once on an office door and we walked in. He whispered to
the man behind the desk who raised an eyebrow and smirked.

"Thanks. Let them stew a little," he told the thin man, who left the room.

Mark DeFrane looked fit, in his early forties, with a closely cropped brown crew cut. He wore a button-down white shirt and red tie, his pressed suit coat hanging neatly on a rack behind his desk next to his gun in a speed holster. Across his desk sat an older, heavy-set man who looked vaguely familiar but I couldn't place him. The office was the polar opposite of Stan Winston's—no obligatory pictures on the wall of DeFrane schmoozing with politicians or plaques announcing commendations, and no visible flags, medals, or brass nameplates with bold, pithy sayings. The Spartan room contained DeFrane's desk, his chair, two visitor chairs, the coat rack, a file cabinet, and the latest computer and office equipment.

I hoped this was a good omen.

Mark DeFrane studied me but didn't say a word.

"I apologize for barging in like this, but two men out there want to kill me. The place will be crawling with Maynard's security people in seconds, demanding to arrest me. You have some difficult decisions to make and not a lot of time."

He considered what I'd said and turned to the older man. "George, would you mind if we continued our talk later."

The heavy-set man nodded, looked at me placidly for a moment like this happens every day, and left the room. I recognized George from Maynard's fundraiser. St. Louis is the epitome of a small, big town, with few degrees of separation.

I handed him my original cell phone and a lengthy hand-written statement from my pocket that detailed my relationship with Lonnie Washington, the conversation I'd overheard between Maynard and Fallon, the transmitter, Rachel Sanchez, agent Winston, and concluded with my suspicions about the duffel bags, their description, possible whereabouts, and destination. I omitted Debbie Macklin's name from my report.

"Help me find the money. I can prove it's counterfeit. It was last seen on a Channel Four news segment two days ago being hefted into the back of a black SUV by one of the men downstairs, Mr. Dodd, the same man who shot me and chased me from the Ritz-Carlton Hotel two nights ago," I said, raising my bandaged hand. I passed DeFrane another paper and said, "This is the license plate number of the SUV in the news segment. It's the same one downstairs that just now attempted to push me into the path of an oncoming truck about fifteen minutes ago that totaled my rental car. It's one of many vehicles currently leased by John Maynard, Jr."

I'd called Tony last night and he confirmed my suspicion that the plates were registered to Maynard.

Counterfeit

I waited patiently for DeFrane's response, when all his phone lines began beeping and blinking. From the commotion outside, I could tell Denise the secretary was under siege from Dodd and the man with the wing-nut ears.

He looked me over, his bright green eyes assessing me. He watched the video twice, he remained so calm and stoic I couldn't read him. At last he said, "When you called, I was certain you were a conspiracy nut. Then I did my homework and checked your background—you

stayed frosty with that psychopath last year and broke the university scandal. Impressive." He held up the phone and said, "You have my interest, Dr. Adams. What's your proof about the money?"

I told him. He still didn't show a reaction.

The commotion escalated to loud shouting and threats in the outer office.

He punched a button on his phone, listened a moment, then chuckled, "I owe you one. Send them in." He turned back to me. "This ought to be good. Roll with it."

The thin man entered first, followed by the two big men. The first was short and muscular, with no neck and a straight dark brown hair bowl cut so close the wing-nut ears were the first thing you noticed. His tie was too short and narrow for that thick body. The taller Mr. Dodd fixed his gaze on me. He still wore his reflective shades and said, "Special Agent DeFrane, there's an APB on this man and a warrant for his arrest. We'll take him off your hands."

"What's the charge?"

"Attempted assault on a high government official under Secret Service protection. After he's questioned, we'll decide whether to add blackmail and attempted murder to the list."

I started to say something but DeFrane shot me down with a look. "When did this alleged assault occur and who was the target?"

Dodd shrugged. "You know who I work for. The incident happened two nights ago." He pointed at me. "This man trespassed and stalked Mr. Maynard. We need to question him."

"Take off the damn shades, Nelson," DeFrane said, "We're not doing a remake of Cool Hand Luke here."

Dodd stood blocking the lone exit and what I saw when he removed his glasses startled

me. His heterochromic eyes—one bright blue iris the color of sky and one dark brown eye flecked with yellow—looked hungry, predatory.

DeFrane put his feet up on the edge of his desk. "Trespass, you say. How does this man trespass in a public hotel?" He scratched his crew cut in mock confusion.

Dodd didn't answer.

"Did you observe this man enter Maynard's hotel room without permission?"

Dodd turned to DeFrane and shook his head.

"Did this man knock on Maynard's hotel room door that night?"
Silence.

"Did this man gain unlawful entrance to another room?"
No answer.

"Did this man gain unauthorized access to Maynard's vehicle, luggage, or his personal belongings?"

Dodd shifted his weight, his frustration showing. "I'm taking him into custody. Now."

DeFrane clasped his hands behind his head and smiled. "There's no trespassing here, Nelson, and you know it."

"That's for a judge to decide. This man stalked Chief Maynard."

"How do you figure?"

"I saw him lurking outside the Prosecutor's hotel room late that night, taking unauthorized videos with his cell phone when Mr. Maynard opened his door. This man is a confidant to a dangerous criminal with an axe to grind against the prosecutor, and must
be questioned as to intent. Blackmail is a very real possibility here."

"I see your point," DeFrane said. "However, your dangerous criminal was murdered in a prison fight."

The look on his face said Dodd didn't know.

"Let me ask you this, Nelson. What do you have to say about the .38 slug we pulled out of a concrete stairwell earlier today at the Ritz-Carlton Clayton Hotel? This man claims you fired that bullet at him. While we're at it, what do you know about an attempted vehicular manslaughter not far from here twenty minutes ago? We have witnesses." He rose and extracted a set of handcuffs from behind his back. I was shocked at the thought that DeFrane was about to cuff Dodd. "If that slug matches your gun or we have a positive paint transfer from your SUV and his car, you'll be wearing these next, Nelson. This man has voluntarily turned himself in to me and, as you well know, I am the alpha dog here. I will handle him."

The wind seemed to go out of Dodd as he put his glasses back on. "You will hear from the chief prosecutor about this."

DeFrane surprised me again by ordering me to turn around. He pulled my arms behind my back and snapped the metal cuffs roughly on my wrists. What's next?

"I look forward to it, Nelson. I'm certain it will be entertaining. If I don't hear from him soon, I will be calling on him myself. Both of you, leave your weapons and keys to the SUV on my desk. I don't care if you left bricks of gold bullion on the front seat, do not return to that vehicle."

Dodd looked like he didn't know whether to shit or stand on one leg. He and his fireplug
partner reluctantly complied and left. DeFrane turned to the thin man and said, "Steve, have Frank impound the SUV and the wrecked white Mustang outside. Have the lab do a paint transfer test on the two vehicles, plus an inventory of both. Make sure the men downstairs escort Dodd and Evans from the premises." The others left. Dodd put the weapons in his desk and called Denise. "Could you bring us two coffees, please?"

"Make mine water."

"Scratch that, make it a coffee and bottled water," DeFrane said into the receiver.

He removed the cuffs and offered me a seat. She brought in our drinks and left without so much as a sideways glance at me for having brought the spooky Mr. Dodd exploding into her office space.

"Running me through that checkpoint before Dodd could get his hands on me probably saved my life. Thanks."

DeFrane blew on his coffee. "Most first-timers are unaware of the security. The next time that door opens, though, Maynard himself may walk through it with a court order and a busload of security and attorneys. I may have to arrest you for your own safety. Show me your evidence."

Afterward he asked, "You said you could identify the counterfeits. Where's your proof?"

I looked down at my shoes. "It's not with me. I hid it at home."

A doubting look came over DeFrane. "If this is true and I was Maynard, I'd hide the money and sit on it."

"That much cash is bulky and heavy. I have an idea what Maynard may do next, but I need your help. We need to act quickly because I think he's nervous and a bit desperate—he may rush into a big mistake."

DeFrane called Steve back in. "Grab Mike and take a drive," he said, giving him my address and key. "Take a close look at the ceiling fan in the bedroom. If there's still anything taped to one of the blades, bring it here. Watch your six, the place has been tossed." He turned to me and said, "Better hope it's there."

A TUM'S MOMENT

Maynard never walked into DeFrane's office the rest of that Sunday, nor did he call.

He did call the holding area to see if I was in jail.

DeFrane brought me home to his lovely wife Angie and their two sons instead of a jail cell. He talked into a secure phone most of the night, nursing a Bud, and making plans for the morning. Angie and I did the dishes and talked about where we went to high school (a St. Louis tradition because the city has seventy-nine separate neighborhoods, not counting the surrounding counties), the latest movies, raising their two teenagers who quickly vanished after dinner, and what it's like being the wife of a Secret Service agent shot defending a former president, and a social worker in private practice who was nearly killed by a madman. By the time she set up the guest room, DeFrane was finishing on the phone and it was midnight.

"Good as it's going to get on short notice. He could always be patient or walk into a new bank and we're screwed."

"I see him using a trusted inside man to clean the money. He's a latecomer to the senate race and wants to catch up. He hates being behind in anything."

"You better be right. I stuck my neck out for you. Our computer and banking men are working overtime. Hopefully we'll have a lead in the morning."

"He's got blood money on his hands. The longer he sits on it, the greater his risk. He knows they're fakes. What he doesn't know is they can be traced."

Counterfeit

In the morning Angie made us a western omelet with toast and orange juice. We left their home at seven and parked in a lot two blocks away from a city Bank of America location. We walked in a back door where DeFrane shook hands with Dominic Lucchesi, a lead agent at the Department of Justice. Lucchesi had no neck, broad shoulders, and a beard like a Norse god. His

wide nose looked like it'd been broken more than once, and I sensed mischief in those eyes that bordered on loosely controlled mayhem. His dark and swarthy complexion fit his carefree demeanor. He was a chatterbox who talked loud and fast, full of energy, life, bullshit, bravado, and opinions. They quickly set up operations, having called in key employees early to get acquainted with the staff and walk them through their roles.

Nine o'clock came and went uneventfully, business as usual for a Monday morning. No sign of Maynard or his staff. No heavy bags, unwieldy trunks, or wheelbarrows of hundred-dollar bills presented themselves for laundering.

Nine became ten, then eleven.

Lunchtime came and went while one of the men re-entered the back door with a boxful of great Italian takeout from Zia's and assorted subs from The Hill.

DeFrane periodically checked ancillary banks Maynard did business with. No activity there, either. We ate in silence while the bank employees continued to help the day's account holders. The later the day grew, the more eyes glanced my way with increasing uncertainty. I overheard DeFrane ask a superior for more time. The call didn't go well.

"I may have to put you in a holding cell tonight if nothing pans out today."

"Does that mean questioning from Maynard and his lawyers?"

He nodded. "Under my supervision."

My mood had plummeted from high alert to hopeful anticipation to questioning my logic to worrying that somehow he'd already laundered his blood money elsewhere to fearing I'd end up like Lonnie.

An hour before closing time, DeFrane was about to call off the mission when a late model black Lincoln Town Car cruised into the bank parking lot. A stranger emerged from the back seat, tall, middle-aged, and thin, with receding wiry hair and glasses. He entered the lobby, glided across the neutral carpeting to the empty teller lane with the long easy strides of a confident, purposeful professional. He wore a tailor-made dark blue three-piece suit and carried a small leather attaché case cuffed to his wrist. Much too small to hold millions, but what caught my eye was the handcuff running from his wrist to the case. *Showtime.*

Then another vehicle, a dark Escalade, cruised into the lot and parked. Two beefy men in sport coats and sunglasses got out, one stood at the rear of the vehicle while the other came inside. He borrowed a cart from the bank.

I tried to watch all three at once but couldn't. The tall, wiry man approached Alice O'Shay. The outside men hoisted two large silver-colored steamer trunks onto the cart. One of them I had never seen before, the other was the stocky man with the wing-nut ears.

Alice O'Shay, a teller in her thirties with long flowing red hair, a warm smile, and a voice that made me think of the Emerald Isle said, "Good afternoon, Mr. Snodgrass. What may I help you with this fine day?" She was a natural, acting like this was just another day.

The man did not return her welcoming smile. "I am here to see Mr. Finch." Snodgrass turned on his heels and walked toward the office of Bruce Finch without waiting to hear her say, "Certainly. I will tell him you're here, sir."

The two big men entered the lobby with the cart. They also made their way toward Finch's office.

Snodgrass opened the door to Bruce Finch's office without knocking, and the three men and cart quickly disappeared behind the closed door. An orchestrated, efficient entrance.

Finch, a senior loan account specialist, wore a rumpled white shirt, dark blue pants, and

yellow tie. His complexion was too blotchy to be considered ruddy, his belly hung out over his

too-tight brown belt, and a fine bead of sweat appeared on his brow. I'd never seen him before today, but he seemed nervous and self-conscious while he sat behind his oak desk. I hoped he wouldn't blow this all to pieces.

Without a word Snodgrass calmly unlocked his attaché case while Finch fidgeted with his water bottle. He shot furtive glances up at the wall behind where the three men sat opposite him.

Don't stare at the camera, Finch!

Snodgrass produced a thick stack of paperwork. "As you know, my client has a wide variety of interests and dealings on many fronts. Taking precedence over them now is the coming election. What you see before you is the first installment of financial contributions from his party constituents and supporters."

"Is it a mixed bag, checks and cash?" Finch said, wiping his brow.

"Cash today." Snodgrass handed the first set of papers to Finch. "I want the amounts listed here deposited directly into these numbered accounts."

Finch looked at the figures on the sheets and his eyes widened. "That's a lot of money. What about the SARs and CTRs?"

Snodgrass raised an eyebrow at this. "By all means, complete the usual paperwork. And I want to watch you do the deed. Same as before."

Finch busied himself completing a stack of applications that took fifteen minutes. Snodgrass sat calmly, occasionally sipping his bottled water. His first task completed, Finch tore the back NCR paper from each application, swiveled self-consciously and awkwardly in his chair, which emitted a loud creak, and shredded every bottom copy in full view of Snodgrass.

Snodgrass stared suspiciously at Finch. "You seem twitchier than normal today,
even for you."

Finch again wiped his brow. "I think I'm coming down with something. I feel sick to my stomach."

Snodgrass frowned and said, "We're on a tight schedule. Keep working."

Finch stared at him, frozen.

"We have more business," Snodgrass said, impatiently. "File the top forms correctly and let's proceed," he said with irritation growing in his voice.

Finch dutifully placed the top SAR and CTR forms in the correct folders to the attorney's satisfaction.

Counterfeit

Snodgrass laid a smaller stack of paperwork on Finch's desk. "Moving on, I wish to acquire the following bank accounts, credit cards, and loan agreements in my name on behalf of my client. Finally, I wish to establish the following corporations, trusts and partnerships as outlined in the pages here, all of which have been duly notarized by my client. As before."

Finch studied the forms for some time, chewing on his thin lower lip. Sweat stained the armpits of his shirt, he reached for his water glass again but he'd already emptied it. He looked in his desk drawer. "I'm sorry, but I've run out of contract forms. I'll be right back, gentlemen."

Finch left the room. Damn! The two young security men looked expectantly at Snodgrass, who looked at his platinum Rolex and shook his head. I thought I detected a growing sense of unease on the face of Maynard's senior lawyer.

Five minutes later Finch re-entered his office with a stack of forms in his shaky hands, a second bottled water, and a container of Tums. He sat down. "I'm concerned about the
size of some of the deposits into the offshore accounts. The paperwork seems a little incomplete. I'm not certain these will get past the manager without explicit written authorization by Mr. Maynard himself. I'm afraid I'm going to need his signature on some of these forms." Finch looked at Snodgrass like he expected a reprimand from the school principal.

The attorney in the three-thousand-dollar Armani suit said, "Don't go soft on us, Finch. You're paid extremely well for things like this."

For the first time, Finch stood his ground and lowered his voice. "I aware of that, sir, but if you wish to continue doing these transactions as free men, everything must be bulletproof." Then, in a more appeasing tone: "Your documentation is flawless, as always, Mr. Snodgrass. I assure you, it's just a formality, but before we may continue I must have Mr. Maynard's signature on these seven documents, since the offshore accounts are in his name. Seven John Henry's and he's on his way. I'll take care of the Medallion signature notaries and the rest, same as before."

Snodgrass assessed Finch for some time, his coal dark eyes trying to peer into the loan specialist's soul for a telltale clue, then said into his Bluetooth, "We need your signature on some forms." He listened for some time and said, "I advise we delay. Yes, I'm aware time is of the essence. No, I don't think it's right." He sighed and the call terminated. "He's coming in."

In the bank parking lot, Nelson Dodd stepped out of the Town Car and opened a back door for his boss, Maynard Junior, who adjusted his tie and smoothed his tailored suit. Dodd and Paul Fallon accompanied him inside. I saw no 100-watt smile until he entered the office of Bruce Finch and closed the door.

Maynard offered his hand. "Bruce, how's the wife and kids?" Not waiting for a
reply and with condescension in his voice he added, "Did I forget to dot an 'i' or cross a 't' again?" Big man in a hurry, talking down.

"An important oversight, sir, but an easy one to fix, and then you'll be on your way. We need your signature approving the amounts you wish to transfer to Bermuda and the Cayman Islands. With these signatures, the forms will sail past my boss's desk and I can do my magic act later." Then in a conspiratorial whisper he added, "So no questions are asked and everyone's happy. Best tax rate money can buy."

Maynard's smile beamed. "That's what I like about you, Bruce. Your strong American work ethic makes you an ever vigilant, and well-rewarded, silent partner."

Finch kept looking across the desk expectantly at the Montblanc pen in Maynard's hand, as if he were trying to will him to sign the forms and be done with it. His nerves shot, Finch was losing it. He wouldn't last much longer. Snodgrass sensed something was wrong and started to object but Maynard waved him off and began signing. I found myself Finch-like, biting my lip and leaning forward in anticipation.

As soon as Maynard signed the last form, the door flew open and DeFrane, Lucchesi, and six other DOJ agents burst into the room. Four had their weapons trained on the two security men with the cart and the other two took down Mr. Dodd. The three men were thoroughly searched and their concealed weapons confiscated. The coordinated, choreographed take-downs lasted a minute and a half.

"John Clayton Maynard, Jr., Paul David Fallon, William Franklin Snodgrass, and Nelson Stanley Dodd, you're all under arrest," DeFrane stated in a voice like he was announcing today's starting lineup.

"On what charge? Do you know who—" Maynard started to say, but Snodgrass shook his head and interrupted. "Don't say a word, Mr. Prosecutor. Let this man ruin his career if he wishes."

DeFrane finished reading the men their Miranda rights.

Lucchesi turned to Maynard and bellowed, "Mr. Prosecutor? Oh, I remember you now. I didn't recognize you without the silver spoon in your mouth. You ladies are under arrest for counterfeiting with intent to distribute and conspiracy to counterfeit." Flashing his best Italian grin, he added, "Two slimy shysters and a little big man with a board up his ass—you're going to be very popular in prison."

Maynard approached Lucchesi who stood his ground and beamed from ear to ear while two agents restrained the Chief Prosecutor. Snodgrass tried but failed to control his client.

Through it all, Fallon sat still and silent, like an alligator in the weeds.

Maynard spotted Bruce Finch, who by now was silently slinking toward the door clutching his Tums to his chest, and said, "Better run home and give your wife and kids one last kiss, Bruce."

DeFrane intervened. "You better stay up nights praying no harm ever comes to him or his family, Mr. Maynard. If it does, I will connect you to it and add it to your growing list of felonies."

Maynard protested, "Don't you know who I am? Besides, I didn't make that money—"

"John, SHUT UP NOW!" Snodgrass screamed. Then: "I told you not to trust the fat bastard!"

Fallon remained quiet as death, only his eyes moved.

Lucchesi seemed to derive special delight in reading these men their Miranda rights
a second time, which he delivered with the excessive flare and stage presence of a Shakespearean actor.

"Gentlemen, I prefer not to be handcuffed when you take us outside," Maynard said.

Lucchesi smiled. "And I want to be married to a young Sophia Loren. Guess that's the first in a long line of arguments you're going to lose, Counselor. Hands behind your back. And no damn sunglasses for any of you. That goes for you too, Incredible Hulk." He tore off Dodd's shades and for a split second appeared ill at ease when he noticed the man's rapacious eyes.

"You'll be writing traffic tickets along St. Louis Avenue or chasing smash and grabs near Jennings and West Florissant when this is over," Snodgrass threatened.

Lucchesi laughed. "I think you'll be the expert on moving violations in the joint, Brillo pad."

During the controlled police action, the few bank customers inside had been safely escorted into the parking lot, which was now filled with patrol cars. The cars in turn had drawn a sizable crowd of gawkers, growing by the minute. Everyone outside assumed the bank had been robbed and they'd have a surprise coming when the truth eventually came out that the criminals were actually caught trying to deposit money.

Life has its enjoyable little ironies every so often.

As agents DeFrane and Lucchesi prepared to lead the six men in custody to waiting squad cars, I stepped out of the bank manager's office next door that had served as command central. I watched and listened to the scenes play out on multiple hidden surveillance cameras, alongside uniformed officers ready to spring into action. Bruce Finch lay sprawled on a sofa with a wet towel draped over his forehead. He fanned himself and chewed Tums like they were Skittles.

I walked up to Dodd and said, "They don't want you. They want the big fish. Do yourself a favor. Cut a deal. Do that and I won't press charges."

His heterochromic eyes stared into mine and that sick, crooked grin appeared like a slice made by a knife blade. "Remember this, Adams, I will eventually be released."

It's a good thing he couldn't see the chill that now crept up my spine.

Through the clear double doors, I spotted a Channel Four news van rumble into the parking lot and screech to a stop near the police barricade. Debbie Macklin and a male crew member hoisting a portable TV camera hopped out and double-timed it to the lobby entrance.

I walked up to Maynard. "I heard you two missed hooking up the other night, so I invited Ms. Macklin to your coming-out party. Or perhaps now it's a going-away party?

"Once I knew the real man behind your public persona, the rest became relatively easy to figure out. Lonnie and the Secret Service helped obtain the proof. From behind bars, even after his murder, he was a step ahead of you. When I learned the 'Big Top' is code for the Secret Service, I knew you had a mole there. An underling of Winston's."

Recognition dawned in those icy blue eyes. "You ... you overheard us."

"Your career is in ruins in part because I had bad tacos for lunch the day you announced Lonnie's capture. Something else to blame on the Mexicans," I said. I held up my replacement phone and watched his eyes grow larger. "I know you and Dodd were concerned about my cell phone the other night. I want you to know that it's in safe hands."

I stepped back so Maynard was in my new phone's field of vision and took a picture of
him in handcuffs. He had that same faraway, dead look in his eyes that I first saw in Lonnie's
mug shot. "That's just how I want to remember you."

"You're no better than he was. I'll be out in a matter of hours once I clear up this little misunderstanding. You'd be wise to keep that in mind," he said, above the protestations of his wire-haired attorney to keep his mouth shut.

I smiled. "I had you pegged for a bully—you don't disappoint. It's good to keep a positive attitude, but my friend Lonnie was a brilliant, meticulous man. He was far more patient than you. He kept records of everything. You'll hear more about that at the trial."

Maynard's tanned face turned to white marble.

"Have a nice day, Mr. Maynard. Good luck with the election. After you settle in, I think you'll be a shoo-in for prisoner representative."

He took a step toward me and spoke in a hushed tone. "You think you've done something good here, perhaps even noble. You think you've stopped me. My cause will endure. I am a patriot. Unlike you, I love this country and will fight for her and the direction she must take. You've just weakened our country."

"Do you even believe that *Mr. Murphy*?"

In a face-saving gesture, he stood about to say more when Snodgrass yelled, "John, keep your damn mouth shut!"

Maynard stood his ground, fists balled, and stamped his feet.

Lucchesi stepped between us, chuckling to himself, and patted me on the back. "That's enough, Big Dog. You talk to him anymore and he'll be on suicide watch."

"Thanks for giving me a minute."

DeFrane and Lucchesi stayed behind to ensure the chain of evidence collection of the subpoenaed bank records and shredded items and to take Finch into custody as a material witness. The special agents called me into Finch's now vacant office and carefully opened the trunks.

"Show me the money," Lucchesi said, rubbing his meat-hook hands together, as the special agents raised both lids simultaneously.

Each contained a large duffel bag with the Green Bay Packer logo on the sides. Inside them were neatly banded stacks and stacks of Benjamin Franklins. It appeared every bill was the 1996 hundred dollar enlarged portrait variety. They looked like the real thing to my untrained eye.

When Lucchesi tried to lift one of the duffels from the large ornate silver trunk he grimaced, his wide face turned red from the effort and said, "Holy Magnolia, one strong MoFo must have toted these babies around."

"That would be Mr. Dodd," I said, remembering my terrifying night in the hotel and dark alley.

DeFrane turned to Lucchesi. "We have the serials of every counterfeit bill he and his crew made, thanks to Dr. Adams."

"That's a quarter of a million numbers, ace," Lucchesi said, looking at me skeptically.

"I can do the math," I said. "The flash drive has more than enough space to contain the randomly generated numbers. So if this passes inspection from the experts—"

"The Golden Boy and his minions will face the charge of intent to distribute counterfeit money, same as counterfeiting. That carries the same penalties Lonnie Washington faced,"
DeFrane said.

"Maynard planned to use the forgeries to help finance his senate run, even though he was worth millions."

"Why the hell would Richie Rich risk it all if he had his own money?" Lucchesi asked.

I smiled. "As they say, you can never be too thin or too rich."

291

BOOK THREE: FINDING THE WAY

In a gentle way, you can shake the world.
Mohandas Gandhi

IMMORTALITY WITHIN REACH

DeFrane's late-night phone calls set in motion a frenzied dash the weekend before the banks opened Monday. DeFrane had enlisted the help of his DOJ friend Dom Lucchesi to investigate Maynard's bank history and patterns. A team of experts in white-collar methods of money laundering intensely scrutinized Maynard's business dealings. They discovered possible past improprieties with Bruce Finch acting as go-between every time. They struck pay dirt when they questioned the excitable Mr. Finch at his home late Sunday. Armed with insider knowledge, it was a matter of exerting the right type of pressure on Finch to testify in exchange for immunity from prosecution and the chance for a fresh start. His nerves and bad acting had nearly compromised the undercover operation, but Maynard's greed caused him to ignore his attorney's recommendation. I hoped he'd come to regret it.

I went home after I helped Finch hyperventilate into a paper bag to alleviate his panic attack. A tiny manila package waited for me in today's mail. Inside it was a storage key and a note which read:

Dear Mitchell,

This is another posthumous letter I'd hoped to avoid. When time allows, go to the Glover Storage facility off south Kingshighway. The items in Unit #10 are my hobby, my personal treasures. I promise there is nothing illegal or stolen within. I decided to store them here when we entered the production phase, in the event of my arrest. I didn't want them falling into unfriendly hands.

They are yours to keep or give away as you see fit. My only request is that they be given away—not sold—to people who will appreciate them. The space is climate controlled and in order to empty unit #10 in one trip you will need a small truck and the help of a discreet friend. Once done, please close my Glover account number listed below and you will receive a refund for the remainder of the year's rental fee. Use the balance for your trouble as you see fit.

    Account #2694746.

LW

    P.S. I wish I possessed your talent with people.

    P.P.S. I was rejected for restorer technician as well. You will understand when you visit #10.

Tony Martin, my former mentor and supervisor at River City State Psychiatric Hospital, owns a truck and offered to help.

We met at Glover Storage late one sunny afternoon. It was an old, sprawling one-level storage facility like many in the area, with rows and rows of units painted basic orange and brown behind rusting metal bars.

When I pulled up the heavy tri-hinged metal door to Unit #10, it rattled in its aluminum track with a rumble like rolling thunder or the groan of an angry god. The first thing I saw was DaVinci's 'Mona Lisa' and her subtle smile. She smirked and laughed at me from an old easel. I wondered how Lonnie could have pilfered it from The Louvre. Past tiny and inscrutable Mona, I saw DaVinci's 'Last Supper,' Monet's 'Water Lilies' and 'The Lily Pond,' Van Gogh's 'Starry Night,' Vermeer's 'Girl with a Pearl Earring,' Rembrandt's 'Blue Boy,' Michelangelo's 'Creation of Adam,' Degas' 'Letoile,' and Goya's 'Nude Maja.' We walked through the private art gallery in silent awe until Tony emitted a low whistle. "Are you seeing this too, or am I imagining it?"

I picked up a smaller version of Botticelli's 'The Birth of Venus' and turned it around. The initials LW had been brushed on the back in the most elaborate calligraphy.

At the back of the storage unit, Tony said, "Your guy had a sense of humor. Look at this one." With a devilish smirk he held up a frame for my inspection.

I saw a large red and black dollar sign splashed on a beige background and behind Tony, one with columns of duplicate green one-hundred-dollar bills perfectly stacked on top of one another in a two-dimensional frame. "A couple knockoffs of Andy Warhol's 'Money,'" Tony said.

I couldn't suppress a sad smile. "He's right, there's nothing illegal here. He created these in his free time."

"Such a talented little felon."

I silently nodded agreement.

"What a waste," Tony said, shaking his head. "He could have used his gifts for good."

He tried. He'd applied for work as an art technician who restores invaluable works of art that have begun to fade due to the ravages of time. Rejected again, he couldn't escape his past to help keep masterpieces immortal.

"I think he changed his little part of the world the best way he could."

Tony stared at me like I'd sprouted a second head.

I couldn't explain everything to him yet, for Maynard's fate was far from sealed and he still possessed many powerful and intricate ties with the police. "A lot of doors closed on him. After the truth comes out, I'll explain it all to you over a couple beers."

Counterfeit

"At the risk of sounding like a racist, did Lonnie help only black people?" he asked, thumbing through a cabinet that contained hundreds of sketches and lithographs wrapped in plastic.

I examined a duplicate self-portrait of Leonardo DaVinci. "Since Maynard's arrest, I've spent time piecing together Lonnie's story. A couple weeks ago, I met a lady who'd taken in her infant granddaughter because the mother's a crack junkie who tried to sell her baby on the street for drugs. Grandma has her own health and financial problems, but couldn't bear the thought of her grandbaby with strangers in foster care. A few days later I met a man who runs after-school programs for underprivileged teens in the city whose ministry was being forced to close its doors due to lack of funding. Both received eleventh-hour financial aid, accompanied by a mysterious letter from an LW thanking them for their selfless deeds. Both are whiter than Wonder Bread, and there are more. LW was color blind. He didn't care about anyone's ethnicity, sexual orientation, or age. All he saw, those he helped, were people in need who spent their lives helping others. But once word started getting out, especially in his own neighborhood, he made more than his share of enemies. I met a few of them who wanted start-up capital for bars, escort services, pawn shops, or cash advance loan stores. He turned every one of them down because, for Lonnie, it wasn't where you came from or who you were, it was what you did and what you lived for."

He held up a brightly colored oil and pastel on thick cardboard. "Damn, this looks just like 'The Scream' by Munch." Still gazing at Lonnie's handiwork, he ruminated, "We've both worked with criminals who occasionally toss money into church poor boxes to help relieve their inner guilt over stealing. Was he one of them?"

"I don't think so. There was a lot more to him." A modern-day Robin Hood comes to mind again. His philanthropy could have made him an intriguing figurehead for the Occupy Wall Street movement if he'd had a political bone in his body. But he shunned the limelight like a blind mole. "The fact is unique, extraordinary people come along, grace the rest of us with their presence, and then are gone." I thought of Kris, whose smiling face flashed before me. "Like shooting stars, sometimes we enjoy them before their light goes out, sometimes after."

Tony eyed another painting. "Hey, could I have this Vermeer for Cindy? She loved that movie about the girl with the pearl earring. We watched it together a lot. She lusts over Colin Firth and you know I have a thing for Scarlett Johansson."

His wife Cindy followed her favorite actors with a groupie-like zeal unusual for someone in her mid-forties.

"As long as she'll appreciate it," I said, with a sudden air of propriety. He turned to look at me, and I felt my cheeks flush. "Which I know she will."

We carefully loaded Tony's truck. While he completed the final rope ties, I walked to the manager's office. It was a stale smelling room made of cinder block walls painted mauve and a water-stained drop ceiling that reminded me of the visiting room at Gateway jail. A morbidly obese black man with mutton chop sideburns looked up and scowled when I walked through the door. He returned his attention to the baseball game on a tiny black-and-white television perched precariously on a warped plywood desk. He fiddled with the rabbit ears on the old TV and made no move to acknowledge my presence.

"I'm here to close the account for unit number ten," I said, dropping Lonnie's keys on the grimy pockmarked counter.

The man's ears perked up at mention of the unit number. He turned off the set, his sullen indifference now sudden attentiveness. He stood up, wiped his hands on his shirt, and said in a soft, high-pitched voice, "I.D., please."

I showed him my driver's license.

"Uh-huh," he said, his droopy hound dog eyes carefully comparing the picture to my face like a wary passport inspector. "I have your refund here. You can be on your way in a minute, Mr. Adams."

"How can that be? I didn't rent the storage unit."

"That doesn't matter," the corpulent man said as he lumbered to a gray metal filing cabinet. He bent to the lowest shelf, wheezing from the exertion. He pulled out a manila folder and wrote a check for over three hundred dollars.

"This is already made out in my name. How did you know I would be coming here?"

"Somebody called ahead, said to be expecting you within the month and for me to cut the check." More wheezing, heavier this time. I noticed an inhaler next to the television.

"Was it Michael Anthony?"

His face was calm but I thought I saw those muddy eyes briefly widen at mention of the name. "I can't say, sir."

"You know who Lonnie Washington is, don't you?"

"Everyone knows him. He's been on the news for weeks. That the most I can say. Have a blessed day."

I noticed his name badge and decided to take a shot in the dark. "Mr. Anthony sure has a sweet, silky voice. A most pleasing accent reminiscent of tropical islands. What do you think she looks like, Reggie?"

For an instant Reggie stopped in his tracks, then suddenly grabbed the inhaler and

waddled through an arched doorway marked "FOR EMPLOYEES ONLY." It barely accommodated his girth, and the red plastic beads hanging in the narrow archway rattled against each other like hollow bones in his wide wake. He did not return. As I left I thought I saw those same sad, hangdog eyes peer at me through the lengthening shadows past the dirty window pane.

While I walked to the truck, I wondered if Reggie was placing a call to Michael Anthony.

IF IT BLEEDS

The next day, life took another bizarre turn.

All the stations had reporters yesterday at the federal grand jury when the Assistant US Attorney prepped the jurors that the law had been violated. The AUSA read the counts of the indictment and witnesses, like me, described the facts. There was no cross-examination because there was no established defendant or defense. The jurors asked questions when they needed clarification. After all the testimony was given, the jurors voted on the spot for an indictment and an arrest warrant was issued and signed by the judge.

Debbie Macklin called my cell sixteen times while Tony and I finished storing Lonnie's artwork in my lower level of my townhouse. While we enjoyed a beer, she left three more messages, each more desperate than the last. I also had multiple land line messages from representatives at Channels Two, Five, and Eleven.

Once Tony went home to give Cindy the Vermeer, I had mercy and called Debbie. She asked the obvious questions and I said, "Okay, but I won't be there early. Ten o'clock. I'm sleeping in."

At half-past ten, she tapped her foot and anxiously looked at her watch while I sat for the makeup artist.

"Today is a sit-down interview," she said in the doorway before she turned and walked to the set where hair and makeup made last second adjustments.

"I'm not talking about Maynard," I called out to her wake.

The young woman patting my face had perfect skin and metal posts in her eyebrows. She looked in Deb's direction then back at me and said, "Good luck with that." Her tone said it all, like I'm going to need it.

When I walked to the set, Deb was fiddling with items on the table between our chairs and reviewed her notes while she settled. The crew and director waited for me to take me the chair next to her. When I did, she straightened her posture, pasted on her television smile, and faced the lens as the red light winked on.

"It is my great pleasure to welcome back Dr. Mitchell Adams, a Clayton-based Ph.D. social worker in private practice, to the team at Channel Four. Dr. Adams has served the community as a professional consultant on numerous occasions covering a broad spectrum of special interest topics. Tonight, we ask for his insights about the David and Goliath relationship between a disabled local counterfeiter and chief prosecutor John Maynard, who was indicted by a federal grand jury yesterday on the same charge of counterfeiting.

"In a dramatic man-bites-dog story, an arrest warrant was issued and signed by Judge Reinholt for John Maynard, Jr. The Chief Prosecutor had been waging a successful war on crime in the city and weeks ago had announced his plan to run for the senate. He instantly became the frontrunner after defining himself as a tough, law-and-order candidate with a spotless record and perfect conviction rate. In the light of these stunning new events, Mr. Maynard now finds himself in a legal hot seat of epic proportions. What can you tell our viewers about the unlikely connection between these two vastly different men, Dr. Adams?"

I saw the camera lens swing my way from the corner of my eye. "I want to preface everything I'm about to say with a caveat: John Maynard is innocent until proven guilty in a court of law. He has not had his trial by jury, nor a chance to answer the charges levied against him. Your question forces me to speculate."

She leaned forward in anticipation. "By all means, our viewers are eager to hear your opinions about these two men."

"The jurors voted by a majority for a True Bill on the indictment. The Assistant US Attorney asked for the indictment to be sealed by the judge to prevent the facts from being released before trial."

I watched her mood sink. "Why was this done?"

"Because the information is sensitive. Other suspects remain under investigation and witnesses could be in danger if their names are released."

Like yours truly. As a witness, my name was recorded as Mitch A. It didn't take long for you and a host of others to ring my phone off the hook, did it?

"What insights can you share with the viewers about John Maynard?"

"Plenty, but this is not the time or forum. Too much happened to risk a tainted jury pool that could result in a change of venue. I'm sorry, but you'll have to be patient and wait for Judge Reinholt to lift the indictment seal, once all the suspects have been identified, indicted, and arrested."

Mark DeFrane had completed his investigation and turned it over to the AUSA for Judicial Action, but before he left he predicted the media would swoop down on me like a flock of gulls attacking Tippi Hendron's character in *The Birds* once they knew I was on the witness list.

She passed a note that read: Help! Toss me a bone. Something, anything!

"So, if Mr. Maynard is proven guilty of counterfeiting, why do you think he chose the path he took?" She almost grimaced.

"Let me tell you the true story of another chief prosecutor. Right here in St. Louis, in the 1980s. He was a ruthless, 49-year-old, law-and-order prosecutor who launched a city-wide campaign to crackdown on prostitution and pornography, closing down porn and video stores. In June of 1991, he endorsed jail time for all prostitutes, pimps, and customers who were second time offenders. For fifteen years he held office until he was arrested, and admitted to, soliciting sex from an undercover policewoman. It was proven he'd spent at least twelve thousand dollars of city tax-payer money over the years on prostitutes. Investigators were likely to have connected him to another hundred thousand dollars of misappropriated city money had he not burned those records first. He'd become such a bold and regular john he sometimes used his real name with pimps and madams. Other times he used the alias Larry Johnson."

She looked puzzled. "So, this prosecutor in 1991—

"Your older viewers will remember his name."

I handed her note back, with the words: "Interview me about him."

"He was a little before my time," she said, smiling for the camera and shooting me a look.

"Mine too. That's what *Post-Dispatch* archives are for."

"If this man was such a tough law-and-order prosecutor who cracked down on prostitutes, why would he be a frequent john and steal from the city to fund his sexual … appetite?"

"The psychological term for this is reaction formation. It's a primitive defense mechanism some people resort to when faced with anxiety-causing or unacceptable emotions and impulses. Someone using this primitive defense mechanism is having intense psychic conflict. They're struggling against strong instinctive reactions and trying to control these unacceptable emotions or impulses by exaggerating the exact opposite feeling. However, the original rejected impulse does not simply vanish. They linger in the unconscious, in their original infantile form. That's why, when he was caught with a prostitute in a police sting in an airport hotel, he was dumbstruck that the media made a connection between his actions and his tough, law-and-order stance against prostitution. I've treated a number of clients who struggle with similar internal turmoil."

She tugged at the hem of her skirt and settled into her chair as if we were in for a long discussion. "So, if someone protests too much about something, they may be actually in favor of what they're protesting against?'

I nodded. "It's possible. The strong antisocial impulses may drive a person to become active in a crusade against vice, crime, and prostitution. The inhibited desire constantly attempts to resurface and sometimes the impulses win out, like when an alcoholic or smoker relapses."

She seemed to be playing along now. "What happened to this man?"

"He was forced to resign amid scandal. He relocated to another state."

"Can you share other examples of reaction formation with us, Dr. Adams?"

"Certainly, reaction formation is one of the most difficult defenses for lay people to understand, in part because of its effectiveness and flexibility as a disguise. There's the well-known Stockholm Syndrome in which a hostage or kidnap victims 'fall in love' with the kidnappers who hold complete power over them, the most famous example being the heiress Patty Hearst. More recently, several well-known preachers and politicians pontificating excessively emotional and moral hard-line stances against homosexuality were later outed as closet gays. The inner conflict eventually comes out.

She nodded, eyed the camera, and said, "Fascinating examples, Dr. Adams. You said earlier that reaction formation is a primitive defense mechanism. Why is it called primitive?"

"Primitive defense mechanisms are usually effective only in the short-term and are typically learned as young children."

"What's another example of a reaction formation that a child would employ?"

Where's she going with this? "I imagine that when you were in grade school, at that age when kids start to become attracted to the opposite sex, there was probably a boy who went out of his way to show everyone in class, especially his closest friends, that he didn't like you at all. Am I right?

She smiled and briefly blushed for the camera. "One or two leap to mind."

"And how did those boys really feel about you?"

"Just the opposite," Debbie said and modestly looked down briefly at her lap for the camera before she continued. "If reaction formation is so effective and flexible, why doesn't it work for long?"

"The inner conflict ultimately breaches the surface, as in the case of the former prosecutor. Most defense mechanisms are unconscious; we don't realize we're using them in the moment. Therapy can help a person identify the defense mechanisms they're using, understand why they don't work, and learn how to use healthier ones in the future."

"I see. Can you give us examples of other primitive defense mechanisms?"

Why the psych 101? I know this will be edited, but what's her angle?

"Ones we've all probably heard before are denial, acting out, and regression. Denial is used to avoid dealing with painful feelings or problems, such as alcohol and drug abuse. A classic example of acting out is a temper tantrum, when one is unable to express feelings verbally and resorts to physical expressions. In regression, one reverts to an earlier stage of development when faced with unacceptable thoughts or impulses, such as when an adolescent overwhelmed with fear becomes clingy and wets the bed."

She gave me a brief wink with the eye not in sight of the camera. She leaned forward and continued. "So, if the charges filed against John Maynard are proved true, he tried to hide his antisocial impulses the best way he knew how, by going overboard to the other extreme and leading a crusade against prostitution and crime, but eventually his antisocial impulses won the internal battle and revealed his true nature."

"I wasn't talking about Mr. Maynard. I cannot comment on his pending trial other than to say he is innocent until proven guilty in a court of law. You're drawing your own conclusions about Mr. Maynard."

She shifted her nominal weight in the chair again and narrowed her eyes. "What can you tell our viewers about your harrowing ordeal of the last few days?"

"I don't know what you're referring to. I had some car problems."

"My sources tell Channel Four you were chased at gunpoint by one of Maynard's security men. That he shot you because you held incriminating evidence against the Chief Prosecutor. I see your hand is bandaged."

I held her gaze. "Then interview your sources instead of me."

"Other sources say an All-Points Bulletin went out for your immediate arrest because you were suspected of being a direct threat to Mr. Maynard. That your home and business were searched and placed under twenty-four-hour surveillance."

I simply stared at her, thinking the dead silence would end the filming, worse than merely a no comment.

"An unnamed source also said Mr. Maynard's men allegedly tried to run you off the road while you tried to seek sanctuary at the local Secret Service office. That the Department of Justice found discrepancies in Mr. Maynard's diverse financial holdings, including illegally established dummy corporations when he attempted to legitimize the stolen counterfeit money."   I stared at her in silence until the red camera light went out.

She noticed it and said, "No, keep rolling!"

She turned back to me. "John Maynard is already a wealthy man. Why would he risk his freedom, his family, and a possible run at the White House for six million dollars?"

"I was talking about the former prosecutor. If you don't like my answer, I suggest you interview Mr. Maynard. Or interview your sources."

Her attention briefly switched to her Bluetooth. Then she turned to the camera.

"We have breaking news. There are numerous reports now coming in from citizens disputing the initial accounts of the responding officers at the scene of Benny Blade's tragic death at the zoo. No witnesses have stepped forward to confirm that Mr. Blades fired a gun or even brandished one in that tense standoff. No one saw a bomb, but one witness watching from a hill with binoculars saw a leather briefcase filled with money fly open at Big Cat Country. The Medical Examiner's initial report is now available. It indicates Mr. Blades was center shot five times in the chest and died instantly before falling into the tiger pit."

I hope that's true, for Benny's sake.

She turned back to me and whispered, "You promised me an exclusive."

I thought about it.

She looked at me and said softly, "Please."

"Roll the damn camera," I said. "We now arrive at the most extraordinary and unexpected part of the Lonnie Washington story, his motivation. From the beginning, the answer seemed obvious to everyone, me included—plain and simple greed, getting something for nothing—but we were wrong. Lonnie Washington *did* greatly benefit from his counterfeit money, but not as you think. He derived immense satisfaction and joy from giving away every dollar he created to people in need.

"He helped good people who found themselves in bad situations through no fault of their own. He helped kids, caregivers, the elderly, the poor, and people of all races. Lonnie Washington gave away all his millions."

She sat with her mouth open, until a staffer caught her attention by making a circular motion with his hand that we were still filming. She cleared her throat. "This is an incredible story, Dr. Adams. Has your life returned to normal yet?"

"This is not about me. It's about Lonnie Washington, Earl Mooney, Benny Blades, and Tyrone Sparks."

"Sources indicate your car was vandalized and rocks were thrown through your home windows. You received hate mail and death threats from Maynard's political supporters, prompting the Secret Service to provide twenty-four-hour protection. Critics are attacking you in the media. They claim you've initiated your own personal witch hunt and fabricated evidence to damage the popular prosecutor's election bid. His PR people are labeling you a hater and calling for jail time once Mr. Maynard is vindicated. What is your response, Dr. Adams?"

I smiled. "I will not debase the story of Lonnie Washington's life by lowering it into the political arena. Two non-violent men are dead for a crime that doesn't carry the death penalty."

She turned to me. "Thank you for your insights, Dr. Adams. I'm sure there will be many legal twists and turns to this case in the coming months."

Then she quickly swung back to the camera lens. "Channel Four viewers will surely remember Dr. Adams from a year ago when he narrowly survived a harrowing standoff with a deranged client who had brutally murdered his girlfriend. Armed only with his quick wits and professional training, Dr. Adams was able to talk the psychopath down and simultaneously

break the infamous Gateway University scandal." She turned to me again. "Are there any similarities between the two cases, Dr. Adams?"

Counterfeit

We'd come full circle. *Kris was right, if it bleeds, it leads.* I should have expected the sucker punch at the end.

I removed the tiny black microphone a makeup artist had pinned to my lapel earlier and walked from the station without another word. From behind I heard Debbie whisper, "Thank you," and, "I'm sorry," in the same breath. I didn't stop or look back.

THICKER THAN WATER

I drove to a nondescript, mid-sized apartment complex not far from the Gateway University campus and rang the bell for apartment 1-A. The front door looked brand new. A few wood shavings littered the threshold and I smelled fresh paint. A tall, attractive black woman in her late thirties opened the door. She had high cheek bones and wore a red kerchief that held her straightened hair from her face. At first she looked happy to see me again, but it seemed I was either calling at a bad time or she wasn't really happy to see me. She hugged me on the front porch and said in a sultry West Indian accent, "Mitch, what a pleasant surprise! I just saw that blonde swizzle-stick grill you on the news. She was out of line, but you did your usual great job. JoJo's not here. Was he supposed to meet you?"

I'd seen no black '95 Cadillac Fleetwood on either side of the street when I arrived tonight, but that was my hope.

"No, I'm here to talk with Mr. Anthony. You've been very busy these days."

Simone tensed and her first eye movement was to the door, as if she wanted to close it. She bit her lower lip. "You know just me and JoJo live here, Mitch."

"Normally that's true, but these are trying times. I think the two of you have taken a ghost writer into your home. May I come in?"

She stepped aside. "Of course, where are my manners? May I get you something to drink?"

"Whatever you're having is fine," I said, knowing she drank water with lemon.

Counterfeit

She offered me a seat in the living room. She handed me a
sweaty glass and folded her
arms across her chest. She waited in this defensive posture, an anxious
smile on her face, not wanting to make eye contact but willing herself to
look at me.

"In my line of work I observe people. What they say and what
they don't say. I develop a feel for their thought patterns, what they
value, and who is important to them. Nothing much fazes JoJo—the
toughest bad guys or the most clueless brass. When I've seen emotion
from him, he's in protection mode, keeping someone he cares about safe,
or fighting to right a wrong. I know he would die for you. I think he
would have died for Lonnie, too. That's what didn't add up. He said he
knew Lonnie years ago in school. Later I saw the fire in his eyes when
he spoke about Lonnie when we rode in his car. I heard his voice break
with emotion when we sat outside the morgue and drank toasts to Lonnie.
I sensed palpable rage when he spoke about his murderer. There's more
history between them."

"What would that be, Cool Breeze?" Baker said, his six foot-
four-inch frame filling the doorway. He stared at me from behind dark
shades.

Simone arched her back like a frightened cat. "He knows."

He ignored her and waited for my reply.

"Blood's thicker than water, big man."

He didn't move a muscle.

I thought back to the very beginning. *There's a little brother in
city lockup.*

"We both know the most effective lies are mixed with truth. The
'little brother' phrase was a clever misdirection on your part—it's how

you talk. I believed your story that you were his childhood protector, why wouldn't I? However, over time the intensity of your emotions outstripped that relationship. Lonnie is your younger half-brother. My guess is you share the same biological father."

Stunned, Simone said, "Sweet Jesus in a manger," and fanned her narrow face with an *O Magazine.*

He remained imposing and silent as a sheer black rock wall.

I climbed out farther on my limb. "And the father you two share is Earl Mooney."

Wild-eyed, Simone crossed herself and kept repeating, "O my God, I am heartily sorry for having offended Thee and I detest all my sins!"

"You think you know all that, Cool Breeze," he said, the same black and impassive wall of muscle looming before me.

I nodded. "I'll tell you why. Little things I heard and observed when I first met Skinny that didn't quite add up when I thought about them later: Skinny and Earl's separation the year before Lonnie's birth, precipitated by a transgression on Earl's part; Shirley and Tyra's reaction when I asked about a father figure in Lonnie's life; and Earl fainting during Lonnie's birth wasn't from the sight of blood since he'd worked as a butcher, rather it was from the sudden shock and surreal sight of watching his common-law wife deliver his baby by a younger woman seven months after a one-night stand." I smiled. "I wouldn't have wanted to be in Earl's shoes the day Skinny found out."

Simone wanted to speak but Baker shook his head.

"You staring at me like you Nostradamus ain't going to make my tongue wag," he said.

Counterfeit

"I haven't had the pleasure of meeting your father, but I enjoyed meeting your mother, JoJo. She's a strong, assertive woman."

I thought I sensed a faint weakening in his impassable façade.

"Skinny and Earl raised you well. Her crusty shell always softened at mention of your name. She once bragged she could put you over her knee any time she wanted. There's a special bond between you, a mother-son bond."

Simone locked her eyes on JoJo, waiting for direction that never came.

I forged ahead. "You're silent because if this ever gets out, you might not be able to help Lonnie complete his life's work. He and you two created the alter ego of Mr. Anthony. You work in tandem taking turns in the role. It was you, JoJo, who called the guard in Virginia and sent her those six annuities. Lonnie may have called her once from jail because he was concerned about her injuries. You probably called in a favor with a DC connection for Rachel Sanchez's new security job while Simone orchestrated the storage facility arrangement and penned those beautifully written letters. The night we toasted Lonnie, LeMaster must have learned you had a personal relationship with Lonnie to suspend you. You put up so little fight because it was true. I hope it doesn't jeopardize your career because you're one hell of a detective."

I looked at him. He didn't move a muscle.

Simone looked like her brown oval eyes were about to pop out of their sockets and roll across the hardwood floor while the standoff continued.

I turned to her. "There's no need to recite acts of contrition. What you're doing is a noble task. You've assumed a huge responsibility at great personal risk—insuring Lonnie's legacy lives on after his murder and, from what I've witnessed, you're doing a great job. No one else needs to know about Mr. Anthony. The right thing to do is get the rest of the money to the people he chose."

She exhaled, seemingly for the first time in five minutes. She turned to speak to me but Baker waved her off again. "Baby, there's a time and a place and this is neither." He still stood blocking the doorway. "What do you think you know about him?" His words a challenge.

"What you wouldn't tell me, you wanted me to find out on my own. I know Lonnie was a dreamer and an idealist, both brilliant and naïve. He had a blind spot when it came to the cruel side of man's nature. He didn't care about money, but was keenly aware of its power for good in the right hands. His father recognized his off-the-chart abilities, hiring him and handing down his knowledge of counterfeiting. Lonnie was perhaps one of the last of a dying breed. His perfect plan derailed early when Benny broke the first rule of counterfeiting by telling others. Prematurely forced to weed out all who would be corrupted by the power of money, he made enemies along the way.

"I know he imagined a world without poverty, where every child is raised and educated in a stable environment. Kids and their caregivers held special places in his heart. He held a deep belief that education and work builds character and social responsibility. He believed everyone who can work, should. His mother had to maintain her sobriety and adhere to his regimen to keep her house. I don't think he spent a counterfeit dime on himself. Toward the end, more abject need confronted him than he had money to fix.

"He was living proof that the American dream's a myth—he did not receive equal opportunity according to his ability regardless of social class or circumstance of birth. His dream job should have been master engraver for the Federal government or an art treasure restorer. He entrusted his artwork collection to me. It's yours. Like you, his older half-brother, he had a highly developed sense of right and wrong and social justice, but he never complained of life's injustices. Not the cigarettes put out on his face and arms by foster parents or their biological children, the psychological abuse, the constant turmoil and upheaval in his group and foster homes, the limitations and pain from his club foot, or the many job rejections.

"Lonnie could have wandered through life full of rage and hate and prejudice, but he didn't. Even in the hostile environment of jail, he took the high road. He was an honorable man in a dishonorable venture. He was driven, motivated by the love of family and altruism. He only agreed to the counterfeiting plan so your father could pay for an operation to save his life. He was patient and kind and humble. I came to respect him and consider him a friend."

Baker walked up close to me. "You came up with this by yourself?"

"Lonnie had your back. He never told me you were family. No one did, if that's what you mean."

Baker's toothpick bobbed up and down.

"He focused on completing his mission. His actions directly or obliquely could have seriously wronged innocent people, but I don't think they did. My sympathies go out to you and your family. He made his choices and knew the consequences of his actions, as did Earl, Benny, and Tyrone. I don't think he directly harmed another soul. He didn't shoot the security guard. I met her in DC. Her wounds were dramatically blown out of proportion by a local source here. Who was it? We'll probably never know." I glanced at Simone. "But Mr. Anthony saw to it that she, her children, and nephews will have the opportunity for a better life and good educations."

I turned back to Baker. "I don't know when you first learned Lonnie had become a counterfeiter, and I don't want to know. He told me he wants his story told. To me that means making sure the world knows he used his money to help people who help others, and to honor those who helped him along the way.

"What's disturbingly curious was my reaction to Maynard's first news conference
announcing Lonnie's capture, especially the pictures of the four men. Being brutally honest, if
Tyrone's picture was the first one shown I probably wouldn't have taken the case. I plead guilty to some degree of racial profiling and stereotyping. If the police had access to other photos of Earl and Benny and Lonnie, I probably wouldn't have taken the case. Those pictures didn't fit with the hardened criminal stereotype Maynard described. That got me thinking something might be wrong."

Baker shook his bald head. "I will not confirm a damn thing you just said." He held out a meaty hand. "My man, Cool Breeze. Wouldn't it be a trip if Maynard moved into the little brother's jail cell instead of a senate seat?"

I nodded. "Good to see you recovered from the head wound."

"Nothing gets through that thick skull," Simone said, staring at Baker.

"I think Lonnie would have made a better senator than Maynard," I said.

Counterfeit

I may write his name on my ballot this year if I don't like either candidate.

Simone cleared her throat. "You may be big and bad and all that, JoJo, but I am going to say my piece here and you will not hush me." She handed me a business card. "This is the name of a friend in Family Services. Mention Lonnie and tell her I sent you. She may tell you something amazing." She kissed me on the cheek. "Thank you, Mitch. God bless."

On my way out the new door, I turned back to Baker. "I'm glad the Secret Service left empty handed, but they will never give up."

Baker didn't flinch. "I don't know what you talkin' about, Breezy. We needed a new door so I put one in. You must be high from smoke inhalation or depressed over your little car." Then he winked at me.

Baker and Simone stood, arms linked. They looked like two puzzle pieces that fit together perfectly. "Keep up the good work," I told them.

The white Mustang now sat totaled in a police impound yard awaiting paint transfer tests. I climbed in the only car the rental company would loan me after I played demolition derby with their GT, a bright yellow PT Cruiser with two hundred thousand miles on it. It looked like a hearse wearing a Haz-Mat suit. The interior smelled of stale cheese and mothballs.

I drove home missing Kris, with Skinny's words in my head: *To live, the spirit must cross over.* What do I need to cross? No matter how hard I tried, I couldn't answer that. Baker said the voices sometimes didn't ring true. That's how my luck's been running.

Scott L. Miller

A THOUSAND WORDS

My twenty-four-hour Secret Service protection ended tonight. I came home to less hate mail riddled with misspelled words, capital letters, and exclamation points than last week. It was like bloggers had somehow stuffed themselves into my mailbox for months. Several mentioned my mother, others suggested I do physically impossible stunts, and some recommended I relocate to Cuba since I clearly was a Communist. The townhouse still stood and my lawn remained free of burning crosses. My office mates in the practice had left supportive messages and invited me to a party next weekend. Marilyn was co-guest of honor since she'd been a jail bird for an afternoon.

I sat on my sofa, in a self-deprecating and ruminative mood, with a cold Rolling Rock in hand. *Sitting here long enough watching television that had become an ideology of watching other people's moments on television will do that.*

I reflected about the case: the whispered conversations; my time with Lonnie; the nighttime trips into north city; T-Bone; the fight with Skinny; car rides with the scheming Baker; meeting Maynard and Fallon; finding the bug; the nighttime chase and being shot; hiding trapped behind a Dumpster hoping not to die; the side of Quinn's head splattering onto my face; pulling Baker from a burning cabin; and seeing Maynard's arrest. The trials of Maynard, Fallon, Earl, and Tyrone could drag on for years, and I worried about the unequal scales of justice.

Regular TV had a reality show about modern-day mail order bride wannabes sharing streams of consciousness, eager to meet and marry their princes. We are doomed. I flipped to cable to catch the latest episode of *The Newsroom* when the phone rang.

Counterfeit

Simone's silky voice filled my ear. "JoJo and I want you to attend Lonnie's funeral in the morning."

"I'd be honored."

She gave me the details.

I had a dreamless night.

Lonnie was laid to rest in a potter's field on a bright warm Sunday morning, with fall in St. Louis a month away. In the first row under the maroon tent LaKeesha sat with her hands in her lap, next to Skinny and Tyra and Shirley and her kids. Baker and Simone occupied the second row, among many others. All were dressed in black save for Skinny, who wore a bright maroon dashiki with her purple turban.

I wore a black suit and came stag. Baker and Simone came over.

Baker was a changed man, wearing a black suit with wide purple lapels and no toothpick in his mouth. Simone wore a long black dress. She reached out and hugged me. I smelled spices and lemon grass.

Baker extended his hand. "Cool Breeze, my man. You being here means a lot. Shoulda brought Blondie. Now you got 'em back, you should use 'em." He smiled and patted my back. "Come back to our crib after. There are some fine sisters be happy to hook up with you, especially now you an honorary brother." They went to greet others.

Birds chirped and sang songs in the branches of the shady elms behind the hole dug for Lonnie. The black hearse arrived, lights on, followed by the longest procession of cars I've ever

seen, short of a freeway jam. Heads of those seated under the tent turned as Baker and five men solemnly carried Lonnie in his plain pine box from the hearse to the empty hole under the largest elm.

Skinny turned to me, staring impassively at first, then smiled sadly and mouthed the words 'thank you' before returning to face the grave site. She held her head high. Tyra and Shirley had started to cry along with LaKeesha, but not Skinny.

Every seat under the awning was filled and the standing areas along both sides and behind the tent packed with people wanting to pay their respects. By the time the preacher began his eulogy, there were so many mourners I couldn't tell how far back the sea of people reached. The vast majority wouldn't be able to hear his words, even though he held a microphone.

The prison chaplain Reverend Mathis was in his late fifties, with a barrel chest and round wire-rimmed glasses. He addressed the gathering in a soothing, avuncular tone. "I didn't have the pleasure of knowing our brother Lonnie Earl Washington for that long. He knew this day was coming and he specifically requested that I keep my words short because life is for the living. Lonnie did not want me to read passages from Scripture that would make his momma cry. He did not want anyone here to mourn him today. He wants us to return to our homes and cherish our family and friends, to hold them closer to our hearts, and to be good to one another. He asked that I use secular words and focus on those who remain. I reminded our brother Lonnie that I am a chaplain and a talker, but promised I would try to keep it short."

That received a mild chorus of laughter.

"In our brief but intense time together, I came to know Lonnie well. He loved his mother LaKeesha very deeply, and he adored his father and looked up to his big brothers for being mentors in their own separate and loving ways. He also counted his co-workers at the printing shop as members of his family."

Counterfeit

Brothers?

The Reverend's voice grew in fervor and resoluteness. "Lonnie Washington was a man of mettle. He shunned personal possessions and the limelight. He was a kindhearted man; he turned the other cheek, even in the most trying situations. He cared deeply for the Jeff Vanderlou neighborhood he lived in and the city of St. Louis. He was passionate about you fine people and wanted you to have every opportunity to achieve your dreams and aspirations. He was a quiet, intelligent man who always thought before he spoke. He overcame many obstacles in life, yet remained focused on the needs of others. As we know, Lonnie had many gifts and talents. I have met thousands of men in my days and Lonnie was one of the nicest, most decent people I have ever known. He was a true gentleman and I will miss him."

The Reverend paused, took a deep breath, and cleaned his wire rims with a handkerchief. "Lonnie was not a religious man in the traditional sense. He believed man incapable of understanding the Universe without using God for his own self-serving purposes. During our last visit, he lamented to me that God had never spoken to him. I want to leave you good people gathered today in your Sunday finest with the same message I gave him. I told Lonnie that I believed the Hand of God moved through him every day, through his mind and through his artistry. That God's love acted through him every time he helped others. May his good works live forever in your hearts and minds. Because of this, I believe Lonnie will live forever. His time on earth will be judged by the Lord God, not by man. Let us take comfort in knowing he is looking down on us now, smiling as he walks straight and true, with no limp, head held high and proud, hand in hand with Almighty God through the Gates of Heaven. Amen."

A hearty chorus of amens followed.

"At this time, anyone who wishes to approach the grave site and pay their final respects to Lonnie today is warmly encouraged to do so, after his family has had the opportunity. Thank you all for coming. God bless us all and may we find peace in our lives."

Skinny stood and escorted a trembling LaKeesha to Lonnie's coffin that sat over the mouth of the grave. LaKeesha placed a worn-to-the-nub set of crayons in a clear plastic baggy on the casket top and said, "I sent these to you when you was little. I couldn't believe you kept them all those years. This was what got you started, boy. They belong back with you now, my Boo."

Skinny silently placed a red rose, and then a wrapped cigar on the coffin on behalf of Earl, who remained handcuffed to a hospital bed under police guard. She placed both hands along the rough, knotted wooden sides of the coffin and leaned back. I almost expected something supernatural to happen, but it didn't. She kissed the lid.

Shirley and Tyra placed a white rose and said their goodbyes. Shirley's kids each released a white balloon.

JoJo and Simone walked up arm in arm and left photographs on the coffin. Simone softly said, "We will see it to the end." At first I thought JoJo would remain silent, but he bowed his head and said, "Peace, little brother," before escorting Simone back to her seat.

As I watched the attractive couple, I noticed movement on a nearby hill. Mark DeFrane and Francis LeMaster were dressed in conservative suits, heading toward their sedans.

DeFrane made eye contact with me and briefly, almost imperceptibly, nodded his head.

I nodded back. On a hill behind them, Debbie Macklin and a cameraman kept their distance, filming the throng of mourners.

Next in line came an attractive couple in their forties, the mystery brother and his attractive friend. *I see the resemblance now. I should have known. This boy, he the runt of the litter.* Next to them stood a small, thin teenage girl. The couple left a framed photograph of the trio and the girl placed an old Etch A Sketch on the coffin. What caught my eye was the drawing on it.

A procession of somber faces followed in orderly fashion. Most of them I didn't know, some I did. Many left a single flower or picture. An elderly black man released a white dove and the handicapped lady with him started to cry.

Coretta Mae Givens arrived with her walker and the help of Shondra McKinney. Coretta gently laid a sandwich with some hard candies in a baggie on top of the coffin. She saw me and stood a little straighter. "I will continue my work in his name until it's my time." Shondra had Dmitri in tow as well. She left a Christmas tree topper of an angel blowing a horn. She said to me, "I brought one of my angels to say goodbye."

Dmitri was nattily dressed in a coat and tie. He told me, "Thanks for helping him."

"You were right about him, Dmitri. It's good to see you again."

By this time, the stacked offerings had begun to slide from the coffin to the mounded earth below. The casket was partially lowered to accommodate the remembrances. Hundreds had come and gone so far and the number of mourners showed no sign of slowing.

Little Ty arrived on his bike and placed a pack of firecrackers on the lid.

Even a decked-out Reggie from Glover Storage arrived using a cane and left the sign from storage unit # 10 atop Lonnie's coffin.

Maurice the burly doorman from Debbie's apartment building paid his respects, leaving one of his hats.

The next mourners I recognized arrived en masse—the guards from Gateway City jail. Sgt. Donnell Collins led the way, followed by Smilin' Henry, Big Daddy Dwight, and Rain Man Marty. Zack and Wilbur Johnson were no-shows.

To my surprise, Sgt. Collins handed me two charcoal sketches—one of my face in profile and one of Lonnie and I sitting around the visitation table, talking. "He wanted me to give you these. I came to respect him. He was a man among men." The other guards shook my hand. Smilin' Henry nearly crushed me with a bear hug and Marty spoke his first words to me, saying, "Lonnie was okay."

Simone returned and introduced me to a tiny white lady who sported a graying page boy haircut, large round glasses, and dark blue two-piece suit. The three of us walked off to talk privately and the lady stepped forward, hand extended. "I'm Yvette Sorkin, a city administrator for Family Services. I compile and analyze city welfare data and other statistical records. My department examines quarterly statistics by neighborhood and evaluates trends, to determine what areas are declining or on an upswing. During the last fiscal quarter of this year in the Jeff Vanderlou and surrounding neighborhoods, there have been major declines in the use of food stamp and general relief programs, school truancies are down eleven percent, and youth and adult crimes decreased sixteen percent despite the hot summer and concerns over growing racial tension in the wake of the counterfeiting arrests."

Counterfeit

"Do your statistics identify the cause of these dramatic changes?"

"No, but I can tell you that this neighborhood and surrounding ones have never had their food pantries so well stocked with healthy basic foods since Nixon first spoke of a war on hunger. Large, sustaining financial contributions poured in from someone with the initials L.W. If we had more LWs on the planet, we would eradicate world hunger in a generation. LW has also provided generous funding for inner city kids' programs to insure they remain in the black for years, and similar donations have been made to area children's residential, group, and foster homes, as well as outpatient psychiatric clinics and agencies. Through my city contacts, I also learned that one hundred art scholarships have been established for children in the name of LaKeesha Washington. Anonymous monies have been sent to local colleges, earmarked for art classes. The St. Louis Art Museum welcomed a sizable donation. Even the police and firefighters embraced substantial donations. All from the mysterious philanthropist LW."

I smiled. "I'm not surprised."

Sorkin glanced back at the grave site. "He bought the least expensive coffin and no marker for himself, but the family has ordered a granite tombstone. The city lost a good man today."

"I agree. We usually get the other kind."

She gave me a quizzical look. "You're right. A good man is hard to find. Pleasure meeting you, Dr. Adams." She gave me a second firm, brisk handshake.

At last the line had dwindled to a scant trickle when the biggest surprise of the day arrived, en masse.

"I didn't recognize her at first because I never expected her to know about Lonnie's

murder, much less make the trip. The attractive young woman wore a black pants outfit and held a baby son in her arms. Clustered near her in a well-behaved tight circle stood four young boys ranging in age from four to eight. An older lady accompanied her and pushed the lone girl, a toddler, in a pink stroller.

Rachel Sanchez walked up to me and said, "Surprise!" One by one she introduced her mother and children. "Mom came along to help with the kids. I thought long and hard about what you said. I want to apologize. When you visited, it brought back bad memories. I was thinking with my emotions. Later I got to thinking that nobody in my family ever had the chance to go to college. These annuities are a blessing and a responsibility. I want my kids to know who Lonnie was and to remember him and his generous spirit. I want them to be that way."

"With a mom like you, they have a good start."

The cute little boys took turns gently depositing their personal crayon artwork in honor of Lonnie onto the mountain of gifts. They bowed their heads and made signs of the cross. Rachel placed a small plastic bag that contained a bullet casing on the festooned coffin. I assumed it was the casing from the bullet that had passed through her arm.

I introduced Rachel and the boys to JoJo and Simone so they could begin their education about Lonnie.

The crowd had dwindled to the last stragglers. Everything was winding down.

I missed my talks with Lonnie.

Then I saw her standing nearby. Sixteen, maybe seventeen. She gradually walked my way.

Etch A Sketch.

With sad, almond-shaped, almost sleepy eyes, she had distanced herself from the adults, seemingly in a moment of quiet reflection.

"That was quite a picture. Did you sketch that?" I asked, smiling, hands in my pockets.

She nodded.

"You have a lot of talent."

Was that a trace of a smile? She had that same faraway look in her face I'd come to know.

"I'm Tanya."

I offered my hand. "I'm—"

"I know who you are," she said, as her long, slender fingers slid into my palm, the only green on them her nail polish.

"I could barely draw a snowman on my Etch A Sketch. What do you want to be when you're an adult?"

"Uncle JoJo is staring at us."

Baker, shades back on, stood next to the man who bore a definite family resemblance. Both looked at us. A toothpick in Baker's mouth bobbed up and down. He walked toward us.

"I want to paint and sculpt in Paris, work in the Louvre restoring works of art. She stood on her tiptoes and kissed my cheek before she lost herself in what crowd remained.

The Etch A Sketch screen showed an exact duplicate of a hundred-dollar bill.

I'll be damned. You're a sly one, Lonnie.

For the first time in more than a year, the smile on my face matched the one in my heart.

Baker approached warily.

"Nice kid," I said. "Just wanted to let you know that I stopped by Stan Winston's office the other day with some of Lonnie's bills." He was mad I'd lied to him about being the station manager's son and almost refused to meet with me a second time. "I told him I'd received the bills at a casino and was worried they might be fake. He inspected each meticulously at his desk, in front of his 'The Buck Stops Here' sign. He pronounced them all legal tender and handed them back."

"Little brother was the man," Baker said, still eying me.

I squeezed his tree trunk of an arm. "What a great kid. I wish her the best."

Baker didn't say a word.

"I'm glad Lonnie's knowledge didn't die with him. It would have been a shame. Right, uncle JoJo?"

He remained silent, staring.

"I hope she achieves her career goals. I guess we'll have to wait and see if the world opens up to her more than it did for Lonnie. She has great potential."

"We take care of our own," Baker said.

"I know you do."

He hugged me and we shook hands.

I walked to my car wondering whether Tanya was Lonnie's daughter or niece. Considering a young life was at stake, I didn't need to know. I like to think she was his daughter and that he experienced some joy and happiness during his brief time.

Counterfeit

Since Lonnie was technically indigent, my code of ethics prevented me from keeping the remained of the money Mr. Anthony had sent, so I made an anonymous donation to the Make-A-Wish Foundation for kids. I decided to keep Warhol's *Money* and find homes for the rest of the artwork Baker and Skinny didn't want. I hung Lonnie's sketches in my study with *Money* in the middle.

The next day, I mailed a certified package containing ten of Lonnie's bills to my unlikely mentor and guardian. I wondered what he'd do with them, but I knew he'd get a hoot out of it. I wished I could see the look on Milton Peebles' face when he opens his thank-you letter. I figure he'll enjoy an adrenaline rush when he passes at least one of the counterfeits to pay for a night of Guinness. I bet he'll smirk each time he sticks it to The Man. I imagine he'll frame one.

That night, I threw myself into writing Lonnie's story, the first of what would prove to be many long nights with less sleep, because my days gradually filled again with challenging, difficult clients who alternately frustrated, disappointed, touched, revolted, and surprised me. I didn't move the practice from my Clayton office, but I wheeled my old leather chair past a bewildered Gus the security guard to the Dumpster after buying a new burgundy-colored one. By the time my first rough draft was completed, I had, irony of ironies, a quarter million words and two interested publishers. The trials kept being delayed, irony part deux, by Maynard and Fallon's legal teams. The election would pass him by and I hoped he'd never be able to vote again.

Counterfeit seemed like a good title.

I thought James McAvoy could play me if a movie were ever made. Idris Elba could play Baker and Donald Glover could play Lonnie.

The day after I started to write, I felt all the way back from my self-imposed exile. The world brimmed with endless possibility.

New excited me again.

I drove my Velveeta-colored Haz-Mat Cruiser to Shaw's Garden to talk to Kris.

A young couple was getting married in the rose garden and I didn't notice the wedding photographer as she backed up quickly for a panoramic shot until it was too late. She tripped over my foot and I caught her in mid fall, looking into the brightest aquamarine oval eyes and the clearest complexion I'd ever seen. Those eyes changed from blue to green and back again. I held her in my arms. I didn't want it to end.

"Thanks. You can let me up now, if you want," she said. Her kind eyes looked into mine
and grew larger. "I know you, from the news."

She stood about five seven, with shoulder-length strawberry blonde hair, and wore matching turquoise earrings and a necklace that highlighted her white blouse and shorts. Her open-toed golden sandals revealed red toenails. My years of training noted the bare ring finger.

She snapped a series of several quick close-ups before I could object. She handed me her card. "I've got to get back to work. Call me, I think you'll like several of the pics. They'll be ready next Friday night after five. On the house." She smiled one last time and returned her attention to the wedding. Also being an observant and trained professional, I noticed her long legs and nice ass.

I made my way to the Joyce Duane bench and told Kris how the case was winding down and of the latest news. The bullets that killed Dan Quinn matched a test round fired from a rifle found in the possession of, and registered to, Nelson Dodd. That sly and slick Maynard had been able to convince and manipulate the major players to agree to a white lie that 95% of the money had been recovered—even special agent DeFrane—to protect the force from bad press and buy them time for their investigation to build a stronger case. That Carter, Malvern, and Downey accepted plea deals in exchange for rolling over on Maynard and Fallon. That the police chief and his assistant were circling the wagons and lawyering up, looking for a deal but finding all the seats taken. Looks like this story will make the St. Louis city towing and the baseball playoff ticket scandals look like small potatoes. Detective LeMaster appeared to not be involved in it at all.

I told her all this, trying to imagine her response. The breeze caressed my back and the sun filtered through the canopy of trees to touch my face, but that was it.

She wasn't here.

I thought of Skinny's final prophecy and grinned. *Crossing over.*

I was sitting on a weathered wooden bench in a beautiful garden talking to myself like a doofus.

I looked at the business card. Miranda Gabriel was a photographer at a studio called A Thousand Words, five miles from my townhouse.

A Thousand Words.

I laughed and smiled. I, Mitchell Adams, former ladies' man and lost soul, had spent the last forty minutes talking to a phantom and realized I hadn't said one word to the beautiful woman I'd held briefly in my arms.

There's always Friday night redemption.

New is exciting.

The End

ABOUT THE AUTHOR

Scott L. Miller is a retired, former licensed clinical social worker who earned his MSW at St. Louis University. He worked extensively with adults, children, families, and the elderly in state and private hospitals in St. Louis City and County, which allowed him to see and work with most every psychiatric diagnosis in the DSM as well as experience a taste of city life while doing home visits.

Long fascinated by the power of the written word and an avid reader, he utilized his acquired psychiatric and medical knowledge to write the Mitchell Adams series, as well as numerous stories and works in progress.

He lives in Chesterfield, MO with his pocket beagle Juliet, the greatest dog ever.

ACKNOWLEDGMENTS

My second foray into the world of writing. Thanks again to Kristina Blank Makansi for initially publishing Counterfeit. I have since regained all rights to this novel. The book received interest upon its release from staff at New Line Cinema and from director Sam Raimi's right-hand man for the movie rights, but sadly, no deal could be worked out.

I received invaluable help on this project from someone who wishes to remain anonymous on the technical aspects of counterfeiting and the Secret Service. He chooses to remain in the shadows, much like my Mr. Anthony character. Any errors in the world of counterfeiting or the Secret Service are mine and mine alone.

Thanks to William Boyd Brown, a now deceased social worker, for his knowledge of the many St. Louis neighborhoods.

Many thanks to Dr. Felix Vincenz, for his private practice acumen and computer knowledge. He should run for president, or at least, be a contestant on Survivor.

Thanks to attorney Mike Schaller, the bulldog, for his help with legal matters in the story. He is a great man.

Thanks are also in order for the staff at New York Book Publishers for creating the new cover for Counterfeit, for my killer new website, and for re-releasing this story. Special thanks go to Lisa Smith (aka: Tokyo, for her support), Logan Walsh, Jessica Cohen, Emma Becker, Jeremiah Hofsted, and any others at NYBP involved with this project.

www.ingramcontent.com/pod-product-compliance
Lightning Source LLC
Chambersburg PA
CBHW051110300726
48981CB00001B/74